Three on a Couch

Norman Malamud

Barringer Publishing, Naples, Florida
www.barringerpublishing.com
Cover, graphics, layout design by Lisa Camp
Editing by Carole Greene
Cover illustration by Judith Malamud

ISBN: 978-0-9839050-9-7

Library of Congress Cataloging-in-Publication Data
Three on a Couch / Norman Malamud

Printed in U.S.A.

This is a work of fiction. All characters, organizations,
and events portrayed in this novel are either products of the
author's imagination or are used fictitiously.

Dedication

To my daughters, Shari and Hillary;
My Hodges University writer buddies;
Dr. George F. Corrent M.D. Ph.D.,
for his invaluable medical expertise
on corneal transplant surgery;
and to Judith, the love of my life.

Prologue

From the moment Dr. Jonathon Kent inserted the key into the lock of his office door, he knew something bad was going to happen. After locking the door he walked to the wall, removed the Picasso painting that hid a wall safe, and carefully set the painting down on his desk. He spoke aloud, hoping the sound of his voice would dissolve the tension that seemed to permeate the air in the dimly lit room. "Fourteen left, twenty-three right, seventeen left, twelve right." The clicking of the numbers as he dialed, combined with the thumping of his heart, sent a shiver through him. *Why the hell didn't I do this during the day?*

A veil of smoke clouded his mind. *Guilt. What do I have to feel guilty about? They knew what they were getting into. Screw them.* He kissed the videotapes, shoved them into the back of the safe, closed the door, and twirled the combination dial. Just then, he detected the sound of someone breathing. He froze. The agitated flutter of the parakeet's wings confirmed his suspicion. Turning quickly, he came face to face with an intruder.

"Jesus," he said, relieved. "You scared the shit out of me. What are you doing here?"

The intruder grimaced with cruel intent, raised an arm, and pointed a pistol squarely at the bewildered doctor.

Panic flashed in Jonathon's eyes; his complexion faded to milky white as the blood drained from his face. A strangled cry rose from his throat. "This is a joke. You're not serious. You wouldn't..."

The intruder glared with hatred. "Oh wouldn't I? You sick, perverted bastard. Just watch me."

The handsome Dr. Jonathon Kent, psychiatrist and sexual healer to the many depressed women who sought his help, begged a final plea for mercy. "I'll make it up to you," he stammered. "Don't do this. I'll be so good to you, I'll..."

The intruder simply smiled wryly, pulled the trigger, checked for a pulse and proceeded to close the dead man's eyes.

Chapter 1

Central Park was a virtual parking lot. The honking of horns could be heard for miles. Cars were backed up from 86th to 72nd Street to Central Park West as sheets of rain beat relentlessly onto the Yellow taxicab.

The frenetic rhythms of the East Indian music jostled Franny Goldsmith's already compromised nerves. "This is worse than the Long Island Expressway," she fumed silently, knowing she would never get to the office on time. "It's market week. Ten more minutes, and I'll miss my first appointment. The buyer will be pissed, and the boss will be cursing up a storm. I'm going to get fired. I better call."

She searched in her purse for her phone. It was then she discovered she had left her phone in another bag. Her heart raced in time with the music, and she shifted into a state of hysteria.

She shouted at the taxi driver. "Sinbad, turn off the goddamn music!" Her once perfectly combed bob began to wilt under the stress perspiration. She impatiently brushed her hair from her reddened face.

The driver was oblivious to her demand.

With clenched fists, she pounded on the plastic divider that separated them. He turned around, lifted his turban, scratched his head, and eyed her questioningly. "You want?" he mumbled.

Peering at him through dark sunglasses, she motioned for him to slide the plastic divider to the side.

Fucking moron, she thought. He reached over his right shoulder and slowly pushed the divider to his left.

"I need a phone!" she yelled, putting her hand to her ear, gesturing a telephone. He bobbed his head up and down.

She rolled her eyes and looked skyward. "Why me, God? Why are you punishing me? All I want to do is get to work." She took a deep breath and spoke aloud again. "You're all right, Franny, keep calm. Don't let it get to you. Say your serenity prayer."

"No good, lady," the driver said. "Cars not move." He pointed to the automobiles that waited impatiently for the traffic jam to ease up.

"Look at me. I'm turning into a beaten-up piñata." Drumming her fingers nervously on her bag, she thought, *what I need is a couple of Valium.* Franny wiped the fogged up window with a tissue and peered out. The tissue shredded in her hand, adding to her already agitated state of mind.

"No damn air conditioning!" she cursed. "Figures." Wiping her bangs away from her perspiring forehead, she muttered, "I feel weak. I'm getting claustrophobic." The Indian music throbbed in her temples. She began breathing rapidly. "I've got to get out of here." She shouted at the driver, "You have a phone! I see it! Give it to me!"

His expression showed indifference, then impatience, hoping the traffic would start moving and he would be rid of her.

She reached through the divider and pointed at the phone, screaming above the music at the top of her lungs, "You bandaged head Buddha - THE TELEPHONE! THE TELEPHONE! MOHAMMED, GIVE ME THE GODDAMN TELEPHONE!" The Indian driver turned off his stereo and gingerly handed her the phone. He muttered discourteously, cursing her in his native tongue.

"Moron," she said. "We're being overrun by aliens. Whatever happened to the nice native drivers?" She dialed her work number and received a busy signal. Her eyes widened as she pushed the end button. "Can't be busy, it's a one hundred million dollar business." Her breathing increased and she felt faint. She tried calling the number three times, then blew out a breath of disgust and dialed 911.

The operator answered, but Franny cut her off. "Listen, police emergency. I'm stuck in a cab, and I'm having an anxiety attack. If I don't get some help, I'm going to flip out. You can save me. Please, call my boss and tell him I'm going to be late. The number is 731-7220. Can you do that for me?"

"I'm sorry, ma'am, but that is not in our jurisdiction. Are you in danger?"

"Listen, fuzz head," Franny shouted, "I pay taxes so you can sit on your fat ass all day and help people like me."

The only thing the operator offered was dead air.

"Didn't you hear me? I need your help! I'm claustrophobic. I'm cooped up in this goddamn taxi with an alien driver, and we're stuck in traffic. Are you listening? I can't catch my breath."

Thinking she was dealing with some kook, the operator said, "Try opening the window, ma'am; it works for me." A distinct click signaled an abrupt end to the conversation. Noticing Franny off the phone, the driver turned up his music once again.

The disturbing music, the unexpected, negative response from the officer, combined with her claustrophobic state of mind set Franny's head into a downward spiral. Lightheaded and nauseous, her mind began to spin out of control. Zigzagging lightning flashes of a myriad colors splashed in her eyes. Incapable of conscious thoughts, Franny Goldsmith opened the door of the taxi, stepped out and fell to the wet pavement unconscious.

Chapter 2

Lily Violet Fitzgerald sat alone at the Plaza Athenee restaurant, toying with her angel hair pasta. She wound the strands of pasta around her fork, tossed her flaming red hair to one side, and then pushed the plate away from her.

The two Phentermine diet pills she removed from her purse were immediately immersed in one gulp as they slid down her throat with the help of a glass of Chardonnay. She mentally noted to call her doctor to get a refill. She was running low on Phentermine. She had planned on telling Dr. Feinstein she had lost her purse and the pills were in them. Sipping the last of her wine, she held the empty glass up to the waiter, who stood attentively at the sideboard.

She remembered what her savvy roommate had told her some years ago when she had won a scholarship and arrived in New York from San Luis Obispo, California. "It can get real cold out there, Lily. It's every man for himself."

She unconsciously finished the wine and signaled for another.

The hotel's lounge, The Bar Seine, offered a romantic setting, an eclectic décor with its exotic atmosphere of combined Moroccan, African, European, Asian artwork in addition to the red lacquered walls, rich velvet drapes, and leather floors. The glances cast by the diners at the attractive lady dining alone did not in the least faze Lily.

She stared hard at her image in the wall mirror. Soft lighting of the dimly lit bistro accentuated her creamy complexion and full red lips, and the silk ruffled blouse; her charcoal grey Chanel pinstriped pantsuit portrayed elegance. She turned her face to view her profile. *You're pretty enough, have a great body, and you're getting rave reviews from th*e critics. So what's your problem, lady? She contemplated easing up on the pills. She eyed her wineglass. *Not the wine,* she mused. She had to leave herself *some* pleasures.

For long minutes, in her mind, the only sounds in the room were her thoughts. Sensing someone watching her, Lily looked at the wall mirror and noticed a mature, well-groomed man smiling at her. She turned away quickly, embarrassed at having been caught admiring herself. She sipped her wine, put the glass down, and stole a glimpse in the mirror to see if he was still observing her.

This time he smiled broadly, toasting her with what looked like either a glass of lemonade or iced tea.

This guy has to be a banker, a stockbroker, or a Texas oil tycoon. Graying at the temples, with deep-set blue eyes and an engaging smile, the handsome gentleman kept his glass raised and waited for a sign of acknowledgement.

She looked down at the tablecloth, and back at him. *What the heck?* she thought. *Tomorrow morning, I'll be gone, and he'll be history. I could use an ego boost.* The rush she felt from the diet pills mingled with the wine kicked in and her courage intensified; still a nod was all she could manage as she tugged apprehensively at her earlobe.

She looked up and there he was, towering over her.

Bending slightly, he smiled a modest, little-boy smile and said, "I could say that I thought you were someone I knew. Or, I could lay a line on you like, 'Haven't we met before?' Or I could tell you the honest to goodness truth. You took my breath away, and I just had to meet you.”

She glanced around the room. “You’d better sit down. After that long, well-rehearsed speech, you must be exhausted. And you’re beginning to attract attention. Five-star hotels do not approve of men being so blatantly obvious.” She thought. *Did I just ask him to join me?*

“Thank you,” he said, sitting across from her. “I’m Bradford T. Tillingham.” He raised his brows, his blue eyes penetrating hers, and waited for a response.

She stared blankly at him.

He persevered. “You *do* have a name?”

Flustered, she gulped the rest of her wine. “I’m sorry, I just remembered I’m late for an appointment.” Before the words had left her mouth, she regretted having said them.

His face showed disappointment.

“I…” she started to say, but he rode over her words.

“That’s what I get for forcing myself on you. I’m sorry.”

He started to rise, but she took hold of his sleeve, stopping him halfway. “Don’t go. The appointment can wait. Please, sit.” She held her hand out for him to shake. “I’m Lily. Lily V. Fitzgerald. Seems we both have middle initials.”

Pleased that she had changed her mind, he signaled the waiter. “Two of the same, please.”

She placed her hand over her glass. “Not for me. I still have work to do. This was my lunch break, and I’ve had more than my quota.”

“Work? What kind of work?”

“I tinker with the piano.”

He lifted her hand gently, and held it. “Tinker? No. This is the hand of an artist.”

She lacked the will to withdraw her hand. “I’m a concert pianist taking a break from a rehearsal. What does the ‘T’ stand for?” She couldn’t believe this brief encounter was actually happening. *Yes, maybe, in novels or movies, but certainly not in real life.* "The "V" is for Violet. My mother pinned that moniker on me."

"Violet. I like it." He leaned closer. "Like the flower. Thank your mother for me. The 'T' is for Tennessee, and don't laugh, or our dinner date for tonight is cancelled."

"Dinner date? Tonight? You don't give a lady a chance to catch her breath do you, Tennessee?" She ran her well-manicured nails around the lace-trimmed tablecloth and then lowered her eyes. "I'm sorry. I have an engagement this evening." Hesitant about her last comment, she waited to see his reaction.

"Break it!" he said.

"I don't know," she said, faltering. "It's business."

"It'll be fun," he said, smiling warmly as he reached across the table and boldly took hold of her hands.

Her mind raced. *This is going too fast. For all I know, he could be a serial killer. But he does have such presence.*

He sensed her dilemma. "Look," he said, "if you think I'm moving too fast, just say so. Honestly, I'm not out to ...you know. We could just enjoy each other's company, have a quiet dinner, and if you like, a dance or two. Here, in the hotel. No pressure. No strings. I'm registered at the hotel. If you feel uneasy, you can have me checked out." He reached into his breast pocket for a business card.

"Stop," she said. "That's not necessary."

He raised his brows. "Trust is a good thing," he said with confidence.

"Do you always get your way, Tennessee?"

"Always," he said, smiling a beatific smile. "But I am not usually so forward with women. Except in business, where I'm known as a monster." He switched gears to make her more at ease. "Let's change the subject. It's just seeing you sitting here, so pretty.... I couldn't resist speaking to you." Feeling he had begun to win her over, he asked, "Is Tennessee going to be my name for the duration of our relationship?"

"Guess so," she said. "I don't have a middle name as unusual as yours. Lily Violet is my professional name."

"You should have kept Violet as your first name. Matches your eyes." He leaned closer to her. "Violet, aren't they?"

She released her hands from his. "I have to go. The maestro can be quite temperamental. By now he must be cursing up a storm. Words a lady cannot repeat." She started to rise.

"Violet, it would be helpful if we'd arranged where and what time tonight. I have a tuxedo. Do you have a gown? If not, we can dine in the Studio Lounge. I just thought it would be fun to dress up. If you don't, it's okay. We can go snappy casual."

She lied. "It just so happens, I do have a gown."

"He spoke with a contrived English accent, "Dinner at eight, madam? In the lobby?"

"Dinner at eight," she mimicked," hoping she would be able to find a gown at Bergdorf's that wouldn't need altering.

•

That evening as she dressed, she kept telling herself she was behaving like a teenager about to embark on her first date, but the warm, exciting feeling inside of her allayed any doubts she might have had.

She gave herself a last-minute check in the foyer mirror, picked up her evening bag and walked to the elevator. Stepping into the elevator, she looked in the Louis XIV gilt-framed mirror and smiled. *Great choice,* she thought. *The Richard Tyler cost me a bundle, but it was worth it.* She admired the classic cut of her plunging neckline, fingering the expensive black fabric of her floor-length gown. The operator inhaled the aroma of Joy and smiled at Lily approvingly, giving her the once-over as she exited.

At the sight of her, Bradford sprang to his feet. His eyes lit up. "You look fantastic. I was right."

"About what?"

"You, sweet Violet. You."

Smiling, she thought, *this is going to be a wonderful evening.*

She took notice of his expertly tailored Armani tuxedo, which seemed molded to his well-built physique, and the graying of his hair at his temples gave him an air of distinction. *Tonight I'm Cinderella and he, Prince Charming, even if it's only for one evening.*

He took her arm and a wave of electricity shot through her. "Want to have a drink at the bar?"

Not one to refuse a drink, she said, "A drink sounds wonderful, but I'd prefer not to sit on a stool in this gown."

"Violet, I was only teasing," he said, waving a beckoning hand at the maître d', who hovered close by. The maître d' selected a secluded table in the corner, led them to it, and pulled out her chair. "Was your appointment difficult to break?"

"I made up a last-minute excuse, and he bought it."

"I'm glad." He reached for her hands as the waiter approached. "What would you like, Violet?"

"I'll leave it up to you. Don't tell me you're having iced tea."

"Not tonight. Iced tea is for the afternoon." He stared at her, but directed his voice to the waiter. "Two of the house's special martinis, straight up, very dry, with two onions and one olive."

"Tell me, Tennessee, what do you do?" she asked, glancing at his hand, searching for a wedding ring.

"For business or pleasure?"

"Business, silly."

"Guess."

She squinted. "Let me see. Your hands are those of a man who uses his brain...certainly not a laborer. You could be a lawyer, or maybe a doctor.

No, you are the C.E.O. of a big corporation, spending the night in New York to close a multi-million dollar deal." She searched his eyes.

"Have you been checking up on me?"

"You mean I guessed right?"

"Violet, can I tell you something?"

"Well, as much as you can in one evening. What's on your mind, Tennessee? Is it that you're married? It's okay. You said it. No pressure. No strings. Just dinner, dancing and then, *au revoir.*"

He stared at her intently. "I know, but I didn't think you would have such an effect on me. And no, I'm not married." His grin was lopsided. "I haven't been able to concentrate on anything except you."

She laughed.

"Go ahead, laugh. It does sound bizarre. You meet a man, and in a few hours the idiot tells you he's nuts about you. No one would believe it. I'm not asking you for anything. Just want to get to know you better."

His blue eyes pierced hers. The waiter served the martinis. They toasted. She took one long pull on her drink, and suddenly, her face turned beet red.

"What's wrong?" he asked.

"I ...drank too fast," she spluttered, trying to catch her breath. "I'm fine, really. The bartender must have poured a double." She silently chided herself for not having known better than to mix pills and liquor on an empty stomach.

He motioned to the waiter. "I think we better get some food into you."

"I feel better," she said, nervously brushing back her hair.

His eyed narrowed.

"All right," she conceded, "anything to soak up the drink."

He smiled. "I've got a little something for you," he teased. "Later, after we've eaten." He winked at her.

"I'm impressed. A man who can order in French," she said after they finished dinner. "I told you all about me, and the world of a concert pianist, now how about you?"

He waved his hand dismissively. "Later. I told you I had a surprise for you." He felt the inside of his breast pocket.

She stammered. "Really, Tennessee, I can't accept anything. We have only just met. I do feel I've known you for a ...but..."

"Violet, I told you no strings, and I meant it. I would like to see more of you. And, I want you to know me, too." He fell silent, watching her reaction. "I know, I know, I'm rushing things but...*please trust me.*" He waited for her to speak.

Confused, she thought, *everything is happening so fast. I can't think logically.* "You've come on pretty strong for the short time we've known each other." With a nervous smile and a warning look, she struggled to come to grips with her emotions. Again her hands nervously sought to straighten out her hair. "Let me at least catch my breath."

He reached into his jacket pocket, and handed her a velvet box. "Here," he said. "This should take your breath away."

"A velvet box, from Cartier?"

"Open it," he encouraged.

Her eyes widened as an emerald-cut diamond ring glittered up at her. "My God," she said. "Is it real?"

"Put it on. I picked it up this afternoon. Now when you play, your fingers will sparkle on the ivories."

Her hands trembled. "I don't know what to say."

"Don't say anything, Violet. I drove the salesman at Cartier crazy, looking for a velvet box with a violet silk lining to match your eyes."

She rose and placed her hands on the table to steady herself. "I really must powder my nose. I mean," she stammered, "I have to put on some lipstick. Damn it! What I really mean is that I have to be alone for a moment." She gently placed the ring back on the silk cushion.

Suddenly, he removed the ring from the box, and held it above his head. "Take it, or I'll toss it!"

"Okay, okay, Tennessee, don't make a scene. I'll wear it," she said and slipped the massive rock onto the ring finger of her right hand and walked away.

•

In the ladies room she held the ring under the makeup light, watching the facets sparkle.

A woman sat down beside her. "Just get it?" the woman asked. "May I?" Lily extended her fingers, and the woman turned the ring back and forth. "What a beauty." She looked up at Lily. "Just get engaged?"

Lily hesitated. "Well, sort of."

"You don't look very happy. Did you expect a larger stone?" She proceeded to tease her hair.

"Oh, no, it was quite unexpected." She turned, and faced the woman. "We only just met this afternoon. I'm sorry, I don't know why I'm telling you this."

"Happens all the time. I guess after four husbands, I've taken on a motherly look. Take my advice and have it appraised and check the guy out. I wouldn't have made three huge mistakes if I'd hired a private detective to run a credit report on the bastards. All they want is to get into your panties, or your bank account."

"I'm not well off."

"Don't be naive. They're all after something. Take my advice. If the stone checks out, put it in a vault before he changes his mind. A girl can't be too careful nowadays."

The woman rose and adjusted her gown, walked to the door, and tipped the maid. Turning to Lily, she said, "Brighten up. Possession is nine-tenths of the law. After all, you're going out with a lot more than you came in with."

Lily stared at the stone. *She's right. I've got nothing to lose. The Cartier box and ring are probably phonies anyway. Still, lots of couples meet and fall in love at first sight. How many newlyweds really know their partners?* She spoke to her image in the mirror, as she reapplied her lipstick. "Go with the flow, Lily."

He rose as she approached the table. She kissed him lightly on the cheek. "I didn't even thank you," she said. "I apologize for my lack of manners."

"I knew you'd come around. You can consider this a get-acquainted dinner. Tomorrow you can tell your people that you need a sabbatical. We'll spend the entire day shopping for…well, anything your heart desires."

"Easy, Tennessee. You're making me dizzy. I just can't spring this on them. I have a tour coming up, and I've worked hard to get where I am. The piano is my life. And besides, they've been very good to me."

"I'm sure you've made a lot of money for them too. Don't sell yourself so short."

"Even so, I couldn't just walk out. I have concerts scheduled."

"Of course. I'm sorry. I'm so accustomed to taking charge, I automatically assume everything has to be my way." He smiled warmly at her. "And now, if you want to thank me properly, just enjoy the rest of the evening." He leaned across the table and kissed her on the lips. "More champagne, or coffee?"

"Neither, Tennessee. I haven't thanked you properly either. But not here." She took hold of his hands and gently squeezed them.

His expression registered triumph. "Your place, okay, Violet? Mine is a mess."

The sun shone through the blinds as Lily stretched her arms and smiled. She had never slept better. She turned, expecting to see Tennessee beside her, but only the aroma of his cologne lingered. She pulled his pillow around her body and hugged it. *He's probably in his room making arrangements for us.*

She showered, dressed, and thought of ordering breakfast but decided to wait for him. The calls to her agent and maestro didn't take long. They were startled to hear she was engaged, and wished her luck, and hoped her newfound happiness didn't interfere with the concert tour.

An hour passed, and Lily became apprehensive. She'd consumed four cups of coffee and downed three diet pills. The phone stared at her, and she decided to call his room.

"I'm sorry, Miss Fitzgerald," the operator said. "Mr. Tillingham checked out this morning. But there is a message for you from *Mrs.* Tillingham."

Lily sat dumbfounded. "Did you say, Mrs. Tillingham?"

"Yes, ma'am, Mrs. Tillingham. Would you like me to read the message?"

Trying to raise herself off of the bed, Lily felt her strength desert her and she plopped back down as the phone fell from her hand to the floor.

"Hello! Hello," the operator said repeatedly. "Ms. Fitzgerald, are you there?"

Lily sat dazed, staring into space, her mind blank, senses numb. The vial of diet pills that sat on the night table magnified ten fold. Devastated, she picked up the vial of Phentermine and emptied the contents into the palm of her hand.

Chapter 3

Elaine Benjamin complained to her husband, Lew. "Why do we need a house in Darien, Connecticut? Forest Hills isn't good enough for you? You're bitching about the drive from here to the city as it is. It's not like you're hanging on a subway strap. You *are* being chauffeured. The ride from Darien is a lot longer…and the traffic, forget it! And what about the girls? I don't think they'll be happy changing schools and leaving their friends." She shook her head. "Uh, uh. That's going to be a problem." She knifed a chunk of cream cheese, spread it on half of a toasted bagel, and then sandwiched it with the other half. "Another thing, Lew, I don't get to see you as it is. It seems like the girls and I are living alone. Mmm, that's good," she said, crunching at a bite of the bagel. She dabbed at her lips with a napkin, and said hesitantly, "Darien, huh. Mmm. Sounds restricted."

Lew eyed her with reservation. "Let's wait until school's finished, Elaine. Then we'll talk. Okay?"

She continued. "Later is not going to change anything." She sipped her coffee, and yelled into the kitchen to the maid. "Celina, what's for dinner?"

Lew Benjamin lowered the *New York Times,* and frowned distastefully. "Elaine, do you have to shout? Celina's not deaf."

The kitchen door swung open, and Celina, a middle aged, pleasantly plump, attractive woman—dressed in her usual attire, a maid's uniform—stood impatiently tapping her foot.

The Benjamins treated Celina as family, and she, in turn, ran the household and the children as if they were hers. Hands placed firmly on her rounded hips, she pushed her jet-black hair away from her eyes. "Dinner? Let's talk about it, shall we? That depends on if the master of the house is dining at home tonight. If not, I could defrost Omaha steaks. Incidentally, if anyone is interested, tonight is my early night." Celina had a world-weary look about her, and spoke with a familiarity that one rarely found in the hired help. She followed up with, "That is, unless you need me."

"We're not your bosses, Celina," Elaine said, shaking her head. "Friends, we're friends. Steak? No. Rosy and Anna hate steak." She looked at her husband. "Lew, do you have a late night?"

"Yes, Elaine. You *know* it's market week. I'll be out with the buyers every night this week. Didn't you say your mother was coming over tonight?"

"I hope not. I can use a breather from her. It's Monday, and Monday is Canasta with the girls."

He stifled a laugh. "Girls? They haven't been girls since Brooklyn was a prairie."

Ignoring his remark, she went on. "Can't the salespeople entertain the buyers? My brother has market week too, and Sara told me that he doesn't stay downtown every night."

Lew folded the newspaper and placed it neatly on the table. "Elaine, my love, you know the boys have to entertain the buyers. You spent half your life in the garment center, and you act like you just moved here from the hinterlands."

Elaine unconsciously stirred the remainder of her coffee, her mind drifting to the past. Their discussion about moving shook loose memories of their first home, a modest two-bedroom, one-bath ranch house her father and mother had bought them in Paramus, New Jersey, as a wedding present. At first, Lew, a house painter by day and security guard at night, vehemently refused the gracious gift; but after many heated arguments and butting heads with Elaine and her intrusive mother, he gave in, promising to pay his in-laws back if it was the last thing he did.

After one year of college, Elaine had decided that it was not for her. Having an aptitude for drawing and fashion, she took courses at The Fashion Institute of Technology, and then applied for a position as a designer/model for an apparel manufacturer in New York City's garment center.

On her way to the restroom the day she met Lew, she collided with him as he exited the elevator. Taken with his good looks and not one to be bashful, she immediately struck up a conversation. Tossing her blond shoulder-length hair to one side for effect, she said flirtatiously, "Trying to sweep me off my feet?"

"Sorry, I was in a hurry. I have an appointment for a salesman's position and I'm late," he said, admiring her attractive face and shapely figure.

"Cool your buns. There's another guy in the boss's office. You'll have to wait."

She thought, *put the bathroom visit on hold, Elaine. This guy's to die for.* "Have a seat." She pointed to a couch in the outer-office and sat down next to him.

He said, "I bet there's been a lot of guys interviewing for the job, huh?"

Edging closer to him, she thought, *not like you, sonny boy.* To him she said, "About five have come and gone this morning, but I'll put my money on you. What's your name? Maybe I can put in a good word with the almighty one."

"Lew. Lew Benjamin. If you would, I'd appreciate it."

"You're on, Lew. But it's going to cost you."

His eyes brightened. "I'll chance it." He couldn't believe his good luck. Feeling self-assured, he asked, "What's your name?"

"Elaine." Her mind working on overtime foresaw the future. *Lew Benjamin. Mmm. Mrs. Elaine Benjamin. Sounds good.* He doesn't know it, not yet, but he's the one.

It wasn't his wavy, black hair that spilled onto his forehead, his athletic build, or his expressive grey eyes that drew her to him. It was the broad, warm smile that lit up his face like the happy-face decal on a T-shirt. Elaine spoke to the boss, telling him that Lew was a distant relative, and the boss bought it. Within two years, Lew bought the business from the owner, who retired to Florida, and in the following two years he and Elaine, as his designer and model, had married and grown the company to one of the top ten in New York.

Back at the breakfast table, Lew asked, "Where are you, Elaine? Somewhere in La La Land? We were talking about my entertaining the buyers because it's market week."

Shaking her head to clear her thoughts, she said hesitantly, "Oh, yeah. I was thinking about when we first met and about the small ranch house we had after we married."

"I don't want to think about that shack."

"We had a lot of happy years there."

"Yes, but it's nowhere near this place. The girls have separate rooms, redecorated, I might add, every year. We have the whole floor to ourselves, and, a wrap-around terrace. And besides, the old place was just too close to your relatives." He reluctantly reached into his breast pocket, took out a Havana cigar, held it underneath his nose, savoring the aroma.

She immediately waved a "no" with her index finger. "Uh, uh, Lew. Nix the cigar. You want to inhale poison," she pointed with her thumb, "do it on the terrace. Let the neighbors inhale your secondhand smoke. Michael cut out smoking. Maybe you should try."

He sighed. "Okay, okay. I'll smoke in the limo. And Elaine, please don't talk to me about your brother. He should pay more attention to his business. That's why we can afford to move to a bigger house while he's still borrowing money from us. And, since I'm on the subject of *your* family, he doesn't get another red cent. Do you realize we've loaned him one hundred thousand green ones, and we have yet to see a nickel? Elaine, I…"

She cut him off. "All right, all right. Don't rub it in. I'm sorry I talked you into loaning him the money. It's my fault."

He stood and kissed her on her cheek. "Don't get me wrong, sweetheart. It's not your fault. You meant well."

Celina spoke up. "Are we finished with, 'All in the Family?'" She looked from Lew to Elaine. "Mmm. I guess so. And now for the $64,000 question. Have we made a decision about dinner, or should I take things into my own hands, as usual?" She didn't wait for an answer. "Let's give the girls a treat. I'll pick up knishes, frankfurters, and corned beef sandwiches from the deli and everyone will be happy." She looked from Lew to Elaine for an answer, but the room remained quiet, so she shrugged and said, "I guess that's settled. Now if you'll excuse me, I have to pick up the mess from the primadonnas." She shook her head as she walked through the swinging doors into the kitchen, muttering in Spanish.

Elaine poured herself another cup of coffee and held the sterling decanter up to Lew. "No thanks," he said. "I'm over-coffeed." He stood, laid his napkin on the kitchen table, and looked toward the swinging doors. "That Celina is something else."

Elaine nodded. "From what I hear from the women at the club and their problems with help, we lucked out. Practically raised the kids. Remember when I had Rosy and was afraid to hold her? Thought I'd drop her? Celina took over."

Lew chuckled. "I remember." He studied the woman he constantly argued with but loved dearly. "What's the matter? Don't tell me after all these years you have regrets."

"You seem to think I'm made of iron. I've always felt guilty, Lew. I loved modeling the clothes, and designing the line…working side by side with you."

"Yeah, sure. Could have fooled me," he chided. "The cleaning people constantly complained about the broken china they had to pick up after you had your daily fit." He held up his left hand. "See, I even have the scar to prove it."

She leaned closer to him and kissed his scar. She laughed. "I never told you, but I meant to hit you with the coffee mug."

"I never drank from a mug again, you nut."

"But I was right."

"Really? Who sez so?"

"I sez so. You and the rest of your fawning followers don't know fashion from borsht. And another thing…"

The banging on the kitchen wall cut her sentence short. Celina sang out, "Time to go to the office. It's market week."

They laughed. "Guess I better hustle," Lew said.

Elaine took a scarf from the standing rack and wrapped it around his neck. "Wear your scarf; it's cold outside." Suddenly, she pulled back, her face paling.

He stiffened. "What's wrong?"

"Nothing," she said wincing. "Just my fingers. Lately I've been getting these stupid shooting pains."

"In your hands? Did you call Dr. Stern?"

"What for? It goes away. Mama had a touch of arthritis at my age. It's no big deal." She poked him playfully. "You better get going."

He flopped into the kitchen chair. "Forget the office," he said, "I'm not leaving until you promise me you'll see Dr. Stern." He shouted into the kitchen. "Celina, I need you."

Celina came out, wiping her hands on her apron. "I heard, Mr. Benjamin. Not to worry. As soon as I finish in the kitchen, I'll make an appointment for her with Dr. Stern." She drew her mouth to one side, scowling at Elaine. "Stop giving me the evil eye, Missy. *We're going!*" She turned toward Lew. "Kissy, kissy, and say good bye, Mr. Benjamin." She slipped her arm through his and escorted him to the door. She held up his coat and he slipped into it." Don't worry," she whispered, "I'll call you." As she double locked the door, a shiver ran through her body. *I know her, she thought. She could be bleeding to death and wouldn't ask for help.*

Celina walked into the breakfast room, hoping her smile concealed her concern. She clapped her hands. "Okay, Elaine, let's see who's doing who on Jerry Springer."

Chapter 4

At the doctor's office, Elaine fidgeted in her seat. "I've never been to a doctor or a dentist who actually took a patient on time." She raised her voice, directing it at the receptionist. "Just once, I'd like to be taken on time, instead of hearing the same old line: 'the doctor will be with you shortly.' Evidently, shortly means at his convenience." She turned to Celina. "What are they doing in there? We've been here at least a half hour."

Celina patted Elaine's hand. She spoke quietly. "Stay cool, *mi estimado,* you're overreacting. We've only been here five minutes. I've never seen you so uptight. Well, maybe when one of the girls was sick." She leaned closer to Elaine, studied her face and searched her eyes. "Are you hiding something?"

"I'm scared, Celina. My fingers have been hurting for a while now."

Celina frowned. "What do you call a while? A week? A month?"

Elaine said nothing.

Celina bit her lip. *"Mierda,"* she said, frowning. "A year?" Elaine nodded. "And you kept it to yourself all this time? Why?"

"I didn't want to upset Lew and the girls, and you."

Celina shook her head. "Now I understand why the nurse was so hesitant when I called for the appointment. She said the doctor wanted to know why you haven't been back. I thought she was talking about your yearly checkup." She eyed Elaine. "He's already examined you, hasn't he?"

Before Elaine could answer, the nurse called her name. "I'm sorry you had to wait, Mrs. Benjamin."

"No, Bonita," Elaine said apologetically. "I'm the one who was out of line."

Elaine walked toward the doctor's office, Celina at her heels. "I'm sorry, Celina…" the nurse started to say, but Celina finished her sentence.

"If the doctor wants to throw me out, I'll understand, but until then, I'm sticking to her like glue."

Dr. Stern's greeting towards Elaine was less than cordial. "Naughty girl. I see you brought your bodyguard with you." He nodded at Celina. "How are you?"

Celina took a seat near the window. "I've seen better days and I've seen worse. The better days are when I don't get heartache from the *princesa.*" She motioned to Elaine. "I guess this is one of the worse days."

"Dr. Bill, I'm sorry," Elaine said. "It was stupid of me to keep putting it off."

His lips tightened as he shook his head. "Elaine, we have to talk." He sat behind his desk, nervously tapping his fingers on the blotter. "Frankly, I had given up on you. I thought by now you would have seen a rheumatologist."

Celina sat up in her chair. "A rheumatologist!"

He leaned forward. "You know, Elaine, I was hurt when I didn't hear from you. I've been your family doctor for more than ten years. I thought we had more than just a doctor-patient relationship. We see each other at the club. We go out to dinner. Lew and I play golf. For God's sake, Elaine, I brought the girls into the world."

Elaine threw her hands over her face and started to cry. "I'm so ashamed." He handed her a tissue. "Not only because I avoided you, but for hiding it from my family."

"I'm sorry to interrupt, Doctor," Celina said. *"Por favor*, bring me up to date. What's wrong with her?"

He looked at Elaine, who nodded. He clasped his hands and gently placed them on his desk. "Elaine has lupus."

Celina rose and took a chair next to Elaine. "I've heard of it, but I'm not exactly sure what it is. Does it have something to do with arthritis?"

"Some cases of lupus start as arthritis, with swelling and pain in the fingers and other joints. There are two types of lupus, but we are concerned with only one. It is called systemic lupus. It's what doctors call an autoimmune disease, in that the body's own defense system goes haywire, attacking the lining of joints and other tissues by mistake. In plain talk, it affects the organs of the body." He paused and looked at Elaine. "We should stop for now. Lew should hear this."

Elaine cried out. "No! Not yet. Just tell me how serious you think my case is."

He frowned. "Well, it goes without saying that we have lost a year that we could have...but that's neither here nor there. I'll recommend a specialist who will start you on anti-inflammatory drugs. Let's not jump the gun. I'm just being cautious. In fact, I was just reading about a possible new cure for lupus, and..."

Three loud knocks on the door interrupted the doctor's words, and the nurse burst into the room. "Doctor, Mr. Benjamin is here, and..." her eyes locked with Elaine's.

Panic immediately overwhelmed Elaine. She shrieked, "Lew? What's he doing here?"

His emotional sensibilities shattered, Lew, his shoulders hunched, his face the color of grey cement, stood in the outer office, sobbing. He tried to control his anguish. Tears ran down his cheeks as he wondered how he would tell Elaine the tragic news.

She ran from the doctor's office into the waiting room, saw Lew's face, stopped short and froze. Little by little, she edged towards him. A cold chill ran through her as she sucked in a quick breath. Her eyes wide with fear, she took one slow step, then another, until they were face to face.

He rubbed his hand roughly across his face, his mouth open but his voice silent.

"Well? What?" she screamed. "Just don't stand there. Talk to me! Can't you talk? Tell me! Lew! What happened?"

He whispered, "There was an accident."

"An accident? Who? Where?" Her body swayed unsteadily from side to side. "Not my girls? Which one? You idiot, why don't you answer me?"

He started to sweat, afraid to let the words escape his lips, then dropped his head. Raising his eyes to meet hers, he uttered, "Elaine, they're both gone."

"Gone?" She grabbed hold of his jacket lapels and shook him. "What are you talking about? They're in school!" She turned sharply towards Celina. "He's joking. Right, Celina? You packed their lunch and put them on the bus!"

Celina's grief-stricken eyes fell to the floor; words now would be futile.

Turning back to Lew, Elaine whimpered, "An accident?" Biting down hard on her finger, she repeated, "The bus…the bus…they were on the bus…my God, my God!" Looking at Lew questioningly, she searched his eyes then cringed, and asked, "Did you say…both of them?"

Lew nodded yes.

Her head wavered as if it were going to disengage from her neck. Moaning, she cried, "Not my babies… my babies…" The blood drained from her face and Elaine Benjamin fell silent, folding up inside herself.

Chapter 5

Fifteen years previous.

The pendulum on the stately grandfather clock struck midnight. Ambassador Theodore Hallsworth Kent, Senior, dabbed his mouth with a hand embroidered linen napkin, placed it neatly on his plate, and walked twenty feet to the other end of the dining room table. He bent down and gave his wife a peck on her cheek. "Happy New Year, dear," he said in a formal tone.

With a half smile, her voice cool, she said, "Happy New Year, Teddy."

The butler carefully pulled her chair out as she rose from the table. "Will you be having dessert in the study or on the terrace, sir?"

The ambassador glanced at his wife. "On the terrace, Radcliff," she said. "After all, it *is* New Year's Eve. Let us try to make it festive." Her husband nodded, held out his arm, and escorted her to the terrace.

The butler rolled his eyes, thinking; *I wonder what they'll do when their batteries die. What a pair of sleepwalkers.* He snapped his fingers and Bridgett the maid appeared with a rolling cart displaying espresso, tiramisu, éclairs and assorted pastries. She poured the coffee and handed it to Mrs. Kent and then to the ambassador.

Melissa Kent sipped her coffee, set the cup and saucer down on the coffee table and eyed the pastry. She smiled guiltily at her husband. "I know I shouldn't, but it being New Year's I'm going to indulge."

The Ambassador shrugged. "Suit yourself, my dear. Personally, I don't understand why you keep to a strict diet. You don't weigh a pound more than when we married. In fact, I think you're a bit on the slimmer side." He cocked his head and shut one eye. "A man likes a little meat on his woman. Makes her sexier."

"Sexier? Really, Teddy. Yes, I suppose you are a connoisseur on that subject. But you know nothing about keeping fit. It's the fashion to be svelte today. You never complained about my figure before." Her eyes strayed to his flabby stomach and waited until he caught her gaze. "It wouldn't hurt *you* to lose a few pounds. A man in your position should keep up appearances."

Bridgett carried the tray of tiramisu and held it out to him. He picked up a portion and immediately devoured it. "Quite right, quite right," he said, waving the maid off, and reached for another serving of the dessert. "Of course, of course. I'll start on a diet right after the new year."

His wife scowled at his lack of manners. "You have cake on your mouth, *dear*. Try using your napkin. And, while we are on the subject of health, you might give some thought to giving up polo? I have noticed that you are breathing heavily after a game." Teasingly, she added, "At your age, you should be careful."

His face flushed. "Give up polo? I just contributed a fortune towards the new indoor arena. Are you suggesting that I'm not in good shape, or are you saying I'm too old to play? I'll have you know I keep up with men half my age." To spite her, he stuffed a whipped crème tart into his mouth and washed it down with a healthy swallow of brandy. "Humph!" he snapped. "If you're looking to find fault, I suggest that you stop watching what I eat and pay attention to what your spoiled son Jonathon is up to." He held the brandy snifter up for Radcliff to refill. "The latest rumor at the club is of his chasing women around Boston." His tone mocked her.

"He's a reckless gadabout, painting the town red, white, and blue. I warned you years ago to tighten the reins on him."

Lifting a teacup, her pinky finger extending delicately, she countered with, "He has to sow his oats. The boy will get it out of his system." She smiled sarcastically. "You forget what it is to be young."

She opposed her husband at every turn. For years his philandering had been a thorn in her side, and each time Jonathon's name came up she held back, not wanting to tell her husband that she was sick and tired of his covert affairs and had no right to criticize her son when *he* so blatantly carried on. Lately, her patience was coming to an end.

"Boy? He's a runaway stallion. God, Melissa, he's a man, not a boy."

She stiffened. "Did you ever think it might possibly be your fault his being so, shall we say, active? You should have taken the time and paid attention to him…gone to athletic activities, bonded with him. Other fathers take time from their busy work schedules. Oh, but not you. You're too busy wining and dining every little…" Thinking she had said enough, she set the teacup down and shifted uncomfortably in her seat. "Let's not get into that again, Theodore, it *is* New Year's Eve."

He ignored her. "Humph," he declared, "You *must* be angry if you're calling me Theodore. Anyhow, what has my playing polo to do with your spoiled son's shenanigans? Can you deny the fact that Jonathon cannot stand up like a man, on his own two feet? He hasn't any ambition, or the slightest desire to accomplish a goal in life. I'd have liked him to follow in my footsteps. But, no, you have to coddle and keep him tied to your apron strings." He emptied the brandy snifter in one swift gulp. The liquor loosened his tongue. "If you have something to accuse me of, why don't you just come out and say it?" He motioned to Radcliff for a refill of the brandy and then, with a wave of his hand, dismissed the butler and the maid. Swishing the brandy around his mouth, he swallowed, inclined his body closer to her, and declared. "And, while we're taking pot shots at one another, I'm not so sure you and Jonathon haven't had more than just a mother-son relationship."

Chastising their son, and the gall that he suggested there might be an incestuous relationship going on, enraged her. Years of pent-up emotion burst from her very being. Slamming her fist down on the table, she shouted, "That's it! That's the last straw!" Her composure hanging by a thread, his accusation pushed her over the edge.

Melissa Kent tossed her napkin on the table, rose from her chair, walked to the terrace, and closed the French doors. She turned on her heels and stared down at her husband, her eyes bulging in their sockets. "Thank you for forcing me to tell you what I've been dying to for lo these many years. How dare you point a finger at me, you pompous, arrogant, podgy excuse for a man? I've news for you. I have evidence of your philandering with women from Boston to Timbuktu. Twenty-five years of indiscretions! You don't think I'm so stupid as to sit around all these years and hide my head in the sand, do you? You want proof? I'll show you affidavits and photographs that will make your hair stand on end. Files and files all compiled by licensed, bonded detectives, and also witnesses who will attest to your infidelities in a court of law."

She paced the floor then spun around and glared at him. "Yes, I spoiled Jonathon. Why shouldn't I? At least *he* gives me happiness. Do you think I would have gone to such extremes if you had shown me one bit of attention…one bit of affection? Oh, I don't care about me, but I do care about my son."

The hatred of her husband consumed her and she continued her tirade. Standing over him, she scowled down at him. "Do you want to know what I drilled into his head every night when he said his prayers?" She walked to the edge of the terrace, opened the French doors and looked up at the stars.

"Now I lay me down to sleep. I pray the Lord my soul to keep. If I should die before I wake, I pray the Lord my soul to take..." She turned towards her husband and finished the sentence. "...And Lord, if I should live another day, keep Father far away."

Theodore sat speechless. Defiantly, she placed her hands on her hips. "Well, Mister Ambassador? Lost your tongue? That's a first. No counter repartee? You must be slipping. I've seen you talk your way out of thousands of sticky situations."

Melissa raised her hand. He drew back and flinched, thinking she was going to strike him, but she lowered her hand and said, "I'll make this simple, Teddy. Frankly, you bore me. You always have. Perhaps it was wrong to go along with your infidelities. But, in spite of you, I've had a good life." Plopping into an armchair, she said, "I'm tired. Let's put this to bed. I am not going to expose you...simply distance myself from you."

He stared down at the oriental carpet, contemplating an answer. Finally he raised his head, and locked eyes with the woman he hardly knew. He looked at her questioningly. "What is it you want, Melissa?"

"I haven't decided. My lawyers will be in touch with you."

He winced.

"Oh, don't worry, Teddy, I won't take you to the cleaners, just sort of shake the money tree and the holdings you have so cleverly hidden. I will not lower myself to let the media in on any of your sordid affairs, although I'm sure your escapades are no secret." She raised her voice ever so slightly. "And one last thing. No, two. Jonathon will not associate with you, and have Radcliff move your belongings to the west wing of the estate."

His face devoid of expression, he held on to the arms of the chair and rose slowly. "Are you quite finished?" he asked.

With a sly smile and an endearing voice she answered, "For now, Teddy, for now."

The following afternoon the NBC Television Broadcasting Network opened their regular nightly program announcing the breaking news of the day.

Ambassador Theodore Hallsworth Kent, Senior, suffered a fatal heart attack while playing polo at the Back Bay Horse and Polo Club in Upper Meadow Lake, Massachusetts.

Chapter 6

Jonathon Kent, Jr. vaulted over the door of his shiny red Corvette convertible and sped down the driveway toward the exit of the massive antique gates that enclosed the Kent estate. "Jesus," he shouted. "Open up, will you!" He made a mental note to ask his mother to have the electricians install a faster, more up-to-date mechanism. As he maneuvered his car through the gates, he didn't look back, but waved a "goodbye" to his mother, who he knew was watching from the window of the breakfast room in the east wing.

He floored the Corvette along the winding highway while the radio blared, and sang, "You ain't nothin but a hound dog," his mind forming pleasurable thoughts of Penelope. The tires screeched as he gunned the sportscar around a sharp turn in the road. *Boy,* he thought, *this baby corners like crazy.* He pulled into a parking spot that read, "Handicapped Parking only," jammed on the brakes, skirted over the car door, gave a finger gesture at the $50 fine warning sign, then casually walked into the beauty salon.

"Hello, Mr. Kent," the receptionist chirped. "You're early. Penny will be finished with her client in just a few minutes." Smiling flirtatiously, she added, "Can I get you something? Coffee, magazine?"

"I'm just fine, Rosie." He smiled, eyeing her ample breasts. But his smile faded fast when he caught Penny giving him an evil eye.

"There, you're done," Penny said to her client. "I think this color suits you much better than the one you had before." She pocketed the tip, handed the lady the bill then sauntered to where Jonathan was sitting. "Flirting with Rosie? Can't you behave?"

"Gee, Penny, I was only kidding around." His eyes roamed from her pretty face to her bosom and back to her innocent blue eyes. "You look swell, Penny. Can you get away after you do my nails?"

She returned his enamored look. "No, Jonny, I can't. It's crunch time. I've got back-to-back appointments until five o'clock" She read his expression. "Now, Jonny, you know I'd love to, but Lottie warned me about the last time I took off." She grasped his hand for a second and looked around. "Don't be mad, but I can't afford to get fired."

"Get off it, Penny. Quit this menial job. I'll take care of you. I told you I would set you up in your own place, and we can be together all the time."

"And *I* told you, Jonny, I don't want to be kept. If you really loved me like you keep telling me, you'd make a commitment. Or is it like I thought from the start, that I'm just a girl from the wrong side of the tracks? Let's sit. We can talk while I do your nails. Lottie has her eye on us." She walked him to her table and plunged his fingers into a tray of soapy water.

He lowered his voice. "Tonight at the hotel, okay? Please, Penny. I'm not leading you on. I love you. Honest I do. I'm even thinking of having you meet my mother."

She rolled her eyes. "Yeah, I'll hold my breath."

"I think about you all day long. Please, Penny, I know you want to be with mc."

"Tonight? Maybe. I have to get another emery board, Jonny. I'll be just a minute." She turned and walked toward the cabinet, thinking, *Should I tell him or should I just have an abortion? His snobby mother will never accept me.*

Chapter 7

Melissa Kent eyed her son. Her voice was strained. "Really, Jonathon, a common beautician? I can't believe you'd stoop..." She stopped short, aware of his hurt expression and decided on a more tactful manner of persuasion. She poured a cup of tea, added a teaspoon of sugar, stirred it, and handed it to him. "Here, dear, drink your tea." She smiled and offered him a finger sandwich.

He refused the tea, grabbed the tray of sandwiches and roughly set them down on the coffee table. Anger flashed in his eyes. "Can't you get off your high horse for once and listen to what I'm saying?"

"Of course, dear," she said aloofly. "I'm listening. It isn't necessary to raise your voice or lose your temper."

"Do you have to be so condescending? I'm trying to tell you something that's important to me. You sound like a recorded message. I don't mean to offend you, but can't you understand what I'm saying without being so unfeeling, so cold? I'm your son, not a stranger."

Her eyes narrowed and she looked squarely into his eyes. "Jonathon, I may come across like I am unfeeling and cold, but I can assure you I do have feelings. I might remind you, all of them have been for you."

"You've just summed up my entire argument. I appreciate everything you've sacrificed for me, Mother, but now it's time for your little spoiled boy to grow up. To spread his wings."

"Spread your wings? From my point of view, you are already flying pretty high. Is there something I've overlooked, besides the entrance gates not working fast enough for you to speed through, or the generous no-limit allowance you enjoy?"

He moved his chair closer to her. "Mother, you've given me everything I've ever wanted...maybe too much. Yes, I agree. I have been a handful lately, but I do appreciate what you've done for me."

"I never sought your appreciation, Jonathon. It was my duty as your mother to see you had whatever I thought you needed." She fell silent for a moment. "It is not easy being both mother and father, you know."

He bit his lip in frustration. "You just said it. You gave me whatever *you* thought I needed. Maybe it wasn't the best thing for me." For one instant, memory flashed through his mind. His tone softened. "Oh, I'm not talking about the closeness we've had." He turned away, trying to erase the thought of their clandestine relationship. "That's in the past; dead; buried. I'm not blaming anyone." He leaned closer to her. "Mother, I'm a twenty-five-year-old man. You still think of me as your little boy."

She did think of him as her little boy; the child she had read fairy tales to; the young person she had spooned her body against, all the while pleasuring him, and herself, until they climaxed; the innocent, adolescent son who lost his virginity to her because she felt it was safer and best for him. His lack of appreciation and his speaking so maturely irked her.

"You will always be my little boy, Jonathon."

He stood over her, his chest heaving heavily. Frustrated, he protested loudly. "For God's sakes, Mother, cut the God damn cord! You're stifling me. I can't breathe."

She delicately placed her teacup in the saucer, set it down on the coffee table, and patted the cushion next to hers. Speaking softly but firmly, she said, "Jonathan dear, calm down. Come sit here, beside me. Evidently, you have developed a crush on this person...what is her name?"

Eyeing her cautiously but pleased that she asked, he said, "Penelope; but I call her Penny. And it's more than just a crush."

"Penny? How quaint. Call it a crush, infatuation, obsession or whatever you wish." She turned her attention to the hand-painted flowers that adorned the Dresden teapot, thinking she could easily handle this situation and get rid of this young woman who was surely after their money. "Very well, Jonathon, if it will make you happy, I'll be delighted to meet Penelope. Is 1:00 sharp tomorrow soon enough for you?"

He registered a sigh of relief; the image of Penny's happy face flashed in his mind.

"Brunch on the terrace would be appropriate, don't you think?" She didn't wait for an answer. "Just the ladies, Jonathon. Girl talk, you know. I'm sure you'd be bored."

His eyebrows shot up. "Mother, you are going to be cordial, aren't you? She's intimidated by us, as it is."

"Honestly, Jonathon. You're speaking as if I were going to tie her up and put her in a dungeon. Really. If you can't trust your own mother, well, I honestly don't know what more I can say."

He eyed her suspiciously, thinking, *Play it cool. Take it nice and easy. Play it her way, for now. When the time is right, then you'll act. The old crow has had it her way far too long. Be smart. Humor her.* He rose, bent over, met her gaze, tilted her face up to his and kissed her sensuously on her lips. Stirring sensations surged through her as inklings of her past indiscretions surfaced.

Apologetically, he said, "I'm sorry, Mother. I was wrong. I should know better. You're right. You have always made me your number-one priority."

Chapter 8

The sky was a serene, azure blue and the billowy cumulus clouds predicted fair skies from this day forward for Jonathon Kent Jr. He was in all his glory. This was going to be the best day of his life.

The Corvette's tires parted the gravel in front of Penelope's trailer park home. He pressed down on the horn to alert her. To Penelope, the horn sounded like a symphony orchestra. Holding the lace curtains to one side, she glanced out the window and waved at Jonathon. "I'll be right out," she called.

Jonathon did a double take, watching her gaily bopping down the three steps of the trailer. His face took on a sullen expression as he held the passenger door open for her. "You look funny," she said. "Your mother didn't cancel, did she?"

He stammered. "I..."

"I knew it," she said, tears welling in her eyes. "She cancelled."

"Penny, she's expecting you at one o'clock. Don't be so uptight."

"I knew it," she repeated. "I got all dressed up, and I took off from work, too."

"You're not listening, Penny. Give me a chance to talk, will you? She didn't cancel. It's not that."

"Then what is it? You don't like my hair. It's my hair, isn't it? We have

43

lots of time. I can do it over. I could wear it up. It'll make me look more sophisticated."

He grabbed her by her shoulders and gently shook her. "Settle down, will you, honey? Your hair looks super. You look very pretty. It's your dress."

"What's wrong with my dress? I spent an hour going through the racks at Sears until I found it. And even with the markdown, it wasn't cheap."

"Don't think I'm being critical, Penny. It's just not good enough for you. Tell you what. We have plenty of time. Let's drive into town and stop at Neimans and pick up something, uh, more suitable." He kissed her gently on the lips. He gazed lovingly into her eyes. "After all, if you're going to be Mrs. Jonathon Kent, you'll have to get used to spending money on yourself."

"Mrs. Jonathon Kent," she said, lifting her head proudly. "I like the way it sounds. In fact, Jonny, I don't think I want to be called 'Penny' anymore." She giggled.

"Why?" he questioned. "I like Penny."

"Okay, I'll make an exception, but only for you."

He pulled away from the curb, laughing loudly. "I love you, Penny; you're so adorable. It's refreshing how honest you are." He took her hand and squeezed it. "I think we are going to change you from an Eliza Doolittle to a Grace Kelly."

"Well," she pouted, "if Liza Doowhatever, is one of your old girlfriends I certainly don't want to look like her."

Walking into a classy boutique or department store had always intimidated Penelope. But when they entered Neiman Marcus to buy a dress that would be appropriate for her meeting with his mother, she lost her shyness. The saleslady held an afternoon party dress up to Penny's neck. "Now," she chirped, "if ever I saw a dress that has your name written all over it, this is it. Red is your color."

A sculptured plaque, hand crafted onto the wrought iron gate at the Kent estate, read, 'Simon Sez' in bold script lettering.

"What does that mean?" Penny asked. "Reminds me of a game we used to play."

"That's what everyone says when they first come here. It was the name of a horse that father owned. He won the top polo honors with her years ago. He died recently." Jonathon pressed the remote control and the gates swung open. "Good job, Mother," he said. "Didn't take long to have the gates fixed."

Penny looked around, amazed at the estate. She shivered. "You mean this is your home? Gees, it's as big as Edmonton Park. How many people live here?"

"Seven."

"Are they relatives?"

He chuckled. "Only mother and I are family. The rest are servants. There's James, the chauffeur, Betsy, the housekeeper, Mamie, the cook, Radcliff the butler, and Bridgett, the maid."

"Wow! They're all servants?" Feeling uneasy, she said, "Jonny, I'm not sure I can do this. I'm too nervous. I'm getting sick to my stomach."

"You're overreacting. Take a deep breath. You'll be okay. Now that I think about it, Penny, you've been acting kind of funny lately. How come you've been getting stomach aches? When did you have your last checkup?"

She hesitated. "Checkups? I don't need checkups. I never get sick. But I should cut down on the greasy food." She pressed her hand to her stomach, wondering if she might possibly be showing.

Radcliff the butler greeted them as they walked up the steps to the front door. "Welcome to Simon Sez," he said, bowing slightly at Penelope. "Jonathon, your mother is waiting on the terrace for you and the young lady."

"Oh, I won't be staying. This is just for the girls." He chuckled at the word "girls." "It's a sort of get-acquainted lunch. I'll be back later."

Penny held onto Jonathon's coat sleeve. "Jonny," she said, trembling.

He turned her towards him. "Now, Penny, there's nothing to be afraid of. When you get to know her you'll like her." She looked at him with uncertainty. He embraced her. "Relax, darling. I promise, if you and mother don't hit it off, it won't make any difference. I don't think you realize how crazy I am about you." He pressed her closer to him. "Listen, Penny, if after your lunch you feel uncomfortable, just say the word and I'll pack my bags, and we'll leave this afternoon. We can elope and have a honeymoon anywhere you say." He searched her eyes. "Tell me you understand, and say you love me. I need to hear it."

Her lips quivered. "I understand, Jonny," she said, but it didn't quell her fears.

"I'll be back for you in an hour. There's some business I have to take care of, and then you and I will celebrate."

Jonathon pointed to the butler. "She's all yours, Radcliff. Take care of her. She's very special."

"Yes, sir."

Penny weakly called out to Jonathon as he opened the door. He turned, blew her a kiss. "Handle Mother just the way you would one of your irate customers at the beauty shop. Just smile. You win everyone over with your smile. See you in a little while, sweetheart."

She wanted to run to him, but the butler's voice stopped her. He smiled sympathetically. "Mrs. Kent's bark is worse than her bite, miss. Follow me, please."

•。

Melissa Kent watched Penny enter the terrace garden. *Attractive young lady,* she thought. *Jonathon must have outfitted her at Neiman's. She could hardly afford to pay for that designer dress working in a beauty salon. God, who wears red in the afternoon?*

"How do you do?" she asked, extending a limp hand. "Please sit down." Radcliff held the chair for her. "Jonathon seems quite smitten with you. And I can see why. You're quite good-looking."

"Thank you, Mrs. Kent," Penny said, the compliment putting her a little more at ease. "Jonny talks about you all the time."

"*Jonny?* Does he really? How nice of Jonathon." She glanced at the butler. "Radcliff, you may serve lunch." She studied Penny. "Is that the new hairstyle being worn nowadays?"

"I saw it in the latest Hair Trends Magazine. Do you like it?"

"Well, it isn't exactly how the young women at the club are doing their hair. But to each his own, as they say."

Penny felt her composure slipping away. "I only did it today," she said. "I'm not sure I like it that much, either."

"I didn't mean to offend you, Penelope. I suppose, when one is as pretty as you, one can overlook small details."

Penny's heart sank. Mrs. Kent made Penelope feel like a flower that had suddenly wilted. She thought, *I knew I shouldn't have come. I don't belong here.*

"I understand that you and Jonathon are quite close. I'm sure you are mature enough to understand how serious a commitment marriage is."

"Marriage? Well, we haven't really gotten that far. We're not even engaged yet. Jonny wanted to get your approval first. He's so proper about everything. I admire him for that."

"Yes, I am sure you do." The maid entered, wheeling a serving cart. "You may leave, Bridgett," Mrs. Kent said dryly. "I'll serve." She picked up a serving spoon and smiled at Penny. "The cook always prepares salads for lunch on weekends. Lobster salad, shrimp salad, or perhaps crab salad?" she asked.

"Lobster salad, please. I love it. I don't get to eat it very often, it being so expensive."

"I'm sure." Mrs. Kent said. She spooned a serving of lobster salad, held out the plate to Penelope, and then suddenly withdrew the dish. "Perhaps I should give you a bit more," she said. "You did say you don't get a chance to have lobster, it being so expensive." Penelope winced. She could feel the perspiration running down her armpits. "Tell me, Penelope. What does your father do for a living? Jonathon never speaks about your parents or your background."

Penny hesitated. "I don't have a father. I mean, I have a father, but he doesn't live with us. I don't even know what he looks like. He left my mother the day she gave birth to me."

"Oh dear, how sad for you and your mother. One must be very careful with whom one becomes sexually involved, wouldn't you say?"

"Yes. But it's not that way with Jonny and me. We trust each other. I would never lie or deceive him." She stared down at the lace tablecloth, admiring the intricate design. "I go to church every Sunday, and sometimes at night."

"Very commendable, my dear." Eying Penelope, she suddenly said," Are you a virgin?"

Penny was taken aback. "I..."

Mrs. Kent smiled. "Which means that you are not, I take it."

Penny dropped her fork. "Wa…well," she stuttered. "But Jonny's the only one."

"Of course, dear, of course. Here, take this fork."

"I don't think I'm very hungry. In fact, I don't feel very well. I need to use the rest room."

Mrs. Kent called out. "Radcliff, please show Penelope to the powder room."

●ₒ

"Are you all right?" Mrs. Kent asked as Penny, accompanied by Radcliff, walked back onto the terrace.

Penny nodded as she sat down. "I didn't want it to be this way. I mean, our meeting for the first time. I wanted so much for us to start out the right way."

Mrs. Kent dabbed the corners of her mouth with her napkin, placed the napkin neatly on the table, and looked at Penelope. "There is no right way, Penelope. I hate to be blunt, but you don't fit into our way of life. Think about it. True, you are attractive. No one can take that away from you, but try to understand our point of view. Look at how we live, the caliber of people we associate with. It's a whole different world than you know. You may not think so now, but I'm trying to save you a lot of pain and embarrassment. You'd be lost here. Yes, Jonathon is infatuated with you, but he's not in love with you. He just thinks he is. Believe me, in a few months he will tire of you and long for the life he was born to. Find someone of your own class. You'll be better off. Chalk this up to experience."

Penny wanted to die. "I don't understand any of this. I only know we love each other." She mustered all the courage she could and looked her adversary straight in the eye. "Jonny told me if you gave me a hard time not to worry. He said he would pack his things and we would elope and go on a honeymoon."

"Listen, Penelope. I can prove he's stringing you along. Do you know where he is at this very moment?" Penny shook her head. "He's with Pamela. Pamela Worthington. The young lady he is going to marry."

"He couldn't be. He told me he would be back to get me."

"All right, if you don't believe me, I'll just have to convince you." Mrs. Kent reached for the phone and dialed a number.

"Worthington residence."

"Hello, Arthur. This is Mrs. Kent. May I speak to Pamela, please?"

"Surely, Mrs. Kent. Just a moment."

"Hello, Mrs. Kent. How are you?"

"Just fine, Pamela. Pamela, is Jonathon there?"

Mrs. Kent held the phone to Penny's ear.

"He walked in the door a few minutes ago," Pamela chirped. "Hold on, I'll call him. Jonathon, sweetie, your mother's on the phone."

"What's wrong, Mother?" Jonathon asked.

Penny gasped in disbelief. She bolted from her chair, plucked her purse from the entrance table. Disoriented and brokenhearted, she dashed out the front door.

Jonathon continued, "Mother, is Penny there? I hope you're not starting any trouble. I'm at Pamela's to tell her that I'm not going to see her anymore. I love Penny."

"Yes dear, I understand. Goodbye." Mrs. Kent quietly placed the receiver in its cradle, smiled smugly and motioned to Radcliff to remove Penny's plate. "Radcliff," she said, "Tell Margot that I wish to see her in my study."

Margot Plantine, Mrs. Kent's social secretary, pencil and pad in hand, sheepishly shuffled into the room. Her stark, ash gray hair, pulled back into a ponytail knotted with a scrungee, hung loosely down the back of her neck. Horn-rimmed glasses perched on the tip of her narrow nose threatened to drop off at any moment. "Good afternoon, Mrs. Kent. Are there letters you wish to dictate?"

In the study, Mrs. Kent found it increasingly difficult to conceal the delight she derived by severing Penelope's involvement with Jonathon. "Margot, I find that I need to get away. Perhaps Madrid. No, I understand it is the rainy season there. Paris! Yes, Paris. Make all the proper arrangements."

"For how many, ma'am?"

"For three, Margot. You will come along to assist me. We'll be staying at the Hotel de Crillon. Reserve a private room for yourself and the Louis XV suite for me and…"

"You did say three persons, Mrs. Kent?"

Without hesitation, she said, "Yes, three, Margot. And instruct Radcliff to pack suitable attire for Jonathon."

Chapter 9

Dora Muldoon pushed the Silver Cross pram along the cobblestone path in Edmonton Park. "Now make sure ya stay close to me all the time, Timothy. It's very important. Ya never can tell who might be lurking about." She stopped walking and looked down at her five-year-old ward. "Are you listening to me, Timothy?"

He grinned as he looked up at her, his large brown eyes sparkling. "Every day we come to the park, and every day you say the same thing." He mimicked her. "Make sure ya stay close to me, Timothy. It's very important." He squinted. "You must think I'm a baby."

She had an urge to pick him up and smother him with kisses, but she knew he would squirm and complain that he was a big boy. "Well, we can't be too careful, young man. Your mother and father would have me head if ya got lost."

"Look, Nana, there's Michael. Can I play with him?"

"Sure, go ahead. I'll be settin' on the bench talking to Maddie." She pointed a warning finger at him. "Remember, I want ya to be where I can see you."

"I promise, Nana."

She sat down heavily, next to her friend. "These feet are begging for me to get offa them." She sighed. "Ah, that's better. How are you today, Maddie?" she said, her eyes focused on Timothy's every move as she automatically rocked the infant in the carriage.

Maddie tucked the blanket securely around her charge. "I've had a wee bit of pain in me back, so I went to the doctor and he gave me a prescription. God' musta heard me prayers 'cause I'm feeling better."

Dora shook her head. "Don't believe in pills, and for sure don't believe in doctors. Once you start on the medications it's not long before you're hooked on 'em. You'll see. You won't be able to do without them."

"But, Dora, they *have* helped me."

"Sure, for the moment. Wait and see. Ya'll be poppin 'em like candy. I'm telling ya, Maddie, there's a secret society of medical bigwigs out there who don't do a damn thing but think up ways to get the public addicted to drugs. Ya know I was a nurse before I decided to become a nanny." She nodded to confirm what she said. "Lord help us, money is the root of all evil."

"Do ya really think there are doctors like that, Dora?"

"Uh, huh. The guy that comes up with a way to cleanse the body without poppin pills is gonna make a fortune." She eyed the children playing near the water's edge. Turning her attention back to her friend, she continued speaking. "Ease off of the junk, Maddie. If the label says, take three times a day; take 'em twice a day, then just once a day. Wean offa them. Don't fall into their trap. It's an old trick that the drug companies play on us. That's why they're so rich."

"Is that a fact?"

"Now what are the children carrying on about?" She stood up and yelled at them. "Boys! Timothy! Get away from the water. Don'tcha be makin me come after ya!"

"They probably saw a fish in the lake," Maddie said. "Anyhow, they're coming back."

The boys ran as fast as their legs could carry them to where the women were sitting. Timothy pulled on Dora's dress. "What's the matter, child?" she asked. "You look like ya seen a ghost."

"Nana! Nana!" he cried, breathlessly. "Down at the water...come."

"Watch the little one, Maddie. I'm goin to see what all the fuss is about." She took hold of Timothy's hand. "Now, young man, I hope you didn't get me up for a wild goose chase. These feet are about to give out. What's all the racket about?"

His eyes wide with fright, he pointed to the lake. "See, Nana, over there. There's a lady in a red dress floating in the water."

Chapter 10

Jonathon smiled as he tossed a tennis ball against his bedroom wall. The trip to Paris with his mother had been grueling but in order to accomplish his goal he knew he had to be patient. *I gave her what she wanted and now it's my turn to collect the rewards.*

A glimmer of sun peeked through the half drawn drapes and mimicked his upbeat mood. He let out a chuckle as his mind flashed to last night's objective when he had donned a hooded grey sweat suit, sneaked down to where the family motorboat was docked and planted a strip of dynamite underneath the starter.

"C'mon ring, will you," he said aloud to the silent phone beside him. "The suspense is killing me." When the phone finally did sound, he laid the tennis ball on the bed and waited for five rings. He picked up the receiver, and said, "And to what do I owe this unexpected pleasure, Trippy?"

His lawyer, Filmore Tripplehorn answered somberly. "Good morning, Jonathon."

"And a good morning to you," Jonathon said briskly. "You must have something important to tell me, or you'd be out on the golf course on such a beautiful Sunday morning."

"Evidently, you haven't heard."

"Heard? Heard what? Don't tell me you finally got that hair transplant?"

His lawyer ignored Jonathon's flippant remark. "Brace yourself, Jonathon. Your mother has been in a boating accident. I'm afraid it's bad news."

Jonathon feigned surprise. "Oh, no! Not mother! Was she badly hurt?"

"I'm afraid she's gone."

"Gone? What do you mean? I can't believe it. I spoke to her last night. She asked me to go boating on the lake with her this morning, but I had to beg off. I had made a previous commitment. It's impossible. In fact she called me from the boat a few hours ago." He pretended to cry. "I can't talk now, Trippy, I'm...I'm...too upset."

He hung up the receiver, picked up the tennis ball and continued bouncing it against the wall. Thinking the servants might be about, he tossed the ball to the floor, and proceeded to check the temperature of his coffee. Displeased with its warmth, he poured himself another cup, walked to the middle of the room, and stared at the picture of his mother that stood on his night table. Their eyes seemed to lock. He raised his cup of coffee in a toast to her. "Now we are even, Mother. Finally even."

Chapter 11

Present day

Franny Goldsmith pulled up her pantyhose and checked herself in the bedroom mirror. "Not bad," she said. "Five more pounds and I'll be back to where I was before."

Joey, her live-in boyfriend spoke up. "There's nothing wrong with your figure. You don't want to look like those emaciated beanpoles they call models, do you? I'd rather sleep with a two-headed gorilla. You're just right." He popped open a can of beer. "Your bod is great; it's your head that's messed up."

She rolled her eyes. "Do me a favor and lay off the sarcasm. I'm nervous enough about going to the new shrink. It took all my courage to make the call." She straightened her skirt. "You men are so lucky not having to deal with cellulite."

He jumped off the bed and grabbed her and teased, "Come on, baby, give me some of that cellulite. It drives me crazy."

She shoved him away. "Joey, stop kidding around. I have to be in the right frame of mind for my session with Dr. Jonathon Kent."

"You're wasting your time and money. There's nothing *that* wrong with you. You're a little hyper, and once in a while you go off the deep end, but so what? No one's perfect."

She raised her hand. "Hold it!" she commanded. "You're not helping me." She sat down on the bed and folded her hands around his. "Listen, Joey, I know you're trying to make me feel better and I appreciate it, but no one knows me better than me. I've got a lot bottled up inside of me. If I don't get some help, I think I'll..."

"Okay, okay. Franny. I understand. I'm sorry. You know me, always kidding around. Want me to drive you? I could wait for you and take you home after your session."

She kissed him on the forehead. "No, I have to do this by myself. And besides, didn't you tell me that you had a meeting with Bernie and Al at the funeral parlor? You know, Joey, Bernie's really pissed at you. He said the accountants need to finish their work on the fiscal quarter, and you're holding them up."

"Screw them. You'd think they would show a little more respect to the top embalmer."

"Don't be such a wise guy, Joey. Save it for the stiffs. Listen, I've got to get moving."

"You sure you don't want me to drive you? Take me a sec to dress."

"No thanks, hon. I'll grab a cab."

"Hey, Franny, go easy on the shrink."

"Very funny, Joey. Wish me luck."

"Wish you luck? Forget it. It's the shrink who's going to need the luck."

Chapter 12

"Here ya are, lady," the cabby said. "Want me ta get da door for ya?"

"Get out of here," Franny said, surprised. Scanning his name and photo on the dashboard, she came back with, "Melvin, you want me to have a heart attack? A cabby holding the door for a passenger! What are you bucking for, cabby of the month?"

"Didn't you read the poster on the back divider? The mayor is cleaning up New York. This month it's the hacks. Last month it was da bus drivers."

Franny chuckled. "What's it going to be next month? Clean the peep holes in the porno joints?"

He guffawed. She placed the fare and a five-dollar tip through the opening of the plastic divider tray as he pulled up to Dr. Kent's address. His brow's arched with surprise. "Hey, thanks. You're okay, lady. Have a good one."

"I'm going to do my best, Melvin," Franny said, closing the taxi's door.

The doorman tipped his cap as he greeted her underneath the building's canopy. "Can I help you, ma'am?"

She glanced at the psychiatrist's business card. "I'm looking for Penthouse A. Dr. Jonathon Kent."

"Follow me, please." He led her to a bank of elevators of which only one had an operator. "Arnie," he said, "Take the young lady to Doctor Kent's suite."

The elevator's purple-tufted velvet banquette and handcrafted teak parquet walls took her by surprise.

The entire waiting room was circular and decorated in myriad shades of white, off white, milk white, ash white, and pale white. Chairs were quilted in a diamond pattern, with overstuffed cushioned seats with tufted backs in a circular design. A large picture by Erte', depicting a gentleman in a top hat and tails escorting a lady in a silver-sequined evening gown, caped by a black fox fur stole, hung above an oversized plush, sandy-white circular sofa. Complementing the sofa, a large, round beveled glass table displaying a huge conch rested above a circular white fur rug. On the adjacent wall over a Bombay chest, a cartoon heroine in an original Liechtenstein looked dubiously down at the patients.

"Phew," Franny uttered. *Place looks like an art deco movie set. Impressive. Tres chic. I should have asked how much a session is going to set me back.*

An attractive receptionist smiled warmly. "Good morning, Ms. Goldsmith. I'm Cynthia. How are you today?"

Franny returned her smile. "Any better and it would be a sin," she quipped. "I know. I'm early."

Cynthia smiled. "By an hour."

Tugging at her earlobe, Franny said, "I'm a little nervous. I didn't want to be late for my first appointment."

"It's understandable." She handed Franny a clipboard. "Just short medical background info. It will only take a minute." She checked her wristwatch. Smiling pleasantly, she quickly added, "Can I get you something to eat?"

"Oh no, I wouldn't want you to go to any trouble. But coffee would be good."

"It's no trouble. We have a full kitchen and a chef. I could have the chef cook up anything from steak and eggs to pancakes to, well, just about anything." She emphasized, "And you *do* have an hour."

"Wow! Breakfast, lunch, dinner? Am I in a shrink's office or a restaurant? I did skip breakfast."

"Good. Let's go into the dining room. And we have a powder room if you would like to freshen up. Meanwhile, I'll get a menu."

"Do you mean to tell me the doctor has a personal chef that works here full time? I never heard of such a thing. And a menu, yet?"

Cynthia nodded. "You're not the first to say that. "Dr. Kent spares no expense to ensure his patients are well taken care of."

"Well taken care of," Franny repeated.

Franny sat on a poof in the ladies room and stared into the mirror. *He must be the only shrink in the world who offers a menu, and an around-the-clock chef while he listens to problems. This piece of real estate must set him back a pretty penny. To hell with my diet. Today I'm going to eat until I bust. I have a feeling this shrink is going to take me to the cleaners.*

"Did you enjoy the breakfast?" the receptionist asked after Franny had finished eating.

Franny placed her napkin on the table, stood, and patted her hips. "Weighted and sated," she joked. "You make coming here a pleasant experience. How about dinner?"

"You're joking, but as a matter of fact, if you have an appointment after work you can call ahead and make dinner arrangements." She pursed her lips. "But sometimes you have to settle for pot luck."

Franny sighed. "What a drag. Must be a bummer to eat leftovers." They both laughed.

"The doctor will be with you shortly, Ms. Goldsmith. Would you like to freshen up? You'll find a fresh toothbrush and toothpaste in the upper left hand drawer of the powder room."

"Franny, call me Franny. Ms. Goldsmith sounds like you're speaking to my mother, and we definitely don't want her in on the conversation. But,

I *will* visit the powder room. Wouldn't want to offend the good doctor with onion breath on my first visit."

"You have quite a sense of humor, Franny."

"That's why I'm here. I have this terrible problem. I just can't stop making people laugh." She shrugged and waved her hands. "Well, that's enough of that. Is it time for my session?"

"As soon as you finish in the powder room."

Cynthia led Franny to a closed door and tapped lightly. "Come," the doctor said. He rose, approached Franny, and extended his hand.

Franny's heart skipped a beat. *This guy is to die for.* Their eyes fastened and Franny felt her legs turn to Jello.

His smile was warm and inviting. "You could relax here," he said, motioning to a chaise lounge. "Or, if you prefer, there's the leather chair with an ottoman, or the straight-back, cushy chair. Wherever you feel comfortable. You choose."

The word *choose* revolved in her brain. *How about on your lap?* she thought, but to him she said demurely, "I'm not sure. They all look good to me." She couldn't resist. "Do I get extra points for choosing the right one?"

His face lit up. "You get extra points for just being here."

She walked to the straight-back cushy chair, sat, lifted her skirt above her knees, and crossed her shapely legs. "Good choice?" she asked.

He nodded, dragged a chair close to her and sat down. "May I call you 'Franny?'" Before she could answer, he added, "And call me Jonathon. First names tend to put patients at ease." He pretended to glance at the questionnaire she had completed but covertly checked out her form and good looks.

The only stirring in the room was his libido, which shifted from first, to second, skipped third and went straight into overdrive. *Mmm,* he thought, *hyper individual. Bet she's a tigress in the sack.*

Chapter 13

The two-months' sessions with Dr. Kent blossomed into more than a patient/doctor relationship.

"I'm famished," Franny said soberly as she stepped out of Jonathon's private bathroom.

"Wow!" he exclaimed. "You look sensational."

She was overjoyed by his compliment, and although the black satin, strapless Vera Wang gown had made a huge dent in her bank account, she felt it was well worth it. "What a workout!" she declared, spraying her neck with Joy. "Are you sure you're up to going out tonight?"

Jonathon slipped into his formal shoes. "I'm raring to go. Now, if I can get this damn tie to lie straight."

"Stop fussing, handsome. Here, let me do it. Psychiatrists are not supposed to know about trivial things, like tying ties. Their area of expertise is to help people solve their problems. Which reminds me. This is our tenth session. Don't I get a report card, or a good conduct medal? I could use a little encouragement."

He spun her around. "A report card on your progress as a patient or as a lover?"

She put distance between them. "Stop that, you animal. I'm serious."

"You…serious? That's a first."

She folded her arms across her chest. "I'm going to hound you until you answer me." She narrowed her eyes. "You're full of secrets tonight. You tell me to get all dolled up, and you won't give me a hint as to where we're going, and you're stalling about my progress as a patient." Looking defiantly at him, she added, "I'm not moving an inch." She raised her voice. "Tell me. Am I making any headway?"

"How do *you* think you're doing?"

She pursed her lips in thought. "I think the combination of you being such a good listener and your voracious sexual appetite is doing wonders for me."

He took her hand and led her out of the office. "You're doing just fine."

She gave him a long, tentative look.

He yielded. "Okay, okay. Stop pouting. You are making progress, but…"

"That's a but with a capitol B, Jonathon."

The tightness of his mouth showed exasperation. He stopped short and faced her. "This is not the time to discuss your progress. Let's forget about business and have some fun." His hands softened around her face. "Okay?"

Melting from his touch, she reconsidered. *He's right. I better drop the subject. I'm getting frustrated and he's getting pissed. Pushing the conversation will put a damper on the evening.*

Stepping into the elevator, Jonathan pulled her against him, reached into his jacket pocket and jiggled the keys to his Lamborghini in front of her eyes.

Surprised, she inquired, "What? Don't tell me you want me to drive your precious baby? You can't be serious."

He nodded. "You have a driver's license, don't you?"

"Sure, but I have to warn you…well, let's put it this way. I was asked to join the Demolition Derby Auto Wrecker's Club. Get the picture?"

He shrugged. "Let me worry about that. I have another one in the barn."

"A barn, for automobiles? What do you feed them, hay?"

He shook his head. "Oh boy, there goes your sense of humor again. No, the barn is part of the estate where I house my new and vintage automobiles."

"And the horses? Did you sell them to make Jello?"

At the parking level he led her to the Lamborghini. "Here," he said. "Push this button on the remote, but stand back, the doors swing up."

She pushed the button and stood in awe as the doors lifted. "Wow," she said, amazed. "If you need a professional car duster, I work cheap. Want to see my credentials?"

He shook his head. "I've already seen your credentials."

She shrugged. "No, huh." She entered the driver's side and sat down as the seat belt encircled her. "So where do I put the key?"

He reached across and placed her hand on his crotch. "Right here," he said.

"Later potato." She removed her hand. "I can't concentrate on this state-of-the-art piece of machinery, my hunger, and you, at the same time."

"Now pay attention. There's no ignition key. Just touch this button, but don't give it gas."

She pressed the button he had pointed to. "Is it on?" she asked. "I don't hear the motor running."

"It's on, Franny. It runs quietly." He stifled a chuckle.

"Stop laughing at me, Jonny, or I'll change shrinks."

He stiffened. "What did you say?" he said sharply, his face showing anger.

"Say what? That I might change shrinks?"

"No. You called me Jonny."

"What's the problem?" She looked at him with concern. "I'm sorry. I'll go back to Jonathon." She stared out of the window. "Jeez, Jonathon. We've been going out for over a month. It's not like we just met, you know."

"Forget it. It's just that no one calls me Jonny. Except for once, when I was young," he said curtly, his mind clouding with thoughts of Penny.

She sighed. "That bad, huh? Only once? You're lucky. I've been burned more than just once."

"Let's go." He felt annoyed as flashes of Penny whirled around his head.

She thought, *Keep the conversation light, Franny; change the subject.* She asked, "Where to? I love surprises! You must have planned something special. Is that why we're going formal?"

He mellowed. "Well, I think so. We are going to the opera to see Die Valkure. You did mention that you like the opera."

Die Valkure, she thought. *Geez, at least Madam Butterfly, or La Boehme. I guess he's not into heavy metal or Madonna. Now that would have been a real surprise.* But to him... "Are you kidding? Of all the operas, it's my very favorite."

"You're joking, right? It's getting so I can't tell when you're kidding around or being straight."

"Just because I kid around doesn't mean I'm not into the arts."

His face lit up. "Good! We'll dine afterwards. I made reservations at Le Cirque."

"Wonderful. I'm famished."

●

Hunger...boredom...climbing over the Berlin Wall to freedom: these were the only thoughts on Franny's mind during the tedious three hours at the opera. Her arm was black and blue from pinching it to keep from dozing off. *If only you would get me something like a corned beef sandwich from The Stage Deli.* Her mouth watered. *Okay, I'll settle for a giant size box of Good n' Plenty. They last longer. Be serious,* she told herself. *Show him you've got class.*

At the restaurant the maitre'd greeted them. "Bonjour, Monsieur Kent. Your table is ready. The usual? Dom Perignon?"

Jonathon looked at Franny for approval. She felt like saying, "Get the damn food on the table, Frenchie, before I pass out from starvation. Instead she smiled sweetly at the maitre'd and said, "Dom Perignon of course. Merci beaucoup."

"Are you all right, Franny?" Jonathon asked. "You seem preoccupied. The opera, right? It's so exciting. Especially the end."

"Oh, yes," she said, wondering when that happened. "It's one opera that I never tire of. That and La Boheme." She placed her hand to her heart. "When Brunnhilde sang her heart out on top of the mountain I got goose bumps."

The waiter popped the cork and poured the champagne. "To La Boheme," Jonathon said, toasting. "It's playing in two weeks." He removed a small notepad from his inside jacket pocket and made a notation. "Just a reminder to tell Cynthia to get tickets."

❦

After dining, Jonathon looked at Franny in earnest. "You should channel some of your pent-up energy."

"Channel my pent-up energy? Isn't that what I have *you* for?" On a whim, she decided to take a stand, feel him out. "I get the feeling you're trying to tell me something. You haven't fallen madly in love with me, have you?"

He finished his champagne and set it down. "Seriously, Franny, all your joking around is amusing to a point, but you overdo it."

"Which means?"

"I didn't want to discuss anything personal tonight, but since you won't let up…"

She sulked, thinking, *Here it comes.*

"You're suppressing your feelings," he said as the wheels in his brain started to rouse. "I've been thinking."

"That's commendable," she wisecracked.

He ignored her ill-timed comment. "I want you to join my group therapy."

She became solemn. "You're not trying to let me down easy, are you?"

"Don't be foolish. This has nothing to do with the way I feel about you." He took hold of her hands. "You believe me, don't you?"

"I want to Jonathon, but..."

"Trust me, Franny. I wouldn't hurt you." He thought. *It's time to put an end to this relationship.* "I'm going to arrange for you to sit in on the group."

Casting a suspicious eye, she removed her hand from his. "What about our private sessions?"

"We'll have to cancel the one-on-one for now. Maybe you'll open up to the group. Our being so close hasn't helped you." He was holding her hand again. "Believe me, I'm doing this for you. Let's finish dinner and go to the hotel."

She brooded. "Do we have to go to a hotel? It's so tacky."

"The Plaza isn't tacky."

"All right," she said reluctantly.

He cast a lustful eye. "I'll make it up to you. C'mon Franny, give us that devil-may-care attitude you're so good at."

Chapter 14

Noisy clatter could be heard from the unsecured shutter that hung loosely from the second story brownstone window on the upper west side of Manhattan. Folding French doors separated the bedroom from a small but functional kitchen. A shiny black Formica counter held an array of black, red and stainless steel electrical appliances. The black and white octagon tiled floor complemented two tall wrought iron stools that stood alongside a café table draped with a red and white checkerboard tablecloth. On the tablecloth, a saltshaker, a peppershaker, and an empty Cinzano wine decanter with dried deposits of candle wax flickered ghostly shadows onto the canary yellow kitchen walls.

Reminiscent of an old-time railroad dining car, flocked wallpaper in a red rose pattern covered one-bedroom wall. On either side of the four-poster canopied bed, a wall sconce lit the room circuitously. Opposite the bed, a shelf of Franny's collectable porcelain dolls sat motionless on miniature chairs, while others stood, braced by armatures, their arms outstretched, their glass eyes staring into space.

It wasn't the chic art-deco office, or the mouth-watering gourmet meals the chef prepared that had Franny enthralled; it was Doctor Jonathon Kent's undivided attention. The clandestine arrangements of the past month had blossomed into a hot and heavy sexual affair, but the abrupt announcement he'd sprung on her suggesting she join his weekly group therapy session left her irritable and short tempered.

Lying in bed, Franny prodded the mound of pillows and watched television. "Say the secret word and win a hundred dollars," Groucho Marx said to a contestant. His thick eyebrows tweaked up and down as his fingers flicked his cigar at the participating guest. Franny popped the last piece of Godiva chocolate into her mouth, placed the cover back on the box and tossed it to one side. "Yummy," she sighed as she licked the chocolate from her fingers then plucked a tissue and wiped her hands.

Joey, her boyfriend, walked into the room, toweling his hair. "I called the super three times. You'd think he'd send someone to fix the damn shutter. Watcha watching? Oh, Groucho. Next to 'All in the Family,' he's my fave. Love those old sitcoms." He tossed the towel over his shoulder and reached for the box of chocolates. Finding it empty, he said sarcastically, "Thank you very much. You ate the whole damn box, Franny! Did you ever think that I might want some?"

"I bought it. I paid for it. I'm entitled to it. If you like chocolate so much pick up some Goobers at the 7-11."

He stared at her. "I can't believe you said that. What's it going to be next? Split the fridge? You keep your food on one side and mine on the other?"

"Suits me," she said, unconcerned. She reached over and picked up her Barbie doll and curled a lock of its hair around her finger.

"What's with you lately? Since you've been seeing Dr. Feelgood, you've been a real drag. Get rid of the quack. Your temperament is getting worse, and your personality is for shit. And another thing, the gang is wondering why you're avoiding them."

"Screw them." She placed her doll by her side and eyed Joey. "Listen, it's my money I'm spending, and besides, who made you an authority on what's good for me? You have a hard enough time aiming your dick when you pee. There's more urine on the floor than in the bowl."

"Is that so? Well, I still think the good doctor is sucking the money out of you."

"Is that a fact? Well, as far as the doctor sucking my money, I have to tell you that's not the only thing he sucks, and a hell of a lot better than you ever did."

His feelings wounded, he stood staring at her. He would have liked to slap some sense into her, hoping she would revert to the old Franny, but he'd never raise a hand to her.

His face flushed a bright red as he walked to the closet and pulled out a suitcase. He shouted. "That's it!" and started shoving essentials into the bag. "I've had it with your talking down to me. I knew you were off the wall, but I didn't think you were a heartless bitch, too. I'm on to you. Coming home all hours of the morning, when you do come home. Wearing fancy getups, smelling of booze. And, you've been holding back in the sex department too. You're getting it at the shrink's office, aren't you?"

She hoped he'd just go, but he raved on. "I never once cheated on you. Go ahead, mingle with the ritzy son of a bitch. But I'm telling ya, you won't find another schnook like me, who would put up with your nonsense."

"Bye, bye." She waved at him. "Don't let the door hit you on the way out."

He jumped into a sweat suit and sneakers, hurried into the bathroom, collected a few toiletries, grabbed his suitcase, walked past her and took hold of the front door knob. Suddenly he turned on his heels. "I'll get the rest of my stuff as soon as I get settled."

"It'll be packed and ready and outside the door in the morning. If you come after twelve, it's a Salvation Army donation."

"You're all heart, Franny."

"Yeah, I know."

He slammed the door and walked to the elevator, grumbling obscenities. Franny picked up her doll and held it to her breast.

Her eyes focused on the television, but her mind was drawing visions of her and Jonathon. *It's better this way,* she thought. *Now I can concentrate on Jonathon.*

Hugging her doll, she focused at the TV and watched Barbra Streisand, in the movie *Nuts*, portraying a woman abused by her father at an early age. She shuddered.

Did I do the right thing by telling Joey off? He did put up with my crazy tirades. She shrugged. *What's done is done. Time to move on.*

In the bathroom she opened the medicine cabinet and removed a vial of Ambien tablets. *Now*, she thought, *if I can just sleep straight through the night, and not get up every three hours, without those horrible nightmares, it would be a blessing.*

•₀

The little girl's father placed the Hans Christian Andersen fairy tale on the dresser alongside his daughter's doll collection. He spoke softly as he stroked her long, blond silky hair. "Daddy loves you very much. You're his little princess."

She smiled adoringly at the most important man in her life.

He snuggled closer to her. "Who loves you the most in the whole world?"

"You do, Daddy."

"And who is Daddy's little princess?"

"I am."

"That's right, you're Daddy's little princess. Now pet it gently, like Daddy taught you." His breathing increased. "That's good, Princess. Daddy is going to buy you the special edition Barbie doll you wanted. Would you like that?"

"Oh, yes, Daddy. You're the best daddy in the whole world."

"And if his little princess does everything Daddy says, he will make sure his little girl will get other wonderful dolls."

"Can we tell Mommy about the games we play?"

"No, sweetheart, I'm afraid not. It's a secret only meant for you and me. You see, I'm the handsome prince and you are the beautiful princess who I have to save from the evil witch."

"Mommy isn't a witch, is she, Daddy?"

"There are good witches and bad ones, and we can't take any chances." He stroked her hair. "You must listen to Daddy, or the handsome prince will not be able to save the beautiful princess." His breathing increased as he hardened against her. "If you tell Mommy she might turn into an evil witch. You don't want that to happen to Mommy, do you?"

"Oh no, Daddy."

"Of course not, princess. This will be our secret. That way we can protect Mommy." He kissed her lightly on her cheek. "Promise?"

"Yes, Daddy. I promise never to tell her or anyone. Cross my heart and hope to die." Her eyes met his. "Am I really a beautiful princess, Daddy?"

He caressed her thighs. "The most beautiful princess in the kingdom. And you will always be as long as you do what the prince asks of you."

"If she doesn't listen to the prince, does she get punished?"

He leaned closer and brushed his lips across her temple. "Much worse than that. A spell is put on her and she turns into a wicked old lady."

"Yuck, Daddy. Is the curse forever, or can she be saved by a prince who kisses her, like in the fairy tale?"

"No one can break the spell. That's why she must always listen to the prince."

The child shivered. "I'll keep our secret, Daddy."

"That's my good little girl. Now lie on your back like Daddy taught you and the prince will show the princess how much he loves her." He sighed with pleasure. "You are the most precious daughter a Daddy could ask for."

Smiling with expectation, she closed her eyes and envisioned the different outfits she would be trying on her special edition Barbie doll.

Chapter 15

All night long, Elaine Benjamin tossed and turned from one side to the other in the king-sized canopy bed. Keeping her eyes closed for any length of time was impossible; her mind would not shut down. Agonizing months had passed since a drunk driver had taken her daughters' lives—and a part of hers too. She had cried bitter tears, shrieked, and fainted in the morgue when she identified their lifeless, waxen bodies. The image of the girls lying on a slab alongside one another haunted her.

Consoling Elaine was fruitless, forcing Lew to move his personal belongings from the master bedroom to the guest bedroom. He had fought the idea but she insisted, knowing her restlessness kept him awake.

"You have enough on your mind, a business to run," she lamented.

She tried working in the showroom, but after five days she stopped going, mindful that her presence dampened the spirits of everyone there.

At Sunday's breakfast, Elaine, in a state of bereavement, buttered a slice of toast, put it to her lips and then set it back down on the bread tray. She glanced down at her rapidly cooling omelet, lifted her fork than stopped and held the fork in mid air.

Lew's face expressed deep concern. "Sleeping pills didn't work, Elaine?"

Placing the fork back on the table, she said. "I wish I were as strong as you, Lew."

He drew back.

No sooner had the words left her mouth, than she wished she could take them back. Reaching for his hand, she shook her head. "I didn't mean it the way it came out, sweetheart. I know you grieve too."

He looked at her, studied her. His expression was one of distress, hers, one of permanent loss. Jerking his head abruptly, as if to toss away their problems, he said, "Why don't you take Celina and go somewhere? Like Maine Chance, or The Golden Door, or one of those spas you went to with Amelia."

"Amelia is wrapped up in her kids, and kids are the last things I want to think about."

"Maybe we should put the condo up for sale. Everything here reminds us of the girls. You don't sleep. At night you mosey around the apartment crying. You need some kind of diversion."

"Diversion? I *don't* deserve to enjoy myself, not when they are..."

He stood, walked to where she sat, pulled her to her feet and grabbed hold of her shoulders. "Now hear this, Elaine. You're heading for a nervous breakdown. I can see it coming. Please, if for no other reason than to make me happy, you have to think of changing the scenery. To hell with the business. I'll take time off. How about we go to Europe...around the world...Hawaii? Would you like that?"

"No, I wouldn't. The way I feel, I'd only make you more miserable."

His panic-stricken expression startled her.

"Uh...well...maybe. Okay, Lew. I'll do the spa for one week."

He sat back down heavily. "A month!"

"Are you crazy? Two weeks at the most."

"Three weeks, and I won't take no for an answer."

"Okay, three weeks with an option to cancel the third week...if we *both* agree."

"Promise?"

"I promise, I promise."

He looked at her skeptically. "Swear on my life."

"Your life? Never. How about my brother Michael? You hate him."

"Done deal," he said, half smiling.

Managing a weak grin, she playfully punched him on his shoulder.

"That's my girl," he said. "You're already coming back to life."

Elaine called out. "Celina, want to go to The Golden Door?"

The kitchen door swung open and Celina came strolling out. "You called, *senora?*"

"You heard?" Elaine asked.

"I heard." Celina mimicked their conversation. "One month. No. Dos semanos. Es usted loco? Tres semanos con option. I thought for a minute you were going to swear on my life. I was just going to check my wardrobe when you called." She spoke seriously. "It will be good for you to get away."

He inhaled, blew out a deep breath. "You forget, Elaine, you were a model before you turned to designing. If you're going to blow twenty grand you better come back a new woman." He waited to see her reaction, hoping he hadn't pushed too hard.

Catching a glimpse of herself in the mirrored sideboard, Elaine admired her image and playfully fluffed up her hair. "I forgot. I did turn heads, didn't I? Okay, I'll give it a shot," she declared, but in the back of her mind the thought of her children and how long the lupus would remain in remission preyed on her.

He smiled triumphantly. "One more thing, Elaine."

"I said I'd go."

"It's not going to be easy to get back to where we were before. We should talk to someone."

She protested lightly. "Talk? You mean a psychiatrist?"

His mouth tightened. "Yes. Elaine, a psychiatrist." He stared her down. "I'll go too."

"I'll think about it. We'll talk when I get back."

He stood his ground. "We'll talk now! It's no big deal. Half the members at the club go. It's becoming the in thing. Amelia has been going to one for years."

She sighed. "Again with Amelia."

"The Doc says he's afraid she might leave him for the psychiatrist, he's that handsome."

"I have you, Lew. You're enough for me."

"You can talk until you're blue in the face, Elaine. Like it or not, you're going! I hear he's booked up the kazoo and not taking on new patients."

Celina broke in. "I have problemas, too. Think he'll give us a family rate?"

Lew smiled, grateful for Celina's timely humor. "I'm sure he will."

Elaine gave in. "We'll all go."

Celina spoke up. "I was only joking. I get enough therapy taking care of the two of you."

"So, what's the Don Juan's name?" Elaine asked.

"I'm not sure. Doc told me his name when we played golf last week. He was kidding around about how rich the shrink is. It stuck in my mind because Amelia said the best part of the therapy was at the end of the session when the shrink puts her into a state of euphoria."

Celina released a low whistle. "Euphoria, huh?"

Lew furrowed his brows. "His name? It's on the tip of my tongue. Trent, or Brent...oh, I remember. Kent. Doctor Jonathon Kent."

Chapter 16

The warm southerly wind carried a promise of better days to come as Elaine and Celina sat under a rainbow-colored umbrella at the spa's trendy outdoor clubhouse restaurant. "You know, Celina, these weeks of dieting, exercising, *and* pounding from the masseuse did wonders for this ancient body. I don't look bad in a bikini, do I?"

"Ancient?" Celina smiled approvingly. "I'll let you in on a secret, Elaine. You measure up to any of those Hollywood glamour girls. Don't let it go to your head, but you've never looked so good in the twelve years I've been with you." She would have liked to have said, "and after having two children also." But that was too painful to mention. "If you're thinking of staying longer than three weeks, you should call Lew and let him know."

Elaine shook her head. "Later. Let's order lunch. I'm starving. This is the first day I'm allowed to eat just about anything I like. I feel like I was let out of jail. The staff is worse than the Gestapo. You're lucky; you can eat anything you want."

Celina shrugged. "After losing and gaining, and gaining and losing, I decided long ago, it's not worth the wear and tear on my body, much less my state of mind. God wanted me this way and that's the way I am going to stay. It wouldn't be right to go against Him, would it?"

"Great philosophy, Celina. As long as you're happy."

"Who said I'm happy? I'd need a million dollars to have a complete makeover, and I'd still come out like someone put me together with crazy glue. She glanced at the menu. "What are you having?"

"Good afternoon, ladies," the waiter announced. "Have we decided?"

"Oh, yes." Elaine said enthusiastically. "I know exactly what I want. I'll have the Grande Caesar salad to start and then the Poulet Alsace Lorraine. Oh, and throw a few anchovies into the salad, please. For dessert, a vanilla ice cream sundae with nuts, strawberries, a dollop of marshmallow, and a mile-high heaping of whipped cream."

Celina smiled. *"Manera de ir muchacha,* or in plain English, way to go girl! You're svelte enough to indulge yourself. I'll wait to order."

"Tell me, Celina, would you consider plastic surgery if you had the money?"

"A new me wouldn't fit my personality."

"You've got a great personality."

"I'm not you. You were in the fashion business. You can be chic and savvy." She hesitated. "Well, in an earthy way. Me, I fall short of those characteristics."

"Listen, I have a great idea."

"No! Whatever it is, no."

"Lighten up. I've been thinking. You and I could go to this Dr. Kent, together. He could screw both our heads on straight at the same time. It could be fun?"

"No."

"Why not?"

"Save your breath. Did you ever hear the expression, 'no, means no'?"

"There must be something you'd like to get rid of."

"The only thing I want to get rid of is this conversation."

Elaine's eye's lit up as the waiter set the food down. "Mmm. Looks scrumptious." She eyed Celina. "Who are you staring at?"

"Just some man that's been checking you out since we sat down."

"Get out of here! Are you sure? What does he look like?"

"I better get the smelling salts. I think you're hyperventilating with curiosity. *Mi dios!* I've never seen such a lack of interest."

"Stop joking, Celina. Should I turn around and take a peek?"

"Sure, if you want to start something you can't finish. I'm dedicated to Lew. Remember him—the man you're married to?"

Elaine had promiscuity written all over her face. "So I do a little dancing and harmless flirting. Helps me forget."

Celina folded and refolded her napkin. She thought, *Trying to keep her from doing something foolish and telling her to enjoy the moment is not going to be easy.* She placed her hand on Elaine's. "Can I tell you something?"

"What a foolish question, Celina. You know better than that."

She put her hand over Elaine's. "You don't fool me for a minute, Elaine. You're just covering up your feelings. The loss was tragic. Give yourself time."

"I thought I was handling it rather well."

"Rather well? You haven't shed a tear since we arrived. You're holding it all inside."

"Maybe I am, Celina. Maybe I am. But I don't know how else to cope. I have this awful pain in the pit of my stomach."

"I'm sorry if I upset you."

She leaned over and kissed Celina on her cheek. "I know you care."

"Are you ready to order, ma'am?" the waiter asked.

"Yes, thank you," Celina said. "I'll have the same sundae Mrs. Benjamin is having, except please add some butterscotch topping and make the ice cream strawberry." *I've got to get her out of the doldrums,* she thought. The man looked their way again. "He's still staring, Elaine."

"Maybe he's staring at you. He can only see my profile."

"I don't think so," Celina mouthed.

"Well, who cares," Elaine said indifferently, but she was curious and intrigued. She drummed her fingers on the table. "Think I should turn and take a quick peek, Celina? No…I shouldn't…should I?"

"Celina crooked her mouth to one side and spoke flippantly, "It must be easy for women to forget they're married, in a place like this. You know, away from their husbands, and soooo lonely."

"I guess," Elaine, said, trying not to show interest or concern. "Would you excuse me, Celina, I have to go to the powder room."

"Want me to go with you?"

"I am capable of going to the ladies room alone."

Celina grimaced. "I'm sure you are." She eyed the man and spoke to Elaine at the same time. "Hurry back, dear," she teased. "You don't want your sundae to melt in the heat of the moment."

Elaine sashayed slowly up to where her admirer sat, gave him a fleeting glance enhanced with a coquettish smile, and continued walking to the powder room.

In the lounge, her image in the mirror signaled caution, but the sudden, unexpected sexual stirring that ran through her was overwhelming.

All at once, a transformation came over Elaine. She decided to put her problems on hold and store them in a filing cabinet deep in her subconscious, and label them, *Later*. But for now, Elaine was going to concentrate solely on Elaine.

Chapter 17

Celina fumed but hid it. It took all her self-control to keep from taking Elaine by the shoulders and shaking some sense into her. "Go ahead," she said. "Tell me I'm only the hired help, but I just can't sit by and let you make a fool of yourself."

"Stop overreacting, Celina. My dates are harmless flirtations. They're employees. They're told to entertain the guests. And it's the event of the season. Everyone is going formal. You're the one who told me to stop mourning and have some fun." She turned from side to side, admiring herself in the full-length mirror, and stroked with her fingertips beneath her chin. "Think I could use a little tightening?"

"It's not your face that needs the work. I never saw a person go from one extreme to another so quickly." She stared seriously at Elaine. "Elaine, *mi querida*. You worry me. I think it's time to go home. We've been here over a month."

Elaine lied. "I already spoke to Lew. Stop begrudging me a little fun. He said we should stay as long as we want. And besides, I'm feeling better."

Celina threw Elaine a disapproving look. "You've been out with a different man every night. Have they been helping themselves to you, too? I'm not your keeper, just your housekeeper, and friend...I hope."

"I've done nothing to be ashamed of. I know you have my best interests at heart, and I appreciate your concern, but tonight's party is the highlight of our stay. It will be fun. Come on. Get into that Scaasi. Lew would be disappointed knowing he spent all that cash on the gown and you didn't wear it."

"I'd be just as happy in the gown I bought at Loehmans."

"They set up gambling tables and an orchestra. You keep harping at me to let go. How about *you* letting go?"

"I let go a long time ago and it left me with nothing but grief."

Elaine stared her down.

Celina conceded, with a heavy sigh. "All right, I'll go. I do have a weakness for the slots." Her eyes narrowed at Elaine. "Did you really speak to Lew, today?"

Elaine crossed her arms defensively across her chest. "Of course," she said, knowing she had avoided returning his calls. "He sends his best to you."

Celina grimaced, wondering how much longer Elaine was going to continue her inappropriate behavior at the spa, and whether it would stop or escalate when she returned home.

The ballroom bustled with excitement. A platinum blond chanteuse held a microphone to her painted red lips and sang, *embrace me, my sweet embraceable you.* The music filtered into the casino where couples danced, chatted, sipped champagne, and gambled. They greeted each other with the usual, "You look fantastic" and "that mud treatment did wonders for you."

"Number three on the red," the croupier called. Elaine picked up her chips and tossed them into a plastic bucket. *That's enough of that. I hate losing.* She glanced past the casino into the adjacent ballroom, her hips swaying in time to the music, as she watched the guests dancing.

A tap on her shoulder startled her. She turned to see a good-looking, muscular young man smiling at her. He held a glass of wine in one hand and munched on an hors d'oeuvre with the other.

"Winning, losing, or breaking even?" he asked.

"Does anyone ever win?" she said, recalling that he was the man who had smiled at her at lunch the other day.

"It doesn't matter," he said. "You are not supposed to win. All the winnings are donated to charity."

"Oh. I didn't know."

"I'm Keith. Keith Handler. And you are...?"

"Elaine. Just plain Elaine."

He laughed. "What are you drinking, just plain Elaine? I was about to hit the bar."

"Hit the bar? I like that. Where are you from? New Jersey?"

"You're psychic. I was born in Paramus and was practically brought up in a shopping mall. My dad used to kid my mother, saying that if she had the baby at Macy's department store she would get a free layette."

She studied this attractive man who radiated sex. "Don't tell me she gave birth to you in a department store?" They both laughed.

His white teeth gleamed as he smiled. "How about a drink?"

"I don't think so, Keith. I only drink at special occasions."

"And this isn't a special occasion? You are dressed to kill." He eyed her up and down then added, "and packaged very nicely, I might add." He cocked his head to one side. A half smile crossed his face. "How about a whirl around the floor? I promise I won't step on your toes."

Casting a wary eye at Celina, she said, "Look, Keith, I don't mean to be short, but I'm not one of the beautiful people. I'm here with my companion, on sort of a sabbatical. You'd be better off with one of the other ladies. God knows, there are enough of them around who would love to dance with you."

"And you wouldn't? C'mon, plain Elaine. It's a Saturday night. I only asked you to dance, not elope." He winked good-naturedly and held up his glass. "Okay, you win the first round. Now, how about that drink? Wine or something stronger?" His eyes registered a you-know-you-can't-resist-me look.

And, she couldn't. "Sure, why not? Vodka on the rocks, and easy on the rocks."

He laughed. "Only special occasions, huh? Gotta watch the ladies who say they never drink," he said, starting for the bar. He called over his shoulder. "If you're not here when I get back, I'm going to page you on the loudspeaker and tell everyone you stole my wallet."

She watched him walk away, telling herself it was his job to make sure the guests had a good time. But she couldn't deny he more than sparked her interest.

She walked to a slot machine and inserted five silver dollars. Three cherries appeared. "Well, I'll be!" she exclaimed.

He snuck up behind her. "Your lucky night," he said.

She placed the bucket down and emptied her winnings into it. "Did you see that?" she said. "I won five hundred dollars. Here, hold the bucket while I take a sip. I think I need it." She downed half of the glass of vodka. "Mmm, smooth," she said. "Good stuff."

"Good stuff, huh? Occasional drinker? Elaine, I think you're putting me on."

"What do you do at the spa, Keith?"

"I'm a masseur. I manage the health club. I've done practically everyone here except you." He smiled boyishly. "I didn't mean that the way it sounded."

"I know what you meant. Guess I missed out. I have Laura as my masseuse." She smiled sheepishly. "Keith Handler...goes with your profession."

"Cute, real cute," he said, smirking at her. "Laura is good, but I could see to it that you get the full treatment. By me, of course." He took her glass. Refill?"

"I..." she started to say, but he interrupted.

He set the glass down. "Let's dance first; we can drink afterwards."

As he led her to the dance floor she wondered if maybe there was something to what Celina had been saying. Maybe it was time to forget. There had to be, or why would her juices be flowing, and her head saying, "enjoy it; you haven't felt this way in a long time?"

Celina sat at a slot machine inserting coins, keeping a watchful eye on Elaine and the handsome young man as they danced. She swallowed hard as Elaine pressed herself against him, her eyes closed, her cheek resting on his shoulder, her fingers dancing soft, affectionate circles around his ear, an expression of pure bliss on her face. The dance ended and Celina stood to get a better view of Elaine and the young man walking hand in hand like two love-struck kids towards an elevator. "Estimados Dios!" she exclaimed, observing them enter the elevator, embrace and kiss as the doors closed, leaving the rest to her troubled imagination.

Chapter 18

A puzzled expression crossed Dr. Jonathon Kent's face as he scanned Elaine's folder. "You can't be fifty two."

"Fifty two? I don't think so," Elaine responded. "Especially since I just got back from a spa where they were supposed to pound ten years off of my life."

Cynthia tapped on the door. "I'm sorry, doctor. I gave you the wrong folder. *This* is Mrs. Benjamin's file."

"Well, that explains it," he said, exchanging folders with Cynthia. He smiled his usual inviting smile. "Take a seat wherever you feel comfortable," he suggested, giving her a fast once over at the same time.

Taken in by his good looks, she took a seat at the far end of the room, where she crossed her legs and hiked her skirt above her knees. "I think your receptionist had my housekeeper's chart. We both had appointments, but she chickened out."

"That would be a first," he said.

Elaine's eyebrows arched.

"I mean having a housekeeper and her employer seeking my help at the same time." He opened Elaine's folder, gave it a quick read, closed it and asked, "Did you enjoy your stay at the spa?"

Her face scrunched up. "It was fun for a while I guess, but..." She paused as her glance focused on the ornate designs of the Oriental rug.

With a knowing nod, he stood, pulled a straight back chair close to her, sat, and waited for her to speak.

For long minutes the only sound in the room was the monotonous tick of the Grandfather clock's pendulum as it swayed back and forth. Finally, she raised her eyes and spoke. "I was only fooling myself. It was just a temporary escape. When I got home reality set in. I shouldn't have gone. And yet, I didn't want to leave…to go home. I was having fun, or so I thought. I'm not making sense, am I?"

He smiled reassuringly. "In time it will make sense. By the way, I prefer a first-name basis with my patients, if you don't mind, Elaine."

God, she thought, aware of the effect his presence was having on her. *I can't concentrate with him staring at me.* She shook her head. "I don't mind, Doctor."

"Jonathon," he reminded her.

"Jonathon," she repeated.

"Cry, scream, curse, carry on if it will help release any tension you're feeling." He frowned. "I'm sorry to bring this up so soon, Elaine, but it is the underlying reason of why you are here. You know, sooner or later you're going to have to talk about the hurt you're experiencing." He stared directly into her eyes and said softly, "I'm talking about the children." He quickly followed up with, "But, as I said before, all in good time."

Tears immediately streamed down her face. "I've been so selfish," she sobbed. "I wasn't there when the accident happened, but I can imagine how awful it must have been for them. My mind relives it over and over and over. I thought going to the spa would help, and for a while it seemed to. I can't forgive myself for being so insensitive. To just take off, indulge myself, and have a good time, while they are buried in the cold earth. What kind of a mother am I, to forget about my sweet, adorable children? I keep asking, why did this have to happen to them?" She broke down and cried uncontrollably.

Dr. Kent walked to her and stood looking down at her. "It was a shock. You couldn't face up to what happened so you tried to erase it, hoping it would disappear. Go on, have a good cry. It will help."

She gasped a sudden intake of air.

Drawing a steadying breath, he grasped her hands, pulled her to her feet and embraced her. He tenderly massaged her neck, then her shoulders, and slid his fingers in a circular motion down her back, as he pressed her body closer to his. He breathed in her ear. "Cry it out, Elaine. I promise it's going to be all right."

Distraught and flustered, Elaine clung tightly to him.

He tilted her face against his, all the while consoling her with reassuring words. "There, there. Let me help you solve your problems."

Sensing that he was becoming aroused, he straightened and pulled back just enough to keep from revealing the situation. "Just put yourself in the doctor's hands," he said. "I'll see to it that you are well taken care of."

Chapter 19

Lily Violet Fitzgerald bit her lip as she pulled into the parking lot of the Sweetwater Shopping Center. *Damn*, she thought, *if I don't get a move on I'll never make it to Jonathon's on time."*

The pharmacist eyed her suspiciously. He laid her prescription down on the counter, looked over his shoulder, then turned back and met her eyes. Speaking in a low, sensuous tone, he whispered. "I had to call your doctor for verification. It seems the date on the prescription for Phentermine has expired. He wasn't in, but I filled it. No charge." He moved closer to her, a gleam of lust in his eyes. "You do realize I went out on a limb for you? I could get canned."

Her heartbeat quickened. *Shit*, she thought, he suspects something. She tossed her long red hair to the side of her head and smiled flirtatiously. "Thank you, but I'm late for an appointment." She glanced at his nametag. "I promise I'll get back to you, Donald. Tomorrow? Rain check? We can have lunch and…. Now, I really must hurry." She picked up her prescription form and the vial of pills, walked briskly out of the drugstore, rushed to her car, thumbed the remote, flung the door open, and sighed with relief as she inserted the key into the ignition.

The car started, but not quickly enough for Lily. *Guess that's the last time I'll be picking up prescriptions from Donald. Just a little too close for comfort.*

Have to find another pharmacy. She gunned her car out of the parking lot and onto the highway toward the Big Apple. *Stupid, stupid, stupid,* she thought, reprimanding herself. *That's the last prescription you swiped off the doctor's desk.* She drove to a gas station and purchased a can of diet, caffeine-free Dr. Pepper, opened the vial of diet pills, and took two. She washed them down with the soda and placed the can in the cup holder. "What the hell," she said aloud. "They'll kill my appetite, and I'll be wide awake and raring to go for Jonathon."

•.

"Good evening, Ms. Fitzgerald. The doctor has been asking about you."

"Hi, Cynthia. I got stuck in traffic."

"Let me take your coat."

"Don't bother. I'll just toss it on the couch." She stopped at the wall mirror, ran a comb through her hair and applied lipstick.

Lily hurried into Jonathon's office, closed the door and leaned against it, her arms outstretched. "I am so sorry. The traffic was unbearable and I had to make a condolence call," she lied.

He walked toward her and embraced her, nuzzling her ear. "You know how I worry about you. You should have called." He reached behind her and snapped the lock. "Are you all right? You seem to be out of breath."

"I like that you worry about me. I'm out of breath because you take my breath away." She thought to herself, *Those damn pills, they're making me hyper.*

He lifted her up and carried her to the chaise and gently laid her down. "I have a surprise for you."

Her mind raced. *He's going to propose.*

She slipped her hands around his neck and pulled him down on top of her.

"And after we make love I thought we would go out to dine."

"If you wish, Jonathon."

"Well, that doesn't sound very enthusiastic."

"I'm not all that hungry."

He studied her body language then broke her hold on him and sat up. "You've been acting rather strange lately. You never eat when you're with me, and the times we go out you just play with your food." He tilted her chin up. "Come on, Lily, talk to me."

She sat up. "I'm sorry. I turned you off, didn't I?"

"I am your shrink and I do care about you. I don't expect you to come clean all at once, but you're not eating and your behavior has me concerned."

She wondered if he might be on to her popping diet pills.

He walked to his desk and opened his humidor. He held up a cigar. "Mind?"

She stood and straightened her dress. "No," she said softly, "but won't your other patients mind?"

"Cynthia will deodorize. Come over here and sit by me. There is something I want to discuss with you."

Oh, no. He's going to tell me that we've been too close, and it's not good for his reputation. And I thought that tonight I'd be engaged. Gees, what a reality check.

"Wipe that sad look from your face, Lily. I'm only thinking of your welfare. I've given it a lot of thought and..." He took her hand in his.

Here it comes, the old brush-off, she thought, remembering an old affair and her most recent one, the Tennessee Tillingham let down: the reason she was seeing Jonathon. *Well, that's two down and one to go. Must be some kind of a record I'm setting.*

"Lily, I can only do so much for you. Maybe it's my fault. Our close relationship may not be the best thing for you."

Lily bolted. "Does that mean...?"

"Now, don't jump the gun. It doesn't change anything between us. What I'm trying to say is that our being so close is not helping your recovery. Actually, it's getting in the way of your progress."

Her look grew distant. "Level with me, Jonathon. You don't want to be with me anymore. Is that what you're trying to say?"

He put his arms around her. "That's your insecurity talking. I do care about you." Suddenly the air in the room seemed stuffy. He walked to the window, opened it and turned to face her. "Believe me, Lily, I do care and only want what is best for you. That's why I am suggesting you join my therapy group. You may not see it at first, but I think you will eventually open up to them."

Relieved that he said he still cared, she nodded. "Whatever you say, Jonathon. Tell me about the group therapy."

"They are intelligent, interesting people, who meet twice a week. Two men and two women. Thomas, Gerald, and Franny. You will be the fourth."

"Only four?"

"I may add one more."

"Participating in this group will be helpful and enlightening. In fact, they usually stay afterwards and dine." He waited for her reaction.

"But you *do* care, don't you?" she asked hesitantly.

His arms reached out to her. "Come here, Lily, and I'll show you how much I care."

Chapter 20

The conductor lifted his baton as a loud cough was heard from someone in the audience. He held the baton in midair until the concert hall was silent, raised his brows at the musicians, and led the symphony orchestra into Mozart's Sonata No.16 in C major. He turned to the featured pianist and nodded for her to begin.

Lily Violet Fitzgerald placed her slender fingers on the keyboard and began playing. Her flaming red hair shimmered under the spotlights, and the feathers that edged the hem of her sequined gown swayed as her foot touched the pedals on the Steinway.

She played well but it was not her best. Her concentration was clouded by thoughts of her fading romance with Jonathon and seeing him less frequently unnerved her. At first it had been four nights a week and Sunday afternoons; then three nights a week and no Sunday afternoons. Now, it came down to no nights a week, just group therapy. True, she had been on tour, but she felt her absence should have made him want her all the more.

As her fingers automatically touched the keys she was aware that her performance was not up to par, but she didn't care. *Like the audience would know the difference,* she thought. It was the last concert of the season and then she would be up, up and away, back to New York and Jonathon. He was caught up with his patients, and if he seemed distant she would try to understand. She would do what he had asked concerning the group therapy but wondered how much she would let the group in on, and how much she would conceal. She paused and rested her hands in her lap as the orchestra played. The conductor smiled questioningly at her mediocre performance, and she smiled back at him.

On the plane to New York, Lily drank white wine non-stop. By the time the plane touched down at La Guardia Airport, she had taken two pills. As soon as she settled herself in the taxi on the way to her apartment she called Jonathon's office on her cellular phone.

Cynthia answered. "Hello, Ms. Fitzgerald. How did the concert go? I bet you had a dozen curtain calls."

She ignored Cynthia's question. Abruptly, she asked, "Is the doctor in? I need to speak to him immediately."

Cynthia hesitated, sensing that Lily was not quite herself. She asked Lily to hold, and buzzed Dr. Kent. "I'm not sure, Doctor, but I think she might be a little high."

"Tell her I'm with a patient and I'll get back to her.

Cynthia went on the line with Lily. "I'm sorry, Ms. Fitzgerald, but the doctor is tied up. He said he would get back to you. Is there something I...?"

Lily fumed, opened the window and threw the phone out of the car. "I'll fucking kill him," she shrieked, startling the driver. Then she reached into her bag and popped two more diet pills into her mouth. "He can't treat me like some common whore." She thought of Tennessee Tillingham and how he took advantage of her. "Oh, no. This is not going to happen to me again," she said. "No way!"

Chapter 21

D r. Jonathon Kent was quite pleased with himself. He knew he had to watch his back, not overdo it, but the intense excitement of controlling the three women was too compelling to relinquish. To say nothing of the great sex he was enjoying. He glanced at Elaine and hummed along to the strains of Saint-Saens, "Softly Awakes My Heart," from *Samson and Delilah*.

Elaine's giving in to him so effortlessly pleased his already inflated ego. He reached up, pulled her tightly against his chest and murmured, "Let's do it again."

"Maybe you should see a doctor, you oversexed maniac," she chided. "If I don't get home soon, Celina will have the National Guard searching for me. As it is, I'm having a hard time thinking up excuses, and Lew's been acting suspicious. Probably wondering why we haven't had sex lately."

Jonathon released his hold on her. A red flag flashed through his mind and a little panic washed through him. *Careful, mister,* he thought. *One thing you don't need is an irate husband nipping at your heels. Time to ease up.* "I know I suggested we spend a weekend at my cabin, but I think we should put it on hold."

"If you're concerned about Lew or Celina, not to worry. I can manage them."

She's too anxious, he thought. *And when they get too anxious they get possessive, and when they get possessive it spells trouble.* "Well, we'll see," he said. "Anyhow, I'm not exactly sure how my schedule shapes up. I'll check with Cynthia."

She read the sudden change in attitude on his face and it disturbed her. "If you're worried about how much time we're spending together, don't," she said. "I've been very careful. Celina and Lew think I have taken on charity work." Her dark eyes searched his face. "Jonathon, is there something more?"

He stood up and tied his robe. "Come on, Elaine, that pretty head of yours is working overtime. Do you think I could stop caring about you?" He snapped his fingers. "Just like that?" He released his grip on her, walked to the bar, and poured champagne into two flutes. Holding one out to her, he said, "Frankly, Elaine, you're becoming too dependent on me." She started to speak but he raised his hand. "Oh, I know you feel safe and secure with me, but if you don't work through your feelings without me, you'll be in real trouble. I'm not ending our relationship, just slowing it down. Believe me, Elaine, right now you feel like I'm deserting you, but soon you will realize that it's best for you."

"I feel so empty," she said. "At least I had you to lean on for support."

"You still have me, but now you'll be doing it on your own. Emotional and mental stability come first."

The pressure of his unexpectedly blowing her off and the sudden tingling in her fingers unnerved her. Her body began to tremble. "I don't know if I can do it, Jonathon. You've been there to fill the void in my life."

You moron, he thought, *that's what you have your husband for;* but to her he said, "I'll always be here for you. You know that."

"I have to go," she blurted. "I'm too upset to think logically."

Contemplating his next move, he watched her pull up her pantyhose, throw her dress over her head, and abruptly stop short as she reached for a shoe. She groaned.

"What's wrong," he asked.

Embarrassed, she said, "Nothing you can fix," but she was concerned about her arthritis returning.

"Wait," he said. "I have to discuss one more thing. Get hold of yourself. Sit for one more minute."

She would have liked to put her hands over her ears and shut out his voice, but instead she concentrated on holding back the tears that waited to fall. After a few seconds she slowly raised her eyes until they met his. A helpless, childlike expression crossed her face. "What else?" she asked.

He took hold of her hands. "This is going to be good for us. I know you're upset, but you're going to find this interesting and stimulating."

Feeling that this was not the end of their relationship, she breathed a sigh of relief.

With self-assurance he said," I know this will benefit you. I want you to join my group therapy class. Patients sometimes open up to their peers more than they do to their doctors. I have a group that meets twice a week at the office. Two men. Two women. Thomas, Gerald, Lily, and Franny. You will be the fifth."

Chapter 22

So this is what it's come down to, Franny reflected. *Group therapy with four other messed up misfits.* She considered it a setback, but Jonathon had left her little choice. She swung her Prada bag haphazardly, greeting Cynthia with a nonchalant, "Hello, how are you?"

"Good morning, Ms. Goldsmith. We are waiting for one more client. The others are in the dining room. The doctor's running a bit late." She smiled smugly at Franny.

Franny questioned Cynthia's cool demeanor. Calling her Ms. Goldsmith, not Franny, left her apprehensive. She wondered how long Jonathon had been sleeping with Cynthia. *She's just the type to sleep her way up the ladder,* she thought.

Just as Franny left for the dining room to meet the others, the outer door opened and Elaine entered.

Cynthia's tone was warmer than it was to Franny. "Good morning, Elaine. Welcome to the group. We are looking forward to your joining us. If you'll come with me," she said, taking Elaine's arm, "I'll introduce you to the others."

Cynthia rattled off their names. "Thomas, Gerald, Franny and Lily, meet your new addition, Elaine Benjamin."

Thomas and Gerald stood. Elaine's eyes darted from the men to Franny and lastly to Lily. She waved a casual greeting.

Franny announced, "The gang's all here, so let the games begin." They all smiled.

Thomas, a tall, thin man in his middle twenties, with a wise-ass smile and a Fu Man Chu mustache, spoke. "Well, the latest addition to our group is the quiet type."

Thomas continued. "Glad to have you aboard." Gesturing towards Franny, he said, "It's good to have quiet for a change."

Elaine nodded.

Franny spoke flatly. "Don't get carried away, Jerry. There's another side to me you haven't seen. The one that sticks pins into voodoo dolls and howls at the moon."

"Turns me on," Thomas challenged.

Franny shot back with, "Save it for the vampires, Tommy."

Thomas, his shoulder-length blond hair, bleached from too much sun, opened his mouth to speak, but Gerald intervened. "Don't mind him, ladies; he's harmless. Likes to upstage everyone." In return, Thomas gave him the finger.

"I see everyone is in rare form today," Cynthia said as she handed out menus. "I hope no one's had breakfast. The chef has prepared crepes today. And, Dr. Kent is on his way and asked that you start without him. I think it would be appropriate if we introduced ourselves to Elaine, after Elaine says hello."

Everyone focused on Elaine. "I'm Elaine, and I can't think of a thing to say."

Lily spoke up. "I'm Lily, and I don't eat breakfast."

"Watching your weight, dear?" Franny snapped.

Lily shrugged. "Constantly and forever."

Franny shook her head. "You look pretty good to me. Bet you don't even wear a bra."

Gerald chimed in. "Do you?"

"Do I what?" Lily said, puzzled.

Thomas flicked a knuckle at the menu. "He's teasing you about wearing a bra. I wouldn't answer; you'll only encourage him."

"Why is everyone picking on me?" Gerald asked sheepishly.

Thomas's head bobbed up and down. "You leave yourself open to criticism." He lifted his knife and tapped it against his water glass. "Mesdames and Messieurs, your attention, please. May I suggest the chef's specialty? Crepes delicately prepared in a special fat free, no cholesterol oil, and with a hint of Grand Marnier." He put his fingers to his lips and threw a kiss into the air. "Voila," he said. "To die for."

Franny closed her eyes. "Mmm, sounds irresistible."

"I'll have a double order of that," Gerald spouted.

Elaine shook her head then licked her lips. "I'm salivating. Bet he makes delicious Balinese, too. Count me in."

All eyes were on Lily. "Okay, okay. I'm not going to be a wet blanket. I'll try it."

Franny eyed Lily. "You're not going to purge afterwards, are you?"

"How vivid," Lily said. "No, I won't purge." She studied Franny. "Why do you remind me of my mother?" They all laughed.

Just as everyone started eating, the door flew open and Dr. Kent stepped briskly into the room. He handed Cynthia his coat and briefcase and smiled broadly at everyone. "Well," he said. "Looks as though we are having a good time without the teacher." Thomas started to speak but the doctor cut him off. "If you're going to make some cute remark, Thomas, save it for the open discussion. Are we all acquainted?" He didn't wait for an answer and didn't expect one. His eyes roamed from Franny to Elaine to Lily, giving each lady a personal glance of affection. "Start eating," he said. "I'll join you after I wash up." He walked toward his office, waving at the group. "Enjoy."

All through breakfast the ladies had a hard time concentrating on the food while stealing glances at Dr. Kent. He in turn made light conversation, avoiding their eyes and slight innuendoes.

After they had finished eating, Lily turned to Thomas. "Evidently, you and Gerald have been in group therapy before. How long does it last?"

Thomas stood and patted his stomach. "Boy, that was good." He wiped his mouth and placed his napkin on the table. "How long? As long as you want it to, or until the conversation gets too hot and someone gets so upset the doctor has to intervene. Or when one of us looks like we're going to punch someone's lights out. I'm one of the mischief-makers. I love to stir up trouble. Pit one against the other. Right, Gerald, you pathetic, frustrated psychology dropout?"

Gerald sulked. "Screw you, Thomas."

Thomas chuckled. "Actually, Gerald and I are old friends. Went to Columbia together. Only reason I hang with him is because I feel sorry for him."

"Geez," Elaine said, directing her conversation to Franny and Lily. "This is going to be tougher than I thought. Maybe we should try for an all girls group."

"Uh Uh," Gerald said. "The men are easy; it's the women who are dangerous. Believe me, I've been in lots of therapy groups with La Femme."

"He may be right," Elaine said. "I've always gotten along better with men than women." Lily raised her eyebrows but said nothing.

"Well," Franny said, "I have no trouble with men."

"I'm sure," Elaine and Lily said in unison.

Franny clapped her hands together. "Okay, ladies," she fired, "time to spill our guts."

Chapter 23

Lew Benjamin tossed the Mont Blanc pen across the desk, breathed a deep sigh of relief, and looked up at the entourage of patternmakers, designers, models and salesmen who anxiously awaited his next move.

He pointed a finger and shouted, "If those buyers don't like the spring line, every one of your asses will be pounding the pavement." His expression tending grim, he raised his voice. "Buyers! Take them out to dinner, get them theater tickets, fly them first class to Puerto Rico, and what do they do? They turn around and give the business to the competition."

He removed a Havana cigar from the humidor, clipped the end and tossed it into the wastebasket. He held a lighted match close to the cigar, inhaled, and watched as smoke configurations circled in the air.

His mind turned from the problems of the day to Elaine, brooding over how distant she had become. Unconsciously shuffling the sketches of the new line, he thought, *what happened to the way we were? Can people change so quickly? Is everyone out to screw you? Even your nearest and dearest?*

It had been a long, tedious month of designing, redesigning, and merchandising the fall line. The weary employees exchanged glances and rolled their eyes, aware of how hard they had worked, and thinking of how each season they listened to the boss give them the same old spiel.

Lew's private phone rang. Knowing it was Elaine, he curled his mouth to one side, picked it up and said, "Hold on, Elaine, will ya?"

Pretending to play the irate boss, he spoke to his employees. "So why are you standing around? You're falling asleep on your feet. Go home." His tone softened and he smiled at them. "Seriously, people, I want to thank all of you for putting in twelve-hour days. You did a damn good job. It's the best line ever. And to show you my appreciation, there's going to be a hefty Hanukkah bonus in your Christmas stockings this year."

The employees started to leave, some tired and ready for bed, and others headed for a nightcap at the Seventh Avenue watering hole. Lew motioned to Jennifer, the receptionist, to stay. He picked up the phone. "What's up, Elaine?"

"I suppose you're working late again," she said matter-of-factly.

"So?"

"What do you mean, so?"

Silence.

"I know you're there, Lew, I can hear you breathing."

He smirked. "You can hear me breathing, huh? Well, how lucky can I get? That's as close to you as I've been in months. Why the call? Celina usually reports your whereabouts to me. Run out of charities to attend?" He winked at Jennifer.

"Don't get smart with me, Lew. I didn't plan for things to get out of hand between us. I can't just put everything on the back burner like you do."

He laughed. "You are so full of shit, Elaine. I grieve for Rosie and Sara just as much as you do. I didn't create this rift between us. You did. And it seems like your therapist isn't helping much either. But I do appreciate your calling me. I almost forgot what your voice sounds like. Feeling guilty?"

"Guilty? What do I have to be guilty for? I just wanted to tell you that Mother and I are going to Atlantic City for the weekend."

"Uh huh. I knew it wasn't a 'how are ya' darling?' call. And since when do you need my permission to go anywhere? Just put a note in an empty milk bottle. I see the milkman more than I see you."

"Is that supposed to be funny?"

"Your mother hates to gamble."

"She likes the nickel slots. Oh, just forget it. I can't talk to you. You make everything a joke. I thought I'd just call and...well, what's the difference. I can see that you're as sarcastic as ever."

"Good bye, Elaine. Have a good time in Atlantic City or wherever. Maybe the sea air will bring you back to your senses." He hung up.

Jennifer frowned. "I shouldn't stay. It's been a long day and you're tired."

He smiled at the pretty twenty-year-old. He thought, *I know I shouldn't get involved with someone who works for me, but I'm lonely...the children are gone, and Elaine is...who knows where.*

"Mr. Benjamin," Jennifer said, "you should get some sleep, and so should I."

He raised his eyebrows. "Sleep? Okay."

She chuckled. "I mean sleep, like in slumber. You're exhausted." She walked to where he sat, stood in back of him and began to massage his shoulders.

He tilted his head backwards, their eyes met, her perfume filled his nostrils. "Don't stop, that feels good. Thanks for staying, Jen. I don't feel like being alone."

She leaned over and kissed his forehead. "You don't have to be alone, Mr. Benjamin."

"When we are alone, Jen, call me 'Lew.'"

She smiled warmly. "Okay, Lew."

He took hold of her hand and led her around so that she faced him. "It will take me a minute to clear my desk. Why don't you freshen up and we'll have a late night snack, and then..."

She smiled affectionately at him as she walked to the ladies room.

In his office, he started to straighten out the clutter on his desk when the gold-framed picture of Elaine and him caught his eye. Reminiscing, he thought, *we were so young, so much in love, so full of hope for the future.* He swiveled his armchair and gazed out the window and down onto Seventh Avenue, watching the people scurrying home. He wondered, *what happened to the dreams we had?* Swinging the chair back to his desk, he stared at the picture. *All our friends became engaged at the same time, married within a few months of each other, and gave birth to our children only a few months apart. We were only kids when we had our kids. We played follow the leader, never stopping to think if we were meant to spend a lifetime together.*

Jennifer walked up behind him and placed her hands around his neck. "Want to come back down to earth?" she said. He grabbed her hands and pressed them to his chest, then raised and kissed them.

"Are you sure you want to go?" she asked.

He stood and faced her. "Definitely. Grab your coat and we're off."

"It's in my locker. I'll get it."

"Just let me wash my hands, Jen." Lew washed his hands and splashed his face. As he toweled dry a strange feeling ran through him. He wasn't quite sure what it was, but it felt good. He walked into the showroom and stopped to look into the floor-to-ceiling mirror. An impish smile shadowed his face. Pointing a finger at his image, he said aloud, "Lew, if you had the balls, you'd get up tomorrow morning, kiss Elaine goodbye, go to the bank, draw out some money, pick up Jen, drive to the airport, hop on a plane, and start a whole new life."

Chapter 24

Elaine's thoughts were not on her driving as she floored the gas pedal on the Cadillac. The speedometer registered seventy-five miles per hour and nearing eighty when she became aware of the siren signaling her to pull over. *Damn it,* she thought, *it's dinnertime. Why isn't this cop freeloading at the diner?* The gravel sprayed from the soft earth as she pulled over onto the shoulder of the road, pulled up the hand brake and lowered her window.

The officer walked casually up to her car, planted both feet squarely on the ground and grinned a, *tell me one I haven't heard, lady,* stare. "Evening ma'am. Late for an appointment?" His eyes scanned the interior of the car. "Know how fast you were going?" Not waiting for her to reply, he followed up with, "over seventy five miles an hour. The speed limit is fifty-five."

"I was rushing to my mother. She's sick and alone. I wasn't thinking."

He cut her off. "Uh huh." His head moved from side to side, mockingly. "Registration and driver's license, please." She handed him the cards and waited impatiently as he examined them. "Stay in the car," he said, walking away.

She called to him. "Officer, you're not going to give me a ticket, are you? I don't have a blemish on my record."

He stopped and called back, "Then this will be your first."

"Listen, my husband donates to the Policemen's Benevolent Association every year, and I belong to the Charities for the Homeless Orphans. And I'm donating my organs, too. Doesn't that count for anything?"

Returning to the Cadillac, he pushed the brim of his cap up and stood leering down at her. Then he bent over and rested both hands on the roof of the car. A *you're so full of shit* leer crossed his face. "Okay, Mrs. Benjamin, tell you what I'm going to do. After you donate an organ to someone you run over, bring me the receipt and I'll erase the ticket from your record. Might even get you a refund." He winked at her and walked to his car.

Elaine sat in disbelief. "Asshole," she muttered.

He turned on his heels, returned to the car and put his face so close to hers she could smell his "Big Red Cinnamon Gum" breath. With his arms folded defensively across his chest, he said, "Why don't we discuss this down at the station, Mrs. Benjamin?"

Realizing she had dug herself into a hole, she decided to throw herself on his mercy. *All I need is for Lew to bail me out of jail. Another thing he can hold over my head.* "I'm sorry," she said. "I was wrong and stupid. Please accept my apology. I know that no matter what I say now you won't believe me, but really, I am sorry. I promise to drive the speed limit."

After he handed her the ticket he pulled away, waving a warning finger accompanied by a derisive smile.

Elaine drove to her mother's house, parked, and sat in the car. The incident with the policeman started her thinking. *Could the children's sudden death have affected me so badly that I'm going off the deep end? Driving like a maniac? What's happening to me?* Jonathon flashed through her mind. *Is this what it's come to: having sex in order to forget?* She shook her head. *I'm going to tell Jonathon it's over. Then what? Lew is suspicious of me and then I'll have no one.* Still, the thought of Jonathon titillated her. She shrugged. *Jonathon has been a little cold lately, but he'll come around.*

The tapping on the car window startled Elaine. She looked up to see her mother's disgruntled face. "Whaddaya doing, sitting and talking to yourself? I've been waiting for over an hour. How'd ya go, by way of Carnarsie? I called Celina and she said she didn't know where you were. Come on in, I'll make you a nice cup of tea."

At the kitchen table, her mother eyed her distraught daughter with concern. "You look like shit, Lainie. Had another fight with Lew? You looked like a million dollars when you came back from the spa." Her mother poured two cups of tea, added two packets of Nutra-sweet, squeezed a slice of lemon in each, stirred, and sat down opposite her daughter. Her heart lay heavily in her chest. Searching for an answer in her daughter's eyes, she asked, "Wanna talk?"

Elaine stared down at the tea. "I hate going home. The memories of the children haunt me. I haven't gone in their room since... And Lew and I have become strangers." A look of despair crossed her face. "I have this tremendous void inside of me. The only pleasure I get is when I spill my guts to Jonathon."

Her mother raised a disapproving eyebrow.

Elaine continued. "Celina's leaving. I'll miss her. She took good care of us for a lot of years."

"It's better she goes. What is she going to do with herself all day with you running around like a chicken without a head, and Lew working night and day at the showroom?"

"I don't know, Mom. Sometimes I feel like the demons are going to swallow me up. I can't seem to get a handle on my life. What's wrong with me?"

"I'll tell you what's wrong, Lainie. You lost two beautiful girls." Tears welled in her eyes. "There's nothing worse than that. So you flipped out.

This is the hardest time." Her head bobbed up and down. Sighing deeply, she repeated almost inaudibly. "It takes time, it takes time." She took hold of Elaine's hands. "Tell me something, Lainie. How is Lew holding up?"

"He seems to be taking it better than I am. The business keeps him occupied. I suppose men are stronger than women."

"And who told you that, some fortuneteller, or tarot card reader? How do you know what's going on inside of him? Lew is a good, solid man. And a sensitive one, too."

"Is that why he works all those hours and is never home? Who knows what he's up to?"

Her mother shook her head. She looked long and hard at her daughter. "Casting stones? Ya know, kiddo, you've been far from a saint yourself." Her eyes narrowed. "I hear things. What's going on, Lainie?"

Elaine sipped her tea and clumsily put the cup down into the saucer. "What do you mean, what's going on? A second ago you told me that I've suffered a tremendous loss. Now you think I'm hiding something from you."

"I know you, Lainie, better than you know yourself. You've always been one to run away from your troubles. Listen, what happened is a tragedy, but you can't replace a loss by getting yourself involved with people who…"

Elaine looked at her mother with surprise. "What are you talking about? What people?" She sprang up. "I think it's time for me to go. You're upsetting me."

Her mother stood over her daughter and pushed her down into the chair. "Sit!" she commanded. "I'm still your mother, and I deserve a little more respect than you're showing me."

Elaine balked. "You never give me any credit. Just once, why can't you side with me? Anyhow, I don't want to argue. I've got a group therapy session tonight and I don't want to be late."

You can give me ten minutes. I gave you a hell of a lot more than that. You may have lost two children. Well, I lost them, too. And so did Lew. But I love you and I don't want to lose you also."

"You're not losing me, Mom, I'm just..."

"You're just between here and there and nowhere, Lainie. All of a sudden it's 'Jonathon'? Something's not kosher. Between you and me and Lew, I don't see you getting better. If anything, I think you're getting worse. I'm sorry if I hurt your feelings, but I'm afraid, afraid for you. Maybe you should think of seeing a different shrink."

Elaine stood and grabbed her coat and bag. "Change shrinks?" she yelled. "For God's sakes, he's the best thing that's happened to me. Without him, only God knows where I might end up. Thanks for the advice, but I know where I'm going, and I know exactly what I'm doing."

From the window her mother watched her daughter scurry down the walk, swiping at the flowers along the path. She whispered tearfully, "I hope so, Lainie. I hope to God you know what you're doing,"

Elaine ran to her car, jumped in and took off like a bat out of hell. After driving for a few minutes she pulled up to a curb and turned the ignition off. She pounded her fists on the dashboard, then rested her head on the steering wheel and wept uncontrollably. "I know what I'm doing...I know what I'm doing...I know what I'm..."

Chapter 25

L ily relaxed in her plush, overstuffed chaise, staring at the glass of wine she held in her hand. *You are my friend,* she thought. *You make me feel better, you make me tranquil, and you help me forget.* The strains of her most recent recording resonated from the speakers filling the room with her rendition of Liszt's "Liebestraum." Suddenly she bolted up, spattering wine on the cocktail table and over an open newspaper.

"Oh no!" she cried. Rushing to the audio center, she restarted the CD and turned up the volume. Listening intently, she visualized her fingers playing on the keyboard, and upon hearing the passage again, let out a sigh of relief. *That's all I need...a mistake on a newly released recording.*

Lily dabbed with a paper towel at the spilt wine that had splashed onto the cocktail table and picked up the soiled tabloid as her eyes caught an article printed in the *New York Times* business section.

She read: **Bradford T. Tillingham Industries buys out Harmony Distributors for one hundred fifty million. Mr. Tillingham, who acquired two companies last year and two this year, is being investigated by the United States Department of Justice for violating the Freedom of Trade Act.**

Lily's jaw dropped as she looked at Tillingham's photo inserted above the article. She spoke to his picture. "Well, well, you sleazy son of a bitch. I hope the government grinds you into little pieces." She carried the

111

newspaper into the bedroom, set the wineglass on the dresser and opened her jewelry box. Removing the ring, she held it up to the light, recalling the night she had held it under the makeup lights in the Hotel Plaza's powder room; the night he had used his modus operandi of smoke and mirrors by professing his undying love for her. She cringed, remembering his words.

"Go ahead laugh if you want to. You meet a man, and in less then a day the idiot tells you he's nuts about you and to boot gives you a diamond ring. No one would believe it."

I believed it, she thought. *God, how I believed it. How we laughed at the old saying, love at first sight does happen, and how deliriously happy I was when I woke up the next morning with his scent still permeating the air. Life couldn't have been more beautiful.* Tears welled in her eyes. She sighed. *And how devastated I was, hearing from the operator that he and his wife had checked out of the hotel.*

Gritting her teeth, Lily walked onto the terrace and thought about Tillingham. "Good riddance, Tennessee," she said. "You're out of my life forever." She walked back into the living room, sipped her wine, picked up the newspaper and reread the article, thinking, *I wish I could teach that bastard a lesson.*

On an impulse, Lily grabbed the phone book and searched until she found the number she wanted, and dialed.

"Tillingham Industries," a cordial but stern voice said. "How may I direct your call?"

"Mr. Bradford Tillingham, please."

"One moment, I'll connect you with Mr. Tillingham's secretary."

"This is Miss Macy. Can I help you?"

"Yes. I would like to speak with Mr. Tillingham."

"In reference to what, may I ask?"

"In reference to *me* speaking with him."

"Mr. Tillingham does not take calls. If you will tell me what your business with Mr. Tillingham is, I will direct your call to the proper channel."

Lily asserted herself. "My business is personal. Just get me Mr. Tillingham's number one secretary."

Another voice spoke. "This is Miss Merziak. How may I help you?"

"Just tell Tennessee that his dear friend Lily Violet Fitzgerald is on the phone. I can assure you, he'll be delighted to speak with me."

"Mr. Tillingham is tied up in a meeting. May I take a message?"

"Please, not one of those 'meeting' excuses. No, you cannot take a message. Just slip my name under his nose. Lily Violet."

"Did you say Lily Violet, as in Lily Violet, the international concert pianist?"

"Yes. The same."

"Oh, Ms. Violet, I have all your albums. Please hold on." Lily waited less than ten seconds before she heard his familiar, charming, boyish voice.

"I don't believe it," he said. "Violet, I thought by now you would have had a dozen hit men out to gun me down. Is it really you? Say something so I can hear your voice." He quickly interjected, "Without cursing the hell out of me."

"I thought of gunning you down myself, but I was in the middle of a tour, so you have a stay of execution, for now."

"You've done very well for yourself. In fact, I went to your concert in Cleveland. Fell in love with you all over again."

"Still Mr. Charm. Was your wife with you?"

"I know, Violet. Anything I say will not excuse what I did. The only saving grace could possibly be the ring I gave you, which I'm sure you have sold by now. I am a bastard and really, I am ashamed."

"You should be, you rat. But, what the hell, we live and we learn. The ring? Sell it? I have it in my junk drawer. I'm sure it's as worthless as your promises."

"My promises may have been worthless, but believe it or not, I meant everything I said to you. I just couldn't follow through."

"Follow through? I guess it's hard to follow through when you're married. Come on, Tennessee, enough of the B. S. I don't have time for another round of love at first sight."

"You had it insured, didn't you?"

"No, I didn't have it insured. Why should I bother? It is most likely a lucky ring you found in a box of Cracker Jacks."

"Tell me why you called. You know I have no conscience. I'll still sleep through the night."

"I know you haven't any conscience," she said. "I only wish I'd had a clue to your devious character before." Taking a sip of the wine for courage, she thought, *why did I call? I better come up with a logical explanation.* "Okay, don't laugh, I'm being serious. I've become a devout follower of a sect that has to forgive their enemies…a cleansing of the soul ritual, so to speak. Believe me, it kills me, but I have to forgive you. And brother, that takes a lot of absolution where you're concerned. So as of this moment, I hereby declare that I forgive you." She sighed. "Well, that's a load off. Goodbye, Tennessee."

"Wait! Don't hang up," he said. "Are you serious about the ritual of cleansing your soul by forgiving? Well, you're not cleansed yet. If you want to forgive me you'll have to do it in person."

"You're pushing your luck, Tennessee. I fulfilled my third step. I did what I had to. Have to run. I'm late for a rehearsal."

●

Having second thoughts about what Tennessee had said, Lily hailed a cab to Cartiers, where she asked to speak to the gemologist.

Mr. Pearlman peered over his horn-rimmed spectacles as he walked toward her, extended his hand, his demeanor displaying one of authority. "How do you do?" he said. "I am Mr. Pearlman. How may I help you, Miss…?

"Ms. Fitzgerald." Lily held the Cartier velvet box up to him. "I need your expertise," she said.

"May I?" he asked. He took the box from her hand, opened it and removed the ring. Eying it with adoration, he sighed deeply. "Ah, I could never forget this beauty. This is the ring that was purchased by Mr. Tillingham. Exquisite gem. I remember when he purchased it. Had the department in a tizzy about having the box dyed violet. Said it had to be perfect because it was for a very special person." He smiled warmly at Lily. "And you must be that special person."

Lily's eyes widened. "I guess I am," she said. "Would it be presumptuous of me to ask for a written appraisal? I'm not sure it's insured."

Mr. Pearlman's eyes popped in their sockets. Visibly disturbed, he spewed out, "My dear lady, are you telling me this ring was never insured? My God! At the time, Mr. Tillingham said he was late for an appointment and would have his secretary attend to it but… In any case, please have a seat in our salon and I will attend to the matter. Would you care for some champagne, or perhaps a snack?"

"No, thank you, but if you don't mind, I *am* in a bit of a rush."

"Of course, of course. It won't take but a moment. I will need your name and address, if you would be so kind." As he departed, he tsked and repeated, "My God. My God, not insured."

Lily sat flipping through a Cartier brochure. *We'll I'll be damned. Tennessee wasn't kidding when he said the ring was authentic.*

Mr. Pearlman returned, handed Lily an envelope, thanked her, handed her his card, shook her hand and stated if ever he could be of service, not to hesitate to call him.

In the cab back to her apartment she opened the envelope, removed the appraisal and read:

"One internally flawless, colorless, Princess cut (quadrillion) six point-fifty carat diamond. With two matching in color and clarity, trillion diamonds, set in an eighteen-carat gold setting and certified by the Gemological Institute of America, appraised at four hundred and fifty thousand dollars. ($450,000)."

Chapter 26

One would have thought the three women chatting in a therapy session circle were close friends, not strangers who had just met.

"Who is Joey? Your boyfriend?" Lily asked.

Franny popped a mint into her mouth. "Used to be, but I outgrew him. He made me feel claustrophobic. You know, like I wanted to go out and dance and socialize, and he opted to stay in the apartment and watch the tube. It was okay at first, but I became bored sitting at home. He had a jealous streak that made me nuts. If I danced with another guy, he'd get ticked. I told him he could dance with other women, but he refused."

"Sounds like he wanted a relationship and you didn't," Lily said.

"More like you were using him and he cared about you," Elaine added.

"Really?" Franny said. "You two mavens know me for two seconds, and you're already writing a thesis on my life."

Dr. Kent entered the room. "I see you are getting along," he said.

Elaine's eyes lit up at the sight of him. "We were just chatting until Gerald and Thomas arrive."

"If that's what you call chatting, this session should prove to be very informative," Dr. Kent said.

Lily tilted her head to one side. "We are supposed to say whatever comes into our minds, aren't we?"

He repeated. "Whatever comes into your mind."

Eying Jonathon, Franny spoke sarcastically. "I don't think I'll have much to say. Nothing exciting has happened in my life, lately."

Gerald and Thomas dashed into the room. "That's what they all say at first," Thomas voiced. "Sorry we're late; the traffic was a mess, and I had to pick up Gerald, and he's never on time."

"Well, we're all here so let's get started," Jonathon, recommended. "Forget I'm here. Speak to each other, or to yourselves, but not to me. Who wants to begin?"

Thomas spoke up. "Ladies first. Want to go by age?"

"You remind me of an ex-husband…if I had an ex-husband," Franny said.

"I'll start," Gerald volunteered. "I met this terrific girl in the Fifth Avenue Public Library when I was doing research. I could tell she was attracted to me because she kept staring at me."

"Did you check to see if your fly was unzipped?" Thomas said.

Gerald ignored Thomas' comment. "I caught her eye and smiled at her, and she smiled back. Then I mustered all my courage and took the seat next to her. She looked down at the book she was reading and…"

Franny interrupted him. "Let me guess. You grabbed her and threw her on the table and jumped her bones. That must have gone over big in the library."

"Go easy, Franny," Elaine said. "We're not judging."

Franny shrugged.

"Well, anyway," Gerald said. "I got her telephone number."

Lily smiled. "That's very sweet, Gerald. I hope it works out. Thinking of Tennessee, she said, "I spoke to an old boyfriend today." She glanced at Jonathon. "He's quite good looking and extremely wealthy. I mean megabucks."

"I had no idea we had a celebrity in our midst," Elaine said. "A renowned concert pianist, no less. I just read an article about you in Newsweek. I didn't let the cat out of the bag, did I? I mean it's no secret."

"Of course not," Lily said. "I don't consider myself any different than anyone else, or I wouldn't be here, would I?"

"What happened with the old boyfriend? Are you going to see him again?" Thomas asked.

"I haven't decided," Lily said, eyeing Dr. Kent. "Now that I think about it, I don't remember why we broke up," she lied.

"Your career, probably," Franny said. "That's the reason I broke up with Joey. That, and he smelled of formaldehyde. He's an embalmer."

"Creepy," Gerald said. "I never go to anyone's funeral. I get queasy when I visit people in the hospital. Most odors affect me."

Franny asked, "What are you going to do if your new heartthrob uses perfume, douse her with Raid?"

Gerald looked at Dr. Kent, who did not acknowledge him. "I guess I'd do what I was taught to do."

Everyone focused on Gerald. "And?" Lily prompted.

He glanced at Dr. Kent for support, but the doctor stared down at his hands. "Well, I would take it one step at a time and go with my gut instinct."

Franny piped up. "Gee, if I had gone with my gut instinct they'd have taken me away a long time ago."

Thomas smirked. "I bet." He leaned over and slapped Gerald on his back. "Have to agree with you, buddy." He ran his tongue over his teeth. "I'd like to set the record straight, folks. Gerald and I may spar verbally, but we have a pretty strong bond between us. He may come across like he's mentally challenged, but he has a scholastic record of straight A's."

Gerald turned to Thomas. "I can speak for myself, you know."

"Geez, what are you two, lovers?" Franny asked.

Thomas' face turned red. He sprang to his feet. "Figures you would come to that kind of conclusion. You're the type that measures your partner's dick before you have sex. Who'd you put the move on after you slept with the football team, the coach? It just so happens we're both straight. And if you need proof, let me be man enough to prove it to you."

Franny waved a hand of dismissal. "Hey, don't get all bent out of shape. I'm not judging, only contributing to the session. Your lifestyle is your business. If you're not that way, why all the anger?"

Dr. Kent raised his hands. "I think we have had an excellent first session. I like the interaction and the openness with which you have expressed your feelings. How about lunch in the dining room?" He looked around. "Come now, why the long faces? What you all expressed was healthy."

Thomas turned to Gerald. "How about it? We can't get a better meal anywhere else in the city, and at these prices, too." Gerald nodded.

Jonathon turned to the women. "You'll have to excuse me. I have patients to attend to. How about it, ladies? Hungry?"

"Thanks for the offer," Franny said, "but the ladies have made other arrangements." She stared hard at Lily and Elaine. "Right?" She locked arms with both of them and steered them to the outer office. "It was hard enough getting reservations, let's not be late."

In the outer office, Lily and Elaine scowled at Franny. "What reservation?" Lily asked.

"Now don't give me a hard time," Franny said. "If we're going to spill our guts to each other, I think we should get to know each other." She narrowed her eyes. "Unless you think I'm some kind of a leper." She frowned. "Okay, I have an ulterior motive. I'm at a low point." An expression of hopelessness darkened her features. "I need some company."

"Well, I'll force myself to eat," Lily said.

"I'm game," Elaine agreed. "Did you really make reservations at a restaurant?"

"Of course not," Franny said. "I just had to get out of there."

Elaine shook her head. "Don't you have to go back to work?"

"No. I don't have any appointments today. So, ladies, where do we eat?"

Elaine shrugged. "What do you ladies like?"

"I can always eat Chinese," Lily said. "But where?"

"Chinatown is the best for Chinese. But it's such a schlep," Elaine said.

"How about this," Franny said. "We can pick up Chinese food at the local China Palace and go to one of our apartments, where we can relax and let our hair down."

"Fine with me," Elaine said. "I would ask you to my home, but I'm sure you don't want to traipse out to Forest Hills."

Franny threw her hands up. "And mine is in its usual state of disarray. Guess you're elected, Lily. I always wanted to see how a concert pianist lives. I bet it's to die for."

As Elaine reached for the office doorknob the door swung open and a flustered looking woman collided with her. "Oh, I am so sorry," Amelia Stern said. "How careless of me to come barging in, like some scatterbrain." She stopped short upon recognizing Elaine. "Elaine, dear, how are you?" She pecked Elaine on the cheek. "Bill and I have missed seeing you at the club." She acknowledged Lily and Franny with a momentary glance. "You must forgive me, I'm late for my appointment, and you know how upset doctors get if you mess with their appointments. Let's do lunch. Do call me." She flew into the office, her hands waving at Cynthia. "I'm here, I'm here, Cynthia," she cried. "The traffic was unbearable."

The three ladies looked at each other and laughed. Elaine said, "That's Amelia Stern, the wife of our general practitioner. She's really very nice, a bit unpredictable but lots of fun."

"What's she coming in for?" Franny asked. "The doc cheating on her?"

"Not every husband screws around, Franny," Lily said.

"Oh yeah? Listen, she may be what we would call 'remarkable for her age,' but she's just at that time of life when husbands lust for the eighteen-year-old embryos."

Amelia Stern waved a fleeting hello at Cynthia and waited for the buzzer that gave her permission to enter Jonathon's office. She stepped into the room, snapped the lock, smiled beguilingly at Jonathon, and proceeded to untie her wrap dress and let it fall to the floor.

The doorman at Lily's condo extended his hand to assist the three women as they alighted from the limo. Lily bent over and spoke to the chauffeur. "I'll call you later, Ralph, if I need you."

In the apartment, Lily closed the front door and hung their coats in the closet. "Elaine," she said. "I'm still angry with you for insisting on paying for the food." Franny nodded in agreement.

"It was my pleasure. Everyone is doing her fair share. We're using your apartment, and Franny's entertaining us with her sense of humor, so why shouldn't I pay? And besides, my husband foots the bills. Better *I* should spend it then some...anyhow, what's money for, if not to enjoy yourself?"

Franny breathed a low whistle. "Check out this living room. Who was the designer, Michelangelo?" She removed her shoes. "Wouldn't want to get the carpet dirty."

A curved, glistening steel railing led up to a bedroom with a glass door and sheets of glass for walls.

Franny eyed the staircase, her arms flailing in the air. "I don't believe this place."

Elaine started opening the containers of food as Lily poured herself a glass of wine and motioned to them with a wine bottle. When they declined, she raised her glass and toasted to them.

"I did it myself," Lily said. "In between hours of rehearsing at the keyboard. "Keeps me sane. Don't worry about the carpeting. I've been thinking of changing the color scheme."

"Get her," Franny exclaimed. "What are you going to do with this stuff when the colors don't match? Give it to the Salvation Army?"

Lily and Elaine exchanged glances. "Why?" Lily asked. "Can you use it?"

"Can I use it? Are you kidding? You should see my place. The only thing that would help it is if I lit a match. It's a mediaeval torture chamber with red flocked wallpaper."

Lily shook her head. "Say no more; it's yours."

Franny gripped Elaine's arm. "Elaine, I want you to be my witness in case she reneges." She strolled around the living room then started to walk up the stairs to the bedroom. "Mind if I look?"

Lily chuckled. "Feel free to explore."

Franny ascended the staircase, stopped halfway, and called down to Lily. "I suppose if you're re-doing the living room you'll be re-doing the bedroom too? The colors should blend from one room to the other, right? Can't have colors that clash. A concert pianist should have tranquility and harmony when she's at the keyboard. Soothes the mind."

Elaine rolled her eyes. "You must be the top salesman in your firm, Franny. What a con artist you are."

Franny did a thumbs up. "Saleslady, Elaine, and the best."

Lily sipped her wine. "You pay for the moving of the furniture and it's a deal."

Elaine walked into the kitchen. "Damn, we forgot to ask for chopsticks."

Lily waved her hand in the direction of the cabinet. "In the server, second drawer on the left."

"I'll get it," Elaine said. "What about the dishes?"

"Up here, Elaine."

Franny came scurrying down. "What about me? Don't I get to

participate?"

Lily chuckled. "Just keep us entertained. It's refreshing."

"Yeah, except sometimes you speak without thinking first. Like today when you attacked Thomas and Gerald." Elaine poked her chopsticks at an egg roll.

Franny's mouth turned downward. "I still think they've got something going on between them."

"And if they do, who cares?" Elaine said.

Franny shrugged. "Hey, who's judging? I've done a few ménage a trois in my time."

"Have you told that to Dr. Kent?"

Franny's eyes lit up. "I tell him what he wants to hear, and what suits me." She eyed Elaine and then Lily. "And I suppose you two confess everything."

Neither Elaine nor Lilly said anything.

"That's what I thought. Lily, you wouldn't want to put it in writing, would you?"

"Put what in writing?"

"The disbursement of the decor," Franny said.

"Franny, we can inventory the stuff later. Take yourself out to the terrace and relax. Promise you won't jump, okay? I'm not sure my accident insurance covers suicide."

"I'm not *that* depressed," Franny shouted from the terrace. "Elaine, get out here. You have to see this view. I can see all of Central Park and clear up to Washington Heights. Lily, can we eat out here?"

In the kitchen, Elaine nudged Lily. "What a character. Always clowning. Still, you know what they say about clowns."

"Uh huh. They make us laugh but they're sad on the inside. Want to take the tray? Let's make the clown happy and set up the table on the terrace." She raised her voice. "Okay, we'll eat on the terrace, little

Princess. Whatever the Princess wants she will get."

Elaine arranged the plates and set the containers of food on the wrought iron table. Elaine and Lily sat down and unfolded their napkins. They looked at Franny. who sat mesmerized, her face drained of blood. "Franny, what's wrong?" Lily cried.

Elaine reached over and rubbed Franny's wrist, then lightly slapped her face. "Come on, Franny," she said. "Wake up, you're okay."

After several seconds Franny came to. "What happened?" she asked. "Did I faint?"

"No," Elaine said. "It's hard to faint sitting up. More like you were stuck in time for a few seconds." She felt Franny's forehead. "How are you feeling?" "I feel fine. And suddenly I'm starving. Sit down, the food is getting cold."

Lily sighed. "Are you sure you don't need a doctor?"

"I have a doctor, dear. And he's more than enough. Can we just eat?" She eyed them. "Are we finished playing hospital?"

Elaine and Lily answered in unison. "Yes."

"Want me to let you in on a secret, girls?" Lily asked. "I'm actually hungry."

"So what's so special about that, Lily?"

"I'm never hungry. I forgot to take my diet pills today. I can't believe I did that."

"What does that mean?" Elaine said.

"Oh nothing, really. It's just that I'm never without them."

Elaine shook her head. "Big mistake, Lily. Once you get addicted to them you're in for a lot of trouble. Have you tried getting off of them?"

Lily refilled her wineglass. "Oh, I can stop anytime I choose to. That and drinking."

"Want to bet?" Elaine said.

"Can we just eat?" asked Franny. "For God's sake, we just came from therapy." She stared at her food.

"Franny," Elaine said. "Are you all right?"

"What? Oh, I was just thinking. I remember Lily saying something about me being a little princess and it triggered something...something from the past..."

Chapter 27

Bob the doorman smiled at Lily. "Taxi, Miss Fitzgerald? No chauffeur?"

"I was thinking of walking. I could use the exercise."

"Isn't this the day you go to the gym?"

"Don't remind me. I haven't been able to get myself back on schedule."

"You look pretty good to me."

"I don't know for how long, Bob, if I don't start working out again. Sitting at the piano for hours doesn't help my derriere any."

"When are you going to play at Carnegie Hall?"

"Next month. Don't worry; there will be tickets at the box office for you and the wife. I *will* take a cab, Bob."

A cab pulled up to the curb and stopped abruptly. The doorman turned to Lily. "We'll wait for another one. This one's a cowboy."

The cab door swung open and a dapper, tall man wearing a homburg stepped out. He bent down and spoke sternly to the driver. "I've got a good mind to report you, my man. Are you sure you have a legitimate license?" He flung the fare at the driver and turned toward Lily. "I would suggest you pass on this one; he must have traded in a racing car for this cab." He tipped his hat.

"Dash?" she said surprised. "Dashel Wentworth. Is it really you?"

He was taken aback. "Lily? I can't believe my eyes. What are you doing here?"

"I live here. I could ask you the same thing. How are you? My God, it must be two...no, three years since we played together in London."

"Three," he said, his eyes sparkling. The flash of gray hair peeking from beneath the homburg gave him a most distinguished look. "And it was Paris."

"Of course," she said. "What brings you to New York? If I remember correctly, you said you would never set foot in the States again."

"I was young and foolish then. I've forgiven the critics."

She narrowed her eyes. "I doubt it. You're not the forgiving type."

"Well, you may be right. Say, how about getting together? I don't want to lose track of you again." He hesitated. "Remember the last time?"

"No, let's not get into that," she said, remembering how she had stood him up, and left that night for the States without even a goodbye, afraid they were becoming too involved. "Whenever you say, Dash."

"Your place or mine?"

The memory of Tennessee saying the exact words the night before he dumped her flashed though her head. "Here's my card. Call me."

He kissed her on both cheeks, his hands holding tightly to hers, not wanting to let go. "I'm so excited, Lily! What a wonderful surprise. I read wonderful things about you. We have so much to catch up on."

"I have to dash, Dash," she said, slightly embarrassed by the play on words, remembering how they used to laugh at the phrase. "I'm late for an appointment," she said, gently withdrawing her hands from his. "Call me."

•

At seven fifteen that evening the phone rang. Lily's heartbeat quickened, thinking it might be Jonathon. "Hello," she said coolly, not wanting to appear too eager.

"Lily?"

"Oh, is that you, Dash?" she said.

"Yes, it's Dash. Did someone die?"

"No. Why?"

"From your tone of voice I thought surely someone had passed on, or you've been playing "Marche Slave." You had the same inflection in your voice that my ex-wife has."

"I'm sure that was not meant as a compliment. You didn't waste any time. We only met this morning. Ex wife? So, you married and divorced? What happened?"

"After you broke my heart I eloped with the first woman that walked through the revolving door at the Ritz."

"That should teach you not to make rash decisions."

"It was either that or slashing my wrists. Actually, I'm waiting for the divorce to come through, so I'm practically free, and may I add, loose?"

His sense of humor was what had originally attracted her to him. She laughed. "You mean now? I just got home from a grueling rehearsal and I was just going to..."

"Defrost a chicken pot pie, right?"

He made her feel at ease. "You remembered," she said.

"Leave it in the freezer. I'm two blocks from Zabars. I am going to pick up Nova Scotia salmon, sturgeon, and chive cream cheese and garlic bagels. We'll have Sunday brunch on Friday night. Do you by any chance have capers, scallions and a lemon or two?"

"No."

"I'll be there pronto. Oh, by the way, you didn't have plans for tonight, did you?"

"Does it matter?"

"No. I'm just so excited to see you. I haven't thought about anything but you all afternoon."

Geez, she thought, *where have I heard that line before, thinking of another thing Tennessee had said the day he dumped her. Two down and one to go.* "You're still a married man, Dash. I wouldn't wish to have my name mixed into a messy divorce. I have to be careful."

"Not to worry. The bitch is in London-town. And besides I know you usually don't fool around on the first date. I'll pick up a bottle of your favorite wine. You still drink, don't you?"

She rolled her eyes. "Like a fish."

"Good. I'll get two bottles. I can't wait to tell you about my new position with the Tillingham organization. Ta ta."

"Hold on!" she said, taken aback. "Did you say, Tillingham, as in Bradford T. Tillingham?"

"The very same. Why? Do you know him?"

"Slightly," she said. "See you soon, and Dash, nix the garlic bagels for me and get a few sesame seed."

Lily placed the phone in its cradle and opened a bottle of wine. As she poured, she envisioned Bradford Tennessee Tillingham's face whirling around the wine glass. *Well, well,* she thought. *This should prove to be a very interesting evening.*

•.

Lily greeted Dashel at the door and quickly turned her face to the side as his mouth aimed for her lips. She gently pushed him away. "You don't want to crush the food, Dash."

"It's you I want to crush, Lily."

"So I gathered by your zealous advance." Hands placed firmly on her hips, she spoke sharply. "We are not going to have one of those chase-me-around-the-house games, are we?" Her eyes narrowed. "Are you going to behave or do I have to throw you out?"

He threw his hands into the air. "Okay, you win. Can't blame a guy for trying." He stared at her. "You look fantastic, Lily. How do you keep so trim?"

"I drink three bottles of wine a day and counteract it with diet pills. Then I let them fight it out."

"Are you serious?" He shook his head. "Do you think that's wise? You at least take vitamins, don't you?"

"Wine has vitamins. Enough about my habits and me. Let me prepare the food."

"No, let me. You can set the table. You know I love to play 'chef.'"

"Be my guest. I already set the table and even lit candles." He raised his eyebrows, but she threw him a warning look.

He held his hands up. "I promise I'll behave."

The sun was setting over Central Park as Dashel watched the lights go on in the office buildings in the distance. "Spectacular view you have here, Lily," he called to her and leaned over the terrace straining to see into the windows of the adjacent building. "If I lived here I would have high-powered binoculars and a telescope."

Lily joined him on the terrace. "If you lived here, your name would be on the ten most wanted list of voyeurs in New York."

"Why begrudge me a little extra-curricular activity? I gave up my apartment in London, I gave up what I loved doing most—giving concerts—and settled for giving lessons to untalented children of wealthy parents." He faced her. "I wouldn't admit this to anyone but you, Lily. I miss it so much."

She placed her hands on his shoulders. "You were a good pianist. Maybe you lacked concentration, didn't work hard enough. You did win competitions."

"You said it, Lily. I was a *good* pianist." She started to speak, but he interrupted. "I want to put all that behind me, but this damn ego of mine won't let go."

"But you said you were excited about this new venture with the Tillingham Corporation."

"Oh, I am. I could be set for life, but that, too, has its drawbacks."

"How so?"

"This Tillingham, he's a cold-blooded, ruthless son of a bitch. He's like a crocodile. He'd eat his children if they stood in his way."

Lily played it cool. "You don't say? All of the above?"

"Uh huh. But he pays huge salaries, and the working conditions, benefits and vacations are fabulous."

"So you eat a little crow and enjoy the perks. What's Tillingham's interest in you?"

"It's strange how things come about. While dining in London town I bumped into an old boyhood chum who happens to be one of Tillingham's hatchet men. I needed the change and so I talked him into hiring me. But it goes deeper than that."

"I want to hear, but since you offered to play chef you'll have to get the dessert and demitasse."

"I can talk meanwhile. You remember my father and the caster company he owned?"

She chuckled. "I remember asking you what casters were and you explained that they were the wheels that were under my piano. By the way, how is he?"

"He died last year."

"I am so sorry to hear that, Dash. He seemed so healthy. What happened?"

He wiped his hands on a hand towel. "Let's go out on the terrace." She poured wine and they both sipped. "Dad ran into a bit of trouble and needed refinancing for his company. The big companies were cutting prices and Dad had to meet the competition. That's how it started. Evidently, the word got out and he was approached by one of

Tillingham's henchmen. In order to save the business, he signed over a portion of it to the Tillingham organization. That was the beginning of the end for Dad. Before long, Dad was out and Tillingham controlled everything. The heartless son of a bitch just about threw Dad into the street." Dashel bit his lip. "Within two months Dad had a massive coronary."

"How awful," she said, remembering that Tennessee had told her how unethical he was in his business transactions. "And you want to work for him?"

He gave her a long, serious look. "Revenge," he said. "I live for the day I can bury the bastard."

She sank back in her seat, her jaw thrust forward, an idea forming in her mind.

"Why the pensive look?" he asked.

She refilled their wineglasses and held hers up to him. "You know, Dash, our meeting might not have been an accident. Do you have any incriminating evidence you could use against him?"

He cocked his head to one side. "I have a few leads that could be detrimental to him, but nothing conclusive as of yet. I'm working on it."

"Does he know who you are?"

"Are you serious? Of course not. That would blow my cover. Why the sudden interest?"

"Because I have a score to settle with the lowlife, too."

"Don't tell me he duped you out of money?"

"What he did to me cannot be measured in money, Dash," she said as she ran her finger along the rim of the wine glass. "I think that you and I are going to help put Bradford T. Tillingham where he belongs."

Chapter 28

The cosmetologist at Macy's beamed as though she had just put the finishing touches on a Rembrandt. She stepped back, scrutinized her masterpiece and said with pride, "That shade is you! The chemists must have had you in mind when they mixed the formula!" Franny studied her face in the oval mirror as the makeup artist stood by, admiring her creation. "Lights up your entire face and goes so well with your skin tone." She edged closer to Franny. "I don't usually say this, but it isn't every day I get someone with your bone structure and natural beauty to work with."

What a line of bullshit, Franny thought. *If you think I'm spending mega bucks for this supposedly free makeup job, you're out of your bird.*

The salesgirl turned to a prospective customer. "Give me one second, madam, and I'll give you my full attention."

Franny's mother, Blanche, waved a hand of dismissal. "It'll take more than your full attention to overhaul this face."

Upon hearing her mother's voice, Franny shrank back on the high stool.

Mrs. Goldsmith approached Franny. "I thought Halloween was over. Why the makeover?"

Franny smiled cordially at the cosmetologist. "I'll think about it," she said, sliding off the stool and grabbing her mother's arm.

"You just made an enemy," Blanche said. "Boy, if looks could kill."

"What are you doing here, Blanche?" Franny asked, miffed.

"What? I can't shop in department stores any more, I have to get a visa to come into Manhattan?"

"I didn't mean it that way, Blanche. You sort of snuck up on me. I just spoke to you yesterday."

Her mother looked at her questioningly. "Your conversation left me depressed…hanging up on me because you didn't want to hear what I was saying." She looked over her shoulder. "That salesgirl is throwing daggers at you. You could have at least bought a lipstick. Oh well. Did you have lunch, and don't say 'yes.'"

Franny shrugged. "I'll buy the cosmetics next time. Anyhow, I was short with you because I have a lot on my mind."

"Don't we all. Chinese, Italian, deli or a Subway hero?"

"You pick. I can tell this is going to be a no-win situation."

"No-win for who? I have yet to win an argument with you."

"That's because we are so much alike, Blanche."

"I'm older, so I should get the respect."

"If you don't get the respect you think you should, it's because you brought me up like I was your sister, not your daughter."

"Don't twist things around, Franny. You have a way of confusing issues. Let's go to the deli next door."

Franny sighed heavily. "Okay, Blanche, let's get it over with."

At the restaurant, her mother asked, "Want to split a sandwich?"

"No, Blanche. You eat yours and I'll eat mine. Egg salad with onions and anchovies isn't exactly one of my favorites."

"I've been thinking. It's about time you stopped calling me Blanche."

Franny eyed her mother. "I can't believe you said that. You're the one who insisted I call you 'Blanche.'"

"That was when you were still a child. Then it was cute, now it's...it's not respectful."

Anger flashed in Franny's eyes. "What are you talking about? I don't respect you? I don't kick in with the rent for your place? I don't take your shit almost every day on the phone?" She shook her head. "Maybe I should make a fucking appointment for you with my shrink."

"Okay, Franny, let's stop right now. Once you start with the cursing I know you're losing it. This can only turn into another screaming match and frankly, I don't have the strength." She took a bite of her sandwich and chewed it slowly. "Ya know, lately I've been having palpitations."

"I've heard that for as long as I can remember. Have you been skipping your medication?" Franny asked, knowing full well her mother's irregular heartbeat was not serious. She decided to humor her. "How about I make an appointment for you with Dr. Shool?"

"Yeah, like he knows what he's doing," Blanche said. "It'll pass." She eyed Franny and curled her mouth to one side. "I'll be fine," she said solemnly. "I'm used to taking care of myself."

The soda made a slurping sound as Franny pulled on the straw. She stared straight at her mother. "Okay," she said. "Give. What's the beef this time? And don't give me the same old spiel that you have nothing to look forward to. Have a fight with your neighbor again?"

Blanche didn't say anything.

"Blanche, I'm not paying your next month's rent until you tell me."

"It's your father."

"He died? We should be so lucky."

"No, he's sick."

"Well, then maybe he *will* die."

"Must you be so callous?"

Franny's eyes widened. "Callous? You must be sniffing hair spray. That son of a bitch ran off with his secretary when I was a child and never even gave you a red cent for alimony or child support. Do you know how many nights I cried because all the other kids had fathers? And you're feeling *sorry* for him? Sick, huh. Maybe he has AIDS? What did he do, start hitting on boys? I know I'm inclined to be a little irrational sometimes but I'm not that far gone. Give me a break, Blanche." She studied her mother. "What? Oh, no. Don't tell me you asked him to come back so that you can be a nurse and a purse until he dies. Let me know when it's time. I'll call Hospice.

Blanche pushed the breadcrumbs into a neat pile on the checkered tablecloth and then prearranged them in one of the red squares.

Franny's eyes widened. "You didn't ask him to live with you, did you?"

"I did," Blanche whimpered. Avoiding her daughter's eyes, she moved the breadcrumbs from the red square into a white square. "Don't hate me, Franny."

"I don't hate you. I'm just disappointed. You know, since the day he left I've had mixed emotions about him. I hated him for leaving and yet for some crazy reason I missed him."

Blanche's eyes grew large. "What do you mean?"

"I honestly don't know."

"That's not all, Franny. There's something more. Something I've been holding back for a long time." She looked down at the tablecloth again and shook her head. "I really tried to be a good mother."

Becoming agitated, Franny said, "Bullshit! You were never around. You were out drinking every night. What kind of a mother leaves a child of five alone, without a babysitter?"

"I wanted to teach you to be independent, not to need other people."

"Now that's a truckload of bull. At five and six years old? The truth is you were always a self-centered bitch and you never really loved me. You're one of those women who should never have kids."

Blanche glared at her. "Since we're playing 'to tell the truth,' Franny. I have to admit something else." Staring at Franny as if she was looking through her she said, "I never really wanted you."

Franny's fraught gaze, already fixed on her mother, stayed frozen.

"You ruined my marriage. After you were born, your father never paid any attention to me. Suddenly, you became the star of the family."

Franny tried to hide the hurt she felt. The weight of her dismay caught her off guard. "Are you just about finished spewing your guilt on me?"

"Actually, there's more."

Franny vigorously shook her head from left to right. "Well, save it! I've had more than enough for one afternoon. I'm quitting while I still have what's left of my sanity." She stood, tossed a twenty-dollar bill on the table and stared down at her mother, the tears rolling down her cheeks. "Listen, Blanche," she said, her voice quivering, "let's *not* keep in touch, okay?"

Chapter 29

The Tudor mansion on the Tillingham estate stood high on a hill overlooking the Hudson River in Tarrytown, New York. The servants scurried back and forth from the kitchen to the outdoor patio where Mr. and Mrs. Tillingham were having breakfast. Rehnquist, the butler, nervously poured Mr. Tillingham's coffee, knowing full well that even though the coffee was piping hot and the taste to perfection, his employer would find something to complain about.

Mariah Tillingham watched her husband as the butler poured his coffee, anticipating an outburst, surely not a compliment. Dressed in a Japanese kimono, she sat under a multi-colored umbrella that shaded her beautiful face and spectacular figure. It was a far cry from her days as carhop, to Miss Sweet Potato Queen, to Miss Louisiana, and then to Miss America, compared to the luxurious life she now led.

Bradford Tillingham held the coffee cup to his nose and smelled the aroma. He protested. "What's this, Mariah, perfumed coffee?"

"Don't complain until you've tried it, Brad. I thought a change might please you. Like tasting wines, experiencing different bouquets."

"Why, Mariah? I've been satisfied with the coffee cook has been brewing. If I wanted a change, I would have said so."

"It's only coffee. Come on, taste it. It is possible that you might like it."

Annoyed at her pursuing the conversation he said, "Why would I want to try another blend when I'm perfectly satisfied with the old one?"

"The same reason that you hire people and then fire them, or buy a company or sell a company. You always preached that one has to test and experience new avenues in order to build and strengthen an empire." She smiled coolly at him. "Go on," she teased. "Try it. I wouldn't poison you...well, not in front of the servants."

He held the coffee cup up to his mouth and peered at her. "You're being quite sarcastic this morning, and bitchier than usual, I might add. What's wrong? Did you run out of places to spend my fucking money?"

"Honestly, dear. Such profanity at the breakfast table! And, it's *our* money, remember? Don't tell me you're worried about finances. Is the rent on the apartments you keep for your stable of whores causing you financial difficulties?"

He lowered his voice and scowled at his wife. "Don't fucking push me, Mariah. I have enough on my mind; I will not tolerate your bitchy sarcasm. Not today."

She inclined her body toward him, smiled slyly and accentuated her southern drawl. "Don't match wits with me, dahrlin. Remember, you taught me everything ah know."

He pounded his fist on the table and raised his voice. "Listen, Mariah, not now! I told you I have a lot on my mind. I don't want to hear any more of your offensive, mindless babbling."

She drew back in her chair, stifling a giggle. "Taste the coffee and I'll behave," she teased, an angelic expression on her face.

He sighed and reluctantly tasted the coffee. "Yuck!" he exclaimed, spitting the coffee into his napkin. "What is this shit? It tastes like poison!"

"I said I wouldn't poison you in front of the servants," she chuckled. "Anyway, what's so earth shattering at the office that's upsetting you? I didn't think there was a problem you couldn't solve or talk your way out of. Anything you might want to discuss with this dumb blond, or is it out of my realm?"

He sat back in his chair, emptied the remains of the coffee into the flowerbed and held the cup out for Rehnquist, who had returned, to refill. "This isn't that faggy coffee, is it, Rehnquist?" Upon tasting it, he said, "Now that's more like it." He smiled with reservation at his wife. "Didn't think you were interested in my business, Mariah."

She scowled at him.

"Okay," he said. *Our* business." He studied her for a moment, wondering why he had lost interest in this almost perfect specimen of a woman. He shook his head, his thoughts returning to the new member of his staff and the problems he might present. "I worked so hard and long to steal this Harmony Record Company run by this man." He sniggered. "Practically stole it from under his nose."

"Bad vibrations with the gent?"

"Actually, he's savvy enough. Can't put my finger on it. He just rubs me the wrong way. But right now I'm stuck with him."

"What's the cantankerous gentleman's name?"

"Dashel Wentworth."

"Sounds British."

"The limey has a contract stating that he remain with the company for one year. I suppose I can put up with him. If I don't feel he's right, I'll find a way to get rid of him."

"Sounds to me like he's competition. You like a challenge. I can't believe that you, the scourge of the industry, are letting some unknown nothing get you so worked up." She looked to see if the servants were nearby, then smirked and said, "You know, Brad, if he gives you a hard time you could put a hit out on him. It's worked before."

He sprang to his feet, walked to where she sat and bent down, his lips touching her cheek. His face remained impassive but his voice rang with cold death. "If you ever, ever breathe what you just said, I promise you, Mariah, I'll strangle you with my bare hands." His hands shook as he placed them around her neck. Aware that the butler was approaching he removed his hands from her throat and placed them gently on her shoulders and pecked a kiss on her forehead. "What are your plans for today, dear?" he asked through clenched teeth.

Waving Rehnquist away, Mariah waited until she heard the butler scurry off and the terrace door click shut. Then like a shot she sprang to her feet and grasped at her husband's suit lapels and yanked him toward her. Her eyes resembling those of a snake stalking its prey, she hissed in his ear. "Listen to me, you pompous asshole. If you have any ideas of doing away with me, you better think twice. There's a full account of all your indiscretions, along with a detailed list of who you used and how you built your empire…and a roster of all the rundown ghetto housing that is unfit to live in, tucked safely away." Her hissing changed to a drone as she continued. "Not to mention the people you had…" she ran her finger across her throat. "They'll hang you by your nuts. The boys in prison would love your cute little butt." She pushed him away, reached down and tapped the bell signaling for Rehnquist.

Taken aback by her sudden actions, Tillingham remained standing; his fists clenched, his knuckles white, the veins in his neck pulsating, glaring at her with hatred, trying to control his anger.

The butler entered as Mariah stepped back, raised her palm to her mouth and blew her husband a kiss. "Won't you please be home for dinner, deah? Cook is making your favorite dish. *Looosiana* fried chicken, and yams topped with marshmallow and molasses."

A loud, emphatic, "No!" boomed from his mouth.

She crinkled her fingers, gesturing a short goodbye at him.

"I'll deal with you later," he called over his shoulder as he walked away.

"Yes, later," she said into the air. After a few moments she turned to Rehnquist and asked, "Has he gone?"

The butler walked up the terrace steps and peered out to see Tillingham enter the Rolls Royce and yell at the chauffeur, "Get me the fuck out of here!"

Rehnquist swallowed a smile. "Yes, Madam. Mr. Tillingham has left."

Mariah stood on the steps of the terrace, serene and confident, surveying the expansive view of the Hudson River, her thoughts focused on the luncheon she had planned with her husband's latest adversary, Dashel Wentworth.

Chapter 30

Droplets of rain bounced off of the outstretched umbrellas and found their way onto the rain-soaked pavement of the Chez Norman restaurant.

Gaston, the doorman, leaned down, hesitated and peered guardedly into the Porsche convertible.

"Yes, Gaston, it's me," Mariah Tillingham said.

Acknowledging with a nod of his head that the lady was indeed Mrs. Tillingham, he said contritely, "Orders from Monsieur Johnson. Just wanted to make sure it was you."

Opening the Porsche's door, he drew back, his finger waving a no to her as she pressed a $100 bill into his jacket pocket. "Gaston," she insisted, "humor me."

Shaking his head dubiously at her, he offered his arm, escorted her past the multi-colored waterfall, through the canopied walkway, and opened the door of the plush restaurant. "Mr. Johnson said to make sure I buzz him the moment you arrive." He touched a button on his beeper to alert his boss.

The owner of the restaurant, Mobley Johnson, a tall, good-looking, blue-eyed, light-skinned man engrossed in conversation with a patron excused himself and hastened to greet Mariah.

Accepting a kiss on her cheek, she took his arm and asked, "How's business?"

"Fantastic. Thanks to you. Flourishing with the rich and famous."

They entered a dining room where celadon walls served as the backdrop for a series of early 19th century botanical engravings. Another wall housed caricatures of legendary French actors. And on an adjacent wall there hung lithographs of celebrated French authors. Subdued lit chandeliers lent a mystical air to the opulently furnished room. Well-known French books lined the shelves and a mahogany ladder stood waiting for a patron to climb in order to reach the top level.

Mariah had liked the proposed sketches the decorator had submitted, but Bradford had detested them vehemently, and so to spite him she gave the decorator her approval. Stopping to survey the surroundings, she said, "Don't you think a cozy fireplace would be perfect here, Mobley?"

Rolling his eyes, he scoffed, "Mariah, what this overcooked, claustrophobic object d'art refuge needs is a touch of arson." She poked him and then laughed aloud.

Art deco was the theme of the next room they entered. This was Mariah's favorite dining room. A romantic, dusky atmosphere lingered in the air. Earth-brown leather, embossed with gold studs in a fleur de lis motif covered the walls that complemented the gold and white boxed, tiled floor.

Mariah and Mr. Johnson ascended a winding Lucite banister that led to a small, intimate balcony.

Dashel Wentworth stood as they approached a circular banquette. Before he could speak she said, "The wig and glasses are my *public* disguise." She tilted her head to the side and spoke to Mr. Johnson. "It isn't necessary for you to hover over me, Mobley. The gentleman is not going to eat me."

Protective of her, Mobley warily shook his head. "As you wish. I'll have

Henri serve."

"We'll talk later," she said, and turned to face Dashel. Extending her hand to him, she said, "Please, sit. I like a man with good manners." She kept her eyes on Dashel but directed her voice to Henri the waiter, who suddenly appeared. "Henri, I'll have a martini, but straight up this time. And have Bernard prepare the duck a l'orange." She removed her oversized dark glasses and adjusted her wig. "How about you, Dashel? What's your poison?"

"I'll have whatever the lady is having, Henri." Admiring her flawless complexion and stunning features, he said, "Your disguise is quite good. I would have never recognized you. The tabloid and society pics do not do you justice. I don't mean to sound obsequious, but you are..."

"Are what? Say it. I never get tired of hearing how attractive I am. You may find it hard to believe, but it's been a while since anyone has paid me a compliment."

He raised a brow. "That *is* hard to believe." He leaned a trifle closer. "And if I am permitted to mosey a bit farther...breathtaking?"

She waited until Henri served the drinks and then lifted her glass to toast. "To well laid plans of mice and men," she said.

"From your rapport with Mr. Johnson, the maitre d, I take it you are a regular at the restaurant."

"Mobley is an old friend of mine from what I choose to call 'my down-and-out days.' He was there for me when I desperately needed a friend." She drew in a deep breath and for a brief moment stared into the past. "A true friend is hard to find in this screwed-up world. I like to repay my debts. So when I married Tillingham and acquired the means, I returned the favor. He is the maitre d and owner of Chez Norman." She spoke softly. "I bought and helped plan this restaurant." Tossing her hair to one side, she smirked. "And Bradford didn't even blink an eye." She sipped her drink, aware of Dashel's good looks and charisma. "Well?" she said.

His eyes searched hers. "Uh…I'm still trying to digest your graciousness in returning a friend's good deed."

"Aren't you going to ask me why I arranged this meeting?"

His eyes widened. "I have been dying to, but you and this restaurant have rendered me speechless. Beats anything I have seen, and I have seen them all…from South Hampton to Timbuktu. In fact, if you don't tell me straight away, Mr. Johnson is liable to have a crazy diner to contend with."

The smooth tones in his voice and his English accent pleased her.

"Yes," he went on, "I have been a nervous wreck since our brief conversation this morning. At first I thought it was a hoax, until you verified certain facts."

Henri cleared his throat, warning them he was approaching. "I took the liberty of serving the caviar that madam enjoys; from the Aquitaine region of France?" he said, and proceeded to top off their martinis.

"Shall we drink, or eat, and talk later?" Dashel asked.

"I can do both," she said. "And I'm sure you can, too." Lips firming, she ran her well-manicured fingers along the rim of her water goblet. "Let me lay my cards on the table, Dashel. I have had you checked out from the day you started masturbating to this morning when you asked the housekeeper at your hotel for extra towels."

He swallowed hard.

"Let's skip your childhood, your concert tours as a pianist, your relationship with Lily Violet, and your father losing his business to my esteemed husband, and your connection with Harmony Records. The latter being the reason we are here having this delicious imported caviar." She winked at him, scooped up grains of caviar with a mother of pearl knife, spread it on a toast point, and edged the caviar into his mouth.

"I'm all ears," he said after he'd swallowed. "I'm becoming more intrigued by the minute."

"I have a good feeling about you," she said, pointing the knife at him, "and my instincts are usually on target. Together we can achieve what we both hunger after. I'll be able to shed Bradford—the creep—spread my wings and breathe fresh air once again. And you, you can avenge your father. Isn't it ironic? Bradford, shrewd as he is, with all his savvy, hasn't the faintest idea what's in store for him." She smiled with assurance. "I have information on him that would send him up the river for an eternity, but I choose to stay out of the limelight, so to speak. That's where you come in. I want the evidence that would incriminate him to come from you. Not to worry, Dashel, I'll help. I just don't relish hassling with the league of lawyers, Internet crazies and the slimy media."

Dashel sipped his martini and listened intently as she continued. "I'll be in the clear, and you, my dear Brit, will never have to worry about a damn thing for the rest of your life. Think about it. As a man of leisure, you could travel the world…even go back to the piano." She waited a moment then lifted her glass, proposing a toast. Her eyes bright with anticipation, she asked, "Is it a deal?"

"It's a bully deal!"

Satisfied with her spiel, she threw her shoulders back and smiled triumphantly, then reached across the table and took hold of his hands. Her eyes twinkled with a hint of mischief. "I think we're going to have a very cozy relationship. To sweet revenge, partner," she toasted.

Their glasses clinked in harmony.

Dashel felt more than an attraction for this captivating lady, and he sensed she felt the same. But as Henri served the duck a l'orange, a foreboding shadow of guilt clouded Dashel's mind, regarding Lily and their recently renewed relationship. The martini effortlessly slid down his throat, helping to dismiss all negative thoughts he might have had. *How did I get so lucky to have this lady help me accomplish my long-standing aspirations, and still be paid so handsomely at the same time?*

Chapter 31

Franny slammed the door of her apartment, threw her coat and bag on the chair, hit the message button on her answering machine, and plopped down on the couch. *I'm going to shut myself off from the fricking world,* she thought, and then wondered why she was listening to her messages.

First message: "Franny sweetheart, please don't treat your mother like this. You're killing me. I know how much you hate your father and maybe I did make a mistake by taking him back, but I can't throw him out now. He's too sick. Maybe I shouldn't have told you that I wished you were never born. Just say 'hello' and hang up. He doesn't answer the phone. And, another thing, I don't care if you call me 'Mom' or 'Blanche.'"

Franny held her hands to her ears and shouted into the room, "Don't you understand? I can't call you Blanche or Mom or anything."

The next message interrupted her thoughts.

"This is Cynthia at Doctor Kent's office, reminding you that you are scheduled for a group therapy session tomorrow morning at nine o'clock. See you then. Have a nice day."

"Up yours, Cynthia," Franny said.

The next message came on. "Hi, Franny, this is Elaine. You must have dinner with Lily and me tonight. She has a new guy, Dashel, and he's going to be there for a few minutes so we can check him out. Let Lily, or me, know. Later."

Next message: "Franny, this is Blanche, your mother. I can't believe you would treat your mother so cruelly. Just wait until you have children and they give you aggravation. I love you, even if you don't love me."

The voices of her mother, Elaine and Cynthia revolved in Franny's brain, echoing...*you're drowning, Franny. You're fucking drowning.*

The phone rang. Knowing it had to be her mother, she hesitated, shook her head to clear it, picked it up and waited for Blanche to speak.

"Franny, have pity on me. I'm going to go out of my mind."

"Okay, Blanche. What's so life threatening?"

"You have a cold? You sound funny."

"I'm fine, Blanche."

"Don't tell me you're fine. I'm your mother; I know when something is wrong. Did you lose your job?"

Franny breathed in a deep breath and let it out slowly. "No, I'm still selling rags in the garment center. What do you have to tell me that's so earth shattering?"

"I haven't had a good night's sleep since you shut me out of your life. You think it's easy taking care of your father and having a daughter who is..."

Franny yelled into the phone. "Get to the point! You have me, for how long I don't know."

"What do you mean, you don't know for how long?"

Franny sighed deeply. "Blanche, I'm hanging up!"

"You never did have any patience. I could come to you."

Franny's outrage boiled over. Her voice, shrill and loud, vibrated into the phone. "Blanche! Why are you tormenting me? Didn't we go through this last week? Enough is enough!"

Mrs. Goldsmith ignored her daughter's tirade. "I'll wait until you come back down to earth."

"God grant me the courage…" trailed off of Franny's lips.

"It won't take long," Blanche said. "I have a pot roast in the oven and I want to make sure it's ready for dinner. How about the Around the Clock diner in one hour? We can sit and they won't bother us. What time do you have?"

Franny's mind communicated thoughts. *You're doing good, Franny. Don't let her get to you. You can do this.* "It's Saturday May 2nd and in exactly five seconds it will be nine o'clock. That means we will meet at ten sharp. Oops, make that ten on the dot."

"Always with the smart remarks. Maybe if you didn't wisecrack so much and concentrated on…"

Franny placed the phone in the cradle, knowing that her mother was still talking. *I'll give it one more shot. It will be my good deed for the day. What could she tell me that'll top last week's confession of, 'I wish I never had you'?*

●

At the diner, Franny's mother said, "You're not so friendly. Not even a hello."

Franny pouted. "I promised myself I'd never speak to you again after the last gems you sprung on me. Start talking."

"I ran it over and over in my head and now that we're face to face…"

Losing patience, Franny said, "Spit it out, Blanche."

"Promise you won't hate me. Promise you'll count to twenty before you get crazy."

"I'm not promising anything, Blanche. What could you tell me that's worse than what you've already said? I'm not your child? I'm illegitimate. I'm a test tube baby. No, I got it. You had sex with an alien from outer space. Okay, I forgive you. Can I go now?"

"I wish they were any of those."

A pain shot through Franny's heart. This love/hate relationship with her mother was taking its toll on her already fragile state of mind. She noticed how remorseful her mother looked. Love her or hate her, she still got to her. "Tell me, Blanche. I promise I won't get crazy."

Blanche blew her nose, looked deeply into her daughter's eyes, tugged at her earlobe and cleared her throat. "You listening?"

It took every bit of Franny's self control to remain calm. "Talk," she droned.

"Okay, here goes." Her voice became a whisper. "I knew that your father was taking advantage of you sexually when you were a child…and I did nothing to stop it."

Franny sat in disbelief, while her mother searched her daughter's face, hoping she wouldn't fly into one of her tantrums. Franny raised her hand, signaling the waitress. "Double vodka straight up," she called. As if in a trance, she stared at her mother and spoke calmly but sternly. "Let me get this straight. You knew what he was doing to me and you did nothing to stop him?"

"Well, I wasn't sure. It wasn't until later that I found out. You never mentioned it; you went to school like nothing happened, and you grew up pretty normal. You didn't complain, so I thought it would just…go away." She looked at Franny shamefacedly.

Franny's mind shut down.

"Franny, say something. You've got that scary look on your face."

Franny looked at her mother but didn't see her. Shaking her head to clear her thoughts, she shrugged, her facial expression mocking stupidity. "I just can't believe it. Did I hear correctly? Did you say you thought it would *just go away?*" She shut her eyes tightly, and then cried out, "The bastard fucked your little girl and all you can say is, you thought it would just go away!"

Patrons in the nearby booths turned to look at Franny and her mother.

Franny took a big swallow of the vodka as a low chuckle emerged from her throat. "I love it," she laughed. "Did you click your heels three times and make a wish too?" She took another sip. "You're not making this up to get back at me for being a bad girl and disowning you, are you?" She shook her head. "No, that's not your style, is it, Blanche?"

"Listen, darling," Blanche said, her voice quivering. "I want you to know that after a while I regretted it and told him to leave."

Franny sighed in exasperation. "After a while? So you do have a conscience. That's good to know. Wasn't that about the time he took up with his secretary and told you he was *going* to leave?"

"I guess so. I know there's no forgiving me. But I couldn't live with myself any longer. I had to tell you."

"Well, the light dawns. Did you ever think that might be the reason your daughter is so screwed up?"

"You were very smart in school—always joking around. You didn't seem to be unhappy."

"Maybe I covered it up so well so no one could see how much I hurt on the inside. Did you ever think of that?"

"I felt bad but I didn't know what to do."

Franny downed the rest of the drink and sank back in the faux leather banquette. She thought for a moment and said, "You know something, Blanche? You may have done the right thing without knowing it."

"How's that?"

"Yep. I always felt that there was a reason I pushed myself so hard, and why I hated the son of a bitch for leaving us; not that you were a day at the beach, ya know. I guess I blocked the problem out of my mind. But now pieces are starting to filter back. The other day one of my friends said something about a princess and it distressed me."

"Distressed you?"

"It triggered something in my subconscious. Now the pieces in the puzzle are starting to fall into place—when I think about the fairy tales he used to read to me before he..." She hesitated then straightened up in her seat. "You know, mother dear, you just unlocked a door."

"Door? What door? You're not making sense." Blanche fingered the fake marquisette, seeded pearl cross she wore and prayed silently. *God, get me out of here!*

Franny pushed her chair out, stood, leaned down, and took her mother's face in her hands "Don't worry your head about it, Blanche. Go home and take care of the old man. Little Franny isn't going to talk crazy any more." She took out her wallet and put a twenty-dollar bill on the table. "No, Blanche," she said with assurance, "my crazy days are over. The old Franny is dead and guess what? A new one is going to take her place."

Chapter 32

Elaine's eyes sparked with fire as she yelled at the telephone operator. "What do you mean the number has been disconnected? There must be some mistake. Give me your supervisor."

"Madam, I *am* the supervisor. The party you are inquiring about has requested a new, unlisted number."

"And I suppose you can't give me that, can you?" She slammed the phone down, reached for a cigarette and held it up without lighting it. "Don't do it, Elaine," she said aloud. "Getting upset is not going to help." But she was angry and frustrated, and wasn't about to let it go. "It's the old heave-ho," she said. "I'll fix him. How could he be so blatantly cruel, professing his love for me one minute and ignoring me the next? I should have known something was wrong when he suggested group therapy." The more she thought about Jonathon the angrier she became. She eyed the telephone and called his office.

"Yes, I'm fine, Cynthia. Is the doctor in? I only need a minute," she said, tapping her fingers on the cocktail table. "Of course, I understand that he's with a patient, but I've been trying to reach him at his private number, which has been disconnected. I suppose you know nothing about that," she said sarcastically. "He *does* return calls to patients that are in dire need, doesn't he? Well, I'm in dire need. I'm not budging from this phone until he calls me back, understand?" She smiled smugly and placed the receiver gently in its cradle.

The phone rang and she immediately picked it up and spoke. "You must be quite a celebrity or is one of your patient's irate husbands out to get you?"

"Elaine, this is Lily. What *are* you talking about?"

"Lily...I wasn't expecting you... I..."

"What was that all about?"

"Forget it. It's nothing I want to get into right now." She lit the cigarette. "What's up? Are we still on for tonight? Your place, right? Is Franny coming?" She coughed.

"You're not catching a cold, are you?"

"No, I lit a cigarette. Stupid me."

"Well, put it out right now!"

"I already did. The damn thing burned my throat."

"You're uptight. Is that why you smoked?"

"I appreciate your concern, Lily, but it's not something I wish to discuss."

"Well, maybe it will come out in our therapy session."

"Fat chance." To change the subject, she quickly asked, "We eating in or dining out?"

"I'm loose."

"What did Franny say?"

"She was in as good a mood as you seem to be. Guess I'll have to take over. Let's get all dressed up and go out. Maybe it will get you two out of the doldrums. I'll make reservations at Le Cirque."

"I don't know. Have to put on my face and get dressed...I'm just not in the mood."

"Well, get in the mood. I'm going to have a hard enough time convincing Franny. Tell you what. Let's meet at my place and we can light a joint before we go. It will relax us. You do partake, don't you?"

"You, smoking pot? Geez, I haven't in a thousand years." She thought for a moment. "Okay, you're on. What about Franny?"

"You must be kidding. She's a flower child from way back." Lily hung up and walked to the grand piano. Her fingers gently touched the keyboard, surmising that the caller Elaine avoided talking about was Jonathon.

Elaine jumped when the phone rang. She made sure that this time she answered correctly. "Hello."

"What's your problem, Elaine?" Jonathon asked, annoyed. "Cynthia said you were quite rude to her."

"My problem is you, Jonathon. Before you give me any of your lame excuses like you had an office full of patients, let me ask you why you changed your private number. What's the matter? Isn't it private anymore?"

"You know, Elaine, you're sounding like a nagging wife. First of all, I had the number changed because I am getting calls from agitated patients."

"Like me?"

"Of course not," he lied.

"Really? What happened to the weekend at your cabin in the country? 'Just you and me,' you said. Come to think of it, you made a lot of promises. If you want to end our relationship, why don't you just come out and say so?"

"Stop carrying on, Elaine? Nothing has changed. My schedule is hectic. I haven't had a chance to breathe. Please, try and understand. There are other patients that need my attention. In fact, I am into a patient at the moment."

She couldn't resist. "How far into her are you, Jonathon?"

He ignored her remark. "Look, just let things settle down and we'll have lunch or dinner. You don't think I would lead you on, do you?" He didn't wait for an answer. "Did you get the two dozen roses I sent? Believe me when I say that nothing has changed between us."

"Roses? I didn't get any roses."

"I can't believe that. Let me ask Cynthia."

"Yes, do. And by the way, Jonathon, what's your new unlisted number?"

"Elaine, I really must go. I promise, I'll make it up to you."

"Jonathon, I…" she started to say, but the dial tone told her that he had already hung up the phone.

Aware that Jonathon was easing her out of his life Elaine became incensed. She thought. *Watch your ass, Jonathan, you no good user, son of a bitch, phony bastard. I'm going to fix you!*

The pack of cigarettes caught her eye. She removed one, reached for a match but was repelled by the unpleasant odor of nicotine on her fingers. Shoving the cigarette back into its case, she walked into the bathroom and proceeded to wash her hands. As the soap coalesced with the knobbiness of her swollen fingers, her heart sank in her chest. Staring at her disgruntled face in the mirror, she raised her dripping hands to the Almighty and pleaded. "I've lost Lew, I've lost Jonathon, and now the Lupus."

Chapter 33

"You're kidding," Franny said. "I haven't had a joint in years. I used to be quite a pothead. Smoked morning, noon and night. Who's your connection? Bob, the doorman?"

"How did you guess?"

"Listen. Aside from the FBI, a doorman is the eyes and ears of the American apartment dweller. They know everything about everybody. Where are you hiding the cannabis sativa?"

"The what?"

"Ganja, grass, weed, boo, Mary Jane, to mention a few pet nicknames. In plain English, marijuana."

"Well, you didn't spend your youth in a convent, that's for sure."

"Get real, Lily. You think the nuns just sit around and pray all day? Where's Elaine?"

"She'll be here. By the way, ease up on the wisecracks where she's concerned. She sounded upset on the phone. Had this horrific nightmare."

"Nightmare, huh. More than likely it's her husband's new love interest."

Lily opened a drawer and removed a Zip-lock bag containing pot and handed it to Franny. "I didn't think you knew her husband."

Franny took the bag and removed a joint. "Who rolled this joint, a blind man?"

"I did. I never smoked pot. Wine and pills are my nemesis. Dashel asked me to get it."

"Stick to your piano, kiddo; this one sucks big time. It's all bunched up in the wrong places." She searched in her purse.

"What are you looking for?"

"A credit card so I can separate the seeds and twigs from the good stuff." Franny looked around. "Can I use this dish?"

"Sure."

Her fingers deftly separated the twigs from the seeds. "Mmm, this stuff is nice and sticky." She put a smidgen up to her nose and sniffed. "Bob the doorman knows the right people." The grains of pot held firmly as Franny pinched them onto the rolling paper then rolled the joint and sealed it with a lick of her tongue.

"You started to say something about Elaine's husband."

"I never met him although I've seen him in the garment center. Good-looking guy. You know, it's a small world. The beautician, who does heads at the salon down the street from where I work, lives next door to me. Well, Marjorie ran out of milk and asked if she could borrow some. So being the good neighbor I am, I asked her in. We get to shooting the breeze about the latest dirt in the garment center—like who's doing who—and she brought up Elaine's husband and his affair with his saleslady."

"And you never mentioned it?"

Franny gave Lily a long tentative look. "It's no secret I have a big mouth, but I *do* have some redeeming qualities too. I didn't want to hurt Elaine."

The faucet gushed warm water as Franny rinsed the residue from the dish and set it on the drain rack, then walked into the living room and sat down next to Lily.

"Why the serious face?" Lily asked.

There was an element of openness as Franny confessed. "Look, I never had close girlfriends. The one or two I had were big disappointments. And to unload my problems on Blanche...well, forget it. I found it easier to confide in men. That is, until now. You and Elaine are my only real friends."

"And vice versa, Franny. I'm sure Elaine feels the same."

Franny raised one brow and held the rolled joint up to Lily. "Now that's a work of art. Shall we light up?"

"Shouldn't we wait for Elaine? Maybe the pot will lift her spirits."

"You're right." Franny walked to the grand piano and plunked at the keys. "I've never heard you play. I'd love to hear you tickle the ivories."

"Sure. Rock-and-roll, ragtime, boogie-woogie or swing?"

"Do you know 'Moonlight Sonata'?"

"Do I know 'Moonlight Sonata'? I'm featuring it at my next concert."

"Okay, madam virtuoso. Play."

The doorbell rang as Lily started to play. Franny sprang from her seat. "I'll get it." She opened the door and viewed Elaine. Ordinarily, she would have said some wisecrack like, "Who's your embalmer?" but having been warned, she held back and greeted the woman with, "Hi, Elaine. Come on in and take a load off." Lily stopped playing as she eyed her friend's disheveled appearance. Dressed in faded jeans and an ill-fitting shirt borrowed from Lew, Elaine seemed to carry the weight of the world on her shoulders. "Bad day?" Lily asked.

Elaine brooded. "Bad day, bad night, bad everything." Casting bloodshot eyes at the joint in the ashtray and her friends dressed in evening attire, she strolled to the piano and reconsidered about staying. "You two are dressed to the nines. Listen," she said, "I shouldn't have come. I just didn't want to be by myself tonight."

She hastily walked to the door but Franny leaped from her chair and blocked her way. "Not so fast, lady! You are *not* going anywhere!" She placed her hands firmly on Elaine's shoulders. "Listen, Elaine, you got troubles, then we got troubles. Would you let Lily or me walk when we needed a friend?"

"Let's stay in," Lily said. "I'll change and give Franny something more comfortable to wear. We can just hang out."

Elaine shrugged. "Well, maybe for a while." She sank down into the couch and folded her arms across her chest tightly.

Lily and Franny exchanged concerned glances. Lily exhaled noisily. "I'm going to pass out if I don't have a glass of wine. How about you, Franny?"

"It's a vodka night for me. Got some cranberry juice?"

Lily nodded. "Always prepared." Eying Elaine, she announced, "You, miss, need a drink!" Elaine pulled back, but Lily insisted. "Do me a favor. Just hold it in your hand for effect, please."

Making conversation to take the chill out of the room, Franny quipped, "We're vodka boozers right, Elaine? Let me fix it. I'll squeeze the Grey Goose till it honks."

"And, I'll get the hors d'oeuvres while you're pouring," Lily chimed in.

Franny headed for the fridge. "I'm getting to appreciate the imported caviar. Nix the pigs in a blanket for me."

"I'll do both. We'll think about dinner later."

"What a hostess. Why didn't I listen to my mother and study the piano? I could have served caviar instead of the cheap fish eggs the supermarket sells. Partaking of caviar's probably the only classy thing about me."

Elaine spoke up. "You have your own special class, Franny, and a heart as big as your mouth."

"I'll take that as a compliment," Franny said. The ice cubes tinkled as she shoved the glass of vodka into Elaine's unwilling hand. She stood over Elaine, tapping her foot, waiting for her to take a taste. "You're not drinking, Elaine."

She took a sip. "I'm drinking, I'm drinking."

"I can breast feed faster than that," Franny said. "So, what's the story? "Not that I'm probing, but..."

Elaine took a deep swallow of her drink, put her glass down and blew out a deep breath. "The lupus is back." She turned her face to the side and pointed to her cheek. "See this butterfly pattern? It's a rash caused by lupus. It was in remission. Now it has flared up again."

"You mean you had it before?" Lily said. "I never noticed it."

"What does the doctor say?" Franny asked.

The lines on Elaine's face were drawn and tight. "The usual spiel."

Franny put her arm around Elaine. "What is it actually?"

"It's a virus that causes the immune system to develop antibodies that attack the body's organs and tissues, which inflame the blood vessels and joints. It's a form of arthritis."

"But surely it can be treated," Lily said.

"If the nervous system is weakened anything can happen."

"Well," Franny said, "we're not ready for a burial. It could go into remission again and maybe never come back. Let's look at the positive side."

Lily smiled. "I think you're right. I need a refill. And so do both of you."

Franny eyed Elaine. "Have you told your husband?"

"What for? His pity, so he'll feel guilty and come back to me? And besides, he's happy with his juvenile conquest." Her eyes were sad as she conceded. "It's my fault. After the accident took my girls, Lew suggested I go to the Golden Door to try and forget. I went crazy there, lost myself in sex. I had an affair, and then another and... When I returned home Lew made me see Dr. Stern, who suggested I get some psychiatric help. He referred me to Jonathon, and, ironically, the sex started all over again."

Startled at what Elaine had divulged, Franny spilled her drink, while Lily's mouth dropped open.

Elaine closed her eyes. "I feel relieved now that I told you about Jonathon and me."

"You had an affair with Jonathon?" Lily said.

"I did," Elaine answered. "The lowlife promised me the sun and the moon and the stars and then dropped me. He still professes his love for me."

"Well, add me to the list of his conquests," Lily announced. "The louse promised me the lunar system too, and I'm also getting the brush off."

"I have to light a joint," Franny said. "This is just screwing my head up." She took a drag on the joint and handed it to Lily, then started laughing.

"Are you laughing at me?" Elaine asked.

"With you, not at you, Elaine." Franny giggled. "I need another toke." She took a puff and handed it to Elaine, who refused it. "You have to take a hit, Elaine. What I have to tell you will knock your socks off."

Elaine took a puff then sipped her vodka. "Well?"

Franny started laughing again. "Hold onto your vibrators, ladies. You think you are the only one that's been banging the sex machine? I've got news for you. So have I, and he also promised me the universe. And yes, I'm getting the heave-ho too."

"You're kidding," Elaine said. "And I thought I was the only one."

Lily stood, filled all three glasses to the brim and edged closer to the women. "That no good pervert. He has to be taught a lesson. Drink up, ladies. Then we can plan our strategy on how to screw the shrink like he screwed us. From now on, there's room for only three on a couch."

The maitre d' at the fashionable Le Cirque restaurant escorted them to a table. "As usual, you have heads turning," he said, deliberating whether he should have seated them further back since they had been known to live it up a bit."

Franny smirked. "If we're turning heads it's because of the diva, not us."

"I suppose it's the price one has to pay for fame," Lily joked. "Your best Chardonnay, Andre." She looked at the other two for approval.

"Wine's good," Elaine said. "I want to stay just where I am."

Franny agreed. "You know, ladies, I can't understand why they don't legalize weed. They give it to people who are depressed or have AIDS. Think it will take the place of Prozac?"

"One thing's for sure," Elaine said, "it would put half the pushers out of business. Stop a lot of crime."

"Never happen," Franny said. "Those holier than-thou, tight ass lobbyists who sneak it on the side would protest. Can't seem to fill their greedy pockets fast enough."

Elaine stood. "Sorry, girls, have to pee."

Lily looked at her, concerned. "Want company?"

"Will you two stop treating me as if I'm going to end it all? I'm glad you talked me into coming. Don't spoil it. I'm mellow, the pot relaxed me, and my bladder wants to go on empty."

They watched Elaine walk away. "Do you think it's serious?" Franny asked Lily.

Lily shrugged. "The lupus or her breakup with Jonathon?"

Franny frowned. "Jonathon we can deal with; it's the lupus that scares me. Personally, I don't think she's telling us everything. I think it's more serious than she's letting on."

"Considering her state of mind, she might not be taking proper care of herself. Maybe we should do a little investigating."

"I don't know, Lily. It's like we're going behind her back."

"Nonsense. We're worried about her."

"Her doctor won't give out any information about her condition. It's unethical."

"I have some connections. Not to worry. I'll be discreet." The waiter filled her glass.

Franny shook her head. "Jesus, Lily. Where do you put it? You practically finished the bottle all by yourself."

"Do I appear to be out of control? Are my pupils dilated? Am I slurring my speech? Stop watching how much I drink."

"Don't get all faklempt, Lily. It's just that we've only been here ten minutes and...I'm sorry; I guess Elaine's illness has me on edge. Suddenly the high I had has taken off to parts unknown."

Lily reached across the table and patted Franny's hand. "I know, Franny. We have to act like everything's copasetic."

"That's what friends are for, right? Think positive, not negative. I..."

Lily rode over Franny's words. "Look, I've already slowed down on the diet pills and I'm working on cutting down on the booze. One thing at a time."

"I wasn't thinking about that, Lily. I was wondering how the three of us let that monster seduce us."

"It's simple. We were vulnerable and he took advantage."

"Yeah, I guess he doesn't believe in the Hippocratic oath he swore to uphold."

"Franny, what does 'faklempt' mean?"

"Didn't they teach you anything in parochial school? Let's see. Confused with a touch of being uptight. Uh oh, here comes Elaine. Why is she walking so fast?"

Lily stood. "Are you all right?"

"Sit down, Lily," Elaine said breathlessly. "You won't believe it." She gulped her wine and stopped to catch her breath. "Take a guess."

"You're making me nervous," Lily said. "Anything to do with health?"

"No."

Franny sighed with relief. "Okay, then I'll play. "You got laid in the powder room by a mysterious stranger?"

"Better than that," Elaine said.

The maitre d' stood nearby holding menus, trying to get their attention. Lily spoke up. "I'm dying to hear what you have to say, Elaine." She motioned at the maitre d'. "Andre, you choose, please." Leaning closer to Elaine, she said, "Give. We're all ears."

Elaine spoke aloud. "Guess who is in a secluded booth in the back of the restaurant? Jonathon and…" The nearby patrons turned to look at them.

"Keep it down," Lily said.

Elaine waved a hand. "I had to go back into the ladies room a second time so I could get a better look at the woman. When I returned they were kissing."

"Is it someone from the clinic? Do we know her?"

"It was my doctor's wife, Amelia Stern. Her husband, Dr. Stern, is the reason I went to Jonathon in the first place. Dr. Stern told Lew over a golf game how happy his wife has been since she started seeing this young, handsome shrink." Elaine stopped to sip her wine. "We did socialize quite a bit. Even went on cruises. Lew felt uneasy because Amelia seemed to push herself on him and so we eased off on the camaraderie. And one time I caught her sniffing the white stuff and it turned me off. Amelia can be the sweetest thing and then again quite unpredictable. She's sort of bi-polar."

"Guess that's why she's seeing Jonathon," Lily said. "He must be doing her, too."

"What a sleaze ball," Franny said, smirking. "Can you imagine us going to a psychiatrist who needs a psychiatrist?" She scowled. "Maybe we should let her in on the sex-machine's reputation."

"I don't think she would bat an eyelash, ladies. She's been seeing

Jonathon for years."

"Okay, let's get down to business," Lily said.

The waiter appeared, unbeknownst to Franny. "I have the perfect punishment for him. Remember that lady who cut her husband's dick off because he abused her? Well, I could do that." She imitated a scissors with her fingers. "Snippety snip, one, two, three and no more dingaling. But I wouldn't throw it where it could be found. No sir, I'd..." She stopped short as she noticed the waiter holding a tray full of food and grinning widely. The three ladies laughed hysterically as the nearby patrons turned to gape at them.

He served the soup and bent down over the table smirking at what he had heard. "Je ne comprends pas l'anglais," he spoofed.

"Listen," Elaine said, "we're pretty savvy, intelligent women, right? Are we sober enough to do some serious thinking?" Franny and Lily nodded. "Let me run this by you. How about each of us comes up with a plan to dispose of him? Then we pick the most logical one and go for it."

Lily raised a brow. "Dispose of him, as in assassinate, electrocute, asphyxiate or a slow torturous death?"

"Whatever," Franny said. "I'm getting all tingly just thinking about it."

"Love it," Elaine said. "Let's drink to it." They raised their glasses.

"To us," Lily toasted.

Unconsciously stirring their soup in a circle, their minds conjured ways to do away with the well-respected, eminent womanizer.

"This is the way I see it," Lily said. "I envision myself sitting in my car waiting patiently outside the restaurant for Jonathon. The moment he walks down the steps I laugh uncontrollably and press the gas pedal to the floor. The impact hurls Jonathon high into the air and before he lands I'm standing outside where he falls at my feet. Then he looks up at me, his mouth frothing. "You're the one I really love," he says as he gasps his last breath. "I bet you tell that to all your patients," I say as I extend my foot and roll him over into the gutter. I get into my car, back up, and drive over him just to make sure the good doctor is kaput." Lily took a sip of her wine. "What's your fantasy, Elaine?"

"I picture Jonathon naked, riding a stuffed donkey in a shooting gallery at a carnival. I give the barker a dollar and he hands me a roll of tickets and a loaded rifle. 'What prize do I win if I shoot the shrink off the donkey?' I ask."

"You get to take the donkey home," the barker says.

"And what about the shrink? Do I get to keep him too?"

"Sorry, lady," he answers. "But there are two women who have first dibs on him." I turn to see you two grinning at me. So I pick up the rifle and aim at Jonathon, who struggles frantically, trying to get away. "Okay," I say as I pull the trigger repeatedly. "It's your ass, you ass."

"No! Oh, no! Elaine, you're the one I really love," he shouts, his eyes staring blankly into space. Then his head drops and he descends into the inferno below. Can you beat that, Franny?"

Franny stared into her soup. "Listen to this, ladies. I see Cynthia on her knees pleading with me to release Jonathon from the torture chamber I have him shackled to. Get this. I'm wearing a black leather halter, short shorts and spiked leather boots that lace up to my crotch. I crack my whip and it snaps at Jonathon's ears, his nose and finally his belly button. I can hear the whip's snap echoing a distinct, whooshing sound. My mind intent on punishing him, I laugh in a frenzied rage and crack the whip three times above my head. I sneer vindictively; then, taking careful aim, I whip off his penis. He screams, 'No! Oh, no! Put it back, Franny. You're the one I really love.'"

Chapter 34

Cumulus clouds hung low over the countryside, blackening the sinister night. Lightning flashed across the ominous sky. An instant later thunder chased a cloudburst of rain onto the rental car of the three scheming women, an omen of impending doom.

Lily steered the rented automobile onto the shoulder of the road and pulled up the hand brake as the car skidded to a stop. The mud soaked earth made a gushing sound as the tires sank into the soggy surface of the road.

"This is as far as we should go," Lily said to Franny and Elaine. "We don't want to get too close. Now remember, we took an oath to go through with this. If you want to back out, now's the time to do it. No hard feelings, no questions asked."

Franny spoke up. "Let's get the fucker!"

"Right on," Elaine said. "This will be our testimonial to the *'I Got Screwed by a Shrink Society.'*"

Lily removed the keys from the ignition. "Franny, you have the gun? And the safety catch is on, right?"

Franny held it up. "It's called a piece," she said, waving it at Elaine.

"Hey," Elaine said, "don't point that thing at me."

"Not to worry. I didn't take lessons at the range for nothing." She blew into the gun's nozzle then kissed it. "I wish we had silver bullets like that old time cowboy used to shoot."

"That was the Lone Ranger," Elaine said. "And don't get so frisky with it. You're making me nervous."

Franny smiled and pointed the gun at Elaine's head teasingly. "Bang, Bang!" she shouted.

"Lily!" Elaine shouted. "Make her stop."

"Chill out, Franny," Lily cautioned. "Get serious. Save the antics for the doctor."

"You're right. I'm sorry."

"Now, do we all know what we have to do?" Lily asked.

Elaine sighed. "Yes, Lily. Let's get the show on the road."

"Yeah, let's go," Franny, said impatiently. "My trigger finger is getting itchy."

Elaine let out a tedious, "Fraaaany!"

"Okay, okay," Franny said.

"This is it, girls," Lily said. "Let's do it."

"Yeah, let's put the pedal to the metal," Franny said.

The air was cool and the light nonexistent as they stepped out of the automobile. With each step they took, their sneakers sucked deeper into the muddy earth.

Lily took a tentative step away from the car. "Are you sure Cynthia said Jonathon would be at the cabin tonight?"

"Yes, I'm certain," Elaine replied as the umbrella she had opened caught the wind and flew into the air.

The three avenging women crouched as they moved stealthily along a winding path that led to Jonathon's cabin. Elaine said, "I can't see my hand in front of my face."

"We can't use flashlights, so why don't we hold onto each other until we get there? Give me your hand, Franny. Elaine, take Franny's other hand."

Elaine shivered as she reached for Franny's hand. The cold steel of the gun startled her.

"What's wrong?" Lily asked.

"She grabbed hold of the gun instead of my wrist."

"You scared the shit out of me, Franny. I've a good mind to turn around and wait in the car."

"Sorry, I didn't mean for you to grab the gun."

Lightning flashed and the night lit up for a split second. "Another 25 feet," Lily said. "Damn it! The wind is kicking up."

A bolt of lightning hit a nearby tree, spewing sparks at them.

"Oh my God!" Elaine said, terrified. "That was close."

"I heard," Franny, said, "if you're struck by lightning and live, you're endowed with special powers."

"I'm beginning to wonder about you, Franny," Elaine mused. "Are we there yet? I'm getting soaked."

"I think it's just around the bend," Lily said. "Elaine, where did you say he hides the pass key?"

"On top of the door ledge."

"Franny said. "It's usually under the mat, or in a flowerpot."

"How do you know?" Lily asked.

"You think you're the only one he's been shtuping at honest Abe's cabin."

"Quiet," Lily said. "We've arrived. Let me peek through the window. Gee, it's dark inside. Maybe he and his latest conquest are in the bedroom."

"Yeah," Franny said. "Probably all tuckered out waiting for the sandman to sprinkle fairy dust and put them to sleep. Anyhow, I can't find the key."

Lily tried the doorknob. "It's open," she whispered. Pushing the door ajar, she peered inside. "It's clear. Let's go in."

The door creaked eerily, and then without warning it flew open.

Jonathon, large as life, gun in hand, stood grinning from ear to ear as the ladies froze in their tracks.

Franny, shocked by his sudden appearance, dropped the gun and bent to retrieve it.

"Don't!" Jonathon threatened. He pointed a revolver at her and kicked the gun inside. He stepped back from the threshold and scowled. "Come right in, ladies, I've been expecting you." He waved his gun to usher them in. "You busybodies must be taught to mind your own business." He yelled into the bedroom. "I need some help, sweetheart." He turned to the ladies. "We were having our own fun and games, but since you have crashed our private party, as a decorous host I will invite you to participate."

Beaded curtains tinkled and separated as Cynthia stepped into the room in a white micro miniskirt with suspenders crisscrossing her naked breasts, white mesh stockings, white platform shoes, her blond hair tucked under a white nurse's cap. Snapping her suspenders, she declared. "Jesus, they're like boomerangs. You keep tossing them away and they keep coming back."

"Give them towels," Jonathon said. "They're dripping on the oriental."

"What is this?" Franny said. "A strip search?"

"Be patient, funny lady," he said. Waving his gun he commanded. "Disrobe! Down to the bare essentials."

The three uninvited guests stood, feet glued to the floor.

Jonathon picked up three bullets from a tray, rolled them in the palm of his hand and inserted them into the chambers of the gun. His eyes narrowed to slits as he flipped the barrel and placed the nozzle at Franny's temple. "Okay, if you want to play games, let's begin with you. The element of surprise can be quite titillating." He released the safety catch and lightly fingered the trigger. "Are we going to disrobe or…"

Terrified, Franny shouted. "Okay! Okay!" She looked at Elaine and Lily.

"We better get undressed." After removing their clothes, the three stood naked, their towels wrapped tightly around their quivering bodies.

Cynthia aligned two chairs and roughly pushed Franny and Elaine down and handcuffed them. "Make the cuffs nice and tight," Jonathon said. "I want to see black and blue bruises."

"Lily," he said. "Remove your towel and sit at the piano. I want background music to accompany my little game of Russian roulette."

He waited until Lily sat down at the baby grand, poured wine in a glass and held it to her lips. "I know that without the bubbly you're lost, so take a sip." Her mouth quivered as she tried to drink, but he quickly took the glass away. "Play something festive." He walked up behind her, twirled the barrel of the gun, placed it at the back of her head and pulled the trigger. A faint click was heard. "Lucky you," he said, "for the moment anyhow."

Cynthia placed her hands on her hips defiantly. "I'm not having any fun. Let me try."

"Later," he said. He sidled up to Franny. "You were most entertaining so I'll make it fast. Facing her, he waved the gun in her face. An eerie glow reflected off the gun as he pressed the nozzle against her ear. He twirled the barrel of the gun and pulled the trigger. The gun clicked. "Lucky number two," he exclaimed.

"Let's see if we can make it three in a row," he said, as he walked to Elaine. "You, you annoying bitch. Always pressuring me." He pushed the gun hard against her nose, causing her nostril to twist to one side, forcing blood to ooze down her cheeks and onto her bare breasts. Her face contorted, her eyes wide with terror, she shrieked as Jonathon grabbed hold of her hair with his other hand and vigorously pulled her head back over the ridge of the chair, and didn't let go until her eyes rolled up in her head. Then he removed the gun from her nostril, placed the nozzle between her eyes, pulled the trigger and listened intently as the bullet exploded.

Her face pale, her lips quivering, Elaine bolted straight up in her bed and screamed so loud a resounding echo vibrated throughout the bedroom. Perspiration trickled down her face and her body shook as she gasped for breath. After a passing glance at the familiar surroundings in the room, she sighed with relief. "Damn nightmare!"

Chapter 35

"Cancel all my appointments for this afternoon from one until three," Dr. Kent said to Cynthia as he handed her his briefcase on the way into his office. "And take that inquisitive expression off your face. I'll contact you every hour on the hour to see if you need me." His face showed strains of anxiety.

"You have a group therapy session in fifteen minutes." she said. He didn't answer as he walked briskly into his office and kicked the door shut with his foot. He picked up his private phone and dialed a number.

"Good morning, Tripplehorn, Thornton, and..."

He talked over her words. "Miss Springer," he said coldly, "let me speak to Mr. Tripplehorn."

"How are you, Dr. Kent? Mr. Tripplehorn is with a client. Can I have him call you back? He should be through momentarily."

"Are you mentally challenged?" he said, raising his voice. "Get him now!"

"Please hold on."

"Jonathon," Filmore Tripplehorn said with a touch of coolness in his voice. "So nice to hear from you. What can I do for you?"

"I need to see you!"

"Of course, my dear boy, of course. Let me check my appointment book. How about this afternoon at the club?"

"No, Trippy!" Jonathon shouted. "In ten minutes at the zoo in Central Park. I'll be at the reptile house."

"Sounds serious. Are you in some kind of difficulty?"

"Just be there!" Jonathon said and hung up.

Filmore Tripplehorn leaned back in his overstuffed leather chair and swiveled toward the panoramic view of New York City. *That son of a bitch is up to no good.* His mind flashed back to the funeral of Jonathon's mother, whose scattered body parts were strewn about Amagansett Bay after her yacht mysteriously exploded. *What happened to that ambitious boy? The carefree, happy lad I used to go fishing and sailing with — the lad that called me "Uncle Trippy"?*

Filmore Tripplehorn stared blankly into space. He sighed deeply and covered his eyes with his hands, knowing when the change in Jonathon had taken place. He thought back to Mrs. Kent, who misled Jonathan's girlfriend, Penny, into believing that Jonathon was only toying with her and that he was going to marry Pamela. He remembered how Jonathon loved the sweet, unpretentious Penny and how he fell apart when she was found drowned in a lake.

Chapter 36

"Hey there!" Franny yelled, as Lily and Elaine got out of a taxi in front of the clinic. "I know, I know, you left a message on my machine but I had to meet Blanche." She placed her hands on her hips and raised her eyebrows. "One of her usual anxiety attacks."

"Let's talk for a moment," Elaine said. "Away from the entrance."

"Yeah," Franny said. "I'm flummoxed out of my bird. We should have met earlier, but with my mother bitching about my AWOL father, the lowlife son of a bitch, and mommy dearest, that leaves you, Elaine. How are you feeling and what did the doctor say?"

"I have to go for chemotherapy starting tomorrow, but there is some good news to report."

Lily flinched at the mention of chemotherapy but concealed it with a half smile. "Tell, tell," Franny said, feeling her anxiety level rising.

"Lew called and wants to get together."

"All right!" Franny blurted. "Bet he wants to come back. And what are you going to do about the harlot he's been keeping?"

"She's left Lew and the job, and is looking for a place to live."

Elaine interrupted. "So, have we come up with a plan to punish our esteemed Dr. Jonathon?" she asked. "I have, but I'm not saying. It's too morbid."

Lily sneered and hissed like a cat. "With the bombshell that came into my life and my concert tour coming up, I must say, I've been pretty busy. But I have come up with a terrific plan." She smiled. "But if Elaine's not telling, neither am I." She gave Franny a fake smile. "How about you, Goody Two Shoes? Come up with anything short of murder?"

"Well, *I'm* not afraid to speak my mind, even if you two wimps are. It just so happens that I did think of a way to murder the snake."

"Really?" Elaine said. "Are you going to go through with it? Or are you afraid you'll have to spend time behind bars?"

A serious shadow passed over Franny's face. "I'm not fooling. I spent half the night working out a fantastic plot. You want to hear about it, or is the reality of murdering the louse too much for your tender hearts to bear? Or are we just plain chickening out?" Lily and Elaine gave *the thumbs up* sign and Franny nodded with satisfaction. "Okay," she continued, "I worked out a great scenario whereby not one of us blows him away but all three of us do." Elaine and Lily looked at Franny questioningly. "Stop with the looks and hear me out. I read it in a book or saw it in a movie...never mind, that's not important. What is important is that no one can point an accusing finger at us, if we all claim to have done it. Think about it, it *does* make sense."

"Mmm," Elaine said thoughtfully. "It might work, but I'd be afraid to do it."

"Geez, Elaine," Franny said, "you have the least to worry about, you..." She stopped short realizing she had spoken without thinking of Elaine's illness. "Forgive me, Elaine. That has to be the most thoughtless thing I ever said."

Elaine took hold of Franny's hand.

Lily shook her head at Franny. "Talk about dumb blonds."

"Forget it, ladies." Elaine said. "I'm not gone yet." Her mouth puckered in thought. "But, come to think of it, I am the best candidate to do it.

Franny, you might have spoken hastily, but you have a point."

"Uh uh," Lily said. "It's the three of us or it's a no go."

"I agree," Franny said. "Remember our motto. 'Three on a couch, no solos.'"

Lily looked at her wristwatch. "We'd better hustle; our group therapy is about to start. Remember; act as if nothing has happened. We love and adore our horny doctor."

"Right," Franny said. "Until death do us part...from him."

The three of them breezed into the conference room ready to do their thing, but the moment they linked eyes with Jonathon their mood changed from high to medium and then to low.

Thomas grinned widely. "You're late, girls. Time is money."

Franny, quick to retort, said, "You know what you can do with your time, buster." She strolled to where Jonathon stood and touched his arm. "How are you, stranger? Keeping all your patients on the straight and narrow?" But she thought, *did you screw anyone before breakfast or are you planning a brunch performance?*

Elaine and Lily eyed Franny with stares of caution as Cynthia asked if anyone cared for coffee or a snack. Jonathon flicked his eye from patient to patient, smiling cordially at them. "I'm glad to see that everyone is ready, so I guess we can proceed. Who would like to start?"

Gerald raised his hand. Jonathon nodded. "I hope all of you don't mind if I begin, but I have been having this awful dream and if I don't get it out, I'm going to..." Everyone edged forward.

"Cut your wrists?" Thomas finished for him. "Give us a break, Gerald. You've been threatening to do away with yourself for years, and you never do."

"Shut up!" Elaine said. "Let the man talk, will you?"

"Yeah," Franny chimed in. "I don't see where you're hitting on all four cylinders. Judge not, lest ye be judged, junior."

"Thank you, ladies," Gerald said, leering at Thomas and eyeing Jonathon for his approval. "Well, I dreamt I was with this lady friend that I told you about at our last session, the one I met in the library. We were at a bar and she slipped some powder from a packet that she hid in her pocket, and then poured it in my drink. " He checked the disapproving expressions of the group. "Well, after all, she started it."

The group rolled their eyes and Franny gestured with her finger to her mouth. "Sounds like a date rape scenario to me."

Lily swallowed a gasp, her body stiffened, her face devoid of color.

Jonathon raised his brows, wondering if what Gerald said triggered something in Lily's memory. "What happened next?" he asked.

"She came out of the bathroom, but we were not in the bar anymore, we were in her apartment. I started tearing her clothes off and then I..."

The group edged forward, but Lily sat frozen in her chair, her eyes glazed and staring into space.

"Well...," he said.

"Say it!" Franny yelled. "Say it!"

"Well, I woke up." He turned to Jonathon. "Gosh, Dr. Kent. I feel better about myself."

Jonathon walked to Gerald and clapped him on the shoulder. "You did well, Gerald." He turned to Lily. "You look like you could use a bit of fresh air, or maybe you would like to lie down."

Lily stood up and then suddenly slumped to the floor. Jonathon ran to her side as she slowly came to. "What happened?" she said, noticing everyone hovering over her.

Jonathon rubbed her wrists. "You passed out, but you're all right now." He took both her hands in his, squeezing them gently and looking at her with false cheerfulness.

"I feel so ashamed," she said. "Please everyone, take your seats. I think it's time for me to open up."

Franny and Elaine eyed each other, wondering what the hell she was up to. "Maybe now is not the best time," Elaine said, looking at Franny for support.

Franny squinted at Lily. "Yeah, Lily, you just passed out. Give yourself a minute to regroup. In fact, I would like to go next."

"No!" Lily said emphatically. "I want to talk."

Jonathon gestured time out with his hands. "Let Lily speak," he said. "This is the purpose of group therapy...to express our innermost thoughts. If Lily has something to say we need to listen to her." His eyes lingered on Lily and then shifted to Franny and Elaine. "I'm glad to see that the three of you have bonded since we began group therapy. It helps to have supportive friends in a time of need."

Bet your sweet ass, Franny thought. *There's strength in numbers.* She eyed Elaine.

Dr. Kent smiled, ignoring Franny's curt demeanor. "Are you sure you want to speak, Lily?"

Franny and Elaine stared hard at Lily, but Lily ignored them. Her voice quavered as she began to relate a part of her past that had long been buried.

Chapter 37

Twenty years previous

"Lily," her mother shouted. "Where do you think you're going?"

"I'm meeting Charlene and Diane down at Frosty's Soda Palace. I'll be back by ten."

"You haven't touched the piano all day, Lily. Your dad works hard to pay for your lessons. Money doesn't grow on trees, you know."

"Gee, Mom, it's Saturday and all the kids will be there."

"I don't care about the other kids, Lily. Remember how you begged and cried for a whole year until we saved up enough to buy you the piano, and now you treat practicing like it was a chore."

"I promise, Mom, I'll practice an extra hour when I come home. Professor Mainbacher said I could play at the next recital. He said I'm really good."

"I know what the professor said, Lily. But you won't get anywhere unless you put your career before running around with those silly, giggly, feather-brained girlfriends you hang out with." Her mother wiped her hands on her apron and walked toward Lily, who stood poised at the open door, dying to escape her mother's frustration. "Listen, young lady," she said. "Don't think I didn't see a boy drop you off in his car last night when you were supposed to be with your girlfriends. I didn't tell your father because God only knows what he would have done, but you're only fifteen and you know that riding in cars with boys is off-limits. And don't even think of telling me all the other mothers let them do it. As long as you are living under my roof you will listen to me." She took a deep breath and let it out slowly, then softened her tone. "Lily, I was once fifteen, too. Now is the time to be careful. Please, watch yourself. It will save you a lot of heartache. Boys will be boys, and it isn't them that will have to raise a baby without a father."

Lily hugged her mother. "Don't worry, Mom. I remember everything you tell me. I'll be careful, and I promise I'll practice until you get sick and tired of me playing. I'll be back by ten, I swear. And thanks for not telling Dad."

Lily kissed her mother and walked down the street, where a young man waited for her in his car. "Did the old lady give you a hard time, Lily?"

"Ronnie, I hate that expression, 'old lady.' She cares about me. She doesn't want me to get into trouble."

"Sure, sure. Let's go."

"Where are the others?"

"There's a cool bar that just opened up in Haggerstown. They're going to meet us there."

"A bar? You mean a bar with liquor?"

"No, a bar with soda pop and milk shakes. Of course, a bar with drinks. Where have you been hiding, at Frosty's Soda Palace with the other teeny-boppers?"

"I don't know, Ronnie. I'm not allowed to go to bars."

"You don't have to drink hard liquor; you can have a Coke. They have a cool nickelodeon and a pool table. No one says you have to drink."

"Are we picking up Diane and Charlene and the guys on the way?"

"No, they're going to meet us there. Stop carrying on. We're going to have a great time."

"But won't they ask me for my I.D.? You know I'm only fifteen."

"Not to worry. I took your picture to a friend of mine and he had a fake I.D. made. Here, take a look."

"Gee, Ronnie, it looks like the real thing."

"Hey Lily, you're playing in the big leagues when you're with Ronnie." He opened the glove compartment and took out a marijuana joint, lit it and offered it to her.

"Uh uh," she said. "I tried it once and it made me sick."

"Have it your way. I don't force girls to do what they don't want to do."

"I'm glad, Ronnie. That's the only reason that I see you. And, also, you are kind of cute. Is this the place?" she asked as they pulled up to a darkened building with a neon sign that read Hubba Hubba Bar. "It looks sort of dark and creepy, Ronnie."

He shook his head, pinched the joint with his fingers and placed it in the glove compartment, then removed a packet and slipped it into his trouser pocket. "Boy, you have a lot of growing up to do, Lily. Come on, I'll buy you a Coke. And hold on to the I.D. just in case they ask to see it."

The smoke hung over the dimly lit bar. An obese bartender in a muscle tee shirt that showed off his heavily tattooed arms blew into a glass and wiped it with a soiled towel. "What's your poison?" he asked dryly as Ronnie took a bar stool and shoved it into Lily's behind.

He grinned at the bartender. "Sit down, Lily," he said. "And take that worried look off your face. No one's going to eat you."

The bartender grinned back, awaiting Ronnie's order. "Draft me a tall one," Ronnie said, "and a lemon Coke for the lady."

Luke, the bartender, pointed to his tattoo that spelled out "Luke" with a serpent entwined around it. "Neat, huh?" he said.

"Yeah," Ronnie said, "I remember it from a week ago. The tattoo is real cool. I'm going to get me one of them as soon as I decide on what I want. Where'd you get it done, Luke?"

"Nevensville, at the end of town, past the White Hen Pantry. Ask for Grunge, and make sure to tell him that Luke sent you. He'll give you a discount." He bent over the bar toward them and adjusted the patterned American flag bandanna that was tied around his sweaty forehead. He winked at Ronnie. "He takes care of me if I push business his way." He looked around cautiously. "And I can slip you a shot or a beer once in a while, when the boss isn't looking."

"Cool, man," Ronnie said, and turned toward Lily, who kept thinking that she shouldn't have come.

"Where're the rest of the gang?" she asked, feeling uncomfortable.

"They'll be here. You know the girls. Takes them forever to put themselves together." He lifted his beer and handed her the lemon Coke. "To you and me, Lily," he toasted.

She reluctantly took a sip and glanced toward the bar entrance, hoping her friends would show. "I have to go to the ladies room, Ronnie," she said, wondering where it was as Luke pointed to the rear of the bar.

"Watch out for the dykes and lock the stall behind you," Luke said with a gruff laugh.

Lily bit her lip as she walked nervously to the ladies room, her mother's cautionary advice flashing through her mind.

Luke leaned toward Ronnie, placing his elbow on the bar. "She ain't no eighteen, you know. Watch your ass; undercover dicks keep hitting this place." He looked over his shoulder and out into the restaurant. "It's cool for now. They hit us last week. They won't show for a month." He watched as Ronnie tore open a packet of powder and poured it into Lily's Coke. "Listen." He leaned closer. "If you need any more, there's more where that came from, and I'll cut the price." His head bobbed up and down.

Ronnie snickered. "That stuff is unbelievable. The last broad I slipped it to went wild. Best lay I ever had."

"Just don't get heavy-handed with it," Luke said, showing a trace of concern. "You don't want a corpse on your hands. And sometimes they remember too much and put the finger on you."

"Not to worry, Luke, I'm a big boy. I can handle it."

Luke refilled a customer's beer mug at the other end of the bar as Lily returned, looking visibly upset.

"Missed you, baby," Ronnie said, handing Lily her drink. "You have to catch up with me. I'm on my third and you haven't even downed your first. Come on, Lily. Get with it. It's only Coke. Grow up, will you?"

"The bathroom was so dirty, Ronnie. I couldn't sit down. Could we please go?" She looked around anxiously. "It's been a half hour and they're not here yet." She started toward the exit.

"Okay," he said. "If you're going to get so uptight, we'll go. But at least finish your drink. It's paid for."

She sighed with relief and finished the Coke. "That's a good girl," he said, winking at Luke and leading her to the door.

As the night air filled her lungs, she started to sway. "Geez, I feel so lightheaded," she said.

"Me, too. The smoke in that place could make anyone sick." He held her around her waist. Pulling the car door open, he guided her toward the seat. "Here, let me help you into the car."

"Ronnie, my head is spinning. I...I think I'm going to pass out."

"You'll be fine," he said as he drove from the bar to a motel, where he rented a room and carried Lily over the threshold. He laid her semi-conscious body on the bed and proceeded to remove her clothes.

"You're better off this way, Lily," he said. "You don't know it, but I'm doing you a big favor. At your age you should have had a dozen guys." He kissed her tenderly on the mouth and ran his hands over her body, starting at her small breasts and working down to her thighs. "Oh, you're so pretty," he whispered, growing more passionate by the second. "You have the body of a woman, the kind I love to take." He rubbed his penis on her sparse mound then gently probed his erection along her vagina, all the time panting breathlessly. He whispered, "Oh baby, you don't know what you're missing." Her closed eyes showed movement but stayed closed. When he could no longer hold back, he plunged deep and hard into her, breaking her hymen, causing her body to quiver as her throat whimpered a low, unresponsive moan. He pumped with all his might and groaned with pleasure as he exploded inside her. After two more sexual encounters he tried for a fourth but gave up when his erection failed him. He lit a joint and fell asleep holding her in his arms.

The sun peeked through the faded window shade of the motel room as Lily opened her eyes. She turned to see Ronnie lying sound asleep next to her, snoring. She gasped and sprang out of the bed only to fall to the floor. She pulled herself up and tried to get her thoughts together, but as she looked down at her body covered with dried blood, she gasped and sank to the floor again. The rattle of the maid's cleaning cart awakened her and once again she struggled to get up. Weak and disoriented, she managed to make it to the bathroom, where she splashed water on her bruised body and hurried back into the room where Ronnie lay sleeping soundly. Her first thought was of how she would explain staying out all night to her parents and was sure that by this time they had called the police. She spotted his wallet on the dresser and removed a ten-dollar bill for the taxi fare back to her house. The thought of facing her parents sent chills through her. In a state of confusion, she dressed and ran out of the motel room. Panic gripped her as the realization of what happened ran though her mind.

She asked the taxi driver to stop two blocks from her house. Lily walked up to the front door and stopped short upon hearing her father yelling. "I told you she would end up like the gang she hangs around with. Stop worrying. She'll be back. I'm going to work. I work my ass off so your little piano virtuoso can stay out all night and become a slut." The front door vibrated from the impact as it slammed shut. Lily held her breath, as her father got into his car and drove away, unaware of her hiding behind the bushes.

"It was the most horrifying experience I ever had," Lily said to the group. "And the strangest thing is that I never remembered what happened to me."

The therapy patients and Jonathon were amazed at Lily's confession. Jonathon walked to Lily and put his arm around her. "I think you have said enough for today. You don't have to continue if it is too painful."

"Are you kidding?" Franny said. "You can't just leave us hanging like this. "I'm dying to hear what your mother said when you walked in the door."

"Franny," Elaine said, "maybe Lily has had enough soul searching for today."

Jonathon started to speak, but Lily spoke first. Shrugging her shoulders, she said, "Might as well, while I'm on a roll. The second I opened the door my mother ran to me. Her instincts told her what had happened."

"Cry if you want to," my mother said, trying to comfort me. My body shook as I sobbed hysterically. "We can talk afterwards," she said. "Let's get you undressed and into a nice hot bath." She put her arm around my waist, and with each step I took up the stairs to my bedroom I groaned. "I know you hurt, Lily," Mom said, the tears streaming down her face. "We will get you settled and see what...what damage has been done. She ran the bath and walked into the bedroom, where I stood hugging a bathrobe about my bruised body. My mother gasped as she opened the robe but gathered all her strength, trying to appear as normal as possible.

"Sit awhile, darling," she said. "I'll be right back."

"You're not going to call Daddy?" I asked.

"No, not yet. Try to relax, Lily. I'll be right back." Her hands clenched tightly as she cursed whoever did this to her child. She picked up the downstairs phone and dialed her doctor. I listened as she spoke. "I have to see the doctor immediately! My daughter has been raped. No, I haven't had time to call the police yet. As soon as you tell me I can come over to have the doctor examine her, I will. Where is she? She's in the bath. What do you mean I should have come to you first? Of course, I know she's been violated. I'm her mother. All right, I'll take her out of the tub right away. It's too late now? Late for what? Wash away the evidence? What evidence? Do I know who did it? Call the police? Listen, I can't talk anymore. A half hour – we'll be at the office in half an hour."

My mother slammed the phone in its cradle and ran up the stairs to me. To her surprise, I was slipping on my jeans and sweatshirt.

"I heard you on the telephone with the nurse, Mom," I said, blinking back tears. "And, yes, I know who did it."

"I hate all men," Elaine said bitterly as she eyed Jonathon.

Gerald shook his head, blowing out a deep breath. "I have to agree. That rotten boyfriend of yours sure took advantage of you. He should be hung."

"By the balls," Franny quickly added, her eyes drifting to Jonathon. "The horrendous things men can pull on innocent women."

Jonathon remained expressionless, but he made a mental note of Franny's evident sarcasm. "Let's put Lily's horrible experience in the right perspective and keep in mind that judging a group of people for one person's behavior is not the thing to do." He looked around for confirmation. Making a notation in his notebook, he raised his eyes toward Lily and nodded, in case she wanted to continue.

But Thomas spoke first. "Did you get the bastard, Lily?"

Her face became grim as her thoughts wandered back in time. "No," she said dejectedly. "When the word got out that he was going to be arrested for raping a minor he took off. Vanished into thin air."

"Too bad he got away with it," Elaine said, looking at the others and resting her gaze on Jonathon for a split second.

Lily frowned. "Yes, I guess it is too bad, but I think everyone gets paid back for the harm they do to others. I'm a firm believer in that." Her eyes lingered on Jonathon.

"What did your father do when he found out?" Elaine asked.

"When I knew I was pregnant we had to tell him...and boy, did he go berserk! He shook his head and waved a finger at my mother, his eyes saying, 'I told you so.'"

"Then he pulled my mother aside and screamed, 'No daughter of mine is going to give birth to a little bastard. Find a doctor and get rid of it.'"

"I'll never forget the look of anguish on my mother's face. 'Not my child!' she said defiantly. 'God would never forgive me.'"

"'Well, then you'll just have to make a choice, won't you?'" my father yelled. He paced back and forth, his hands clasped tightly behind him. His breath came in gasps of intense rage. When he pulled up short directly in front of me his eyes widened and he sneered. For a moment I thought he was going to hit me and I shrank back. Confronting my mother, he gave her an ultimatum. 'It's the Lord or me. Let Him pay the bills and the piano lessons that I, like a damn fool, worked my ass off for.'

"He stood waiting for my mother's answer, sure that she would submit to his demands. But his demeanor changed when he saw her expression. He raised his voice. 'I'm not backing down,' he said, hoping she would acquiesce. But she would not answer. She simply walked toward me and took me in her arms, watching him stamp his feet heavily as he ascended the stairs, the veins in his neck ready to burst in a fit of rage. An hour later, we watched my father, suitcase in hand, walk out the front door and out of our lives forever."

Lily stared into space. "You can add the finishing touches to my saga," she said, half smiling. "The baby died at birth. After that, I lived only for my piano."

"And it sure paid off," Franny said. "Sort of a bitter sweet ending. *My* father walked out of our lives, but the bastard had the nerve to come back. You were lucky, Lily."

Lily shrugged. "What was it that Gilda Radner used to say? 'If it's not one thing, it's another.'"

Jonathon checked his watch. "I have to tell you all that this was one of the most productive sessions we have had."

Lily stood and stretched her arms. "Gosh, I could sure use a drink."

"I need more than a drink," Franny blurted. "Let's go, girls. Duffy's tavern awaits us." She looked at the men and smiled. "I don't want to appear rude, gents, but it's ladies only."

Jonathon stood. "Just a moment," he said dryly. "I want you all to check with Cynthia. I have decided that we should meet once instead of three times a week. Anger flashed in his eyes toward the three women.

In the elevator, the ladies huddled close to one another. "He's onto us, girls," Franny said. "Did you catch the look he gave us?"

Elaine nodded her head. "Oh, yes. He's easing us out, slowly but surely."

Franny crooked her mouth to one side. "More than likely he's got younger bait to hook on his line. We are now yesterday's news. I can't get over the way he glared at us. You watch. In a week, he'll be telling us that there is nothing more he can do for us and that he's terminating our therapy."

"This calls for action, ladies," Lily said. "After talking about the rape and my father, I refuse to let another man use me. How about it, you guys ready to commingle?"

"I'm ready," Elaine said.

Franny's eyes flashed anger. "I'm more than ready to do away with the two-faced asshole shrink."

Lily burst out laughing. "Leave it to you to say it like it is."

"Get you," Franny said. "Well, I for one do not wish to *commingle* with any of your heads. In fact, I think it would be more exciting if we did our own thing, like we planned. Whoever gets to him first in their own inimitable style will be the winner."

"The winner of what?" Elaine asked.

Franny shrugged. "I can't think of it now. I'm too hyped up. I'm in high gear and I'm not about to shift into low. I'm revving to go into action. We can decide later."

"Me, too," Elaine said. "I can't wait to put him out of commission."

"I'm way ahead of you," Lily said.

Elaine smirked, closing one eye. "Wanna bet I get to him first?"

Lily and Franny eyed each other. "You're on," they said in unison.

Chapter 38

Detective Nicolas Salvatore Pagliara felt a sense of discomfort as he pulled up to the massive iron gates of the Kent estate. The once impressive sculptured plaque etched into the wrought iron gate's facade that read *SIMON SEZ* was now oxidizing, the flaking rust giving it an eerie outer shell. *Boy, if these old bastions could talk, what stories they could tell.* He snickered. *And probably put me out of work, too.* He shook his head, wondering why he felt ill at ease when called on a case that involved the rich and famous.

It was a far cry from the small 1930s wood and brick house in the Bronx, where Nick's grandparents had lived, he had grown up, married and now resided. He wondered if wealthy people, in spite of their means, have more problems than those who just about make ends meet.

The policeman waved Nick onto the extended driveway lined with rows of tall Island Pine trees originally imported from New Zealand and transplanted at the Kent estate twenty years ago. A flurry of newspaper reporters and television crews were cordoned off to one side of the road. Shouts of, "Hey, Nick, got any leads on the shrink?" and, "Think it was suicide?" could be heard as Nick pulled his vintage 82 P 1800 Volvo up to the entrance of the palatial estate.

Along with the other law enforcement vehicles, Nick parked at the entrance of the mansion, lifted his six-foot-two-inch frame out of the low-slung sports Volvo and uttered an aggrieved groan. His sidekick, Clancy, greeted him with a stifled snigger. "Don't even think it," Nick sneered. "I joined a gym last month. Just haven't had time to go."

Clancy nodded, knowing that Nick would pay but not use the gym, since the rowing machine in Nick's bedroom was a clothes hanger for strewn garments. "Sure, Boss," he scoffed. "You don't mind if I go in your place, do you?"

Nick ignored him. "What do you have on the shrink, Clancy?"

"The forensic people are in there now. Looks pretty clean so far. No sign of a struggle or break-in. The lab results should come up with fingerprints and other evidence. And for sure, you'll come up with something."

"Where are the servants?"

"In the skylight room."

"The what?"

"It's a room with lots of windows and a glass ceiling."

"I'll want to speak to the servants in a few minutes." Nick's eyes searched out every surrounding detail as they walked into the living room, where the coroner was kneeling, examining the corpse of Dr. Jonathon Kent. Nick clapped his hand on Clancy's shoulder. "You could have been in the movies, Clancy. Why did you pick homicide?"

Clancy followed his boss into the room. "I wanted to follow in your footsteps. You're my role model."

Nick's piercing blue eyes seemed to dance and his mouth twisted to one side as he smiled at his sidekick. Again clapping Clancy on the back, he said, "Keep sucking up to me, Clancy; it's great for my ego."

Merve, the coroner, in a stooped position, his eyes focused on the corpse of Dr. Jonathan Kent, gestured to Nick with a back wave of his hand and acknowledged Clancy, with a "Hi Clancy."

"Whadda-yuh-got?" Nick asked.

"Can't tell you too much, yet. He was bludgeoned with that," he said, pointing to a bronze Erte' statuette, "that piece of art. Beautiful, isn't it?"

Nick picked up the artifact, which was labeled and sealed in a plastic bag. "Looks like a lady snake," he said.

"Ya just ain't got no class, Nick," Merve joked. "It's a work of art done by the master of Art Deco himself." He shook his head. "It's called, Le Jalousie."

"Yeah, yeah," Nick said, studying Jonathon's lifeless form. "Work of art, huh?" Jonathon's head, cradled in a pool of drying blood, lay on the stained Oriental rug. "The snake lady did a good job on him, Merve. Got a handle on the time of death?"

"Sometime between 10:00 P.M. and midnight. Whoever did it was careful and neat. No signs of a struggle. As you can see, nothing's been touched or moved. Looks to me like there was only one other person besides the victim." He stood up and held his hand to his side and groaned. "I'm getting too old for this. More will turn up when the technicians search through the fibers of the furniture and carpet, if it wasn't cleaned recently." He shrugged. "They may find traces that go back hundreds of years. The carpet is older than Methuselah. Just in case you're not familiar with collectible items handed down from generation to generation."

Nick grinned. "As always, you are a world of information. Any other enlightening tidbits you want to share with me?"

Merve's face became sober. "Whoever killed the doctor was no stranger to him. No forced entry. Now, my friend, I have given you enough to go on. Do some work on your own. The body-baggers are ready to take the corpse when you're through." He removed his plastic gloves, stuffed them into a police trash bag and jabbed Nick in the ribs. "By the way, is the Volvo still running? I'll still give you $500 for it. Better take me up on it before they recall it again. The old wreck still stalling in the middle of the Long Island Expressway?"

"No, Merve. I had it fixed. There was air in the gas line."

Merve stood, grabbed his black bag, waved a goodbye and headed for the door. "I'll be in touch, buddy," he yelled back.

"Any ideas, Boss?" Clancy asked.

Nick stroked his chin thoughtfully as he bent over Jonathon's expressionless face. "Something's not kosher," he said. "I can see a bell ringing, but I can't hear it."

Clancy eyed his boss. "Excuse me?"

"Just a thought in my brain that's stuck."

"Weird, real weird," Clancy mouthed.

Nick's face brightened. "Got it!" he exclaimed. "I knew it would come to me." He stood up and smiled. "This guy is the son of the woman whose yacht exploded years ago. Married to an Ambassador. At the time, it jammed my mind because of the large amount of money the son inherited. About five hundred million."

"Phew," Clancy said. "Doesn't do him any good now."

"There was a lot of hush-hush talk at the time because the case was closed real fast. Too fast."

"We've seen it work before, Boss. Like they say, money talks, somebody walks." He added quickly, "I know, I know. You want a detailed list of names and addresses of all his patients and I should set up a meeting with his office employees pronto. And you want to interrogate the servants immediately."

"Almost perfect, Clancy. Send out for some doughnuts and coffee."

"Boss, there's nothing around here. The closest town is five miles away."

"Okay, forget it. I'm sure the cook can rustle up something to nosh on in this palatial estate." He hesitated.

"What?" Clancy asked. "You've got that odd look about you."

Nick ran his hand over his chin. "I have the feeling this case is going to prove very interesting, Clancy."

A police officer poked his head into the room. "Sorry to interrupt, Detective, but the butler insists on speaking with you."

"The butler…" Clancy began.

Nick rode over Clancy's words. "Don't even think of saying it. If you pull that old cliché, I'll…"

Clancy scurried out the door and down the hall as Nick heard Clancy's echo reverberate, *the butler did it!*

Chapter 39

The shrill ringing of the telephone interrupted the stillness of the night. Her eyes closed, Franny held the receiver to her ear.

Lily shouted into the telephone. "Do you believe it? I can't get over it. Was it you?"

Franny rubbed her eyes and glanced at the clock on the night table. "Lily, it's five in the morning. What the hell are you talking about? You can't get over what?"

"Then you haven't heard."

"Heard what? At this hour I'm not at my best, even when I'm at my best."

"Are you lying down or sitting up?"

Franny lifted her alarm clock and shook it. "Clock's working, maybe I'm still sleeping." She sat straight up in bed. "My phone is beeping. Oh, my God. It's Elaine. Her face paled. "Something's wrong with Elaine! Hold on, Lily." Franny pressed the hold button. "Hello! What?" she yelled into the phone.

"You heard," Elaine, said. "I can tell by your voice. How did you pull it off?"

Franny rolled her eyes. "Mama told me I was emotionally disturbed and I'm beginning to think she was right. This is not happening, I'm still asleep. Lily's on the other line talking crazy and you're on the line...my lines must be crossed. Listen, are you all right?"

"I'm fine, I wanted to tell you that..."

Franny cut her off. "Hold on, Elaine, I'll see what Lily wants and I'll get back to you."

"But, Franny..." Elaine insisted.

"Lily, I have Elaine on the other line. Why did you say she's not well?"

"I didn't say anything about her not being well. You did."

"I did? Listen, I'm not very good at three-way conversations. You people are coming at me from all directions. Can we start over?"

"Franny, just shut up and listen, will you! Jonathon's dead."

Silence.

"I know you're still there, Franny. Cut the conversation. Hang up and come to my place, ASAP! Now pull yourself together and tell Elaine to be at my apartment, too, and bring all the tabloids you can carry."

The morning shower clouded the windows of the unmarked police car that sat parked across the street from Lily's apartment house. Detective Nicholas Pagliara dipped his powder sugared donut into his grande vanilla latte, let the excess drip into the coffee container and quickly bit into it.

Clancy sat alongside his boss, watching and waiting for the sodden donut to make contact with Nick's shirt.

"Damn windows are fogging up," Nick said. "What's the scoop on the shrink's receptionist? She might have had a motive to do away with the Romeo, too."

"Trust me, Boss, the Don Juan had a harem of patients larger than the national debt. The receptionist is scared shitless."

"Yeah? Which means she has something to hide. What's her alibi? Don't tell me she took the fifth. Is she a dog or over sixty?"

Clancy envisioned Cynthia in his mind's eye and a huge smile spread across his face. "Uh uh. This Cynthia lady is really something else...and what a body. Never would have taken her for a receptionist. She admitted having an affair with the Doc. In fact, she came right out and said, 'The reason I stayed with him was that the money was outstanding.'"

Nick wiped the car window with a paper towel, his eyes focusing on the entrance to the apartment building.

"And get this," Clancy continued, "she had an American Express card that was paid for by the Doc's accountant. You should see the charges. Can you believe spending a thou on one dress? And her salary...fifteen hundred a week clear, no shit."

"Seems like he needed a cohort Girl Friday. Someone he could trust and do more than just secretarial work, and since money was no object he thought nothing of paying for it." Nick turned the blower on high and shook his head, showing impatience with the fogged-up windows. "Is that how you narrowed it down to the three suspects we're staking out?"

"It's only the tip of the iceberg. I figured if I started from the middle instead of the beginning I'd save a lot of precious time. According to Cynthia, his sexual affairs with his patients were getting out of hand lately. She prefaced it by saying, 'It was like he couldn't control himself and was trying to fill a void...that his sexual needs were never satisfied'. She said she thought he actually hated women and at the same time was obsessed with them. The three patients she particularly pointed a finger at are the ones who she said became close friends and had recently turned a cold shoulder on him. Flip the page over; they're the ones on the second sheet of my report. The person we are staking out is a well-known concert pianist, the second is the wife of a wealthy apparel manufacturer, and the third is a saleslady who works in the garment center. The other one of interest the secretary mentioned is a doctor's wife. She's a little older. Give me a month and I'll read the rest of the patients he screwed around with." He let out a "yuk-yuk," and followed up with, "The shrink musta had some shlong."

Nick threw a quick glance at Clancy and then returned a watchful eye to Lily's apartment building. "First thing I learned when I became a cop, Clancy, is never overlook the slightest clue or the least suspicious person. Looks like the shrink was one sick puppy." He furrowed his forehead. "Keep digging up dirt on the Doc and also the accidental death of his mother. There's more to the shrink than meets the eye."

Clancy opened the window but shut it quickly as the rain blew in.

"Get on it now," Nick said. "I'll wait another fifteen and then pay the lady a visit. I'll see you back at the station." Clancy opened the car door as Nick yelled after him. "And make an appointment for me to talk to this Cynthia receptionist sometime tomorrow morning."

Nick tilted his coffee cup, drained it and placed the empty container in a plastic shopping bag that hung on the open ashtray. He thought back to when his wife was alive and prepared breakfast for him every morning before he took off for the precinct. He brushed the dust crumbs off his jacket and looked up to see two women rushing past the doorman, who waved them into the building.

The doorman must know them, he thought. He scanned the notes Clancy had given him. *The pianist lives there so that must be... Elaine Benjamin and Franny Goldsmith.* He smiled, thinking of the name, *Franny.* The only other woman he'd known with the name Franny was his mother.

The doorman was not surprised when Nick flashed his credentials at him. The early newspapers with Lily's picture on the front page sat on the counter of the entrance to the lobby.

"Don't sweat it, pal," Nick said. "Just a routine check on a tenant."

•₂

"Crazy! There's just no other way to describe what's happening," Franny said. "After I spoke to the both of you, I took a couple of Valiums and ducked under the bedcovers. I was still in a daze when I dressed, trying to figure out which one of you two did it."

They leered at her.

Her expression grim, Franny said. "So what's with the evil eyes? Are you intimating that *I* took the shrink out? Believe me, I didn't." Her nose wrinkled up. "But I am kinda bummed that I didn't get to do it." Her eyes narrowed at Elaine. "I think it was you. You did say you had nothing to lose, because of your condition, remember?"

"I did say it, Sherlock, but I didn't do it."

"Let it go," Lily said. "Stop the second guessing. We all agree that we didn't do it." She poured herself a glass of wine.

"Geez," Franny snapped. "It's eight in the morning and you're drinking?"

"If you can take Valium and who knows what else, I can have a drink." Franny swallowed a humph.

Elaine shook her head. "This bickering is senseless. I'm calling time out. I'm hungry. I need some fuel. Can I play chef, Lily?"

Lily shrugged. "Be my guest. Shall we dine on the terrace?"

"I could eat," Franny said, gaining her composure once more. She took a handful of chocolate covered almonds from a candy dish, popped them into her mouth and continued talking. "Besides us, who else would want to do him in?"

Lily raised her brows. "You're not serious?" She took sterling silverware and linen napkins from a Bombay chest and spread a tablecloth over the wrought iron table. "How about Cynthia? Or Thomas or Gerald from the therapy group?"

"Cynthia?" Franny shook her head. "Uh uh. Thomas maybe. Gerald never! Elaine, how about your doctor's wife?"

Elaine's chortle was heard from the kitchen. "Amelia Stern? Her idea of an ideal marriage is to make sure the doctor's dinner is okay, play bridge every Thursday and take tennis and golf lessons. Cheating on her beloved would be like tearing a page out of the Bible. Her luncheon with Jonathon was nothing special."

Elaine took the butter out of the refrigerator, set it on the counter, stopped, examined her swollen fingers, put the butter back into the refrigerator and replaced it with whipped cream cheese. Upon hearing the toaster pop, she removed the bagels and thought that Amelia did get rambunctious after a few drinks, but shrugged the thought off with a shake of her head. She called to the women. "I made it simple. We're having toasted sesame seed bagels, cream cheese, scrambled eggs, Turkey bacon and high-octane coffee. We need the caffeine."

"Whatever," Franny said. She glanced at the newspapers that were spread out on the living room floor. "Do you believe the attention the papers are giving the murder?" Lifting the paper, she remarked. "Look at you, Lily. Great photo!" Her mouth curved mockingly to one side. "Mmm. Maybe a little airbrushed, but so what? Hey, there's none of me or Elaine."

"Just wait," Lily said. "You will be the talk of the garment center, and you, Elaine…"

Elaine broke in. "I don't want to know."

Lily continued. "You know the media; they will blow this up and we will come out looking like debauched women. Let's turn on the TV. Maybe something more is breaking."

Elaine called from the kitchen. "Breakfast is ready. Let's not let the food get cold. We can watch TV from the terrace. Franny, give me a hand, will you?"

The buzzer sounded. "Damn it! Now who could that be at this hour of the morning?" Pressing the intercom button, Lily said, "Yes, Bob. Who? Detective Pagliara? Just a moment." She turned to Franny and Elaine. "Get the papers off the floor and get rid of the wine. It has to be routine questioning of Jonathon's patients. Remember, we have nothing to hide." She pressed the intercom. "Bob, tell the detective to give me five minutes to slip into something and then buzz me when he's on his way up." She looked intently at Elaine and Franny. "I wonder if he knows the three of us are here."

"Let him wait. I'm eating," Elaine said. "The doorman must have told him we're here. But, so what? Lily's right. We have nothing to hide."

"Yeah," Franny said, as she split the bagel apart, spread the scrambled eggs on the seeded side and took a healthy bite. Wiping her mouth with a napkin, she said, "They don't put you in jail for having sex, do they?"

Lily sipped her coffee with forethought. "No, but for murder they do; and one of us is lying."

The elevator reeked of Chanel No. 5 from an overly dressed, overly made-up and overly perfumed tenant. By the time the elevator stopped and the lady exited, Nick was ready to throw up. "How do you stand it?" he said to the elevator operator as he undid the top button of his shirt and pulled his tie down a notch. "I'm about to pass out."

The operator smiled. "I don't even smell it. After five years of her, I'm immune. But I have to tell you, I've lost more lady friends because of her."

Nick let out a *phew!* "I'd get another job."

"She's leaving at the end of the month and guess what. She's marrying a man who manufactures deodorant." They looked at each other and burst out laughing. "This is your floor, sir. Miss Fitzgerald's apartment is the third one on the left."

Nick stepped out of the elevator, stopped at a wall mirror, rebuttoned his shirt, pulled up his tie, and checked his persona for any remaining donut remnants; then he called Clancy on his cell phone.

At headquarters, Clancy sipped his Pepsi, swished the straw around the ice cubes and placed the container on his desk. "Yes, Boss," he said.

"Listen. Meet me outside Fitzgerald's building in…" Nick glanced at his watch, "about an hour. We might have gotten lucky. I spotted the ladies the pianist hangs out with, going in. Gonna pay them a visit. What'd ya come up with?"

"Remember the shrink's mother who was in the boating accident? I'm sure it was pre-meditated. And there's more."

"Keep talking."

"Does the name 'Regent Smyth' ring a bell?"

"Yeah. He's the one they indicted for taking graft for doctoring phony death certificates." Nick took in a deep breath and blew it out slowly. "And you're going to tell me he's the one that was in charge of Mrs. Kent's autopsy, right? No wonder the investigation shut down faster than a clam's ass. What else ya got?"

"I started compiling facts on the shrink's patients, including the three ladies we're checking out. Except for the usual nonsense most screwed up broads exhibit, there's nothing incriminating. So far, they're clean."

Nick was aware that Clancy grew up on the lower eastside of Manhattan, where drugs and gangs were a way of life. He admired the determination the twenty-five-year-old demonstrated. Leaving the ghetto, he had worked three jobs, finished night-college, and enrolled in the police academy. He kept an eye on Clancy's progress but didn't openly praise him, mindful of the exceptional ability the young man showed. Being a father figure was not his job. His job was to prepare his assistant to be a top-notch detective; babying him was for parents. Still, the men shared an unspoken bond of respect.

Nick's face soured as he sighed into the phone. "Do you want to sit behind a desk or do you want to become a first-class detective? I'm accountable for your progress. Don't make me look bad. Number one. There is no such thing as a screwed-up broad. It's all an act. Never underestimate them. When it comes to playing head games, they're smarter than any guy on the planet. And the three ladies in question, who you say are clean...they're the ones you have to watch."

"I hear ya, Boss," he said, but he thought, *don't tell me to keep digging.*

"I'm at Fitzgerald's apartment door. Listen, there has to be some dandruff flaking off of them. Keep digging!"

His ear tuned to Lily's apartment door, Detective Pagliara listened, stepped back and then thumbed the buzzer. Lily greeted him with a cordial smile, and a "Good morning."

"Good morning, Ms. Fitzgerald," he said, flashing his credentials at her. "I'm Detective Nicholas Pagliara with Homicide. I'm running a routine check on the deceased, Doctor Jonathon Kent."

Pausing with her hand on the halfway open door, Lily stepped aside and motioned for him to enter.

At the sight of the detective, Franny brushed Lily aside and sidled up to him. Smiling enticingly, she said, "Well, don't just stand there dripping like a wet umbrella. Here, let me take your raincoat, sergeant."

"Detective," he said, correcting her.

"Well, of course, Detective," she said, taken in by his rugged features and deep blue eyes. "You're too tall and impressive to be a sergeant." She swung around to face Elaine and Lily, smiled approvingly, and then turned back to him. "We were just having breakfast. I bet you haven't eaten." Trying to feel him out in the marriage department, she said, "No wife wants to get up early and make breakfast when everything's so fast food today."

"I hope I haven't interfered with your morning coffee klatch, ladies."

Franny led him into the living room. "No problem. We klatch together every other Friday."

Closing his eyes to her last remark, he said, "I had coffee and a donut."

Not one to give up easily and hopeful he was single, Franny stepped behind him, pulled off his wet raincoat and tossed it over Lily's sixteenth century Chinese hand-painted silk loveseat.

Lily's eyes shot daggers at Franny.

Taking hold of his elbow, Franny steered him onto the terrace. "Sit here," she said, and moved a chair next to hers. "Elaine is a super chef. She can throw anything together in no time at all, can't you, dear?"

Mindful of her flippant personality, he decided to acquiesce for the moment.

Elaine shouted from the kitchen. "We wouldn't want you to think we're inhospitable." She walked to the terrace and extended her hand. "I'm Elaine Benjamin and this is Lily Fitzgerald, the famous pianist, and this *introverted* lady is Franny Goldsmith." A smile cloaked the group. He shook hands with all three, but his handshake with Franny was firmer and lingered a trifle longer.

"Well, back to the kitchen," Elaine said.

"So how many little darlings do you have, Nicholas?" Franny asked.

"Detective," he corrected again. "None. I'm not married."

Franny chattered on. "Well, who wants to be married anyhow? Nine out of ten end up in divorce court. Enough small talk. How about some food?"

Flipping an omelet onto a plate, Elaine yelled from the kitchen, "Move over IHOP. Cheddar-cheese omelet, and a buttered toasted bagel coming up. I hope you don't mind turkey bacon; we're always on a diet. Anything else, just give me a shout."

Franny flailed her hands aimlessly. "Don't mind her; she's always trying to upstage me."

He thought, *like anyone could upstage you.* "Really, Mrs. Benjamin, it's not necessary to go to any bother."

Lily poured coffee for him. "Milk, sugar, cream?"

"Black is good, thank you."

Placing the food in front of him, Elaine said, "We're so upset about Dr. Kent's death."

Franny blurted out. "Let the man eat, Elaine! Can't discuss business on an empty stomach."

The women made small talk, eyed one another, refilled their coffee cups, munched on bagels, played with the brittle bacon, and forked the chilled eggs around their plate.

For the moment, he put up with their irksome behavior, but as soon as he took his last bite he wiped his mouth and switched from his congenial to his sleuthing hat. For effect, he gritted his teeth. "Now, just a few preliminary questions. Mrs. Benjamin, how long have you been Dr. Kent's patient?"

"Gee, I'm not sure. I'd have to think back. Let's see…the girls are gone almost eight months now…"

"The girls?" he questioned.

Elaine lowered her eyes.

Lily spoke up. "Both of her daughters were killed by a drunk driver."

"I'm sorry," he said, and quickly turned to Lily. "How long for you?"

"Five months. Give or take a week. I started a month after Elaine."

Franny piped up. "I started four months ago. Two months after Elaine and one month after Lily. I started later because I didn't need as much help as they did." She giggled.

He ignored Franny. "Had you known each other before your visits to Dr. Kent?"

"No," Elaine said. "We met at the group therapy session. We became friends later. And we get along so well. More coffee?"

He came to his senses with a submissive groan. *This is going nowhere. I'm being conned by three shrewd, attractive vultures that are joined at the hip. I need to pry them apart. There're trying to get away with murder by turning this into a three-ring, three-woman circus. But I'll be cracking the whip and have them jumping through hoops before long.*

He took three business cards from his pocket, handed one to each of them, and smiled cordially. "Thanks for the hospitality." Slowly, he moved out from behind the table and walked to the foyer to pick up his raincoat.

Franny's chair screeched on the terrazzo patio floor as she pushed herself away from the table and dashed to where he stood. She grabbed his raincoat and held it up to him. "By the way, Detective, isn't it illegal to divulge psychiatrist's records?"

He snapped. "Not when they're dead!"

"Oh, really?" Franny said. "Well, so what, we've got nothing to hide. Right, girls?" She held the door open, her eyes searching his, her hand briefly touching his arm. "Bye. I guess we'll be hearing from you?"

He was beyond annoyed at their role-playing antics as he walked into the hallway and called over his shoulder, "You *will* be hearing from me."

Franny closed the door, turned the lock and leaned against it. Sighing, she said, "Did you see the way he looked at me? He likes me, I can feel it." She hugged herself.

"Get away from the door," Lily whispered. "He might be listening."

Elaine started to clear the table. "Did you ever see anything as crass as that display of throwing oneself at a man? Really, Franny. Why didn't you just unzip his fly and..."

Franny cut her off. "Say what you want. I might not have had the highbrow education you had, Lily, or made trips to Europe like you, Elaine, but I know one thing. You have to fight for what you want. If you just sit around waiting for Mister Right to snatch you up onto his white stallion, and carry you off into the sunset, chances are you'll develop calluses on your ass before the sun sets." She plopped down on the chaise lounge. "I know what you're thinking. 'She's a slut.' Well, if that's what it takes to get a man, maybe I am. All I know is, the guy just blew me away."

Elaine pulled a chair alongside Franny and sat down. "If you're a slut, Franny, then so are we. We let Jonathon manipulate us. No one held a gun to our heads. We knew what we were getting into. And getting it regularly didn't hurt either, did it? Real friends support and are there for each other."

Lily nodded. "I couldn't have said it better, Elaine. We need each other. We're carrying on as if we are being accused of Jonathon's murder."

Eyes wide, Franny stared into space.

"Thinking about the detective, are we?" Lily said smugly. "Listen, we need a distraction and I have the perfect solution. The American Musician's Federation wants to honor me with a black tie gala at the Waldorf Astoria, as the virtuoso performer of the year. They are giving me carte blanche. This is going to be the party to end all parties. I'm going to invite everyone I have ever known."

"Wow! That is quite an honor," Elaine said. "Congratulations."

"That's fantastic, Lily. Can I bring whoever I want?" Franny asked.

"Of course." Turning to Elaine, Lily suggested, "You could ask Lew."

The thought of asking Lew to the affair was painful to Elaine. Suddenly she stood and announced, "I almost forgot. I have a doctor's appointment. I'm out of here."

"You were just there," Lily said. "Are you going twice a week?"

Elaine headed for the foyer. "I'm late; we'll talk later."

Franny grabbed Elaine's arm. "Uh uh. We'll talk now." She eyed Lily. "We're getting the brush off, Lily." Confronting Elaine, she said, "You have that guarded look about you. What's up?"

Elaine walked back into the living room and sat down. She drew in a deep breath, exhaled, and drew in another, then shook her head and said, "All right, I'll confess. The lupus has spread. Stop looking like the world has come to an end. I had the same thing last year and it went into remission." Concealing the fact that the Lupus was terminal, she lied.

"The doctor says I have a good chance of getting it under control."

Lily grabbed her jacket and stood in front of her friend. "I'm going with you." She eyed Franny.

"So am I," Franny said. "You're not shutting us out. We made a pact to share the good times and the bad times. It will be hard to grab a cab. How about your limo, Lily?"

Lily called her limo service. "Five minutes. By the time we get downstairs he'll be there." She looked at Elaine, taking notice of her swollen face.

"Slow down, girls," Elaine said. "I'm not about to give birth." Opting to change the subject, she said to Franny, "I suppose you're going to ask Nick to the party; and Lily, is Dash going to be your date?"

"Lily nodded. Why don't you ask Lew? You did say the best years of your life were with him. He might be repentant."

The expression that washed over Elaine's face was one of discontent. "We did have a fabulous marriage—until I went berserk." Her heart ached, thinking, *sure, he'll come back…but it will be out of pity.*

Chapter 40

"Ashes to ashes, dust to dust..."

The day grew dark as a gust of wind from the east blew the rain in circles about the mourners, adding to the already dismal day.

Lily, Franny, Elaine, Lew, and Dashel, huddled together beneath umbrellas, looking at the casket. Franny snickered. "I'm all tingly. What's taking the minister so long? I can't wait to shovel the dirt over him."

Elaine nudged Franny. "We have to lay a rose on the coffin first. Show a little respect."

Franny protested. "Respect? The only respect the bastard will get from me are the thorns of the rose up his butt."

Lily intervened. "Franny, cool it. You're attracting attention. Now is the time to forgive your enemies, to cleanse the soul, become a better person."

Franny winced. "Spare me the sermon. Not in today's world." Disgust flashed in her eyes. "Ya can't even slap your kid on the ass for fear of winding up in court. If my kid brought me up on charges he'd be out the door before it opened."

Elaine uttered a labored "OH!" followed by a shiver as dampness penetrated her swollen fingers. She found comfort in knowing that Lew was there. She thought, *it was humiliating at first, but I'm glad the girls called and convinced him to forgive and forget.*

Lew immediately tightened his grip around her waist and moved closer to her. "Elaine, you shouldn't be standing in the rain. I think we should go."

"No."

"Why are you being so stubborn?"

She forced a smile. "I wouldn't miss this for anything, and besides, the pain is passing."

"Hey, dig Gerald and Thomas," Franny said. "I still think they're an item."

Lily shook her head. "Not nice, Franny. He looked up to Jonathon like he was his savior."

"Okay, okay, I take it back." She buttoned the top button of her raincoat and pulled down the brim of her rain hat. "Why does it always rain at funerals? I have never been to one where I didn't get drenched, catch a cold, and ruin a good pair of shoes."

Lew inclined his head at the women. "Don't look now, but the law is giving you ladies the once-over. Could be he thinks you're a little too joyous for a funeral."

Franny spouted. "Get outta here. He's just checking me out. I'm going to ask him to escort me to Lily's party. I know he's got a thing for me. Anyhow, what do I have to lose? If he says 'no' at least I'll know where I stand."

Lily noticed Mariah Tillingham leaning forward, acknowledging Dashel with a nod. "The lady is giving you the eye," Lily said.

Dashel smirked. "I can't wait to get the goods on her husband and have him put away."

"What goods? Put whose husband away?" Franny asked.

"I'll tell you later," Lily said. "Can't Dash and I have a private conversation? We *are* going steady."

"Going steady was in yesteryear, Lily. And besides, if we're such good friends, how come I had to hear it second hand from Elaine—about how this Tillingham guy ditched you after a one-night roll in the hay?"

Dashel spoke up. "I hate to be the one to break it to you, Franny, but husbands and contenders take precedence over girlfriends." He nudged Lew.

Eyeing Elaine, Lew agreed. "Right!

She concurred with a squeeze to his arm.

Franny raised her head. "I feel sorry for Cynthia. She had a huge crush on the Romeo. It wasn't pleasant for her to sit all day and watch Jonathon charm his patients into the sack." A chill ran through her. "Listen, forget about shoveling the dirt. We're getting soaked. He's not worth our getting sick over. And this has to be the worst weather for your condition, Elaine. The minister's about finished with the same old rehearsed spiel. Let's go."

"You're right about Elaine, Franny," Lily said. "But why give the law more to write in their little black notebook?"

Teasing Franny, Dashel said, "Don't you want to place a rose on Jonathon's casket?"

"The rose has wilted," Franny said. "It's as limp as his dick must be."

Like the visible rain, the minister's voice droned on. Gerald wiped the raindrops from his face with a sopping handkerchief. *A person's life is very fragile*, he thought. *It seems like only yesterday Dr. Kent told me how well I was doing. Who is going to help me come out of my shell now?* His hand trembled as he placed a rose on the coffin, but he swallowed a gasp as the flower slid down to the soft earth. Attempting to retrieve the flower he lost his footing and landed face down alongside the casket. Thomas laughed aloud as he gripped Gerald's arm and helped him up. Except for Gerald, not a tear was shed at the gravesite.

"Poor Gerald," Elaine said. "He'll be lost without his mentor."

"I need a drink," Lily chanted. "Let's go to my place and dry out."

"Pass," Lew said. "Elaine, I'm taking you home and then I'm going to the showroom. I've already lost a morning's business."

"I'm fine, Lew. Go to the showroom. The girls will see to me."

"Count me out, too," Dashel agreed. "What a waste of time this was."

Lily shrugged. "I guess it's us against the world, girls," she said, taking hold of Elaine's hand. She looked up as Detective Pagliara headed towards them. "Franny, guess who's coming our way? Think he might want to frisk you for concealed weapons?"

"Frisking works for me," Franny said. "And, just in case he wants to give me a ride in his Batmobile, ladies, you do have your own transportation, right?"

Surveying everyone with a keen and inquisitive eye, Detective Pagliara walked toward the women when suddenly a man engaged him in conversation. Lily eyed Franny. "Guess you'll have to take a rain check. Oh, oh. He's pointing the man in our direction."

A uniformed chauffeur attended the distinguished gentleman and sheltered him with an oversized umbrella. Droplets of rain slid from the gentleman's brim as he tipped his Homburg at the women. His British accent evident, he said, "Please forgive the intrusion at such an inopportune time. My name is Filmore Tripplehorn. I am Dr. Kent's executory solicitor. I have written to you and have yet to receive a reply. And since we are in such close proximity, I am taking the liberty to inform you that I have information concerning Dr. Kent's estate that could be of interest to you." Reaching into his breast pocket he removed business cards and handed one to each of them. He shivered and said, "Beastly weather!" He tipped his hat again, intimating that the business at hand was concluded.

Lily, Elaine and Franny stood mystified, watching the distinguished gentleman turn and hasten to his limousine.

The attentive chauffeur opened the rear door of the Rolls Royce

Phantom, and once Mr. Tripplehorn was comfortably seated, he neatly positioned a mink comforter over his employer's lap. He then placed a linen napkin on top of the comforter, retrieved a thermos from a paneled enclosure and poured hot chocolate into a Staffordshire mug. Taking a step back, he offered a two-fingered salute, and closed the limo door.

At the rear of the congregation, a mourner gripped the hood of the poncho, attempting to secure it. *There isn't one sorrowful person at this funeral. They're all here for the same reason I am...sweet revenge.* The mourner eyed Detective Pagliara. *As far as he's concerned I'm just anther patient who sought Jonathon's help. This case will be filed and shelved into the archives of unsolved murders.*

Chapter 41

The Yellow Cab pulled up to the curb in front of the police station. "Thanks, lady," the driver said, eying Franny's tip. "If ya need a legit bail bondsman I got it covered. He flashed a business card at her.

She waved her hand. "I'm cool, but thanks anyhow," she said, walking up the steps of the precinct.

The sun peeked through the warped aluminum blind of Detective Pagliara's office. The dust rag made a whooshing sound of resistance as he attempted to polish the marred wood surface of his distressed desk.

Across the room, Clancy sat at his well-organized desk, eyebrows raised, watching his boss fuss, wondering, *What's with the sudden urge to clean?*

Clancy's ears perked up as the desk sergeant announced, "Miss Goldsmith is here. She's waiting in the outer office."

Nick threw some crumpled papers and an empty coffee container into the trash basket and held up five fingers at Clancy.

Clancy tapped the intercom button. "Give us five minutes, sergeant."

A cheeky smile crossed Nick's face. "Clancy, it's time to rope this lady into the corral. Knock some of the chutzpah out of her. Let her stew awhile. Waiting makes them nervous. It worked with the other two."

After five minutes, Clancy opened the door and motioned Franny into the office, then closed the door behind him and left, speculating his boss had a reason to question her alone.

Franny took a seat across from Detective Pagliara, aware of the pangs of guilt that jabbed at her conscience. Justifying her promiscuous behavior with the shrink was not going to be easy. *Don't be stupid,* she thought. *For once, try to keep your mouth shut.* She imagined Elaine and Lily waving a warning finger at her.

But no sooner had she sat down when she blurted out, "I don't usually throw myself at guys, you know."

The detective's intimidating glare unnerved her.

Her voice faltered. "And we had nothing to do with Dr. Kent's murder."

His voice flat and expressionless, his look one of distrust, he said, "No one has accused you. Not yet."

Knowing her expressive, live wire personality to chatter, he sat and waited. Pushing back a lock of her fallen hair from her forehead, she said, "It wasn't like you think. We were extremely depressed, vulnerable. We needed someone to talk to—comfort us—to..." She glanced sideways trying, to avoid his eyes. "It's hard to explain. You have to be a woman to understand." She looked at him, trying to read his facial expression. "Do you know what I'm trying to say?" She didn't wait for a reply. "You probably hear the same old sob stories a hundred times a day. Anyhow, we had nothing to do with the murder."

"I haven't implied that you had anything to do with Dr. Kent's slaying. You have already made that very clear—at least five times in the last five minutes. Your friends gave me the same story." He placed his elbows on his desk and leaned a trifle closer to her. "No doubt rehearsed? You have admitted more than just a dislike for the doctor."

For long seconds the only sound in the room was the whirring of the air-conditioner.

The fact that she had slept with Dr. Kent struck a jealous chord within him. He swiveled his chair away from her then quickly swiveled back and raised his voice at her. "No one forced you to get involved. He must have been very good at what he did." A furtive smile crossed his face. "Uh, I mean with his counseling."

Franny felt as if he were drawing her into his eyes and holding her captive there. *I can't think. He's trying to trick me by saying how good Jonathon was at what he did. Did he mean sexually or psychologically? He's trying to trap me into a confession. And his comment about no one forced us to have sex...*

Snapping at her, he asked, "Were you with him the night he was murdered at the estate?"

Stalling for time, she smiled, but it didn't quite come off. "The estate? Murdered? Why would I do a thing like that?"

"I ask the questions! You answer! Okay? Let's start over. Are you saying you were never at his estate?" He stared questioningly at her. "That's hard to believe." He paused. "Where *did* the affairs take place?"

Franny, being Franny, spoke up. "Listen, I have nothing to hide. What you hear from my mouth is pure Franny Goldsmith." He swallowed a chuckle. "Sure, I hated the bastard. We all did. And yes, I did it at his house when the servants were out—and at his cottage in the country—and yes, at the office too!" She stood and placed her hands defiantly on her hips. "Happy now?" She felt he was baiting her, and the urge to defend herself took over. "No, not all of us at once, if that's what you're thinking. We weren't even friends then. He led us to believe that his intentions were honorable. When he realized that we were on to him, he dropped us like so much excess baggage."

Nick leaned back in his chair. He found himself taken with this outspoken but appealing lady.

His smug look annoyed her. "Yes, we let it happen. And you know what? We got stoned when we heard of his demise. And what's more, we are going to have a party to honor Lily, but it's really to celebrate his death." She blinked back tears. "And another thing. I checked it out. Even if the three of us did kill him, you can't convict all of us."

He walked to her and handed her a box of tissues. He wanted to laugh but held back. "Are you quite finished with the scene?" he asked.

She balked at his amused expression. "I pour my heart out and you think it's a big joke. Do you know how humiliating it is with the media making us look like wanton women?"

"Seems to me I saw that in a movie once," he said. "Not being able to convict three suspects at the same time is pure unadulterated bull."

She rose abruptly. "Listen," she huffed, "is there someone else I could complain to? Someone higher up than you?"

His hands came down on his desk blotter and he burst into laughter; but he quickly simmered down when he caught the hurt expression on her face and the tears rolling down her cheeks. "Sit, please," he said.

"What?" she asked, dabbing at her cheeks with a tissue. She sat down and played with the snap of her purse.

This is not going the way I had planned, he thought. *What's going on? Get hold of yourself; you're letting your feelings take over.* But he found himself losing his resolve and did something he had never done before. Walking up behind her he placed his hands gently on her shoulders. "I'm going to be upfront with you. I know I'm out of line, but I've been interrogating suspects for a long time, and I have to tell you, I have never met anyone quite like you."

His touch sent a tingling sensation through her. She would have liked to jump up and hug him, but for once, used her self-control. "I've heard that before. Is that a good thing?"

Intrigued by her, he stood behind her, nodded and silently mouthed, "Yes." His brain sent out a warning signal, but his emotions chose to ignore it.

Thrilled at his touch, she thought. *I don't care. I'm going to say it.* "Does that mean there might be chemistry in the air?"

He moved his fingers a few inches up the nape of her neck. "Maybe," he whispered, experiencing a sensation he hadn't felt since his wife had passed away.

"You mean, like we could maybe be an item?"

She couldn't see his conflicted smile. "We'll see."

She placed her hands on his and turned toward him. "Don't mess with me, Nick. I'm unable to exert control."

"Let's take it one step at a time."

Her face lit up. "Then you can be my date at Lily's party?"

"Uh uh. I don't think that's a good idea."

Her face fell.

"There could be complications. This is not going to sit well with the Department. They might take me off the case."

"Well, so what? You know, I've been thinking of how to snare you since you walked into Lily's condo."

He shook his head. "Did anyone ever tell you that you are nuts?"

"Are you kidding? Ever since I was born. Why do you think I went to a shrink? Now that that's out of the way," she said, "I suppose we are no longer under suspicion?"

He removed his hands from her neck, walked to his desk and sat down. Resting his elbows on the blotter, he knotted his fingers tightly. His voice inflexible, his cold, blue eyes piercing hers, he said, "Make no mistake, lady. I busted my ass a lotta years to get where I am. I have never mixed business with pleasure. I want you to know I'll be walking a very thin line because of you."

She felt a tiny jolt of fear run through her.

His face unyielding, he stood, walked to where she sat, hovered over her and poked a threatening finger into her face. His voice like solid ice, he threatened, "Heed my warning, Ms. Goldsmith. If I think for one minute that you and your buddies are fucking with me...watch out. I'll haul the lot of you into the cell block so fast your asses will sizzle crispier than McDonald's French fries."

Chapter 42

The limousine gently eased into the designated parking area at Lincoln Center. Tension and excitement permeated the air as the musicians and theatrical people greeted each other at the stage entrance of the concert hall.

The professor smiled warmly at Lily. "You are going to kill them tonight, Lily." He took a deep breath and shook his head as he envisioned a standing ovation and deafening applause. "I feel the electricity in the room. It's going to be a night to remember. Are you in good shape?"

"If you're referring to my nerves, yes, I'm psyched."

He shook his head. "I meant your physical shape. I want you to be able to endure all the curtain calls you are going to get."

She kissed him on both cheeks. "I haven't had a drink all day. Thanks for suggesting I take my frustrations out on the grand." Stepping out of the limousine, she stopped to sign autographs for the fans that had gathered at the stage door.

As she entered her dressing room the scent of the floral bouquets that crammed every available corner of the room took her breath away. "Renee," she said to her attendant, "I can't breathe. Please remove all the flowers except the ones from the girls, Dashel and the professor." She eyed an enormous floral arrangement in the shape of a piano. "Isn't that beautiful," she commented as she plucked the card from the decorative creation.

Good luck, Violet. I'm still hopeful. Love, Tennessee.

She threw the card in the wastebasket and stared at her image in the makeup mirror. She remembered every detail of their night at the Plaza Athenee, where he had insinuated himself into her life at lunch, then at dinner and finally in her bedroom, where he made her feel as if the gates of heaven had opened to her and her alone. She hadn't forgotten the genuine five-and-a-half-carat diamond that she thought was a cubic zirconium from Jolie Gabor's on Madison Avenue, or the pain she felt in her gut when she discovered the next morning that he had checked out of the Plaza Athenee, without as much as a note saying, "had an emergency—you were something else—I'll call you."

"Dumb Lily!" she shouted at her image. "First you get raped, then you let Tennessee screw you, and as if that wasn't enough you add Jonathon to the list of the three most stupid things a woman can do."

"Talking to yourself?" Dashel asked from the doorway.

She looked up, startled. "Not anymore," she said quickly. "Come here. I need you to hold me."

"Hey," he said, rushing to her side, concerned. "What's wrong? Shouldn't you be relaxing before you go on?" He gently massaged her neck. "What's wrong?"

"Too much to go into now," she said, turning abruptly so that his hands lost their grip on her. *This is not what I need right now,* she thought. "Please, don't soothe me. I need to be agitated."

"Excuse me?" he said, visibly hurt. "Am I missing something here?"

"Don't ask and don't placate me, not now, Dash." She looked at him as if he were a stranger. "You wouldn't understand and please, I don't have the time to explain." She turned toward the mirror, picked up her mascara and started applying her makeup. "Don't stand there like a dolt. We'll talk later.. please go."

"But Lily..." he protested.

"Just go, Dashel!" she said harshly. "I told you, I'll explain later. Please!"

He turned and walked out of the room, leaving the door ajar. "What the hell was that all about?" he muttered.

"Renee," Lily shouted. "Get in here and close the door!"

Her attendant ran into the room and stood bewildered, wondering what had happened. "I took most of the flowers out as you asked me to. I didn't have time to get them all because you had a visitor. I'll do it now."

"Forget the flowers, Renee. I don't want to see anyone. I don't care if it's the Messiah Himself." She took the arrangement Tennessee had sent and hurled it against the wall. It landed on the floor upside down. Renee started to pick it up but Lily shouted at her. "Leave it there, Renee; I need it to fuel my hatred for the male species."

Despite the applause, the moment Lily stepped onto the stage she was paralyzed with fear. The piano, which had always been her friend, a comfort to her in times of stress, now stood staring menacingly at her. As the house lights dimmed and the klieg lights focused on her, Lily had the strangest feeling, imagining that she could hear the audience laughing, heckling, and booing her. Beads of perspiration sat on her forehead, waiting to find their way into her eyes.

"Lily, what's wrong?" the conductor asked.

She slowly raised her eyes toward him. "I don't think I can continue," she said. "I feel sick."

"I can play an overture until you get yourself together, but you will have to leave the stage or it will appear awkward." He thought fast. "Sit tight, Lily. I have an idea." He left the podium and walked center stage, bowing his head in acknowledgment of the applause and held his hands up. A hush came over the audience. "Ladies and gentleman," he said. "As it sometimes happens, we are experiencing an electrical problem." Murmurs of disappointment could be heard throughout the theater. "Please, do not leave your seats. Miss Fitzgerald and company will return shortly and I promise you it will be well worth the wait." The audience applauded as Lily, the conductor and the musicians left the stage.

Franny, Elaine, and Dashel turned to one another. "Do you believe it?" Franny said. "You would think they would check the freaking wires before the concert."

Elaine shook her head. "I hope this doesn't upset Lily. She was nervous enough."

Dashel shook his head doubtfully. "I was at the opera here in New York years ago and we had a blackout. Now that's a real catastrophe." He looked around, and then leaned closer to the ladies. "And I am not so sure there is something wrong with the electrical system. I think there's something going on with Lily."

"Everyone gets the jitters before they go on, Dash. You were a concert pianist. Didn't you get terror stricken before each performance?"

"Of course, but that's not what I mean. I went to wish her luck before the concert and she practically threw me out of her dressing room."

"Get out of here," Franny said. "She's nuts about you." She nudged Elaine. "Right, Elaine?"

"That's right, Dash. She even told us about your proposal and she was really happy."

"I'm telling you, ladies, she was positively rude. I couldn't believe it."

"Hmmm," Franny said. "You know, Elaine, we couldn't get past the attendant to wish her luck." She looked thoughtfully at Elaine. "Maybe there is something to what Dash is saying. Now I *am* worried."

● ●

The professor knocked lightly at Lily's dressing room door. "Lily, it's me."

She closed the bathroom door and looked down to see if she had stained her gown when she had thrown up. "Come in, Professor," she said, noticing the sad look on his face. "Don't blame yourself. This is entirely my fault, but I know you must be disappointed in me."

He walked toward her slowly, his face drawn. "What makes you think I am disappointed in you? Listen to me, my child," he said warmly. "One can only do what one can do. We are fragile human beings who are sometimes required to carry very large burdens. It is not your fault that you have such a heavy load to carry at this time."

"I seem to have gotten sidetracked. I just can't concentrate. In fact, I know what's wrong."

He raised his eyebrows, waiting for her to speak, but the conductor tapped at the door. "Lily, we can't wait any longer. What do you want me to do? Cancel?"

Lily hugged the professor and opened the door. "I am ready, Maestro. You can turn the phony electricity back on." She laughed nervously. "Thanks for stalling the audience. The hall must be empty by now. I owe you." After the musicians settled themselves and the conductor nodded, Lily walked on stage aware of two ladies in the front row who stood and applauded. She could hear Franny shout, "Go, Lily!"

She sat down on the piano bench, adjusted her gown beneath her and placed her hands on the keys. "You can do it, you can do it, you can do it," she mumbled. The conductor tapped his baton at the orchestra and glanced at Lily, a smile and a wink to give her the courage she needed.

·•·

The concert was a stupendous success. The thunderous applause and the standing ovation left Lily at a loss for words. They would not let her leave the stage. With tears streaming, she handed her roses to the conductor and held her hand out to the audience, indicating that they could stop applauding. "I can only thank *you* who have come to hear me play and our dear maestro, as well as the orchestra and the man who has stood by me throughout all my difficulties, Professor Gottlieb. And to show you, my faithful audience, who cared enough to wait patiently while we got ourselves together, I am going to break with tradition, by asking the conductor to let me do an encore, especially for you."

Chapter 43

The enormous crystal chandelier in the grand ballroom of the Plaza Hotel that had witnessed many a legendary social affair radiated down on the festive couples as they laughed, drank and danced at the distinguished achievement award gala in Lily's honor.

One would have thought it was a celebration for a head of state or a foreign dignitary. Hundreds of guests were invited. No expense had been spared by the sponsors of the Amalgamated Musicians Union in choosing The Plaza to honor Lily as the *virtuoso of the year.*

The reviews of Lily's latest concert were outstanding and the media took full advantage of the pianist's success by publicizing her association with the recently murdered Dr. Jonathon Kent, making it front-page news.

Thinking it would make an interesting mix, Lily made sure her closest friends—and a few not so close friends—were seated at the main, horseshoe-shaped table.

Franny wore a pale blue silk organza Oscar de la Renta gown she had borrowed from Lily and had her hair done in a chignon, accented with opaque beads. She stared at Nick as he squirmed in his tails. "Stop fidgeting," she said, poking him playfully. "You're the most handsome dude in the place." Turning to Elaine, she said, "Do you believe it? He's complaining because I made him wear tails. I told him how great he looks, but he doesn't believe me."

For Elaine, Lew had called his friend Vera Wang, who designed a chiffon ecru off the shoulder halter gown with beaded sea pearls running down the front. He had gone to the bank vault and removed Elaine's diamond tennis bracelet, which she wore over her elbow-length, ecru lace gloves to veil her crippled fingers.

Elaine kept an upbeat pretense in spite of what her last visit to the doctor revealed. Smiling at Nick, she said, "You do look handsome, Nick," and then turned and held Lew's hand.

Franny bounced up to Elaine while nodding at the two gentlemen. "Check out the hotties at the bar? Boobs galore."

Arching one brow, Nick faced Lew. "Maybe we should check out the bar, Lew."

After the men left for the bar, Elaine said, "Good, now we can talk. You didn't waste any time, did you?"

Franny's face brightened. "It all came together when he interrogated me at his office. He made a move…no…I made a move…or did he make the first move? Well, anyhow, it was like a tsunami hit me."

Elaine said, "That heavy, huh?"

"He told me he's never met anyone like me. I guess we bonded after that."

"I never met anyone like you either, Franny. You are unique, in a class by yourself. I'm happy for you."

"I know you are. I just wish that you…well…"

"I'm coping, Franny. Let's not put a damper on Lily's evening. Lew and I are back together and he's been wonderful about everything. I have Lew, you, and Lily…that's a lot more than most people have." She took Franny's hand and held it.

Franny's insides sank as she touched Elaine's arthritic fingers.

"Looks like we're special," Elaine said. "Lily has us seated at the main table." She glanced around. "Who else do we know at the table? I know Dr. Stern and his wife, Amelia. You've seen her at the clinic. She's the one that I saw at the restaurant with Jonathon." She giggled. "Too bad Jonathon couldn't make it. And there's Cynthia. She doesn't look very happy."

Franny waved and smiled half-heartedly at her mother, but ignored her father. "Why the hell did she ask Blanche to invite him?" she said, her mouth turning down to one side with disgust. She eyed Bradford Tillingham. "Now there's a distinguished, handsome man. And the lady with him must be a movie star. Beau-ti-ful."

"That's the guy that broke Lily's heart. You know, the millionaire that gave her the big diamond—the one she calls Tennessee. And that's his wife, Mariah."

"Catch the baubles on the lady. She's a walking Harry Winston display showcase. Well, at least that one time roll-in-the-hay paid off for Lily."

"I don't think Lily would agree with you. Don't forget that after the heartbreak hotel affair, she landed on Jonathon's doorstep."

Franny sighed. "Didn't we all. But the diamond ring isn't bad for a couple of hours of sexual promiscuity." She noticed Elaine's expression. "Okay, okay, maybe it wasn't worth the heartache. You know, the mix at the table has the makings of an Agatha Christie novel."

"You are so full of it, Franny. But to know you is to love you."

Franny looked toward the staircase. "So when is the diva going to make her grand entrance? I'm dying to see what she's wearing. She doesn't know, but if she wants this creation back she's out of luck." She stood and struck a model's pose. "I should have brought my camera."

"I don't think so. There are professional photographers here."

Franny sat down. "It's more personal doing it myself. Elaine, throw a casual eye at the bar. Like you're just looking around. I don't want Nick to get the idea that I'm worried about him cruising other women."

"Are you?"

"Of course I am, but he doesn't have to know it." She leaned closer to Elaine. "You know, Nick can be real tough. He told me that if he found out we were lying to him he would slap us in the slammer so fast we would burn like MacDonald's French fries."

"Put yourself in his place, Franny. He has a difficult job. What if one of us did kill Jonathon? Getting involved with you is not making his job any easier." She turned to the bar and back to Franny.

Franny eyed Elaine. "Level with me. Did you do it because...well, you know, because of your condition? You can tell me. After all, I am your best friend in the whole world, right? Not counting Lily, of course."

"Tell *you*? You must be out of your mind. Telling you that I killed Jonathon would be like telling *The Inquirer*. And I suppose you would keep it a secret from Nick, right?"

Franny sat back, offended. "You don't trust me to keep your secret? I can't believe what I'm hearing. You're my best friend, next to Lily, of course."

"Franny, if you tell someone a secret it's not a secret anymore."

"Does that mean that you might have done it? I mean, you're not denying it." Her eyes narrowed at Elaine.

Elaine smiled smugly. "I'm not telling. You might divulge it to your boyfriend and then I would have to spend what little time I have left in prison." Placing her hand to her forehead, she feigned fainting.

"That remark is in very bad taste, Elaine. Tell me you're playing with my head."

Lew and Nick came up behind them. "Who's playing with your head?" Nick asked, laughing. "I'll punch their lights out."

Franny straightened up in her chair. "Geez," she said, startled. "You scared the hell out of me."

"Just girl talk, Nick," Elaine said.

A plainclothesman appeared and stood at Nick's side. "What is it, Rafferty?" Nick asked.

"From Clancy," Rafferty said, handing Nick a sealed envelope.

"Excuse me," Nick said. He stood, turned away from the table, opened the envelope, read the contents and then slipped the letter into his inside breast pocket. A concerned look crossed his face. He thought, *At-a-boy, Clancy!*

"Please, don't tell me you have to leave," Franny said.

His face remained impassive, but since reading the message his concern about his growing attachment to Franny preyed on his mind. "Just business as usual," he said, and adjusted his jacket, making sure his shoulder holster was concealed.

Franny's heart sank as she read the tension in his face. She leaned forward. "Did you boys find any hot mamas at the bar?"

Sensing the uneasiness at the table, Lew said, "Do you think we would tell you? That's one thing men don't discuss."

Elaine spoke up. "Really? Men happen to be the biggest gossips. A scientific survey showed that men gossip more than women."

Lew asked. "Who took the census, Gloria Steinem?"

"Never you mind. We can't blame men for everything. After all, they do make us happy," Franny said, placing her hand guardedly on Nick's arm.

"That's right," Nick said, picking up his drink and causing Franny's hand to fall away.

Her nerves frazzled, Franny thought, *Maybe Elaine did kill Jonathon. That must be what Nick read in the letter.*

At the other end of the table Bradford T. Tillingham chatted with Dr. Stern. Mariah Tillingham listened attentively as Doctor Stern conversed with her husband. "I have worked in the most prestigious hospitals in the state and I tell you, Mr. Tillingham, Park Central with all its state-of-the-art apparatus and expensive designer offices leaves a lot to be desired. The doctors would do the patients a greater service if they paid as much attention to them as they do to their golf games. They are running the place like a country club, not a hospital. That's the reason I left."

Mariah Tillingham smiled broadly. "Careful, Doctor Stern, my husband is the majority stockholder in the corporation that owns the hospital."

Amelia Stern's jaw dropped. She spoke apologetically. "My husband is very dedicated when it comes to his practice, and he takes it quite seriously. Sometimes I think a bit too much."

Mariah smiled. "Don't apologize, Mrs. Stern. I think it's admirable and rare to find a man who has his patients' best interests at heart." She eyed her husband, enjoying the anger that flashed in his eyes. "Wouldn't you say so, *dear?*" she said.

Showing exasperation, Tillingham glared at his wife then directed his conversation to Dr. Stern. "Your ego lets you believe you're entitled to all the privileges in the world because you falsely think you are helping mankind. Well, let me set you straight. If it weren't for men like me who keep the hospitals from going bankrupt, you good Samaritans would be working your tails off in ghetto clinics."

Mariah Tillingham quickly jumped into the conversation. "My, my, Bradford. Remember this is a celebration." She put her hand on Dr. Stern's arm. "You have to forgive my husband's crassness, Doctor. He's cynical when it comes to discussing finances."

Bradford waved a hand of dismissal.

Mrs. Tillingham smiled at Doctor Stern. "Your wife mentioned that you love to dance," she said, as she rose and took his arm in hers. Heads turned as he escorted this breathtakingly beautiful woman to the dance floor. "Don't pay any attention to my husband," she said, inclining her lips to his ear. "He's an asshole."

As magical and blissful as Franny felt at the beginning of the evening, the message that Nick had received from Clancy and his sudden change of attitude turned her mood into one of despair, and it reached an all-time low as she watched Nick and Cynthia walk to the dance floor, arm in arm. Franny turned to Elaine. "I need support, Elaine. Do you see what I see?"

"Don't panic," Elaine said.

"What do you mean 'don't panic'? I'm going to die right here in the Grand Ballroom of the Plaza. Is he my date or am I hallucinating? Did he or did he not ask Cynthia to dance?"

"Take it easy. There has to be a reason. Lew, darling," she said softly. "Amelia is sitting all by herself. Ask her to dance, would you?" She tugged at his jacket lapel, bringing him closer to her, pretending to kiss him. "And put an ear on Nick and Cynthia, without being obvious. You understand what I'm saying?"

"Gotcha," he said, kissing her neck.

Elaine poked Franny's arm. "Your face is flushed and you look like you're going to burst into tears. Get hold of yourself. You know what a drama queen you can be. Do you want Nick to come back and see you like this? Maybe Lew will pick up on some of their conversation. He's most likely asking her something pertinent to the case. His demeanor did change after he got the letter. I'm sure it has nothing to do with you."

Franny shrugged, her eyes narrowing at Elaine. "You think I'm being overly dramatic?"

Elaine pushed herself away from the table and stood. "Come on, let's go to the little girl's room. I can't very well shake the hell out of you in front of all these people."

Franny pouted. "No, I'm not going. I might miss something."

Elaine sidled up to Franny and smiled through clenched teeth. "Franny, darling, get off your ass and walk like a lady with me to the powder room or I swear I'll go straight to your father and tell him you want to make up with him." Her teeth still clenched, she added, "I swear I will." She made a half turn toward Franny's parents as Franny sprang from her chair.

"Bitch," Franny said under her breath. "You win."

Lew tried inching toward Nick and Cynthia, but the crowd on the dance floor kept him from getting close enough to hear their conversation.

Amelia leaned her head on Lew's shoulder. "The last time we danced was at the country club when they awarded you and Bill trophies for winning the golf tournament. I miss you and Elaine. Too bad about Dr. Kent, isn't it?" She tilted her face toward his. "And what about you, Lew? What happened to you and Elaine? Mid-life crisis? Elaine should have just let you screw your head off; then you would have come back to her. What is it with you men when you get to that age?" She snuggled closer and breathed in his ear. "You should have come to me; at least we could have kept it in the family."

A fanfare rang out and everyone turned toward the Art Deco flower-patterned spiral staircase. Lily, in a sheer silk lilac Balmain gown, her red hair falling gently about her shoulders, and Dashel, looking every bit the proud escort in his cutaway, stood posing as photographers snapped away at them. The guests stood and applauded as Lily curtsied and blew kisses at them.

For the moment, Elaine and Franny forgot their problems and applauded with the rest of the guests. "Just look at her," Elaine said. "She could be on the cover of *Bride.*"

"Brides do not wear lilac and she's too composed to be a bride," Franny said, thinking that her own chances for marriage were dwindling rapidly.

Lew and Nick walked up behind them. "So, what have you two been up to?" Nick asked.

"*We* have been scouting the room hoping to find someone to dance with since your dance cards seems to be booked solid," Franny snapped.

Elaine pinched Franny's arm. "Franny, please," she said, glaring at her. "Don't make a scene."

Nick grabbed Franny's arm and spun her around. His expression rigidly impassive, he stated, "Stop this foolishness! You have no right to be angry. I danced with Cynthia for reasons that are none of your damn business. Just cool it and stop acting like a jealous, self-centered, spoiled brat. Think before you open that big mouth of yours." His eyes flashed anger at her. "You are not the center of the universe. Do you understand what I'm saying?"

Franny was taken aback. Her mouth dropped opened with surprise and her eyes widened. She stammered, "Sure, Nick...anything you say."

Elaine stifled a giggle and winked at Lew, whispering, "Boy, does he have her number. He's just what the doctor ordered." But her face grew sad as she remembered that she might not be around to be a bridesmaid when and if Franny did get married.

"Here comes the guest of honor," Elaine said as they gathered around Lily and Dashel, who were hugging and kissing.

"What a night," Bradford Tillingham said. "We are so proud of you, Lily." He tried to kiss Lily on the mouth, but she quickly turned her cheek as Mariah Tillingham moved in and shook Lily's hand. "The concert was extraordinary," she said with sincerity. "Bradford didn't even fall asleep." The group laughed but Tillingham inwardly seethed.

"I see Franny got you to wear the monkey suit, Nick," Lily said. "I hope you are not going to practice your sleuthing techniques tonight. I would like my guests to enjoy their dinner without worrying if they've paid their parking tickets." She glanced at Franny then back to Nick. "The cutaway suits you, Nick." She turned toward Doctor Stern and his wife. "Amelia, Bill, glad you could make it. Amelia, I haven't seen you since our visit to…you know who. Elaine talks about you all the time." Lily spied Lew. "And now I am formally getting to meet Elaine's one and only." Lew extended his hand as Lily pulled him to her, kissed his cheek, embraced him, and whispered, "I know you'll take good care of our girl." His smile told her he would.

Lily waved a fleeting hello to Cynthia, who appeared visibly shaken. Lily turned away from the receptionist who had been Jonathon's eyes and ears. A shiver ran down Lily's spine.

The orchestra struck up a fanfare and everyone turned to the podium where the professor stood waiting to introduce Lily. Elaine and Franny exchanged glances, puzzled at not having been greeted by Lily. On the way to the stage, Lily plucked a glass of wine from a passing waiter's tray. Before she stepped up to the podium she downed the first and then grabbed another. She squeezed the maestro's arm. "God, I needed that," she said, eyeing another waiter, but the maestro tugged at her arm playfully.

"The evening has just begun, my dear. I know you can handle the bubbly, but go easy." She rolled her eyes, thinking she had heard him tell her those exact words more times than she cared to remember. He continued, "You said you would play a selection from your concert after dinner. We want to finish the evening on a good note, don't we?"

She pressed his arm tightly against hers, knowing that he had spent many a sleepless night worrying about her drinking before a concert and had patiently nursed her through the not so sober ones.

"I know you can play well under most conditions," he said tactfully, "but this is a special night. Remember, Lily, this is my night too. Do it for me, *liebling*."

"Maestro," she said, giving him a peck on his cheek, "You're right. I owe you more than this night. You have been mother, father, teacher and the keeper of the keys to the liquor cabinet, wrapped up into one neat package. Don't worry, I won't let you down."

Nick's voice mellowed as he took Franny's hand and led her to the table. He read her mind. "Take that hurt expression off your face," he said. "She hasn't forgotten you or Elaine."

"I guess so," Franny said, still reeling from Nick's tongue-lashing. She eyed Elaine. "She's nervous...the concert and all the excitement."

Nick winked at her as he held her chair. He bent over her, kissing her tenderly on her mouth. "I still feel the same," he whispered softly, "but I'm caught in a bind. Don't confuse my job ethics with my feelings for you."

It was as if a kindred spirit had swept through Franny's soul and lifted her into heaven itself. Her eyes filled with tears as she thought of Jonathon's using her, Joey's leaving her, and her mother's turning a blind eye to her father's abuse of her. All now vanished into thin air by Nick's kiss and reassuring words. The rest of the world seemed to fall away.

Dashel walked up to Franny and Nick. "Lily talks incessantly about you two. Don't you think it's about time we became better acquainted?" Nick tried to answer, but Tillingham raised his voice from the other end of the table.

He spoke with a sense of urgency. "Dashel," he said sternly. "I would like a word with you!"

Dashel frowned. "Excuse me, ladies, I promise I shall return. Regrettably, my master's voice beckons." As he started walking away, the professor's voice resounded from the podium and Dashel raised his hands and shrugged at Tillingham, who scowled.

Glancing at Lily warily, the professor concluded his introduction, praising Lily and her accomplishments. "And now it gives me the greatest pleasure to introduce the talented guest of honor, Lily Violet Fitzgerald."

Holding the microphone with one hand, Lily smiled at the guests, who applauded as they looked up at her. But all she could think about was Cynthia and how disturbed she had appeared. She opened her mouth to speak but didn't utter a word. The professor stood alongside her, placed his arm around her waist and spoke into the microphone. "Our guest of honor is so overcome with joy, she cannot speak." He tightened his grip on her and added, "Who can blame her? She is overwhelmed." He stepped to the side and clapped his hands, signaling the guests to applaud.

The cheers and applause brought Lily back to reality. Winking at the professor, she smiled graciously. Raising her hands, she motioned to the audience to stop applauding. "I'm going to make this short. I know you must be starving by now. Thank you for being so kind. If I have played well it was because *you* have given me the inspiration, motivation and encouragement to keep striving for perfection when at times I was so frustrated I wanted to give it all up. And thank you, Professor, for your patience and discipline in the face of my artistic tantrums. Without you, I probably would be playing the piano on the mezzanine at Bloomingdales." Laughter ensued. "To the maestro who makes me sound better than I am, many, many thanks. And I would like to give special thanks to my two dear friends, Franny Goldsmith and Elaine Benjamin, who kept my spirits up when I have had too many of the other kind of 'spirits.'" The audience laughed and applauded. "Ladies, take a bow." Franny and Elaine stood and waved at Lily. "And now, ladies and gentlemen, enjoy, and as I promised, I will play an encore after dessert." She paused. "That is, if the bubbly doesn't do me in first."

Kissing and greeting friends and fans, Lily was happily rescued by Dashel, who took her arm and whisked her to the main table, where everyone stood and applauded. "I could get to like this," she said, pausing in front of Elaine and Franny. "Thought I snubbed you two, but I wanted to give you an honorable mention." She hugged them both. "We have to talk," she said in a serious tone, her back to Nick. "Now, who is going to pour me a drink?" Dashel held up a glass of wine and she took it. "Dance with me, Dash. I have to catch up on the festivities. I may never have a party like this again."

On the dance floor, Dashel held Lily firmly. "You were magnificent last night, Lily. I was concerned about the power outage. I know what it's like to be ruffled just before a performance."

She nestled her nose against his ear. "There wasn't any power outage," she admitted. "The outage was with me. I did something stupid."

"Are you going to tell me or do I have to squeeze it out of you?" He eyed her suspiciously.

"Later," she said, nipping at his ear. "Isn't there something you want to ask me?"

"You know there is. Will you?"

"Will I what?"

"Don't play with me, Lily. Marry me."

"Yes, Dashel Rushmore Wentworth, I will marry you." She tilted her head upward and they kissed.

"Tell me, what happened to delay the concert?" he asked.

She pulled away from him. "I want to be honest with you, Dash. I have a few...habits you may not be comfortable with."

"I know about you and your habits. When you are ready, I'll stand by you."

She looked at him with surprise. "You know?"

"Everyone knows. Except you."

"And you want to saddle yourself with an addict? What if I can't stop?"

"One step at a time, Lily." He kissed her cheek. "Listen, Lily, I have great news."

"Make it fast, Dash, the dance is coming to an end."

"Okay."

"Be careful of Tillingham, Dash. The man is a piranha. He can have you eradicated from the face of the earth quicker than you can bait a hook."

"I know. Until last week he had been rather friendly, then suddenly he started giving me the cold shoulder. He might have gotten wind of my inquiries into his past. And Lily, some of the business transactions he has made...phew...you would not believe."

"I believe, Dash. I was one of them."

"What? You did business with him?"

She paused for a moment before speaking. "You might call it that, but that's for some rainy night by the fireplace. I won't go there."

He shrugged. "I can't figure out if he suspects that I'm gathering information on him. I cover my tracks so well."

"How did the meeting with Mrs. Tillingham go?"

"Oh, yes. We met and really hit it off. The woman flat-out hates him. She is not only beautiful but smart as a whip." He looked around. "I could ask her to dance, but I'm afraid Tillingham would get suspicious. By the way, did you know that she was a patient of Dr. Jonathon Kent and that they had affairs?"

Lily shut her eyes. "No."

"She said she never went to his office. They met in some remote place. She was quite open about it. I like her."

"What's not to like? She's a spectacular looking woman with an awesome body and more wealth than the Sultan of Brunei." She tugged at his earlobe. "Watch yourself. I know how vulnerable you are when it comes to the rich and famous."

"Hey, you," Franny said as they approached the table. "It's 'girl time' in the ladies room after this course, okay?"

"Right," Lily said, noticing Nick's grim expression. She put the wineglass to her lips and felt a pang of guilt as Dashel eyed her watchfully. *Damn*, she thought, *I've got the detective on one end of the table and the wine police at the other.*

As the women excused themselves and headed for the ladies room, Franny turned to Nick. "I'm not jealous. You can dance with anyone you want."

He simply shook his head and waved a goodbye with his fingers.

In the ladies room they made casual conversation and applied fresh makeup. The guests flocked around Lily, making it impossible for them to have a private conversation. Elaine motioned to them with a tilt of her head and they left the room, turned into a hallway and took an elevator to a room reserved for Lily.

"Listen," Franny said, concerned, "we have to make this short. I don't want to upset Nick. He can be the sweetest guy, but if I cross him, believe me, he will end our relationship without any chance of a rain check. I've seen him in action and the man can be like ice."

"I think you're getting paranoid, Franny," Elaine said. "He's crazy about you."

"He's what you would call an honest cop. He'd turn his mother in if he had to." She bit her lip. "I'm screwed, I know it. I can just feel it."

"Let's think logically," Lily said. "One thing at a time. Okay, maybe he suspects one of us. So what? None of us have anything to worry about." She eyed them suspiciously. "He's just doing his job, and his attraction to you, Franny, isn't making it any easier for him. Evidently, Cynthia has told him something that links someone to Jonathon's murder. Did you see her? She's as nervous as a cat on a hot roof. It can't be us. His attitude is too friendly."

"We don't know that," Franny said. "That's pure conjecture on your part. He's too smart to let on even if he suspected one of us. I tell you, girls, if I lose him, I'm taking the gas pipe."

"I thought we were going to talk logically," Elaine said. "Stop your hysterics, Franny. If he accuses either you or Lily, I'll admit to the murder." Franny and Lily started to speak, but Elaine held her hand up. "Don't even say a word. I hate to say this, especially at Lily's celebration, but I don't have forever, anymore. No tears, no big emotional scenes, please. I need you both and Lew to be brave for me, to help me through this. If you fall apart, I swear I'll end it all before..." She hugged them, trying to keep from crying. Finally, Elaine pulled away. "Okay," she said. "Now that we have released our tensions, let's head back to the ladies room and repair. We can do a primal scream later if we need to."

"And by the way," Lily said, "we seem to have forgotten to make an appointment to see Mr. Tripplehorn, Jonathon's lawyer."

"Yeah," Franny said. "Maybe the stiff left us one of his vintage automobiles."

Elaine spoke up. "Let's make this a wonderful night for you Lily; you deserve it."

Chapter 44

After the entrée had been served and eaten, the guests clinked their knives against the water glasses. "What's happening?" Franny asked.

Lily gulped her wine before answering. "It's music appreciation time. To thank my fans for their support."

The professor stood behind Lily. "Are you sure you want to play?" he said. "By now most everyone has had too much to drink." He tightened his grip on her arm. "And, *liebling*, so have you. You don't want to end the night on a bad note."

"I like that," Lily said. "End the evening on a bad note. Not to worry, Professor, I'm not playing anything serious." She pinched his cheek. "I'm going to do a medley of Porter, Gershwin, and Berlin. What do you think?"

"I think you are one clever lady."

She looked at him musingly. "We alcoholics have hollow legs, you know."

"And all the time I thought I was teaching *you*," he said. "Hollow legs, huh? Get your act together, 'cause I'm going to announce you in fifteen minutes." He shook his head then rolled his eyes. "Hollow legs. I must remember to add that to my vocabulary."

Dashel rose and faced Lily. "The professor's got your number. Want me to escort you to the piano?"

"Don't think I can make it on my own?"

"Lily, please. It's just that after you have had a few…Are you really going to do a medley of Porter, Berlin and Gershwin?"

"Bad idea?"

"Are you joking? I think it's fantastic. They will love it." He leaned closer to her. "And so will I. Now that we are officially engaged when can we consummate the relationship?" His hand slipped slowly down her back and rested on her buttocks.

Franny interrupted. "Stop with the schmaltz already; the professor is ready to bust a gut."

"Come on," Lily said to Dashel as she lifted a glass of wine to her lips. "Take me to my leader."

He stopped her hand in midair. "That's mine." He took her glass of wine and finished it. "And besides, I want you willing and sober when we make love tonight." He crooked his arm for her to grasp. "Shall we?" he said, escorting her to the grand piano.

•。

Franny gulped the vodka. "My insides are churning like a blender. I almost wet my pants. I think we should go to the ladies room, Elaine, and check me out."

Nick frowned. "I thought we might sneak in a dance before Lily starts to play."

Franny rose, taking Elaine's hand. "Nick, honey, I have to regroup. You know, girl talk."

"How about man talk?" he said, sounding miffed.

She fluffed him off. "You're such a big baby." She patted him on the back and gave him a light peck on his cheek. "I'll make it up to you." She winked at him.

Nick moved next to Lew. "Crazy broads," he said. "Never know where you stand from one minute to the next."

"Don't fight it," Lew said. "You won't win. They've bonded. Anyone that tries to break up their friendship will be eaten alive. It could be a good thing. Look at it this way. You won't be burdened with all the talk women conjure up. They will discuss us and come to a conclusion without you or me having to get involved, and their get togethers will give us some free time."

"I know what you're saying, Lew, but I want her to come to me with her problems, not her girlfriends. I want to be the main cheese in her life. That's the way I was raised." He shook his head.

"You were married before. I'm sure you had arguments. And in your work you must deal with every type of woman God put on this earth. I think you're jealous. You feel that the ladies are a threat to you." He eyed Nick. "Right?"

Nick smiled thoughtfully at Lew. "You got it. But do me a favor. Let's keep this between us. If you told Elaine and Elaine told Franny...God knows what she would make of it. Franny tends to be a little high-strung."

"I will admit that you picked the one with a short fuse," Lew said. He pushed a few crumbs into a pile on the tablecloth then flicked them with his finger. "I'd settle for what you have in a minute," he said, staring into space.

"Elaine, huh?" Nick asked, noticing Lew's forlorn expression.

Lew sighed. "You go along assuming that nothing will ever happen to you, and then one day, boom, the bottom drops out and you lose everything. No warning, not even a sign that your world is going to fall apart."

"Talking about your children, aren't you?"

"My children yes...and now Elaine." He shook his head and sighed. "She's deteriorating fast. I feel so helpless watching her...slip away. That's why I spoke so frankly to you. If there are three things I have learned in my lifetime they would have to be…understand…overlook…and forgive."

Nick put his arm on Lew's shoulder. "I'll remember that. Being in charge of an investigation in which Franny is a suspect makes me damn uncomfortable. If I had any brains I'd take myself off the case. I could get into trouble; you know, conflict of interest. It's not in anybody's best interest, for either myself or the law."

Wanting to lighten the mood, Lew suggested. "How about we grab a dance with Mrs. Tillingham and Cynthia before the ladies come back? Give them something more to bitch about." He poked Nick good-naturedly.

Nick spoke quickly. "You take Cynthia. I danced with her before. And try cheering her up."

•

"Come on, guys," Franny said, tugging at Elaine's arm. "The crowd is starting to gather around Lily at the piano, and we should be close to her, not in the bleachers. Why the gloomy face, Nick? I saw you dancing with Mariah Tillingham, and I'm not in the least bit jealous, so there."

Nick winked at Lew. "You were right, Lew. Thanks for the words of wisdom."

"Hurry," Franny said. "Let's get closer to the piano."

Nick shook his head. "We're not worried. With you leading the way, the crowd will part like the Red Sea."

Chapter 45

The Executive Banquet Manager of the Plaza, Mr. Davis White, gloated over the spectacular evening he had worked so hard to make a success. He listened intently to his favorite concert pianist, Lily Fitzgerald, as she began playing a medley of songs.

The lavatory attendants left their stations and hummed along with the familiar strains of Cole Porter's, "Just One of Those Things." But when they caught the eye of Mr. White, they quickly scurried into their designated lavatories.

"Sarah, Igor," Davis White called. "Come here. We may not have the opportunity to witness this caliber of performance again. You do enjoy her playing, don't you?"

They nodded.

"Then go and join the crowd. No one is going to use the bathrooms at the moment." They smiled appreciatively. "And, Sarah," he added, "remove your cap for now."

Unnerved to the point of nausea, Cynthia sat alone at the dinner table, turning her napkin into a twisted rag. Lily's playing didn't soothe the throbbing in her head. She was thinking of her conversation with Nick when they had danced; about the threatening phone calls and the notes with pasted cutout letters she had received that warned her to keep her mouth shut.

She lied when she said she hadn't the faintest idea who was harassing her. When he asked her what she did with the letters, she lied again and told him that she was too frightened and upset, so she burned them. When they left the dance floor Cynthia was a nervous wreck thinking Nick was suspicious of her for not reporting the incidents to the police. Frightened, and lightheaded from drinking, she placed her hands on the table for support, stood up and walked to the ladies room.

Relieved that no one was in the powder room, Cynthia removed a hand towel from a basket, ran it under cold water and pressed it to her forehead. Suddenly nausea gripped her. Rushing to the stall, she flung the door open, not bothering to secure the latch. She lifted the toilet seat, sank to her knees and bent over the bowl to vomit, but all that came up was saliva and bile. A cold sweat followed by dry heaves reminded her that she had too much wine on an empty stomach.

At the rear of the atrium a woman spied Cynthia entering the powder room. She withdrew from the guests, who sat engrossed with Lily's playing, and stealthily walked from the atrium, through the ballroom, opened the brass door of the powder room, stepped in, and quickly closed the door.

Cynthia, aware of someone's presence, peeked beneath the stall and gasped as her eyes focused on the intruder's shoes. Her breath caught in her throat and panic gripped her.

Before Cynthia had a chance to think, the intruder swung the stall door open and pointed a gun at her. "Well, thank you," the woman said. "Your getting sick was not what I had planned, but the timing is perfect."

Cynthia's eyes widened with terror. She stammered weakly, "I didn't tell the detective anything...honestly...I swear...Jonathon destroyed them when his office was remodeled. You have to believe me. There aren't any photos or videos."

"Liar! You know where they are!" the intruder snapped. "Never trusted you, you smug bitch. Always reporting back to Jonathon. I made a mistake by not taking care of you at the same time I disposed of him. It would have made a fabulous lovers' suicide pact. Well, we learn from our mistakes, n'est pas? Sorry we can't talk, but time is running out...for you, anyhow. I'm giving you one last chance."

Her ears picked up a sound and the intruder turned toward the door. Cynthia took advantage of the pause and swung the stall door at her adversary, throwing the woman off balance and to the floor.

Cynthia rose from her hands and knees and sprung up, but in her haste to flee her dress caught on the latch of the stall door and she lost her balance. Her assailant quickly regrouped, retrieved the gun, pounced on Cynthia, and brought the butt of the gun down on her jaw.

Conscious of the elapsed time, the intruder lifted Cynthia and propped her up on the toilet seat. Cynthia's body slumped and her head drooped. The intruder acted quickly, attached a silencer to the gun, picked up the wet towel, placed it on Cynthia's head and squeezed the trigger. Cynthia's body jerked up from the impact of the bullet, as the blood splattered onto the silvery wallpaper. She slipped off the toilet seat and slid to the floor like a disjointed rag doll.

The intruder stood up, ran to the mirror, checked her gown for blood, and hurried out of the ladies room. She looked around cautiously and then walked nonchalantly to join the guests, their heads swaying in rhythm, entranced by Lily's playing.

A piercing scream from the ladies room rendered the ballroom silent.

Detective Pagliara was the first police officer to witness Cynthia's lifeless body lying face up on the cold tile floor. With his cell phone, he alerted Clancy and then headquarters. Flashing his badge, he shouted at the hotel security personnel, "Keep everyone away from this area!" He checked Cynthia's neck, hoping that by some miracle she would still have a pulse. Overcome with guilt for not keeping a closer eye on Cynthia, he fought the burning sensation in the pit of his stomach and vowed to detach himself from Ms. Franny Goldsmith.

"What's happening?" Franny asked, looking at Lily, who sat dumbfounded at the piano. She turned to Elaine. "The place is in turmoil. I don't smell smoke. Can't be a fire." She looked around for Nick.

"It's not a fire," Elaine said. "Something happened in the ladies room. Nick ran over to check it out, and Lew and Dash followed him."

Clearly upset, Lily looked around. "I can't believe this is happening at my party."

"This will be a night to remember," Elaine said.

Franny lifted her gown, gripped the side of the piano and stepped up onto the piano bench. She searched above the crowd that surged toward the ladies room. "Yeah. Something *is* going on in the little girls room."

"Help me up," Lily said. "I have to see."

Elaine extended her hand to Franny and Lily. "Make room for me," she said, as they helped her up, and she stood alongside Lily and Franny.

"Who screamed?" Lily asked.

"We'll soon find out, girls," Elaine said. "Lew and Dash are coming this way. They'll tell us."

"Are you nuts?" Franny said. "This view is great." She waved at Lew and Dashel. "Hey, guys, over here."

Dashel held his arms out to Lily and lifted her off the bench.

Lew, frustrated at seeing Elaine standing there, shouted, "Are you crazy, Elaine? Let me help you down."

"In a minute, Lew."

"What's the story?" Franny asked as Dash helped her off the piano bench.

Lew's brows contorted. "It's Cynthia."

Franny's mouth scrunched up. "Yeah, she didn't look so hot. I bet she

253

fainted."

Lew shook his head. "If only that were true," he said.

The three ladies faced Lew. "She's dead, isn't she?" Lily cried.

"She's dead?" Elaine said, losing her balance. Lew caught her and sat her on the piano bench alongside her friends.

A squad of police officers secured the exits as Nick brushed by them and hurried to the podium. He picked up the microphone, cleared his throat and tapped to see if it was on. "Ladies and gentlemen, may I have your attention please? I am Detective Pagliara." A murmur ran through the room. His voice hoarse, he continued. "You are being detained for a short while. Remain at your tables until you are called. There is no cause for alarm and no immediate danger. You will be asked a few routine questions by the police and then will be free to leave. I can tell you only that a homicide has occurred." The guests stood nervously murmuring to one another, wondering who the victim was. Nick raised his hand. "Settle down, please. Cooperate and we will get this over as quickly as possible. I must warn you that anyone who resists will be taken into custody. Thank you." He noticed Franny looking at him and immediately avoided her gaze. He nodded at Clancy, and they left the podium and walked to the crime scene.

"Is the area secured?" Nick asked.

"The hotel security is sealing it off as we speak," Clancy said. "Our boys are on the way." They walked briskly to the ladies room as Franny sidled alongside them, trying to keep up.

"Hey, hold on a sec, Nick," she said. "Can't you stop for a minute?" Nick stopped in his tracks. His eyes squarely on hers, nostrils flaring, his voice coolly precise, he said, "Listen! I can't stop to chat. Get one of your friends to take you home later." He nudged Clancy. "Are the exits secured?"

"Already covered, Boss."

Nick turned on his heels, shook his head and rushed toward the crime scene.

Franny stood dumbfounded. She pictured herself sitting in bed crying, waiting for the telephone to ring, and hoping against hope that it was Nick, but knowing it would be Lily or Elaine.

Elaine and Lily approached. "What did he say?" Elaine asked, noticing Franny's dejected expression.

Franny didn't respond.

Crying, Lily said, "My beautiful night, ruined. What a mess." She eyed Franny. "You look like you're dying."

"I wish I were," Franny said dismally. "Cynthia's the lucky one. Her worries are over."

Chapter 46

All the next day and into the night, Franny holed up in her apartment and watched old movies on television. Her dearest friends couldn't shake her out of her depression. The Prozac the doctor had prescribed didn't seem to help, and when she called the precinct to speak to Nick she was told he was out.

Lily shouted outside of Franny's door. "Come on, Franny. I know you're in there. You can't hide forever."

"Go away," Franny shouted, her voice cracking. "I'm not receiving today. I'll call you...whenever. Just leave!"

"Listen," Lily shouted back, "I could have this door opened in two seconds. All I have to do is yell 'fire' or slip the super ten bucks."

Silence.

Lily bit her lip and whispered to Elaine, "You sure you don't mind? You know how she can get."

"Do it," Elaine mouthed.

Lily tapped on the door. "Well, Franny, I wasn't going to tell you, since you're so depressed...but it's about Elaine. She's..."

Suddenly the door swung open and Franny, hair disheveled, her bathrobe wrapped loosely about her, started to speak. But Lily and Elaine pushed past her and shut the door.

"Geez," Elaine said, holding her nose as she walked from window to window opening them. "What is that exterminator's number?"

"Now listen, you two," Franny started to say but was shoved down on the couch by Lily.

"No, *you* listen, lady," Lily shouted. "What happened to 'one for all and all for one'. Remember our pledge? We promised to suffer together, not alone. What gives you the right to go back on your word? If it had been me or Elaine, how would you react?"

Franny sat back. "What a cheap shot. You two finagled your way into my apartment on false pretenses." She looked up at Elaine, quizzically. "Lily was kidding when she said there was something she had to tell me about you, wasn't she?"

No one said anything.

Franny sprang up, placing her hands on her hips defiantly. "Well?" she snapped. "Don't fool around. Tell me!"

"You're like a rubber band," Elaine said. "You snap right back. I'm, shall we say, status quo. But we had to get to you so we could have some peace."

Franny shook her head. "Geez, you scared the shit out of me."

"Oh, so you *do* care about your so-called friends, whom you seem to have forgotten?" Elaine asked as she started putting the dirty dishes into the dishwasher.

"Don't clean, Elaine. I'll have the cleaning service do it."

Lily ran her finger over the dusty coffee table. "And when do you intend to go back to work, madam? Or are you taking an early retirement?"

"Listen," Franny pleaded. "I know that you mean well, but I just can't..."

Elaine rode over her words. "Can't what? Get over Nick? Don't tell me about heartbreak. I don't have all the time in the world, and I'm not going to waste what precious time I do have on things I can't control." Elaine and Lily sat on either side of Franny. "Lily had a falling out with Dash. She's suspicious of his actions. Seems, through the grapevine, she heard he's been cheating on her. And I have Lew, but for how long I don't know. You could still have a shot with Nick. Remember what he said about mixing business with pleasure?"

Franny showed surprise. "Lily, is that true?"

"If it's true that Dash is fooling around, I'll kill myself," Lily said.

Franny sighed. "Which means that I'm not alone in my misery, right?"

"Right!" Elaine and Lily said in unison. Lily smiled. "Now get yourself into the shower. We have an appointment to keep."

"I know," Franny said, a half smile on her face. "We're going to get facials at Georgette Klinger."

Lily shook her head. "No, we can do that later. We are going to meet with the dear, departed Dr. Jonathon Kent's lawyer, Filmore Tripplehorn. Remember, he told us at the cemetery he had information about Jonathon's will that might interest us? Well, I called him, but he was tighter than a clam about revealing anything over the phone."

"You don't think he left us a couple mil, do you?" Franny inquired. "We could cruise the world and toss all the men overboard."

"I don't have a good feeling about seeing the lawyer," Lily said. "The will was read last week and if we were included we would have been notified. But I sure am curious."

Elaine stared into space. "I could be overreacting but..."

Franny cut in. "Don't overreact, Elaine. That's my shtick. You analyze."

"That's true, but the last few weeks before he died, Jonathon didn't seem to care about our little remarks and innuendoes. In fact, now that I think about it, he smirked at them. As if he was on to us, laughing at us."

"Didn't do him much good, did it?" Franny said. She looked toward the heavens and raised her voice. "You listening, you pervert?"

"He did help us," Lily said.

"You mean, helped himself to us," Elaine said. "The thing that really helped was the group therapy sessions and the meditation periods after his private sessions with us. You know, I felt like I had awoken from a deep, satisfying sleep. So relaxed, so..."

Franny shook her head. "I always woke up feeling like I had been sedated. When I told him about it, he said I fought it. After a while I stopped the meditation. It gave me the creeps."

"I feel like Elaine does. I loved it," Lily said.

Franny rose from the couch and walked behind Elaine and Lily, cowering low, imitating a witch's snarling voice; "I am the illustrious Dr. Hardon, who is going to inject you with my latest invention, Sperma-sleep. It will relax you while I play in your garden. When I count to five you will awaken and remember nothing, but you will feel relaxed and happy."

Elaine and Lily turned to Franny, their minds connecting, and looking at each other as if a light had been turned on in their heads.

Chapter 47

A bove the jam-packed shelves of law books loomed the head of a stuffed moose whose glassy eyes pleaded to be closed. The odor of Bay Rum mingled with the aroma of freshly cut lavender roses in a Lalique vase gave the impression that the gentleman was a man of wealth, dignity and impeccable taste.

Filmore Tripplehorn rose as the three women, escorted by his middle-aged secretary, entered the room. His unruly eyebrows rose slightly in approval of their attractive appearance.

"Ms. Goldsmith, Ms. Fitzgerald and Mrs. Benjamin," his secretary announced, awaiting further instructions from her employer. He greeted them with a nod. She walked to the massive windows and drew back the heavy velvet drapes. "It is a perfectly glorious day. Why don't we let a bit of it in?" she said with the tenor of a doting grandmother.

"Miss Prudence has been with me forever," he said, extending his hand as he greeted each of the ladies. "I thought I would have heard from you before this, but with the ongoing investigation into Dr. Kent's death and the homicide at Ms. Fitzgerald's party, it is understandable."

He focused on Lily. "My congratulations on your last concert, Miss Fitzgerald. You were outstanding."

"Thank you. How good of you to attend."

"Actually, I am a frustrated pianist, unfortunately lacking the talent to reach the heights you have attained." He sighed. "And so, I turned to law. I am quite sure the critics breathed a sigh of relief at my choice."

Franny checked out the expensive decor. "From the looks of things, you made the right choice." She glanced at the moose head. "What a magnificent deer, and get those horns. Did you bag it?"

He eyed her warily, not sure if she was teasing. "It's a moose. And they are antlers." He chuckled. "And, yes, I *bagged* it on a hunting trip in Canada. Do you hunt?"

"No, but maybe I should give it a shot. I haven't been too successful with the two-legged animals."

Elaine and Lily gave Franny the evil eye. "Ms. Goldsmith means well," Elaine said. "She just has this habit of saying whatever comes into her mind."

"I find some of your chutzpah refreshing," Mr. Tripplehorn said, smiling at Franny. "This is a serious matter, so restraint is good under these circumstances. I'm not your lawyer and these records are yours per his last request."

Franny's face lit up. "You see!" she said, turning to Elaine and Lily. "Would you believe it, Mr. Tripplehorn, these two are constantly reprimanding me for my big mouth. I like the way you think."

"That is kind of you to say, Miss Goldsmith."

"I learned the word 'chutzpah' from Elaine," she continued. "Don't tell me it's in one of these law books."

"I was brought up in a multicultural ghetto in London, Miss Goldsmith."

"Call me, Franny. I hate my last name. And your wife, what does she call you?"

Elaine and Lily could not believe Franny's brazenness.

His smile was genuine as he diffidently covered his mouth with his

Norman Malamud

hand. "Trippy. She called me Trippy. I have been a widower for many years now."

Franny started to speak, but Lily cut her off. "We are very anxious to know why you wanted to see us," she said, rolling her eyes at Franny.

"Yes," Elaine chimed in. "It can't be that he left us money. I understand the will was read recently."

"Quite so, quite so," he said. "I am not sure if you are aware, but Jonathon...Dr. Kent, had a...well, what one might call a 'split personality.'"

"We're aware," Franny burst out. "A sick shrink with a split personality, giving advice to sick patients. What a hoot."

He hesitated, processing what Franny had said, and then concurred with a nod. "Unfortunately, we cannot put every doctor through an x-ray screen to prove his intentions before he adversely affects his patients." He half smiled. "Although, that might not be a bad idea."

Lily shook her head. "You knew of his complexities?"

Mr. Tripplehorn rose, walked to the window and stared at the courtyard below, his mind forming thoughts of times past. With a soft utterance, he forced his attention away from the view and looked down at the three faces turned up to him. He pulled a chair alongside them and sat down.

A low, mournful sigh parted his lips. "I have known Jonathon from the day he was born. I was his Godfather. A finer lad one couldn't find. Yes, he was feisty and spoiled...but intelligent, handsome and compassionate, until..."

"Until?" Lily asked.

"I'll get right to the essence of Jonathon's history. Jonathon was deeply in love with a very pretty girl, whom his controlling mother said was from the wrong side of the tracks. Mrs. Kent maliciously and verbally degraded the young lady to such a state that she committed suicide. Her suicide broke Jonathon's heart and spirit. I can only assume that the incident triggered Jonathon's misogyny."

Franny screwed up her face.

He clarified. "Dislike for the female gender. He set out to punish all women, probably thinking he was getting back at his mother. Since his demise I have uncovered…uh…how shall I put it? Well, let us say, matters that are pertinent to his patients. Which leads me to why I have asked you here."

They leaned forward in their chairs, eagerly watching as the lawyer reached into his desk drawer and withdrew three marked envelopes and handed one to each of them.

"I must in all honesty tell you that you are not the first to receive this kind of…" He pursed his lips. "I don't really know how to put it, but I imagine the contents to be self explanatory. They are similar to envelopes I have given other patients. Therefore, please brace yourselves, as the contents will be rather unpleasant."

"Boy," Franny exclaimed, "this is better than a Hitchcock movie. What's to worry? We didn't do anything wrong. I can't wait to open it."

"Don't be too sure, Franny," he cautioned. "Don't be too sure."

Lily slid the photographs from the envelope. Her eyes widened and her mouth dropped open in disbelief. "I can't believe it!" she exclaimed.

"Holy shit!" Franny shouted upon opening hers.

"Oh my God!" Elaine blurted.

The lawyer stifled a chuckle but feigned a serious face. "What do you have to say now, Franny? Still think it would make a good Hitchcock movie? Do you consider posing nude just an everyday occurrence?"

Franny shuffled through the photographs. "Let me see yours, Lily."

"Not a chance in hell!" Lily said.

They sat dumbfounded. Finally, Franny spoke up. "Look at this. He had to take me portrait size. When did the pervert take them? I swear, I never willingly posed for these." The others agreed.

"Let me enlighten you," the lawyer said. "Actually, you three are the last of Jonathon's patients that I have had the misfortune to hand these to, so I have a clue as to what might have transpired. Did you have a meditation period at the end of your private sessions?"

They nodded, and then eyed each other. Elaine said, "We were just discussing the meditation periods the other day, but we thought nothing of it. We felt relaxed afterwards. Except you, Lily. You said it made you uncomfortable."

"So what? He still managed to get me in focus." She bit her lip. "But wouldn't we have woken up or been aware of the camera? It wasn't like we were drugged."

Tripplehorn smiled knowingly. "Oh, but there's the rub. Have you heard of the drug, Rohipnol?"

"Sure," Franny said. "Everyone knows about it. It's called the 'forget pill' or in the better circles, the 'date rape drug.' But listen, we're not virgins. Why would he invade our privacy when we were unconscious? He could have had us anytime."

"Tell me about it," Lily offered. "I've lived through that scene."

"Would you have permitted him to photograph you nude when you were conscious?" he asked.

They shook their heads in unison.

"I thought not."

Elaine stood and paced the room, slapping her envelope against her thigh. "We were consenting adults led to believe that each of us was his one and only. It wasn't like we didn't know what we were doing when we had sex with him. He made us feel special at a time when we needed to feel special."

"And the sicko made out like he was shooting a porno film," Franny said. Elaine and Lily cringed with embarrassment. Franny's eyes connected with Tripplehorn's. "How many of these do you think are floating around?"

"That is what his other patients asked, and I will tell you what I told them. I don't know, but..."

"There's more?" Lily asked, alarmed.

"Son of a bitch," Franny said, under her breath. "I bet there are videos too. He was sick enough to do something like that."

"You were going to tell us what the other patients asked." Elaine sat again and leaned forward.

"When Detective Pagliara questioned me, he thought there were not only photographs but videos as well; Franny beat me to it." He smiled warmly at Franny and she returned his smile.

Thinking of Nick, her expression faded quickly. "So, the illustrious Sherlock Holmes has made an appearance, has he? Did he tell you that the three of us are under suspicion? And was Doctor Watson with him?"

Lily eyed Franny, smiling sourly at her, but Franny ignored her. "Can we get back to reality here?" She turned to the lawyer and asked, "Did Nick...I mean Detective Pagliara, shed any light on the case?"

Mr. Tripplehorn was about to laugh at Franny but quickly controlled himself. "Well, it's not for publication, but I see no harm in telling you." He directed his conversation to the ladies, but his eyes lingered on Franny a trifle longer.

"Detective Pagliara said, in so many words, that Jonathon might have suspected something was going to happen to him, that he had crossed the line, so to speak. Nick intimated that the reason Ms. Connors— Cynthia—was killed was because she knew who murdered Jonathon. And that she might possibly have a clue to where he kept more pictures and perhaps videos."

"God, videos, too! Then every one of Jonathon's patients is a suspect," Lily said.

He again pursed his lips.

Franny waved a hand of dismissal. "Anyhow, who gives a damn if they find them and publish them in the *Requirer*, the *Ladies Home Journal* or the *Kansas City Sentinel?* We didn't know he was taking them. We were innocent victims."

Elaine's anger was written all over her face. "*You* may not care, Franny. To you it would be what you call a 'hoot.' But how do you think it would affect Lew, having it spread around the garment center? He'd be embarrassed to death." She placed her hands on her hips. "And how about Lily? Can you see the headlines?" She held her hands up as if reading a newspaper. "Concert pianist plays Death March at shrink's demise." "All right, all right," Franny said, flailing her hands about her. "So I got carried away." She looked questioningly at Mr. Tripplehorn. "You're the lawyer, Trippy. What do you think?"

"First of all, I hate to see such close friends squabbling," he responded.

"Who told you we were close friends?" she countered. Never mind; it had to be Nick," Franny said. "Well, we *are*, despite our slight disagreements now and then." She looked at Elaine and Lily for confirmation.

"True," Elaine said. "So, what do we do now? Hire you as our attorney?"

"I'm afraid not. First, I am fairly certain that Jonathon would not make duplicate copies. It probably was one of his fetish pranks."

"That's a relief to hear," Lily said.

"Secondly, I represent the Kent estate. I would be disbarred." He narrowed his eyes at each of the women. "Why? Is there a reason for us to have a consultation?"

"Definitely not," Lily said sternly. "We're clean." She glanced at her friends. "But if there were, we would want you."

"Yeah," Franny chimed in, turning on her charm once again. "You wouldn't bankrupt us, would you Trippy? After all, I'm only a working girl."

"I understand," he said. "But, as I explained, that would be out of the question. There is one matter I would like to put forth. When this is over and you get back to living normal lives, you might consider suing the estate." He winked facetiously. "Of course it would be unethical for me to even suggest such a thing since I am bound to protect my client's interests."

"Sue?" Elaine asked. "On what grounds?"

"Offhand, I can think of some very valid grounds, but as of this moment, ladies, we never had this conversation."

He stood, suggesting that the appointment was concluded and politely distributed his business cards to Lily and Elaine. But he smiled fervently as he handed one to Franny. Their eyes locked as his mouth curled up at the edges. "Feel free to call…anytime."

Chapter 48

At the Hacienda Restaurant, Franny excused herself and walked towards the ladies room. She glanced over her shoulder at her friends, veered towards the bar and asked permission to use the phone. She sighed a "yeeeeess" as she rummaged through her purse, snapped up Filmore Tripplehorn's business card, and dialed his number. After she identified herself to Ms. Prudence, he answered. His voice almost melodic, he said, "Well, hello there. You didn't waste any time."

"You're right on target, Trippy," Franny said. "Listen, I thought we had a connection back at your office and being the impulsive, headstrong nymph that I am, I..."

He cut her off. "I'll have my chauffeur pick you up at your apartment at eight sharp. I have your address. We will dine at the Four Seasons. Dress accordingly and don't be late. Cheerio for now!"

Franny placed the receiver gently on its hook, smiled smugly, and said aloud, "Way to go, Trippy!"

"Win the lottery?" Lily asked, as Franny sat down at the table all aglow. "You're all lit up like the Christmas tree at Rockefeller Center. What gives?"

"*I'll* tell you what gives with 'Miss Hot To Trot,' over here," Elaine said, focusing on Franny but replying to Lily. "She's found a new '*Mister Gorgeous*' to concentrate on. A little past his prime, but if anyone can bring out the best in him, our girl can."

"So what if he's a little older than I am?" Franny said defensively. "I hate being alone. I need a new love interest to help me get over Nick. I know myself. If I don't fill the void, I'll slip back into my old depression." She looked to her friends for support.

Lily sipped her Margarita. "A new love interest, huh? Does that imply that you're using him to help you forget Nick? I suppose you think that *Trippy* doesn't see through your little game."

"Get over the Mother Teresa bit, Lily. Everyone uses everyone. It's a matter of giving and taking. He gives and I take. If it were the other way around I would be doing the giving. It evens out."

Elaine shook her head. "You lost me, but if it will get you over the bumpy road, good luck."

"And besides," Lily agreed, "it's only temporary. Like you said, Elaine. It will help our little lost lamb."

Elaine eyed Franny. "I'm not sure I trust your judgment, Franny. You have been known to do some pretty wild and crazy things. I wouldn't put it past you to make your relationship with your latest victim a permanent one."

Franny shrugged. "So? 'Que sera, sera,' as Miss Day sang it. You got something against older men with younger women? Look, if he and I can make a go of it, what's the harm? He's nobody's fool. I know he's onto me. I'm a challenge to him and he likes my style. He said so, remember?"

Lily sighed. "Well, I, for one, think we are picking the flowers before we plant the seeds."

"Mmm, I like that," Elaine said. "But we know our Franny. Anything is possible. Franny, dear, you wouldn't throw us over for a member of the opposite sex, would you?"

"Are you for real?" Franny countered. "I'd sooner cut my heart out. We're family. The guys are just window dressing."

Her phone rang and Lily reached into her bag, looked at the caller ID, her expression changing from jovial to sober. She put her finger to her lips and mouthed, "It's Nick." After a few seconds, she said, "Your office at three this afternoon?...Yes, I'll tell the ladies. Has something new developed?...I understand." She clicked off and stared at her friends.

"What?" they said in unison.

"He sounded serious. He's been trying to get hold of you two, but without any luck. Seems I'm the only one with a cell phone."

"Did he seem upset because he couldn't get hold of me?" Franny asked, a hint of hope in her voice. "I left my phone in my other bag."

Lily rolled her eyes. "You're going to drop Trippy and..."

"Oh back off, Lily. I was only..."

Elaine talked over them. "Drop it, ladies. What did he say, Lily?"

"That he wants to see us at three this afternoon at the station."

"Maybe they know who murdered Jonathon," Franny said. "Or Cynthia."

"I doubt it," Lily said thoughtfully. "If he wants to see us, it must concern us."

"That doesn't give us much time," Franny said. "It's one o'clock, and we haven't eaten. We better order."

Elaine spoke up. "What's the hurry, Franny? Want to hit the salon before you see Nick?"

"That's ridiculous," Franny said coolly. "I'm over him." Elaine and Lily rolled their eyes.

"Anyhow," Franny said, wanting to change the subject, "think we should call Trippy?"

"What for?" Lily asked. "We have nothing to hide. Are you forgetting that Trippy told us it would be a conflict of interest? And why, may I ask, would you ladies want to cover your asses with an attorney? We swore that we didn't do it." She looked suspiciously from Elaine to Franny. Her eyes narrowed. "Oh, no, please, don't tell me that one of *you*..."

Chapter 49

With Clancy looking over his shoulder, Detective Nicolas Pagliara drew outlines of suspected persons on his sketchpad and listed their names alongside the drawings in relationship to the data compiled concerning Jonathon's and Cynthia's murders.

Clancy asked, "Did you forget that Lieutenant McCarty wants to see you?"

Nick continued to focus on his sketchpad, deep in thought.

"I know how you hate to be disturbed when you're concentrating, but he had that bulldog look on his face. Better see what he wants."

"Let'im wait," Nick barked. "I want to finish this before I lose my train of thought. I know what he's going to say; that we're dragging our feet and the mayor and the governor are on his ass, because they're getting heat from the media. So, naturally, it has to trickle down to us. It's the same old bullshit. Damn media always looking to exploit a situation, even if it means ruining someone's reputation. Remember Avery, the CBS News dickhead who concocted that phony story and got the wrong guy sent to the slammer? God knows how many others are innocent and doing time."

Clancy nodded. "Yep, I remember that one. You got the guy off, right?"

The door swung open and the red-faced lieutenant, burst in, arms waving at Nick. "Picasso," he shouted, observing Nick's sketches as he slammed the door behind him. "I'll see that you're demoted down to desk sergeant if you don't give up doodling and get me some results on the Kent case, and pronto! Do you know the heat I'm getting from the top brass?"

"Yeah, yeah, Boss," Nick said nonchalantly, still working on his sketches.

"Don't pull that 'yeah, yeah' shit with me, Nick. I'm still the boss even if you don't like it. What the hell's going on in that egotistical, over inflated head of yours?" He snatched the drawing Nick was working on and studied it. "Mmm, what are these drawings, Rembrandt?" he asked, knowing full well that Nick was the best detective in the city, probably the state.

Nick shook his head and waved a finger at the chief. "Not nice," he taunted. "Didn't your mama teach you any manners? I was going to see you as soon as I finished my investigation, which, I might add, is coming to an end. Give me two days." The lieutenant started to speak, but Nick cut him off. "Relax. You can tell his holiness the captain, the mayor, the governor, and the divine powers that be, that your illustrious staff is on top of things and will be wrapping this case up within a few days." He smiled smugly.

The chief slapped Nick on the back. "I was just messing with you. I knew you were onto something. Just want to keep you on your toes." He turned and winked at Clancy. "I like the way you handle yourself, son. Keep up the good work." His hands deep in his pockets he stood over Nick and with a somber tone, said, "The wife has been after me to slow down or, as she put it, 'retire before the job does you in.' I've given a lot of thought to taking an early retirement. Maybe take a trip around the world." He waited for Nick's reaction.

Nick stood. "You should listen to your wife," he said, knowing that the lieutenant's health had been rocky. "After giving your all to the job, it might be a wise decision."

The lieutenant smiled warmly at the man he respected and admired, the man he watched grow from a young, cocky rookie, into an honest, dedicated, brilliant deputy chief detective. "And, Nick, I'm going to recommend to the board that you take my place. And incidentally, there's a meeting in the captain's office in an hour."

Nick embraced the man who had been a father figure and mentor to him. "I'll never be able to fill your shoes, but if I'm offered the job, I'll give it my best shot."

"You're so full of it, Nick. I can see you counting the days until I leave so you can put your feet up on my desk." He walked toward the door, not wanting them to see the tears that filled his eyes.

"Take it easy," Nick called out as the lieutenant faced the outer office, nodded and waved an affirmation. Nick came face to face with Clancy. "Okay, hot shot, let's get this show moving. Call the three ladies and cancel our appointment with them," he said, thinking there wasn't any valid reason to question them, but merely an excuse to see Franny. "Let's see if we can put this case to bed." He picked up the phone, put it to his ear, then slammed it down into the cradle.

"What's wrong?" Clancy asked, knowing that Nick had been feeling pangs of guilt over his icy treatment of Franny.

Clancy walked closer to Nick and stood over him. "I may be talking out of turn, but why don't you call her, Boss?" Nick's eyes widened, but before he could answer, Clancy spoke. "Go ahead, take my head off. I know I'm stepping over the line, but since you decided to write her off, you've been...well, a real ball buster. You're just kidding yourself. I have eyes, you know."

"She'll hang up. I did a stupid thing by mixing business with pleasure." His voice was flat. "I'll get over it. We have more important things to attend to." Still, he felt his heart was heavy. He wasn't over her.

Chapter 50

The Rolls Royce convertible took command of the road as it sped along the Bronx River Parkway. Franny untied the ribbon that held her ponytail in place and let the wind take over.

"Happy?" Trippy asked, his heart full of admiration for this young, attractive lady at his side.

Placing her hand on his knee, she snuggled closer to him, leaned her head against the headrest and reminisced about the whirlwind relationship that had blossomed from their dinner at the Four Seasons two weeks ago.

Lily made sure Franny was molded into an elegant, black silk, high-neck, above-the-knee creation by Oscar de la Renta. Franny had balked at the plain little black dress, but Lily, with Elaine's help, won out and convinced her to dress chic for her first date with Fillmore Tripplehorn. His radiant smile when the chauffeur held the limo door open for Franny proved the ladies right. During dinner the conversation was light, and they avoided talking about legalities, her girlfriends, and Detective Nicolas Pagliara.

At his country estate the following weekend the stable hands saddled up Arabian stallions for an afternoon of riding, and the chauffeur followed them by limo into the countryside with picnic baskets of food, cheese and wine.

Friday evening, after a candlelight dinner on the terrace, he took her hand and led her into the master bedroom, where he held her at arm's length, drinking in her youth and loveliness. In a slow, sexual manner he removed each item of her clothing and kissed her there, and led her to the floating island. They lay for long moments facing each other in the huge waterbed…naked…not speaking…not touching…eyes locked…bodies in a deep undercurrent, ebbing and flowing…together…apart, drifting in the awareness of each other's desires until the passion became too great to resist.

"Why are you so distant, Franny," he asked, as he covered her hand with his. "Are you happy?"

Shaking her head to clear her thoughts, she squeezed his hand. "Happy? I'd have to be out of my bird not to be happy."

"You certainly have a way with the English language," he said, then added before she could respond, "not that I'm complaining. I adore your manner of speech and your frankness. In fact, as I mentioned before, it's refreshing."

"Yeah, but there's a heluva lot of people who would disagree with you, Trippy. And maybe they're right. I do mouth off more than I should. But even when I try to control myself, somehow words just slip out before I realize it. You have no idea how many times I've regretted saying the first thing that comes into my head."

"Therapy didn't help much, did it?" he chided.

"Are you friggin nuts?" She gestured with her hands. "You see? Now there's a perfect example."

He shook his head. "People will just have to accept you for the virtues you have. And Franny, you have many," he said, his smile warm and loving. "I'm glad you're happy."

"Like I said, Trippy. Why shouldn't I be happy? I'm riding in style. You take me to the finest restaurants. Shower me with gifts and you want to set me up in my own apartment in Manhattan." She snuggled closer to him. "A girl would have to be insane not to be happy."

"You have given me back my youth, Franny. It's what most older men would give anything for."

She pulled away from him. "Why do you always bring up your age? You know it irritates the hell out of me. If I don't care, why should you? Besides, the only thing about you that's old is your antiques. You look a good twenty years younger than you are, and your performance in the sack is a hell of a lot better than a lot of studs half your age. And where am I going to find a lawyer who gives me free advice?" She moved closer to him, caressing the nape of his neck with her fingers.

He took in a deep breath and let it out with a long mournful sigh.

"What's with the heavy sigh, Trippy? Something on your mind?"

He didn't answer.

She teased. "You've found a younger woman! Is that it? I should have known better. I get the picture. Just wanted to get into my panties and now I'm yesterday's news." His silence disturbed her. She became serious. "C'mon, tell me. What's wrong?"

He spotted a rest area and pulled the car into the parking space. "Let's sit," he said. "It's so beautiful here."

"Sure." She dreaded his next move as they walked hand-in-hand to the picnic table and sat down. She spoke non-stop. "Just love the smell of the fresh cut grass and the picturesque sight of cows grazing. My mother used to take me to the country when I was young. We picked all kinds of berries. I'd eat them and get sick. I especially loved the blackberries. Hated camp—all those dumb kids trying to outdo each other. Did you go to camp?"

"Stop it!" he said sharply.

She looked away from him. "Stop what? Talking? Why? Don't you like blackberries?"

"Franny, stop rambling!"

The ultimate victory over her demons fell apart as the tears started to trickle down her face. "I don't want to hear anything you have to say." Not able to hide her true feelings she started sobbing. "I know what's coming. If you want to break up, it's all right. No hard feelings. There's nothing to discuss. We don't have a contract that says you have to stay with me." She took a deep breath, trying to control her emotions. "Please, Trippy, I don't have the courage or strength for this. I can't do it. I just can't take another rejection."

He removed a handkerchief from his pocket and dabbed at her eyes, and took hold of her hands. "You are the most unusual woman I have ever had the good fortune to know," he said, his eyes showing more than compassion. "Why in the world would I want to leave you? If anything, I am the one that is playing for time. You speak of our age difference as if it doesn't matter, but it does. Face it, Franny, I'm more than twice your age."

She started to speak, but he shushed her. "Listen to me. I want you for as long as you want me. I have no intentions of getting married again. Not that I wouldn't marry you in a heartbeat. It's your future I'm thinking about. You're young; you'll want to have children, a family, and that's how it should be for you."

"I'm going to be thirty five. And I'm not sure I want any dirty diapers in my life."

"At the moment, I'm someone who can show you a good time. Help you forget your problems, but I'm benefiting too." His fingers tightened against hers. "You've made me happier than I thought I could ever be. We're using each other...but in a good way. You don't love me, Franny. You love someone else. I'm what you would call a temporary shelter from the storm. I'm a father image with whom you can find refuge. Oh, I don't mind. In fact, I'm selfish enough to hold onto you for as long as you will let me. And then, when you find the right person, I'll send you off with my blessings. I promise."

A small spider crept along the crack of the redwood table and stopped between Franny and Trippy. "Look at her," Franny said, pointing to the insect. "She's not sure which way to go."

"What do you think she should do?" he asked. "What would you do if you were her?"

Studying the spider, Franny said thoughtfully, "I think she's frightened. Like me, she's unsure of herself. I guess her first impulse would be to go where she's safe...secure, and loved."

Trippy opened his arms to her. He smiled warmly. "Come to me, Franny. I love you, and I'll keep you safe until it's time for you to go."

Chapter 51

The tennis balls bounced relentlessly at Amelia Stern, but she paid little attention to them. "Don't you think you should shut the damn machine off until I perfect my swing?" she asked the instructor.

He placed his hand over hers. "Concentrate on what I'm telling you, Mrs. Stern. The machine spits the balls out automatically. No extra charge." He leaned his body closer to her, his hardness pressing lightly against her buttocks. "Don't let the racquet control you," he said. "Now bring the racquet back and go for it." He stepped away as she hit the ball over the net. "That's it," he said. "You're doing well. I have a feeling you've played before," he said, having seen her volleying with her lady friends on the courts. "Your husband is an excellent player." He placed his body in back of her again and gripped her racquet. "That was good. Now keep the racquet at this angle. Try it again."

"My husband is too busy at the hospital," she scowled. "I have to take care of my extracurricular activities all by myself." She shifted her buttocks against him.

"You shouldn't neglect your body, Mrs. Stern. Let your trainer take care of you. That's what he gets paid for."

She turned toward him, her face close to his, her look intense. "Exactly what I've been thinking, Max." She wet her lips and glanced down at the bulge in his shorts. "I don't intend to neglect my body."

He quickly followed up. "You know, I not only teach tennis but I give massages, too. Best thing to keep your body in condition after a game or lesson."

"Versatile, aren't you? I could use a rubdown after this grueling lesson. Do you have time, or are you booked?"

"Well, if we cut this lesson short I could manage to fit you in." He glanced at his watch. "Guess not. I am pressed for time. Can I do it at our next session and just concentrate on practicing your serve for now?" He smiled. "We only have about twenty minutes."

"Now!" she said, her voice sounding like a drill sergeant.

His brows lifted with surprise. "Yes, Ma'am!" He brushed a towel across his forehead. "But the massage rooms are taken. We could use the gardener's cottage. It's clean and private." He looked at her questioningly.

"Well, don't stand there wasting time," she ordered. "We only have twenty minutes." She eyed him. "I'm not easily satisfied, Max."

His crooked smile showed insolence. "I think I can handle whatever you toss at me."

"Don't come crying that you didn't know what you were getting into."

"Tell you what, Mrs. Stern. Let me make a call and see if I can cancel my next appointment. Here's the cottage. You, uh, relax while I call the assistant pro. I'll just be a minute."

The door squeaked as he led her in, turned, then stepped outside and called the clubhouse on his cell phone. "Burt, dude. I need you to do me a huge favor. Can you cover for me with Mrs. Hartman's three o'clock lesson?…Yeah, got a quickie at the cottage….Give her the usual serving techniques. Wouldn't hurt if you nuzzled up a little. Her history is on my agenda chart. Thanks. I owe you."

He entered the cottage, locked the door, and stood over her, ready to pounce; his lean, muscular, six-four frame and insolent smile challenged her.

Propped up on an elbow, eyes beckoning him, she purred, "Time's a wasting. Come over here. Let's see what you've got."

Chapter 52

Daylight faded as the last speck of light vanished from the horizon, leaving the office dimly lit. Clancy turned to Nick. "You going to wrap it up for today?"

No answer.

Clancy walked to the light switch and flipped it on. He prompted, "Light would be good here." Nick stared into space, ignoring Clancy, but Clancy continued. "Right. Guess it's going to be one of those all-night sessions. I'll go to the deli and pick up some dinner. Anything special you want? Thursday is chicken ala king or goulash at The Grill. Any preference?"

Silence.

"You want me to make the decision, right?" Clancy shrugged. "Right," he repeated. He waved his hand in front of Nick's face. Not getting a response, he walked toward the door.

Nick called after him. "Hold on, Clancy. Where did you say you were going?"

"I think you've been working too hard, Boss. I've been trying to get your attention, been waiting for you to come back down to earth. Want to share your thoughts? This case is wearing you down." The wooden floor creaked as Clancy stepped to the door, hesitated, and then turned on his heels. "You know, Boss, I hate to tell you but it's getting me nuts. I gotta say it."

Nick raised his head, making eye contact with Clancy. "Yeah? Say what?"

Clancy took in a deep breath and blew it out. "Okay, here goes. This thing with Franny…"

Nick winced.

Clancy, thinking he had spoken out of turn, quickly changed the subject. "Did I hear you tell the lieutenant this case is practically wrapped up? Where did that come from?"

No response.

Oh, boy, Clancy thought, *he's zoning out again.* He shook his head. "I'm going for the food."

Nick ran his hands over his face. "Hold on, Clancy! I need to talk." He folded his arms defensively. "All I want is to do my job, and then from out of nowhere, boom, she pops into my life. What the hell is wrong with me? Why did I let myself get involved with a woman who's a suspect in my case?"

"Come on, Boss. Things happen." He looked down and scratched below his ear. "The truth is, since you've given me permission to express my opinion…" He waited to read Nick's face, walked to Nick's desk, swung a chair opposite him and sat down.

Nick gave him a long, serious look. "What?"

"Face it, Boss. It's not only Franny that's jamming up your head. It's Teresa. She's been dead for over two years. Maybe it's time to move on. Do you think she'd want you to mourn the way you are?"

Nick cocked his head to the side, stood, reached across his desk and clapped Clancy on his shoulder. "Get you, Father Clancy. You should have been a priest."

"Funny you should say that. I thought of entering the priesthood."

"What changed your mind?"

"I knocked up a girl. And after my dad beat some sense into me I realized I was heading in the wrong direction. My parents thought the world of me and I felt bad for having disappointed them. Especially Mom. She counted on me to be president. I guess the guilt got the better of me." He grinned at Nick. "Anyhow, the priesthood wasn't for me, and no one was asking me to run for president."

A half smile emanated from Nick's face. "I know you mean well. Now, how about some food? I'm hungry. Don't go out. Call the Grill for a delivery. I want to run something by you."

"Chicken ala king or goulash?" Clancy asked.

"Neither. They give me heartburn. Make it a hot pastrami and chopped liver combo on seeded rye."

Clancy rolled his eyes and dialed the restaurant. "Hi Alice...Fine...No, delivery...Yeah, we're working late again. I'll have an order of goulash, heavy on the gravy and a couple of slices of that Italian bread to soak up the gravy, and a small salad...Russian. And a hot pastrami-liver combo on seeded rye, mustard and mayo on the side, two Heinekens, and a large Tums....You think that's funny, huh? And Alice, don't forget the pickles."

He sat down facing Nick. "What's up, Boss? You onto something?"

"Know anything about psychics, Clancy?"

Clancy grinned. "Funny you should ask. I interviewed people with psychic ability for a thesis assignment in college. It was interesting and, at times, eerie."

"I take it you don't believe in psychic ability or the hereafter. Why did you decide to do a thesis on that subject?"

"I didn't pick it. The professor assigned it to me. I wanted to trade with another student, but the professor nixed it. At first I dreaded the assignment, but after a while I really got into it. I felt myself being drawn to the subject more and more. You wouldn't believe the number of books that have been written about clairvoyance, spiritualism and the like. Do you know that we all have psychic ability? We just don't put it to use."

Nick stroked his chin thoughtfully. "I knew there was more to you than meets the eye. What do you think about us using a psychic?"

"You're kidding, right?"

"I'm serious."

"Am I missing something, Boss? You *did* tell the lieutenant you'd have this case sewn up in two days? What gives?"

"I had to get him off my back. He's getting hounded and I knew I was next in line to get reamed out."

"I figured you were stalling him. You sure put your hand in the oven."

"I've gotten burned before. Our problem is lack of evidence. The forensic people haven't come up with anything concrete. All the trace evidence lifted from Kent's body—the fingerprints, stray hairs, etc.—are from too many different people. Anyone of his patients could have done it. Or maybe someone who wasn't a patient."

"What about the three ladies?"

"Do you know how many women used the ladies room at the party? At least seventy-five, and that's not counting other events that took place at the hotel. And it didn't help that some idiots contaminated the crime scene before we had a chance to secure it. And…all the suspects have alibis."

Is that what made you come up with the psychic?"

"Maybe."

"The department has used them before."

"Not with much success."

"It's worth a try, Boss."

"We'll have to keep it under wraps for a while."

"Yeah, I know a few guys who would love to razz you about it."

Sometime later the intercom rang. Clancy walked to the door and took the bag of food from the desk sergeant. "Grub's here, Boss."

Clancy unwrapped the food and set his order of goulash on his desk and placed Nick's sandwich in front of him. "You won't mind if I dine at my desk?" he asked. He screwed up his nose. "Hot pastrami and liver don't mix with goulash." He loosened the cap on the beer bottle and handed it to Nick. "Have anyone in mind?"

"I researched a woman in New Jersey who's had success locating lost children, like the kids you see on the milk cartons and flyers. I've been thinking about contacting her. Discreetly, of course."

"I hate to think of what would happen if this leaked out. Especially since the lieutenant is expecting us to close the case in two days."

Nick unwrapped the sandwich, opened it and spread a thick glop of mustard and mayonnaise over the pastrami, closed it and took a big bite. "Yum," he said. "The Grill makes the best combo. How's the goulash?"

"It isn't like Mom's, but it's okay." He shook his head, wondering how Nick could eat this concoction. "Want me to check her out?"

Nick wiped the mustard off his lips with his napkin. "Yep. Start the ball rolling. I understand she's retired. Contact her and convince her it's her duty as a concerned citizen to use her abilities to help us find this double murderer. Then after you get her to agree to work for us we'll set up a meeting."

"You want me to contact her first? You're the one with all the powers of persuasion."

"Not this time. You have the youth and boyish charm that women find irresistible. And besides, you're already familiar with the world of parapsychology."

Clancy's brows questioned Nick's remark. "Boyish charm, huh? It would help if I had her name and address."

"I just told you, New Jersey. How much info do I have to give you? Do I have to do all the work?" Nick chomped on a pickle and then washed it down with the beer.

"C'mon, Boss."

Nick grinned. "I have to get rid of you, Clancy. You're onto me." He winked at his assistant. "Her name is Marcy Pinchic, and she lives in Totowa. Get on it first thing in the morning."

"Nobody likes to be bothered first thing in the morning, Boss. I'll go to her house and check her out first. She'll probably be working in her garden. I studied horticulture, too." He screwed his mouth to one side. "Boy, we need more time."

"Time is running out, Clancy. We've gotta get something going."

Chapter 53

The imposing New York City skyline gave way to the tree-lined cliffs of the Palisades, and the sun reflected off the waters of the Hudson River, as Nick and Clancy drove over the George Washington Bridge to New Jersey. "Do you believe it?" Nick said. "I remember my dad telling me how angry he was when they raised the toll from a dollar to two bucks. Now it's eight freaking dollars."

"It's actually four dollars each way. You just pay going into Jersey, not coming back."

"What if you don't go back?"

"Then you lose four dollars. I think it's done to ease the rush-hour traffic."

"Could've built a dozen bridges to relieve the traffic with the money they squeeze out of the commuters."

"Well, they tried. The upper level is called the Martha Washington." He glanced at Nick. "Martha on top of George, get it?"

Nick rolled his eyes. "Was the psychic agreeable to having lunch? From what you told me, she didn't warm up to you all at once."

"Like *I* told you, Boss, she's devoted to charities and social work. Spends most of her time working with mentally challenged children and in her garden. Wants to forget about any psychic abilities she possesses.

Says they interfere with her life. Her husband left her well off. And we are very lucky, too."

"Yeah? How come?"

"She was very emphatic about not wanting any publicity. She said she would help us if she had our word on that. In fact, she asked me if you could be trusted to go along with it."

"Why? What did you say that would make her think otherwise?"

Clancy flinched. "Yeah, Boss. I told her you were a hard-nosed detective." He hesitated. "Tell you the truth, she said she had a cloudy impression about you."

"Now who's playing with whose head? What'd you do, show her my high school yearbook?"

"No. I didn't have to. She asked me who else would be working with me and I told her you were and that you were my boss. And I gave her your statistics. Then she closed her eyes and said that she had a cloudy impression about you and that you're confused."

"You didn't mention she said that I was confused a minute ago."

"I thought the timing was bad. You know, because of your situation with Franny being a suspect and all."

"Well, you can rest your mind. I didn't call Franny. I got cold feet and chickened out." He glanced fleetingly at Clancy and then back to the road. "I'm having her watched."

"You lost me. Having who watched?"

"Franny. And the reason I decided not to call her is because I got word she's seeing someone."

"Get out of here! Who?"

"Filmore Tripplehorn."

"Kent's lawyer? No way. He's old enough to be her father."

"I thought so too, but it's been hot and heavy between them." His mouth tightened. "Listen, I don't want to talk about her anymore, okay?

Tell me more about the crystal ball lady. She must be good if she read me without seeing me…although…they use trigger words—like everyone has problems. What does she look like? No, don't tell me. Scraggly blond dyed hair, weighs two hundred pounds, is short, has a round face and talks incessantly."

"How did you know all that?" Clancy asked, lying. "From research?"

"No, from years of experience. When do we turn?"

"Have to watch for the Union Boulevard exit. It's partially hidden by the overgrown foliage. There it is. We go straight here and turn on Maple Lane. It's a gated area. She said she would let the guard house know."

"Very impressive," Nick said, observing the large homes and manicured lawns. "Is she divorced or did her husband pass away?"

"They were in the throes of a divorce."

"Divorce can be a ball buster. Once they find out you're not coming back, forget it."

"There's the gate."

"We're here to see Mrs. Pinchic," Nick said, half smiling at the guard who looked them over warily.

"I'll announce you if you'll just wait a minute, please," the guard said politely. "Yes, Mrs. Pinchic. I'll direct them to your home." He eyed Clancy. "You were here the other day, right?"

Clancy nodded. "I know the way, thanks." The guard placed a visitor's card underneath the windshield wiper and pressed a button allowing the gate to open.

"That's it at the top of the hill," Clancy said.

The aroma of flowers hung heavily in the air, complementing the stone-carved angels that seemed to cast a protective aura over the house and its inhabitant. Nick raised his hand, reaching for the doorknocker, when the door swung open revealing an attractive woman dressed in a Chinese kimono.

"Mrs. Pinchic," Nick said inquiringly. "We have an appointment with Mrs. Pinchic."

The lady smiled as Clancy poked Nick. "This *is* Mrs. Pinchic."

"Marcy," she said, smiling, "and you must be Detective Pagliara." She eyed Nick. "Uh huh, so you're the one who's troubled."

She led them through the entrance hall and onto the terrace. "I hope you don't mind the outdoors. I hate to lose even one minute of daylight."

Nick whispered to Clancy. "I'm going to get you for playing with me."

Mrs. Pinchic waved a warning finger at Nick. "Hostile, too," she said with a grin. "We don't allow such thoughts in this house. Creates bad karma."

Clancy lowered his head, avoiding Nick's eyes.

Nick spoke. "Quite a garden you have, Mrs. Pinchic. I suppose you have gardeners helping you." He inhaled. "And the aroma...I imagine the Garden of Eden had the same heavenly fragrance."

"Marcy. Call me Marcy. My husband said that. He compared my garden to the Garden of Eden." She frowned and added, "Until I discovered the essence he really liked was the marijuana he was growing in the back acre. Anyhow, I'm glad to know that you appreciate the finer things in life, Detective."

Nick smiled. "At least you picked up on my good vibrations. Call me Nick."

She studied Nick as she set a tray of sandwiches and iced tea on the table. "Help yourselves, gentlemen. As I told Clancy, I'm not thrilled to take on this assignment, but Clancy convinced me to help." She took a bite of her sandwich and chewed it slowly. Then she patted her mouth with her napkin, placed it delicately on her lap and smiled demurely, her blue eyes sparkling. "Oh, don't for one minute think I didn't know he was trying to sweet-talk me, but in spite of it I did receive good vibrations from him. No, compelling vibrations."

Nick looked at her inquiringly. "Compelling?"

"It happens, but not usually as quickly. I felt a connection and that's a good sign."

Clancy looked at Nick, wondering if he should ask what she referred to. "Join in, Clancy," Nick said. "Mrs. Pi...uh...Marcy has good vibrations about you. You're one of the chosen people."

She tossed her flaming red hair to one side and smiled. "Now, Nick, don't pout. You have redeeming qualities as well. It just so happens that Clancy is one of the chosen people. Well, on his mother's side anyhow." She arched her eyebrows at Clancy for confirmation.

Nick stared at Clancy. "Did you tell Marcy that your mother was Jewish and your father was Irish?"

Marcy placed her hands on her hips. "Really. If that's all the faith you have in me..." She motioned with her thumb towards the door.

Nick and Clancy looked bewildered.

"I was only teasing. All right, down to business." Settling her shoulders against the back of her chair, she took a deep breath. "I feel connected. Did you bring the articles I asked for?"

Clancy sprang to his feet. "They're in the car. I'll get them."

She waited for Clancy to leave then asked Nick to hold out his hands. He felt a warm, tingly sensation pass from her hands to his as she touched his fingers "You're not doing yourself or your job any good, Nick. You have to separate business from pleasure."

"Tell me about it," he countered.

She spoke with conviction. "I'm quite serious. I feel your skepticism and I forgive your ignorance, but you would be wise to heed my advice." She met his eyes. "Forget everything else and concentrate on your job. Your personal issues will work themselves out. Chalk it up to bad timing. Until you clear your mind, and the other party finds her way, there is nothing you can do to rectify the situation."

Nick's eyes widened. "But I was the one who ended the relationship."

"Do I get a reading, too?" Clancy interrupted as he entered.

Marcy maintained her grip on Nick's hand. "You don't need a reading, Clancy. You're doing just fine." She stood. "Let's go into the study and get started. I think we're in for a thunderstorm."

Clancy looked out of the window. "Thunderstorm? Not a cloud in the sky."

She stared straight ahead, her eyes wide. "Now, who shall I begin with?"

"Why not start with Dr. Kent," Nick answered.

She shook her head with annoyance. "I wasn't asking you. I was thinking aloud. Please, while I am ruminating do not speak to each other or to me. I am centering myself so that the information comes. It takes all my concentration. Interruptions only hamper me."

The room turned dark as the sun slid behind the clouds. With eyes closed, Mrs. Pinchic opened the envelope marked Cynthia Connors and withdrew an earring, which she rubbed between her thumb and forefinger. She sat very still for one minute then spoke. "This is the earring the lady wore the evening she was murdered," she said, her voice husky, an octave lower than usual. "There's restlessness within her soul. She can't understand why she cannot cross over. Others around her are trying to comfort her, but they're not able to reach her. She is trying to get to us, to tell us what she knows."

Nick and Clancy looked at each other.

Marcy slumped back in her chair as a streak of lightning flashed through the room and was followed by a clap of thunder. She placed her hands to her face and sat still for a moment, when suddenly her eyes snapped open. Blinking repeatedly, she announced, "That's it, gentlemen. Mother nature has cancelled today's session. I'm sorry, I cannot continue." She looked at their dejected faces. "Now, don't pout. I'll be in touch."

Nick's face dropped. "Are you sure? I know this must be very trying for you, but I can't tell you how important it is that we have this information...not that we want to impose on you...but time is of the essence...with all due respect..."

She held her hands up. "Stop right there! "I understand what you are saying and I sympathize with your plight, but there is nothing more I can do right now. Even if I wanted to, I couldn't. I'll be in touch as soon as I get word from the beyond."

Nick bit his lip. "Well, if you can't, you can't. I'm sure you did your best. We appreciate your help."

"You will hear from me."

Nick turned to Clancy. "Well, we better get going. I'll just gather up the envelopes."

"No!" she stated. "Leave them. I'll need them when I feel the time is right." She eyed Nick. "You do trust me, don't you?" She stared him down. "Or you could stay and wait..." she gestured eerily with her hands, "until the spirits contact me."

Nick shrugged, knowing she was teasing him. "We're available twenty-four hours a day," he countered, pressing his business card into her upraised hand. "Just send us a telepathic message and we'll appear on your doorstep quicker than you can say, 'there's no place like home' three times."

Chapter 54

At five o'clock the next morning, just as Nick finally fell asleep after a night of tossing and turning, the shrill ringing of the telephone awakened him with a start. "Pagliara here," he said.

Three sharp clicks resounded over the phone and a voice said, "There's no place like home, there's no place like home, there's no place like home."

He bolted out of bed. "You're connected," he said excitedly. "I'm on my way. Just have to throw on some clothes."

She laughed lightly. "I should hope so; otherwise you might be arrested for indecent exposure."

He looked down at his genitals, wondering if she could see them, too. He stuttered, "I'll pick up Clancy and see you soon."

"I'll call the gate to let you in. I'll have coffee ready and I whipped up a cake to nosh on."

"Don't tell me you baked at this hour of the morning," he said, poking his leg into his trousers.

"Don't be ridiculous. I just waved my magic wand and 'poof,' apple crumb cake appeared."

•

"Wow! On wings of song," she exclaimed, opening the door for them. "You made it in twenty minutes flat."

"There wasn't any traffic at this hour and we had the emergency flashers on until we got to the Jersey side," Clancy said. "Mmm. Smells like my grandma's been baking here. Makes my mouth water."

Marcy acknowledged Clancy's compliment with a smile. "I set up a snack. I know you men are always hungry and I feel comfortable working in the den." "A psychic and a baker, too," Nick said. "I have to admit, you aren't at all what I expected." He gritted his teeth, wondering if maybe he shouldn't have said that. "I mean..."

"I know what you meant," she said, pouring the coffee into mugs. "Help yourself to cream and sugar, and..." she hesitated, "but you both drink it black and no sugar. The cake's sliced. Help yourselves." She glanced at them as they both took two helpings of the cake at once. "Vanilla ice cream goes great with crumb cake," she suggested. She went to the refrigerator, removed the ice cream from the freezer, scooped two healthy servings into a dish and placed it in the microwave. "Bachelors," she said, shaking her head, "and for breakfast, no less."

"You're right," Nick said, wondering if he should take another piece of the cake. "It's fast food most of the time. We wolfed down Egg Mc Muffins from the twenty-four-hour joint on the way over." He eyed the cake then decided against asking for another helping. "We can always eat." After taking a sip of his coffee he asked, "We're eager to hear what you've turned up."

She pushed two pieces of the cake toward the men then stood abruptly and sat back down. She eyed the men with concern. "Cynthia is distraught and keeps trying to contact me, but she can't seem to get through to me. I felt with you here, and the articles you brought, I might be able to have more success.

"Let me set the record straight. I've read about the murders in the paper and seen clips on television, but I don't put much faith in either of them. The media captures the public's attention and manipulates the news just enough to keep us interested." She stood, pushed her chair away from the table and circled the room. "I say this so you will know that I am in no way influenced by the media. To them, it all comes down to money. The television and news media are only interested in boosting their ratings and circulation even if it hurts someone badly. I want to keep my life as private as possible." She stopped and faced Nick and Clancy. "Had enough?" Both men nodded. "Then let's go into the den."

Clancy rose, picked up the dishes and mugs, stacked them noiselessly in the sink and turned on the water. Marcy glanced at Nick. "Where did you find him? No, better yet, let him stay after you leave."

The room was as somber as Marcy's mood. Picking up a lock of Cynthia's hair, she stared at it, placed it in the palm of her hand and covered it with Cynthia's handkerchief. Sitting perfectly still, her body rigid, she sought answers from the beyond.

When at last she showed signs of movement, Marcy mumbled incoherently and her hands trembled. The men leaned forward, waiting anxiously for her to divulge something, anything. Her closed eyes quivered, her sealed lips revealed nothing and they sat back in their seats. After a few minutes, she stirred and let out a deep moan. "Who are you trying to describe?" she asked. "What kind of box? Stay with me. Don't go, don't go."

Nick and Clancy edged forward. Marcy shook her head and opened her eyes. She placed the lock of hair and handkerchief back in the plastic envelope. "Cynthia, Dr. Kent's receptionist, is not at peace. She's trying to tell us about a box or person that would shed light on who the murderer is." She shrugged. I'm losing her. She's gone for now. I kept getting signs that Cynthia is trying to warn us about something…someone close by, and…"

Nick leaned forward. "And?"

"And…that's it for the present."

"Damn it," Nick said. "And you seemed so close."

"Funny you should say that." Clancy's eyes darted around the room. "I have had the strangest feeling that someone's been watching us."

"So have I," Marcy said. "But I get so many messages that I can't account for. One thing is sure. Cynthia will be back. She has to or she won't rest in peace." Nick and Clancy's faces showed disappointment. "You're wondering when, aren't you? I'm sorry, but these things can't be rushed. I believe Cynthia is trying to tell us who the murderer is. Help me out here, gents."

Nick stroked his chin thoughtfully. "Well," he said, "we know that the doctor took nude photos of his patients while they were under sedation, and there could be videos. We're not sure about that, though three of his patients have said they thought he sensed they might be onto him and hid the evidence. Maybe that's what she is trying to tell you."

"I think there's more. Cynthia would not be as adamant. She was killed because she recognized the murderer."

"That's a given," Nick said. "But you're right on target when you said that you think there's something more. We know that Cynthia was not only in love with Doctor Kent but was also having an affair with him. She thought his murderer might have had an accomplice. She told me that the night she was murdered at the party given for Ms. Fitzgerald. And I felt there was more, but maybe she was too frightened."

"How about the patients themselves? How do they check out?"

Nick turned toward Clancy. "Well," Clancy said, "they are all what you would call 'upstanding citizens.' No prior arrests...clean records, except for the usual speeding tickets and the like. Naturally, they're screwed up, but not in a pathological way."

Marcy kept her expression impassive as she listened to Clancy, aware of Nick squirming in his seat.

"You know," Clancy continued, "like not being able to cope with things.

The three women had nervous breakdowns. Mrs. Benjamin, the wife of a successful manufacturer, because of the death of her children in an automobile accident plus her own bout with lupus; Lily Violet, the well-known pianist, because of previous male rejections that left her devastated, and her addiction to diet pills and drinking. And the third, Franny Goldsmith." Clancy paused as he caught Nick's uneasiness, but went on talking. "And, uh, Franny Goldsmith, who was sexually molested by her father. Doctor Kent had sex with all of them. There are a few others. Mrs. Tillingham, a former Miss America, whose husband, an industrialist billionaire, is incidentally now being brought up on fraud charges. And then there's Amelia Stern, the wife of a prominent doctor. They all have some kind of troubled personal history, but not enough evidence to arrest them for murder. Who knows how many other patients he molested?"

"Do you think we could get a few of them at a time where I could be close by but out of their view? I might be able to pick up some vibrations that way."

Nick smiled. "A la Agatha Christie? I'm willing to try anything. How about getting in touch with Cynthia again?"

"Oh, I'll keep trying. But I can't say when. Perhaps in an hour and then, maybe, a day." She raised her eyebrows. "Want to hang around? I have guest rooms."

"Wouldn't that be putting you out?" Clancy asked innocently.

"Not if you promise to clean up after yourselves," she joked. "What about the department? Will there be a problem when you don't report for work? And will you still be able to keep my involvement under wraps?"

"Problem?" Nick said. "I run the department. There's only a couple of people above me, and I've got them under my thumb." He smirked. "And if you come up with something, it will be well worth it."

"Good," she said. "I'll show you to your rooms. I have everything you need." She eyed Nick. "Unless you don't need pajamas."

He smiled appreciatively. "I'll make an exception this time."

"How about you, Clancy? Need anything?"

He smiled shyly. "Yes," he said. They both looked at him with surprise. "Some more of that wonderful apple crumb cake."

She smiled, but it faded fast. "The lady called Franny...the one who was abused by her father. When you spoke about her I received a premonition of danger...bad karma surrounding her."

Nick's jaw dropped. "Danger?"

She studied him. "Also, I sense a connection that goes deeper than friendship between the two of you," she said, waiting for him to confirm her insight.

Nick glanced at Clancy and then turned quickly back to Marcy. "You're probably going to read me anyhow. Yes, we became close." He stuck his hands into his trouser pockets. "It wasn't supposed to happen. You know, me working on a case and falling for one of the suspects. But it did."

"You have a problem," she said. "Let's hope she's not the one who did the killings."

A short distance away, with his collar turned up, a private investigator sat behind the wheel of his car, munching on a powdered sugar donut and sipping a Starbucks caramel macchiato, while keeping a watchful eye through his binoculars on Marcy Pinchic's house.

Chapter 55

"You're going!"

"I'm not!"

Franny waived a defiant finger at Elaine. "I'm not taking no for an answer, Elaine. If I have to handcuff myself to that monstrous iron bedpost of yours, I will. You've been moping around this dreary house for over a week. What are you trying out for, *Saturday Night Live's* recluse of the month? You've been holed up in this damn room, not taking calls, unconcerned that Lily and I are worried sick about you, not knowing if you were alive or dead."

"I wish I were dead."

"Well, you're not! Sure, take the easy way out. Listen, we're all going to die. So why don't you just pull yourself together and stop drowning in self pity. Did you see Lew?"

Silence.

"I guess not. You're too busy thinking about yourself. He looks a hundred years old. And why did you cancel the private nurse? I have to tell you, you're aging me, and I can't afford to have myself overhauled. When did you comb your hair last? Or are you cultivating dreadlocks?" The second the words left Franny's lips her heart sank, knowing how hard it was for Elaine to move her fingers.

This isn't working, Franny thought as she looked at Elaine's crippled hands and deteriorating body. She fought back the tears that stung her eyes as she visualized Elaine a few months ago—so vibrant, so pretty, so full of life—with her knockout figure.

Her heart heavy, Franny decided to cool the tough love and try another tactic that she had rehearsed. Sitting close to Elaine, she took hold of her hand. "Look, sweetheart, I know you hurt, and my heart goes out to you. What's happening to you is *your* pain, not mine. But I don't know what else to do. You and Lily are all I have in the world. If you go, a part of me goes with you. I'm hurting, too, Elaine. I'm hurting real bad." She had to gulp before continuing, then spoke in a hushed tone. "I know you're depressed, but can I ask you something?"

Shifting in her chair, Elaine inwardly gritted her teeth, clasped her hands in front of her and lifted her head to meet Franny's eyes.

Franny drew a deep breath. "Would it be terribly selfish of me to ask you, just for a little while, to shelve your pain and help me get through mine?"

Knowing Franny and her shtick, Elaine guardedly waited to hear her out.

Franny enveloped Elaine with her arms. "What if it were me instead of you?"

Elaine's impaired fingers slowly moved up and touched Franny's hair. Her eyes filled with tears. "I've always loved your kinky hair, Franny, it's so...*you.* Okay, you crazy nut, I'll try."

Franny's face brightened. "You will? Promise? Great! I've been practicing that speech for hours. And I had to schlep all the way out here to Armonk, no less. And Lew doesn't look a hundred years old. Maybe seventy-five. So where should we go? Let's celebrate." Franny spoke nonstop. "Did I tell you that I've changed jobs? Terrific boss, and a hell of a lot more moola. Guess who my boss is? Never mind, you'll never guess. It's Lew, your husband. The place needs a woman's touch. You don't mind? Of course you don't. And Trippy and I are hitting it off really well. I told you I needed an older man. And I haven't heard from Nick, so I guess that's kaput. Guess what? They arrested Tillingham on fraud and a million other things....I have to call Lily to let her know about us going out. She's been really anxious about you. Probably sitting by the phone and..."

Franny dropped to her knees and buried her head in Elaine's lap and sobbed. "You can't be that sick. Miracles do happen. Please, Elaine, tell me you're going to get better. You have to. It's not fair. It's not fair. I love you so much. There have to be three of us. Three on a couch, remember?"

Elaine's crippled fingers tilted Franny's chin upward. Their tear-stained cheeks touched. "It's all right," Elaine said. "We'll help each other. Help me up. I am going to give you the honor of helping me bathe. And you can do my hair." She held out her arm to Franny. "If I ask you something, Franny, will you answer me truthfully?"

"Of course. Cross my heart and hope to die. What?"

"You really think I would look bad in dreadlocks?"

Chapter 56

"Hi, it's me. Got some hot news for you."

"Aren't you being a bit reckless by phoning me?"

"No problem. It's cool. We have to talk."

"So, if it's no problem, talk. You're already on the phone."

His voice had a rough, gravelly quality to it. "I didn't realize the chances I'd be taking and the expenses I'd be running up when I took on this job."

"So it comes down to money, huh? Okay, I'll up it a thousand. What's the hot news?"

"A thou? Forget it. Do you realize I could lose my license, and be put away for aiding and abetting a...you know what. Five grand and not a cent less, or find yourself another private eye."

She twirled the phone in a circular motion above her head. She could hear the voice on the other end of the line shouting with frustration. "What's going on? Are you there?"

Retrieving the phone, she spoke into the receiver. "Now you listen to me, you pathetic loser. It's not like the department retired you with honors because of your heroic deeds. The fact is you were caught with your pants down around your ankles screwing a lady driver you pulled over for speeding. You should have just given her the ticket, moron.

Didn't look too good to the chief when she brought you up on charges, did it? And the cocaine you pocketed on that drug bust didn't sit too well with him, either. You've got a pretty shitty record for a cop."

Frustrated and embarrassed, he decided to back down. "That's all bullshit," he said, hoarsely. "I don't know where you picked up that crap, but there's not a blemish on my record. I left the department clean. You can check it out."

"I already have, skuzzball. Who'd you pay off to erase it from your record? They were so glad to get your sorry ass out of there, they gave you your walking papers with their blessing."

"Okay, okay. I'll take the extra grand, but I'm submitting an expense report." he said. "When can we meet?"

"Yesterday," she said. "Half an hour…on the steps in front of the Fifth Avenue Library next to the lion. And you better have something good to tell me."

"Which lion?" he said with a laugh. "There's two, you know."

"The one you resemble," she countered.

"Don't forget the money."

She placed the receiver in its cradle and walked to her dresser drawer, opened it, felt underneath her lingerie, removed a gun, ten one-hundred-dollar bills, wrapped them in a rubber band and stuffed the gun and the money into her purse. Fingering the dresser counter top thoughtfully, she closed the drawer, opened the one beneath it, felt beneath her scarves, and retrieved a packet of powder and a brownish glass vial of cocaine. *Just in case*, she thought.

For the last two years, the sessions with Jonathon only increased her anxieties. His promises, which turned out to be as phony as he was, had taken their toll on her state of mind.

Leaning over the two lines of cocaine she had laid down, she sniffed one with a rolled up dollar bill and quickly inhaled the other. Her eyes rolled back in her head as the cocaine hit, giving her a sudden rush, but an unexpected twinge of pain accompanied it. She wiped the remaining residue over her teeth with her finger and ran her tongue over them, enjoying the numb sensation.

Better get a move on, she thought. *Can't wait to hear what that two-bit private eye has to tell me.*

Walking into her closet, she selected an auburn wig, shook it and adjusted it on her head. The vial of cocaine on the table caught her eye and she picked it up and put it in her purse. As she entered the elevator she felt lightheaded, and an ache in the back of her head told her that something was not right. *It's the coke,* she thought. *As soon as I hit the air I'll be fine.*

As the taxi pulled up alongside the lions in front of the Fifth Avenue Library, her head started to throb and double vision assaulted her eyes.

"Hey, lady," the driver called, as she handed him the fare. "You didn't mean to give me three twenties, did you?"

"Keep it," she said, unconcerned, and stepped out of the taxi and saw two identical private detectives coming towards her. Losing balance from the cocaine, she grasped the private eye's hand for support.

"You don't look so hot," he said, leading her to the library steps, where he suggested she sit and rest for a minute. "Geez, you're as white as a ghost." He noticed a speck of white powder etched in the corner of her mouth. "Want me to get you a drink?"

She shook her head. "Just let me rest awhile. I took some medication and I got a bad reaction. It will pass."

"That happened to me once and I ended up in the hospital. Had to have my stomach pumped. What a bummer." He gave her a serious look. "I think your color is coming back. Feel better?"

She straightened up. "I'm okay now. Help me up."

"I wasn't going to approach you, but I thought the cabbie was giving you a hard time."

"I over tipped him."

"I wasn't sure it was you. Did you dye your hair?"

"Uh uh. It's a wig. I needed a change. Like it?"

He shrugged and looked around. "You look great, as usual. Let's get out of here. Just to be on the safe side, maybe you should get something to eat. There's a restaurant down Forty-First Street. We can talk while we eat. What do you think?"

Still feeling shaky, she took a deep breath and let it out slowly. Relieved that she was feeling better, she took hold of his arm and nodded. "You actually showed concern, Carmine. I'm beginning to change my opinion of you."

"Does that mean you'll up the ante, too?" he asked hopefully, tightening his grip on her arm.

"I may be shaky, Carmine, but I'm not stupid. Don't push your luck. But, if your information is that good, I'll give it some thought."

He grinned. "Oh, it's better than just good." He held the door of the restaurant for her and led her to a booth in the rear. The waiter approached and he looked at Amelia.

"Decaf," she said. "And a toasted cinnamon bagel with a smear of cream cheese."

"BLT down, on white, fries and a Coors," Carmine said. He clasped his large hands together and placed them heavily on the table. "Now that we have developed a better relationship, I can honestly tell you I'm not worried about you taking care of me as far as money is concerned. You have to understand that I deal with a lot of degenerates, and if I don't get the payment up front, sometimes I never get it at all." He held his hands up. "Don't get me wrong...present company excluded. Know what I mean?"

The waiter set the bagel and coffee down. "Your BLT is on the way, sir."

"So where's my beer?" Carmine said, sounding annoyed, just as another waiter rushed over with the beer and a glass. "Just put it down. I'll drink it from the bottle."

She shook her head. "Didn't anyone ever tell you that if you're nice to the help you'd get better service?" He started to reply, but she waved a hand at him. "So, what's the earth shattering news, Carmine?"

He leaned forward. "Well, you know the detective who's on the Kent and Connors cases, Nick Pagliara?"

"He interrogated me," she said, grinning. "He's kind of cute."

"Right. He and his assistant, Clancy, have hooked up with this psychic. I checked her out. They had a few meetings at her house in Jersey, and she's most likely trying to get in touch with the spirit world or some other kind of voodoo magic to help them put the finger on the murderer. There was an article about her in People two years ago."

She wiped her mouth with a napkin. "Don't believe in them," she said.

He shook his head from left to right. "Not so," he said flatly. "I used to think that, too, until I saw some of their predictions materialize. I sat in on a few of their sessions."

She frowned. "It's phony. Bunch of hocus pocus."

"No shit," he said. "Blew my mind." He paused and looked at her for a few moments. "You never did tell me why you hired me in the first place. I know you were a patient of the doctor's..." he stopped short. "So are you one of them armchair detectives? That's what you told me, right?" Suddenly he became serious, and it hit him; could she be linked to the murders and using him? Forwhat, he wasn't quite sure. He became more suspicious and distrustful of her by the second. "Anyhow, from what I can piece together, they didn't have much luck at the psychic's house, so if they are going to make any headway they have to get the psychic closer to the crime scene. My guess is that they're going to hold a session either at the doctor's office or at Connors' residence."

"Cynthia, huh." Amelia said thoughtfully.

"Yeah, that's the one. Cynthia Connors, the doctor's receptionist who was blown away in the Plaza Hotel bathroom. There's another tidbit you might be interested in hearing. This one lady, Franny Goldsmith, had some heavy conversation with Cynthia about Dr. Kent before he was murdered." Amelia's eyes narrowed as he continued. "I wouldn't be surprised if that's why Cynthia was blown away. And if the Goldsmith broad has any brains, she better take off before she gets bumped off, too. Evidently, they both had a pretty good idea as to who the culprit is." He noticed Amelia's tense expression. "Well, anyhow, I'm warning you, Mrs. Stern, don't take the psychic lightly."

"Why should I take her lightly or seriously? I'm an armchair detective, right? I guess by now you've surmised that I'm doing all this research for a mystery novel I'm writing."

His breathing quickened and his heart raced as he caught a glint of satisfaction in her eye at the mention of Cynthia's murder at the Waldorf. As far as he was concerned, her interest and involvement in the murders were too coincidental to be dismissed with this bullshit about research. And why did she look so odd when he mentioned the other lady? Then it hit him. *What the hell did I get myself into?* he thought. *I'm playing with fire. Jesus, I bet she...*

Amelia read his concerned look and stared at him suspiciously. *Is he onto me? And why has his complexion changed from ruddy to chalk white?*

He edged warily toward the edge of his seat. "Listen," he said, a hint of anxiety in his voice. "I just remembered a call I forgot to make. I'll be right back."

"Why don't you use your cell phone?" she asked, her voice sharp, her look suspicious. "Or is it too personal?"

"Yeah," he answered uneasily. "My girlfriend...she gets nuts when I forget."

He started to rise, but she spoke quickly. "Wait, Carmine. Sit a minute," she insisted with a half smile. "I want to pay you for the work you've done. And there's a bonus, also. Finish your beer and then you can make your call."

He sat down reluctantly. "Sure," he said, his forehead showing beads of perspiration. "Let her wait. Show her who's the boss, right?"

Amelia smiled and looked deeply into Carmine's suspicious eyes. From beneath the table, she reached into her bag and felt for her gun. Then suddenly she changed her mind, thinking that even with the silencer it might attract attention, and so she went back to plan A: cyanide.

"Let's toast to better times," she said. "And here, drink from a glass. Beer that's drunk from a bottle loses its flavor." She poured the Coors into a glass and moved it toward him.

Distracting him by dropping her purse on the floor, she kicked it so that it rested between his legs. "Oh, how clumsy of me," she said. "Do you mind?"

As he bent to retrieve her purse, she quickly tore open a packet of powder and slipped it into his glass of beer.

He groaned as he handed her the purse. "My back is going to be the death of me," he said.

Her dark eyes searched his face. "Thanks, I'm becoming so clumsy. Let's toast to good times." Raising her glass to meet his, she said, "Come on, Carmine, chugalug, down the hatch."

He took a big swallow, set the glass down with a thud and grabbed his chest. Contorted from the bitterness of the cyanide, his lungs gasped for air. His eyes rolled back in his head as he slumped in his seat, his head falling to one side.

Rising nonchalantly, she placed a twenty-dollar bill on the table, straightened Carmine's head and spoke to him as if in casual conversation. "Thanks for the information, Carmine. You've been a great help. Forgive me for running, but I must attend to a couple of ladies."

Unhurriedly, she strolled from the restaurant, head bent, and walked up the street. She sat down on the library steps, where she waited until she heard the clamor of an ambulance followed by a police car's siren heading up Forty-First Street to the restaurant. Then she hailed a cab and told the driver to go through Central Park.

After going two blocks, she addressed the driver. "Stop here," she said abruptly. "It's so nice out, I'll walk the rest of the way." As she exited the cab she felt the throbbing in the back of her head again. "Fuck, fuck, fuck," she called aloud. The bench at the bus stop was a welcome sight. She sat down and massaged her head and neck. *At least my vision is okay,* she thought. She opened her purse, removed two Advil and swallowed them dry. She shoved the packet back into her purse, her eye catching the vial of cocaine. Better not, she thought. *Let the Advil kick in.*

A bus pulled up to the stop and passengers exited. The bus driver leaned toward her and shouted, "Well, lady, are you or aren't you getting on?" Amelia gave him the finger. The driver scowled at her, shut the door and drove on. *Have to think, but this damn headache is driving me crazy. I wish Bill were home. He could prescribe something to ease it.*

She signaled for a taxi, entered the cab and as it pulled away from the curb, her voice rang out, "The damn double vision is back." The cabbie, startled by her sudden outburst, turned around. Agitated, she yelled at him, "Keep your eyes on the road, you moron. Move this piece of shit!" The light suddenly turned red, and he jammed on the brakes, causing her to lunge forward. "Go, you idiot!" she yelled.

"Listen, lady," the driver said, "I don't know what your problem is but I stop for red lights. Maybe you should get another cab. One that caters to crazies." When the green light came on he pulled to the curb and waited for her to leave. "Bye, bye," he said. Then muttered, "Fucked up fruit cakes...they're infesting the city!"

Amelia saw particles of red, white, blue and streaks of yellow scatter in her eyes.

"Forget the fare, lady," he said. "Just get out and we'll call it square."

Her eyes popping and her face flushed with rage, Amelia shouted, "Crazy fruit cakes infesting the city, huh? Who do you think you're talking to?"

"Hey, don't give me any shit," he said. "Get out before I throw you out!"

She stepped out of the cab, slammed the door, and quickly opened the front door and slid in next to the surprised driver. "What makes you think I was going to pay you for the ride?" she sneered. She looked at his license, "Huh, Anthony?"

"Listen, you loony," he said sharply, "that's it. I've had it with you. Guess I'll have to throw you out."

"Now you're asking for it," she said, flashing her gun at him as he sank back in his seat.

Smiling coldly, she pointed the gun at the dumbfounded driver and fired. "What's one more or less?" she said, shrugging her shoulders. "Two in one day; I'm starting to enjoy it." She unscrewed the silencer and dropped it and the gun into her purse, exited the cab, leaned into the open window and waved at the bleeding corpse. "Bye, bye," she said. "Fruitcake has to plan her next move."

Chapter 57

"Mrs. Pinchic?"

Marcy answered hesitantly. "Yes, this is she."

"Do forgive me for calling so early in the day, dear."

"Who is this?"

"This is Della Connors, Cynthia's mother," she said with a hint of sorrow in her voice.

Puzzled as to why Cynthia's mother would be calling her, yet not wanting to appear rude, she said, "My deepest condolences, Mrs. Connors. Is there something I can do for you?"

"I received a call from Detective Pagliara. He mentioned that you were going to meet at Cynthia's apartment and he asked if I could be there. The loss of my daughter has drained me of all my strength. He said it was important...you know...to help with the case...that if I were there my presence might make it easier for you to get in touch with..." Her voice faltered. "...My poor baby." She hesitated a moment, then finally found her voice. "Do you think we could have a cup of coffee a few moments before the scheduled meeting?"

"I was just about to leave for the city, Mrs. Connors," Marcy said, feeling compassion for the woman. "But our meeting with Detective

Pagliara isn't until later."

"I'm so distraught...so confused. If you are going to speak to my little girl...you know, when you make contact with her...I thought we could meet and spend a few minutes. Perhaps I could feel Cynthia's presence through you." She sniveled. "I miss her so much. The doctor has me sedated with who knows what...and my husband just sits and stares." She blew her nose. "The pills don't take away the pain. Just for a few minutes. It would mean so much to me."

An uneasy feeling crept through Marcy, torn between her rational instincts and her compassion for the woman's grief. "Well, I could see you briefly before the meeting."

"You're very kind, Mrs. Pinchic. Where and when?"

"How about in front of Cynthia's apartment? We could chat for a bit."

"Oh no, I couldn't...not in front of her building. It would bring back too many memories. There's a coffee shop just down the block called, The Three Buccaneers. We could meet outside."

Marcy looked at her watch. "How about in an hour? Can you make it by then?"

"No problem. And thank you. You're a good soul."

I better get a move on, Marcy thought, uncomfortable with the negative vibrations she was receiving. She dialed Nick at the station. "I'm sorry," the sergeant answered, "but Detective Pagliara is unavailable. Do you want to leave a message?"

"Tell him his friend Miss Marcy called and she must speak with him."

"Does he have your telephone number, Miss Marcy?"

"Yes. Thank you."

With a bit of weariness, Marcy applied herself to her driving and drove down the West Side Highway toward Manhattan to meet Mrs. Connors.

Pleased with her conversation with Marcy Pinchic, the caller laid one line of cocaine, inhaled, and continued her course of action. She dialed Franny Goldsmith.

Chapter 58

Franny put one foot into the foaming tub as the phone rang. "Damn, I'm not going to answer it," she said, annoyed. Thinking it might be Trippy, or, way back in the deepest corner of her mind, Nick, she made her way to the phone and listened to her recording. *"If it's you, Blanche, I don't have time. If you're a salesperson telling me I won a television if I sit for two hours while you sell me a swamp in New Mexico, I suggest you hang up or suffer the consequences. If my Aunt Mamie died and left me a huge inheritance, stay on the line."* When it ended she picked up the receiver.

Amelia covered the mouthpiece of the phone with a handkerchief. "Is this Franny Goldsmith?" she asked timidly, with a quiver in her voice.

Something about the caller's voice sobered Franny. "Yes, the one and only Franny Goldsmith. Who's this?"

"I hope I didn't catch you at a bad time, dear. This is Cynthia Connor's mother, Della Connors."

Geez, Franny thought, *I'm a real asshole.* She spoke softly into the phone. "I'm so sorry, Mrs. Connors, I didn't mean to be rude. How are you doing? Do you remember me? I spoke to you at the funeral."

"Of course I do," she said. "I wonder if I could impose upon you."

"Of course."

"I don't know how close to Cynthia you were. I do know that you saw her at Dr. Kent's office, since she was the doctor's right hand."

"That's right."

"I wonder if you would do me a favor. I'm trying to deal with my baby's death, but it's so hard." She sniffled.

"I'm sure," Franny said, not knowing what else to say.

"Would it be too pushy of me to ask if we could meet and talk about Cynthia? My doctor tells me that it would be helpful to speak to Cynthia's friends. I'm on so much medication, and I'm so sedated...sometimes I just don't know if I'm coming or going." She sniveled again. "Could we meet and just talk? It would help me get through this trying time."

"Sure," Franny said, thinking that she never liked Cynthia, and they were not close. "Where and when?"

"Now would be a perfect time for me. I'm at such a low point." Her voice cracked. "I know that you live downtown. I could be there in no time at all. It would mean so much to me. But if it's an inconvenience, dear, don't worry, I'll get by." She blew her nose. "Would the Three Buccaneers restaurant down the block from Cynthia's apartment be convenient? I could be there in fifteen minutes."

"No problem."

"Good bye, dear, and thank you. I feel better already."

Franny hung up the phone, thinking how she would have liked to soak in the tub, but the least she could do was be there for someone in need. She slipped into her jeans, threw a cotton sweater over her head and slung her DKNY denim jacket over her shoulder. Determined to get this unexpected get-together over with, Franny reluctantly shut the door, thinking of having a relaxing dip in the tub when she returned.

●.

The cocaine she had sniffed took effect. "Phew! That was strong shit!" she exclaimed. A deafening ringing pierced her ears as her brain constricted. Clasping her hands over her ears, trying to stop the ringing, she slammed her fists hard on the vanity table. For a moment, her mind went blank.

After removing her makeup, she checked her image in the mirror. Her thoughts confused, her faculties shaky at best, she found it hard to concentrate. She sat down on the sofa, trying to pull herself together. *Did I make an appointment with that psychic...or that Franny woman?* She adjusted a charcoal gray curly wig, on her head and thought, *I'm getting to be a master with disguises. Psychics, mediums, they're nothing but a bunch of phonies. Still, I can't take any chances.* Studying herself in the mirror, she was certain no one would recognize her.

The cocaine gave her courage and she smiled confidently as she loaded her gun and slipped it along with the silencer, into her tote bag. "Don't know why I don't go to red," she said aloud; "gray hair just makes me look like an old lady."

At the elevator she hesitated before pushing the buttons. "Up or down, down or up," she chanted, pressing both buttons.

As she flagged a taxi she told herself it was not only easy but also justifiable, getting rid of anyone who stood in her way. My husband *will be coming home tomorrow and he'll get the shock of his life when he finds me gone!*

Her eyes wide with expectation, she giggled, wondering whether Mrs. Pinchic or Franny would be waiting for her at the restaurant. She sing-sang, "The lady or the psychic...the psychic or the lady...the lady or the tiger...the tiger or the lady."

Chapter 59

The word *Three* on the coffee shop's neon sign, The Three Buccaneers, flickered as if each flutter was going to be its last. Marcy checked her wristwatch, tapped her foot nervously, and then went into the restaurant to see if Mrs. Connors was there.

After checking the restaurant, and not seeing her, she turned and walked out, sensing the same uncertainty she had felt when speaking with Cynthia's mother on the phone. Bad karma, she told herself. My intuition is warning me to be careful. Goose bumps sprang up on her arms, and the hair on the back of her neck bristled. "That's it," she said aloud. "I'm leaving." She got into her car and hastily drove away.

At the same moment, Franny stepped out of a cab and strolled up to the door of the restaurant. She nodded a hello to a waitress who had previously served her. "It's getting real hard to find a place to grab a smoke these days," she said, waiving her cigarette into the air. Franny looked around for Mrs. Connors.

A moment later the lady pulled to the curb and upon seeing Franny, called to her. "Yoo-hoo, Miss Goldsmith, it's me, Mrs. Connors," and motioned for her to come closer. As Franny approached, Mrs. Connors leaned over the passenger's seat. Her voice tearful, she pleaded with Franny, "Forgive me, dear, I just can't go in there. Cynthia and I used to come here for coffee. I should have known better. There's another place just a few blocks from here." Dabbing at her eyes, she reached across the seat and opened the car door.

Franny peered into the car. "You look different than when I saw you at the funeral," she said.

"It's the wig. I've been so flustered I haven't had time to think of doing my hair."

The moment Franny sat down in the automobile she became queasy and ill at ease. "I don't feel well. I need some air. Give me a second to compose myself." She reached for the door handle to exit, but the woman pressed the door locks on the master panel and immediately floored the gas pedal. The tires screeched and the car took off, narrowly missing an approaching SUV.

Taken aback by the sudden display of Mrs. Connor's aggression, Franny yelled, "Hey, what are you doing? Slow down! I know you're not yourself, but if you don't want this car to smell of puke you better pull over and let me get out."

Mrs. Connors kept her foot glued to the gas pedal.

"Stop! You're going to kill us. What's wrong with you?" Franny yelled.

Mrs. Connors reached into her tote bag and removed her gun, which she pointed at Franny.

Franny paled. Words stuck in her throat as she sat transfixed, her gaze riveted on the gun, which stared threateningly in her face.

Running a red light, the car raced onto the East River Drive. Mrs. Connors, oblivious to the merging traffic, veered into the left lane, the car narrowly missing an automobile that swerved to avoid hitting them. "Sunday drivers," Mrs. Connors crowed.

"What the hell's going on?" Franny shouted, looking back to see the cars swerving in order to avoid them. "Why don't you exit and let me take over? You're in no condition to drive."

"No one's taking over." She pulled at her wig and tossed it into the back seat.

Franny's eyes widened. "My God, you're not Cynthia's mother. You're Amelia Stern, Elaine's friend, the doctor's wife from the clinic. Have you flipped out? What's with the wig and the gun? The car swayed to the right and Franny instinctively grabbed the steering wheel, trying to keep the car in its lane. "This has gone far enough," Franny shouted. "Pull over or I'll..."

"You'll do nothing. Take your hands off the wheel," Amelia shouted and spontaneously pulled the trigger on the 38 revolver. The bullet made a short pinging echo as it hit the roof of the sedan and ricocheted onto the back seat. Pointing the gun at Franny, she warned, "I mean business. Cynthia found out about me, but I wasn't sure about you."

"Me? You got the wrong lady. Cynthia and I were never in cahoots. I didn't even like her."

"Bullshit! I paid good money to find out about you and Cynthia."

This is a deranged woman, Franny thought. "You've got this all wrong."

"Maybe you don't and maybe you do. That's yesterday's news." Amelia winced as a sharp pain shot through her head.

"Headache?" Franny asked. "I have aspirin."

"Well, get it!"

"You better slow down. You're all over the road. Pull over to the shoulder I promise I won't try to escape."

"Yeah, sure. Forget about stopping. I've got to finish what I started."

"Finish? My God. Did you kill the doctor and Cynthia?"

Amelia tried focusing. "Yeah, I killed them. And I did away with two others, too. And guess who's going to be next? " She waved her gun recklessly.

Franny shouted. "You're all over the road. You can't steer with one hand. Let me at least steer for you."

Franny dug into her purse and took out the aspirin, removed three and held them out to Amelia. "How are you going to take them?"

Amelia opened her mouth. "Throw them in."

Police sirens blared behind them. As Amelia looked into her rear view mirror her double vision saw four police cars.

Franny advised. "They're not going to let us get away."

"I haven't done anything!" Amelia's head felt as if it were gripped in a vise.

Franny yelled, "Do you want to die in a car wreck? I know your head aches and you can't see straight, but stop and think for a second."

"Stop, so you can get away? So you can be a witness against me?

"Pull over," a loudspeaker roared.

"Pull on this, you retards," Amelia yelled and fired a shot out the window. "So you want to play, huh?" she yelled and stepped hard on the gas pedal.

Franny screamed. "You wanna commit suicide?"

Amelia didn't answer. She was in a daze. "Catch me if you can, catch me if you can," she repeated. Holding her finger on the horn she sideswiped automobiles and swerved precariously from one lane to another. "I'll lose them," she babbled as the pounding in her head increased.

•₀

Nick and Clancy turned onto the West Side Highway in pursuit of the woman's wild rampage. Nick spoke anxiously to the helicopter pilot that followed Amelia up the West Side Highway. "Where are they now?"

"At 42nd Street," the pilot replied.

"Keep the air open," Nick said and then spoke to Clancy. "Who tipped you off about Franny getting into the car?"

"I just this second hung up with headquarters. The waitress at the Three Buccaneers restaurant was having a cigarette outside the restaurant and saw a lady get into a car that took off like a bat out of hell. She recognized her as one of her customers, named Franny, and called the station. The waitress said the lady tried to leave the vehicle. Also, I just got word that Marcy Pinchic has been calling the station upset about a phone call from Cynthia's mother wanting to meet her. She said to tell you she got in touch with the lady, 'from above' and guess what? Amelia Stern is the culprit. Where's your cell phone, Boss?"

Nick fumed. "I should have put a tail on Franny. Did you get any more info on the car and driver?"

"It should be coming in as we speak. This must be it now."

"Sergeant Pagliara…sedan rented from Budget Rent-A-Car on 62nd Street in Manhattan to an Amelia Stern. 714 Shoreline Drive, Cedarhurst, Long Island, New York."

"Shit," Clancy agonized. "Can you beat that? Marcy was right."

Not expecting a reply, Nick asked Clancy, "Did you ever hate yourself?"

•.

"Did you see that cop's car do a flip?" Amelia said. "Not to worry, I'll lose the others. Then I'll get you out of my life."

"You're talking crazy," Franny said. "You'll either kill us or be caught by the police. Personally, I prefer the latter. How do you expect to get away with this?" The driver narrowly avoided a collision with another car. Franny shrieked, "Watch out!"

The car swerved into the left lane, forcing another car to careen into a third automobile as Amelia headed for the next exit. "They don't know who I am. Only you do." Amelia cut off two more cars, gunned the engine of the rented car and sped off the Eighty-Sixth Street exit ramp. "Bill always told me I drive like I'm the only one on the road."

She blinked rapidly, hoping her vision would clear, but as they exited, the sunlight reflected off the windshield blinded her. She jammed on the brakes and was instantly rear-ended, causing a chain reaction of crashing automobiles. Franny pulled at the door handle, but the master lock prevented the door from opening.

Amelia shifted into reverse and unlocked bumpers with the other car, then shifted into drive, leaving the stunned passengers in the cars behind them in a state of bewilderment. "Never should have gotten off the Drive," Amelia said. She floored the gas pedal, made a U-turn over the divider. The undercarriage of the car scraped against the cement separator and the oncoming cars crashed into one another. Then she headed uptown again.

"I think you left the transmission back there," Franny said. "And I smell gas. Not a good sign. And there's a helicopter following us."

Amelia's face tightened. "I'll lose that whirlybird. Give me some more aspirin and open my purse. I need a snort." She waved the gun at Franny. "Make it fast and no tricks! Hey, what's that dragging noise?"

"Must be the bumper of the car that rear-ended us. It's hanging on. And there's a strong gas odor. Pray we don't blow up. Why don't you pull over and give up this roller coaster ride?"

"I don't smell anything, and I'm not pulling over."

The helicopter pilot announced to Nick and Clancy, "Suspect made an unauthorized U-turn over the island and is now heading south. She's driving like the devil himself is after her and leaving a trail of damaged vehicles in her wake. Traffic is at a standstill going uptown because of the collisions and the chaos the driver has caused. You're not going to get through. We've closed down the entrances and are rerouting the cars off the Drive. And we have backups at all exits. Uh oh. Lost her. She's got shelter from the overhang, but she has to come into the open at Eighty-first Street. Where are you now?"

"Damn it! She's now going downtown and we're going uptown. We're at 61st Street. Over." Nick yelled into the mike as he pounded the dashboard with his fist. "Shit! We're stuck here. We'll never get through the mess of traffic up ahead. Might as well get out and run."

"Wait a minute," Clancy declared, "aren't they doing construction on the island between here and the 96th Street exit? And if I remember it should be..." His face lit up. "Yep, there it is. Now we have to pray there's an opening for us to cut through."

"It's going to be a bitch getting across the divider with the oncoming cars blocking the road downtown," Nick said as he eased the car into the work lane.

A muscle-bound bruiser of a man in a sweaty T-shirt with a bandana tied around his forehead confronted them. "Hey, officer," he yelled, "this here's a work area. You can't make a U-turn. We're fixing the divider."

Nick and Clancy exited the car.

"What'sa trouble?" the man asked.

"Runaway car coming through the downtown lane any second. Have to get over there!" Clancy, shouted.

"No problem. Listen up guys," he yelled. "Emergency! Get the boys to stop da traffic. The fuzz is on a chase." The crew flashed, "SLOW DOWN! DANGER!

The cars came to a halt with the sound of screeching brakes and crashing bumpers.

•.

With the distant police sirens blasting a warning to unsuspecting motorists, Amelia, in a blind rage at seeing the barricade set up by the construction workers, made a sudden U-turn across the divider. A worker tried to get out of the path of Amelia's oncoming car, but he didn't move quickly and her car's impact flung him into the air. He came down with a hard thud on the hood of Amelia's car. His head shattered the windshield and his blank eyes stared at Franny through the opening of the shattered glass. The rented car swerved wildly as Amelia, now starting her trek uptown, maneuvered the car from side to side, trying to shake the worker from the hood of the car, but his head was wedged into the broken glass of the windshield. She shouted obscenities at the man whose body blocked her vision. "Get off my car, you idiot. I can't see!" Then she screamed at Franny. "Do something!"

Franny, her eyes transfixed on the dead man, whose blood now oozed through the splintered glass onto the dashboard and spilled onto the legs of her jeans, didn't hear Amelia.

•

Having been cleared to turn around and go uptown again, Nick and Clancy took off after them. "Jesus Christ," Clancy called, rubbing his hands over his face with anguish, "she's hit one of the workers and he's riding on the hood."

Terror raced through Nick at the thought of Franny riding with crazed Amelia. "Let's see if we can cut her off before she kills Franny and half the population of New York. I don't believe it. There's no traffic going uptown. Now, when we want it to be at a standstill, they get it moving. He shook his head. "Never a break. How the hell is she driving with the guy stuck on the hood?" At that moment, the headless body slipped from the car's hood, the victim's arm fastened itself to the hanging bumper, his torso flailing like a rag doll, his blood spraying at the shocked on-lookers, who cringed at the hideous sight.

"Look out!" Clancy shouted as Nick's patrol car sideswiped an automobile. The startled passengers screamed as the driver lost control, spun around, and broadsided Nick's patrol car, ramming it into a cement pillar.

Clancy's heart pounded. His face drained of all color as he looked at Nick slumped over the steering wheel, blood dripping from his face. "Nick," he said, gently touching his boss's shoulder.

Nick groaned. "What happened?" He raised his head.

"Don't move," Clancy said. "You're hurt."

"I'm okay. Just a little woozy."

"I'm calling an ambulance."

"Stay put, Clancy. I hit my head, nothing serious. Stop overreacting."

"You're bleeding. Don't play the martyr. You *could* have a concussion."

"Just shut the fuck up, Clancy! I tell you I'm okay. Can you reach the first aid kit?"

Clancy shook his head. "Here, use my handkerchief; the kit is buried under the..." He hesitated as he sniffed the odor of gas that permeated the air. "Something tells me we better make tracks, Boss. The gas tank must be punctured." He reached for the door handle but found it jammed. "My side's stuck. Can you open your door?"

"It's jammed, too. I'm pinned in. Can you knock out the window?"

Clancy pressed his body hard against the back of the seat and kicked with his heels at the window. The window shattered, but the wire mesh that reinforced the glass, held. "Damn, it's not giving," he said fearfully. "We have to get out of here...the gas fumes are real heavy." He used all of his strength and finally the mesh gave way.

Nick yelled, "Listen, Clancy, get out!"

"I'm not leaving you here alone. Let me see if I can move your seat back. You're pushed into the tightest seat position. First responders are seconds away. I'm staying till you're ok."

Nick shouted. "I'm giving you an order. Get out while you can."

"No!"

A firefighter from the emergency crew pried the door open, cut Nick's seat belt and eased him out of the cramped quarters. Without wasting a second, they dragged Nick away from the car, Clancy at their heels. They fell to the ground as the car exploded, flames and debris billowing into the sky.

Rising, Nick waved away a medic who was approaching him. He

tightened Clancy's handkerchief around his head and motioned with his thumb at two officers to vacate their patrol car, and he and Clancy took off after Amelia. "Check with the copter and the station. See if we can get a line on them."

"We've lost a lot of time, Boss. By now they're either driving upstate or have been picked up by one of the squad cars posted at the exits."

The helicopter pilot's voice aired. "Perpetrator broke through the barrier, totaled the squad car at the exit and is headed upstate."

Franny held fast to the door strap, trying to regain her composure. "Listen," she said, in a last effort to get Amelia to come to her senses, "stop and think. If you give up now you can save yourself from the electric chair. The trail of bodies you left behind is not going to disappear. You can plead insanity."

Amelia's face tightened and her eyes bulged. "Insanity? Listen, Miss Know It All. The only crazy one here is you. The only reason you're still alive is I might need you as a hostage. If I don't, you're a goner. You think I can't pull this off? All I have to do is lose these idiots, get you out of my hair and I'm home free."

"What about your husband?"

"That shmuck? I wasn't happy with my husband from the day I met him. None of my three kids are his. What a joke. Listen, don't try to get on my good side by getting me to talk." She winced with pain. "I cleaned out the vault and the safe in the house." Her voice faded. "Then it's off to..." Her brows furrowed and a stupefied expression crossed her face. "Now where are my tickets to...? Oh, yes, the Caymans."

Franny curled herself against the front seat, trying to come up with something—anything—to escape.

Amelia rambled on. "I went to Jonathon because of my depression, but when he tried to ease me out of his life, I lost it. I hid in his office closet and watched as he kneeled at his safe. Then I confronted him, and suddenly, he became all the men in my life who hurt me, rolled up into one. God, but I felt so good after I shot him." She waved the gun at Franny.

Franny stared at the gun and imagined it growing larger and larger. She envisioned Lily and Elaine crying as they shoveled dirt over her casket. Shaking her head in order to clear her mind, she reasoned with Amelia. "Think rationally. You'll never get away with this."

Amelia said nothing.

Franny listened. "There's very little traffic and I don't hear the helicopter."

"Told you I'd lose those suckers. I am going to slow down, but I'm warning you, no tricks."

Franny wondered. *So far God has been on my side, but for how long? I've got to do something and fast. Either I grapple for the gun while the car slows down and take advantage of Amelia's confused state, or hang in until the police catch up with us, if that ever happens.*

"Give me more aspirin," Amelia said, her voice wheezing. "And make it four this time." Slowing the car to thirty miles per hour, Amelia pointed the gun threateningly at Franny. "Hurry up," she yelled.

I'll never have a better chance, Franny thought, and sprang into action. Thinking to distract Amelia, she tossed the pills at her, clipped her on the chin with her fist and lunged for the master door lock. Caught off guard, Amelia swung wildly, butting Franny with the gun, as the car careened sharply from one lane to the other.

Franny regained her balance and grabbed for the gun, but Amelia, with one hand on the steering wheel and the other wielding the gun at Franny, pulled the trigger. The bullet singed the hair on the side of her head and ripped through her earlobe.

"I told you I wasn't fooling around," Amelia shouted. "The next one will be between your eyes."

Franny, acting on impulse, stretched her foot across Amelia's and hit the brake pedal with all her might. The car lunged sharply back and forth as Amelia tried to control it.

Franny quickly reached across for the unlock button, pulled it up, swung the door open and jumped from the moving vehicle. Hitting the earth, she rolled over and down an embankment, and landed in a watery marsh where she lay unconscious.

The car screeched to a halt as Amelia slammed the brakes and sprang out of the car in pursuit of Franny. "Fuck you, Franny. Fuck you to hell." Her double vision made it difficult to focus as she followed the path of broken twigs and shreds of clothing that clung to the thorns and bushes marking Franny's descent.

She spied Franny's outstretched form lying partially submerged in the marsh. Gun in hand, she raised her arm to shoot, but wavered. Steadying the gun with her other hand, she aimed directly at Franny's unconscious torso and fired until the only sound was the clicking of the firing pin.

She climbed up the embankment and slid into the driver's seat aware that the helicopter had spotted her. Ignoring the pilot's warning to stay put, she gave him the finger, floored the accelerator and sped off.

Chapter 60

Dazed and disoriented, Franny lay in a pool of murky marsh water and wondered where she was and how she had gotten there. *It's so quiet,* she thought. *I can't hear or see a thing. My eyes burn and my ear aches.* "I must be dead," she moaned as she slipped in and out of consciousness.

The day was bright, and the scent of blooming flowers transported Franny back in time. It was when Blanche had told her about her headaches, and it wasn't until Franny was older that she learned that the headaches were hangovers and the special drink Mommy took from a thermos wasn't a vitamin concoction, but vodka with a splash of orange juice.

Through a mist, Franny saw a huge iron gate and her father holding her hand tightly as they walked into a building where women were screaming. When she asked her father if Mommy was coming home he told her she would, eventually. She remembered when her father had left them—how she waited outside the A. A. meetings for Blanche, making sure she would go straight home and not to a local bar. Suddenly she saw her father, Joey, Lily, Elaine, Trippy, Jonathon and Nick all in a circle waving a warning finger at her as they faded in and out of her confused mind.

It was Clancy who broke the silence. "This is where the copter said they parked." He pulled up to the burnt-out tire tracks Amelia's car had left. "Looks like she's taken off again."

Two squad cars in pursuit of Amelia stopped. One of the policemen leaned out the window and shouted at them. "Just got word. One of the ladies jumped from the car and tumbled down the ravine. Ambulance is on the way. We're going to chase the other lady down."

"They'll nab her," Nick said, wincing with pain. "Let's get down the hill." With Clancy at his heels he started down the ravine, all the while praying that Franny was alive.

Chapter 61

Elaine waited in the kitchen, hoping it was good news concerning Franny, but the thud in the living room confirmed her worst fears.

Trippy's voice faded on the other end of the phone as Lily, hearing of Franny's abduction, dropped the receiver and fainted. Elaine rushed into the room and cradled Lily in her arms. Patting her gently on the cheeks, Elaine said, "You're all right. Wake up. You passed out."

The telephone cord dangled from the table as Trippy's anxious voice kept repeating. "Hello, hello. Lily! Lily!"

"I'm here, I'm here," Elaine shouted at the receiver. "Hold on. Hold on. I'll be there as soon as I can."

"What's going on?" Trippy's voice echoed from the phone.

Relieved to see Lily open her eyes and the color in her cheeks return, she sighed. "You're all right, baby. You had me scared to death. What can I do for you?"

"Nothing. I'm okay," Lily said as she sat up slowly.

Elaine picked up the phone. "Don't spare me, Trippy. What happened to Franny? She's not..."

"I wish I could tell you that she's safe, but I don't know. All I know is that Amelia Stern, the doctor's wife, went berserk and held her hostage during a wild automobile chase."

"Amelia? Why would she kidnap Franny? I'm at a loss. How did you get wind of this? Is it on the television?"

"One question at a time, Elaine. No, it's not out yet. How I received the information isn't important. What is important is Franny's condition. I understand the automobile Franny was in totaled more than a dozen cars during the chase and was, as of an hour ago, still headed upstate."

Elaine sobbed into a tissue. "Lily's okay. What can we do?"

"Just sit tight. I'll inform you the minute I hear anything." He sighed. "By the way, I understand that Nick is trying to stop the mad woman. Just as well."

"What do you mean by, 'just as well'? Are you thinking that the old flame between them will rekindle?"

"I think so, Elaine. It's bittersweet. I knew she would have to leave me sooner than later. I was hoping it would be later. But I have no regrets."

"Poor Franny," Lily said, noticing how deformed Elaine's fingers had become.

Elaine immediately hid her hands from view. "I forgot to wear my gloves. I'm so ashamed."

Moving closer to Elaine, Lily held her hands out. "Come on. Let me hold them. There's nothing to be ashamed of. We need each other now."

"If we knew Franny was okay…" She sighed heavily. "But that's a big if."

Chapter 62

Rushing blindly down the gully in search of Franny, Nick slipped, lost his footing and plunged downward. In the few seconds before he blacked out, images of Franny's lifeless body riddled with bullets whirled around his brain, reinforcing his deep-rooted guilt at not having protected her.

He opened his eyes as Clancy's voice drifted toward him. "You took quite a fall, Boss. You were out for a minute. Stay put. The medics will be with you as soon as they take care of Franny."

Nick shook his head, groaned with pain and looked around. "Franny! Where's Franny?"

"They're working on her. She's alive but unconscious."

"Help me up. I wanna see her." He tried standing but yelped with pain as his leg gave way. "Damn, I think it's broken." He raised his arms toward Clancy. "Clancy give me a hand."

Clancy shook his head. Nick raised his voice at Clancy. "Get me up or I swear I'll fucking kill you!" An alarmed medic ran to Nick's aid, but he pushed her aside.

"Listen, detective," the medic warned, "you want a shot to calm you or are you going to behave? You've got multiple bruises and a gash on the side of your head. And your leg is probably broken."

She stood her ground, but Clancy, knowing Nick's stubborn side, intervened. "Let me handle him," he said.

Leaning on Clancy for support, Nick hopped to where the medics were lifting Franny onto a stretcher. His heart sank. He wished it were he, not Franny.

Clancy felt Nick's concern. "You need medical attention."

Nick paled as he stood watching Franny, her kinky blond hair now muddy and matted with blood, as her body lay motionless. "Jesus," Nick said in a hushed tone to the medics, "how bad is she?"

"She's in shock, detective. A bullet nicked off part of her ear. Her eyes are filled with blood. We have to get her to the ER real fast. Her blood pressure is extremely low." He motioned to the other medics. "Watch the IV line as we go up the hill, guys. There's a copter waiting to take them to the hospital. And you," he said, pointing at Nick, "you don't look so good."

Nick's knee buckled but Clancy caught him and sat him down. "What's all the fuss?" Nick asked. "Get me out of here. I want to be with Franny. This time, I'm not going to let her down."

Chapter 63

"If I didn't know you personally, Nick," the surgeon said, "I'd have you tied down to the hospital bed so fast you wouldn't know what hit you." His thumb stroked his chin thoughtfully. "It's been a few years, hasn't it?" he said, thinking of the day Nick's wife had died from cancer.

Nick stared expressionless into space. "Almost two years since we lost Terry, Doc."

The surgeon leaned closer to Nick. "The rumor circulating around the hospital is that the macho Detective Pagliara carried on like a love-sick kid at the scene of the shooting." He raised his eyebrows questioningly. "Does that mean the mourning period is over and you're ready to move on? I hope."

"You mean people are talking?"

"You forget you're well known in the hospital. At least once or twice a month for the last six years we get to see you and your crew in the shoot-em up emergency ward." He winked. "It's a small world, and gossip is like dessert. We love to feed on it." He glanced at Clancy, who turned away, snickering.

Nick opened his mouth to speak, but the surgeon raised his hand. "I know. You want to know how Miss Goldsmith is doing. And I'll tell you what I told you five minutes ago. She's still in shock. We will have to reconstruct her ear, but that's the least of it. Besides the lacerations and bruises I'm afraid...I don't want to say anything more until I confer with the team of ophthalmic surgeons."

Nick sat straight up. "Ophthalmic surgeons?" He grabbed the doctor's coat lapels, bringing their faces within inches of each other. "Oh no, you don't," he barked. "You're not going to leave me hanging. Tell me. Is it that serious?" He raised his voice. "Well, is it?"

"Take it easy, Nick. Her vision's impaired."

"Her vision? What do you mean, her vision? She'll be able to see, won't she?"

"It's too soon to tell. The eye specialist and I have done only routine examinations." Avoiding Nick's eyes, he said, "but there's definitely a problem." He turned to Clancy. "Make sure he stays put." To Nick, he said, "Listen, I'll personally be monitoring her condition. I promise you."

"You're upset," Clancy said to Nick. Then he turned back to the doctor. "He needs to get some sleep. Right, doc?"

The surgeon patted Nick on the shoulder. "I'm late for my scrub up. Just leave it to me." He faced Clancy. "Stay with him for a while. Clancy nodded and slipped the surgeon a folded piece of paper.

In the hallway, the surgeon read Clancy's message:

"Miss Goldsmith is under twenty four hour surveillance. Her assailant has not been apprehended. Detective Pagliara is overwrought and can be difficult if provoked. He might try to sneak a visit to Miss Goldsmith. That's the last thing we want him to do. Make sure he stays in his bed."

The doctor walked to the nurse's station and approached the head nurse. "I want Detective Pagliara sedated. I'll write out the order." He inclined his body close to hers. "Nurse Tucker, I mean seriously sedated."

Chapter 64

At midnight the stillness in the hospital corridor magnified the echo of the wall clock's TICK! TICK! TICK! Officer Stubbs placed the *Playboy* magazine on his lap, yawned, then stretched his arms to the ceiling. The chair creaked as he stood, tucked the magazine under his arm, and walked toward room 201. Noiselessly, he opened the door just enough to check on Franny, who lay in a state of semi-consciousness. Peering into the room, satisfied that she was all right, he turned to leave when the magazine slid from under his arm.

"Who's there?" Franny moaned.

Groggy and heavily sedated, she slipped from the real world into a dream world, not able to capture either one for more than a few seconds. Her mind struggled to hold onto bits and pieces of images that flickered like lightning flashes through her head and all too quickly faded away.

⁕

Her cries resounded throughout the noiseless corridors. "Stop it! Stop it!" Franny screamed. Officer Stubbs ran into her room. Throwing her arms about his neck, she shouted, "Don't let him make me do it." Tears streamed down her cheeks as the breath caught in her throat. "Don't let him."

"I won't, don't worry," Officer Stubbs said. "You had a nightmare. There now, take it easy."

Franny slowly raised her head from his shoulder. "A nightmare? It was my father asking me to…Yes. A nightmare," she said softly between sobs. "Where am I?"

"I'll take over, officer, thank you." A nurse hurried to Franny. She took Franny's hands and held them. "You're just fine. You mustn't exert yourself," she said, making sure the bandage on Franny's ear was secure. "You had an accident."

"Accident," Franny repeated. "What accident?" Then it came back to her. "Oh yeah. Amelia…she tried to kill me. The last thing I remember is jumping from the car and falling down an embankment."

"You have a lot of people worrying about you. I'm going to give you a shot. This will calm you. You're going to feel better."

"What are you, a nurse in training?" Franny blurted out. "What's with the tape on my eyes? My ear is killing me and my body feels like I was run over by a cement mixer. She tore at the bandages that covered her eyes. Is there a blackout? Or did the hospital forget to pay the electric bill." She stretched her arms out to the nurse. Panic seized her. "Hey, what's going on? Where are you? Turn on the lights."

"Now, just take it easy," the nurse said. "The doctor is on his way."

"What is this, the loony bin? I don't belong here," Franny ranted. "You have no right to keep me here! Where's the doctor? I demand to see the doctor!"

"Just keep calm," the nurse said. "The doctor will be here very shortly."

"Calm! I can't see anything!" she bellowed. "Get the doctor, now! I want to see him, now!" She rubbed her eyes. "Why can't I see?" she screamed. "What's wrong with my eyes?"

"The doctor is on his way," the nurse said.

Within seconds, Franny's body relaxed. "I'm afraid of the dark. The nightmares will come back and I can't take any more. Put the light on, will you?" Her voice gradually faded into a whisper. "Where are you, Nick? Where are my ladies? Weren't they just here? Did I dream them? And Lily's piano, here in my room? Am I going mad? Why is it so dark?"

•

"Clancy? Stubbs here. We have a problem with the Goldsmith lady. You're screaming in my ear, man…No, she's okay. Nothing's happened to her. Just a nightmare; then she got all bent out of shape when she found out she couldn't see. Yes, I know she's Detective Pagliara's lady friend. The doctor? He should be here any second. They gave her a shot to calm her. She was wild…. Don't bite my head off. Don't worry. I won't let her out of my sight…. It's up to you. I don't think it's necessary to have two men on this job. I do go off duty in an hour. Sure, I'll stay on. Clancy, I will not leave her even to take a piss…. What do you mean where am I? I can see her room from here. The doctor just whizzed in…. Which doctor? The same doctor who was here before. Excuse me, the surgeon…. You're coming down? …I'll check every person that goes into her room. Gotta hang up. The doc's raising hell with the nurse."

"I'm right here," Officer Stubbs declared upon hearing the doctor ask about the officer on duty. "I was just checking in with my boss, sir. Never had my eye off the room for a second."

"The doctor scowled. "You do know the patient is in danger, and she's also related to Detective Pagliara."

Officer Stubbs nodded in agreement. "I understand. She's family." He rolled his eyes as he walked out the door. *Thinks this is my first day on the job.* He looked around, embarrassed by the *Playboy* he thoughtlessly left on the folding chair. The chair again squeaked from the weight of his large frame as he shoved the magazine underneath his buttocks. Knowing Clancy would be there any moment, he stood up, walked to the visitors' room, and slipped the magazine under a pile of tabloids that sat on the table. He patted the stack of newspapers. "Don't you go nowhere," he said. "I'll be back for you as soon as it quiets down."

As soon as he sat down, he heard footsteps clicking on the tile floor, signaling Clancy's approach. Clancy smiled broadly. "Good news, Stubby," he said, "the crazy lady who was trying to kill Miss Goldsmith— she drowned in her car in the Apache River."

Officer Stubbs stood. "Guess she ran out of luck. Well, now that it's over I'll just mosey on and get something to eat." He stopped short, noticing Clancy's expression. "What?" Stubbs asked.

"I'm uneasy about leaving her in there unprotected."

"But the perp is no longer a threat. Seems like an open and shut case to me." He eyed Clancy.

"I know, but Nick has been on our ass, and he would want someone watching her just to make sure."

Officer Stubbs sighed deeply, then stood at attention and gave Clancy a snappy salute. "Sir, yes sir."

"Good man," Clancy said, slapping Officer Stubbs on the back. "And to show the department's appreciation, I'll have a porterhouse steak, rare, with mashed potatoes sent up. And a bottle of Gatorade to top it off. You don't want dessert, right?" Stubbs pressed his lips together.

"I have to get downstairs and tell the crowd of hysterical friends and relatives they can rest easy. Miss Goldsmith's mother is kicking up a storm. What a mouth on that woman."

Stubbs smiled guardedly "Detective Pagliara must be on cloud nine with the good news. I hear he's up for the lieutenant's job when the old man retires."

Clancy winced. "Where'd you hear that? That's supposed to be top secret." He shook his head. "Yeah, like anything at the station could be kept under wraps for more than ten minutes. Anyhow, Nick is too sedated to know what's going on. First, I have to speak to the surgeon and then I'm off to deal with the others downstairs." He started toward

Franny's door and turned toward Clancy. "So where did you stash the *Playboy*, Stubby?"

Stubbs looked around. "How did you know?"

"Come on, Stubby. You never go anywhere without your bible. He waved a finger at the embarrassed officer. "I'll make sure the cut of porterhouse is real thick, and maybe I'll surprise you with a gooey dessert."

Chapter 65

Officer Stubbs belched loudly and looked around to see if anyone had heard. Clancy kept his word. "Mama Mia, what a meal," he said as he scooped up the last morsel of mashed potatoes with the last chunk of bread, wiped the plate clean, placed the napkin over the tray and searched his pockets for the candy bars that Clancy had sent up with the dinner. Reaching up, he pushed the off button on the television and watched the screen's light flicker and shrink to a small white spot. "Cheap set," he muttered.

Hearing a moan from across the hall, he listened intently, pulled his *Playboy* magazine from the stack of newspapers, and walked to see if Franny was all right. *If they're so goddamned worried about her they could at least keep a nurse with her,* he thought. Cracking the door slightly, he peeked inside to see Franny asleep.

The hands on the wall clock indicated 2:45 AM when Officer Stubbs nodded off outside Franny's room. He didn't hear the sound of the white sneakers as they squeaked on the tile floor; nor did he see the dowdy figure dressed in a white starched uniform until she was upon him. He quickly sat up in his chair. "Bout time someone looked in on her," he said. "She's been moaning in her sleep."

"Thanks for the advice," she said curtly. She smiled snidely and placed the tray she had been holding on the table. "Hittin' the department for overtime, are we?" She stood, empty tray in hand, an impatient expression on her face and waited for him to move his chair, which blocked her way into the room. "Today, sonny," she said dryly, her tone demanding immediate action.

He rose slowly, thinking it would give him the greatest pleasure if he could just zap her into oblivion. *These nurses are going the way of the flight attendants*, he thought.

"Thanks," she said, making no effort to hide her disgust, as she brushed past him, pushing the door open with her foot.

She walked over to Franny and leered down at her. "I've been waiting for this moment, Franny dear," she whispered. "There isn't much time to get you out of my life once and for all." Movement outside the door startled her, and she listened intently as she tiptoed to the door. Satisfied that all was well, she walked back to the bed, gently lifted Franny's head and removed the pillow from beneath her. "Sorry I can't stay longer and shoot the breeze," she said, "but time is of the essence. You know what I'm saying, sweetheart?"

Franny moaned.

"Bye-bye," she said as she placed the pillow over Franny's face and held it down.

Franny fought to breathe, but her body was too weak and sedated to fight back and within a few seconds her body went limp from the lack of oxygen.

Sensing something was not right, Officer Stubbs entered the room. Shocked to see the nurse holding a pillow over Franny's face, he sprang at the nurse, grabbed the pillow from her hands and tossed it across the room. "Crazy bitch," he yelled. "I'll fix your ass." The woman turned toward him and kicked him in the testicles. He groaned and crouched with pain as the intruder ran from the room. He shouted, "Nurse! Nurse! Get in here, quick!"

"Pray she's not dead," Stubbs said, as the nurses ran into the room. Aware that every second counted, Stubbs called security to see if the woman could be stopped before she left the building. He called for backup and began to search the area for the trespasser. Visualizing himself sitting behind a desk for the rest of his career, he took a deep breath and called Clancy.

The assailant dashed down the hospital stairs, ran through the kitchen, and out the side entrance of the hospital, then jumped into her automobile and took off. She drove two miles to a dumpster in an isolated neighborhood and parked the car. Shedding her brand new white sneakers, white starched uniform, white cotton stockings and nurse's cap, she hurriedly changed into a skirt and blouse. The lid of the dumpster creaked as she lifted it and tossed the nurse's uniform into it. She picked up discarded newspapers, lit a match and stood transfixed, holding the burning newspapers in her hand for a brief moment, then flung them into the dumpster. The flames distorted her face and she resembled someone making a sacrificial offering to an evil deity.

Chapter 66

Dashel, his face remorseful, avoided Lily's eyes. "I know I'm a bastard but I wanted to be honest with you."

Lily glowered at him. "You're walking out on me? I can't believe what you're saying. I didn't expect this from you." She fought to hold back the tears that filled her eyes. "Franny's in the hospital. A part of her ear was hanging by mere threads, and God knows if she'll be able to see again. Elaine's condition is deteriorating, and now you drop this bomb on me. Great timing."

"I'm sorry, Lily. I really am. Better to get it all over with while..."

Overriding his words, she cried, "While I'm at my lowest point? Is that what you're telling me?" She poured herself a glass of wine. "And here I thought I finally found the right one. I guess I'm just destined to pick losers. I'm surprised I haven't been contacted by the Guinness book of records for being the woman with the most rejections in the shortest possible time." She paced back and forth and stopped short within inches of his face. "Who is she?" He stared down at the floor. She took him by the shoulders and shook him. "You poor excuse for a man! You're leaving, so why don't you just tell me?" She gulped her wine and poured another. "I'd offer you some," she said, her eyes ablaze, "but I don't want to share anything with you. Not any more." She tilted her head to one side and glared at him. "So, who is she? Anyone I know?"

He held out his hands. "Please, Lily. Does that matter? The Tillingham package put a million in my pocket. I want to continue playing the piano. I can do that now. You said I was good."

She threw her head back and laughed wildly. "Sure, I said you were good. But I never said you were good enough. Anyhow, I thought I was in love with you when I said it. I guess the money is more important than me."

"You got over me fast. Remember London, when you ditched me?"

"Not as fast as you've gotten over me. So give, who's the new love?"

"Can't we just part like civilized human beings?"

She eyed him. "You call yourself civilized? Come on, you owe me."

"Mariah Tillingham."

Lily's eyes widened. She walked to the door and flung it open. "Out!" she shouted. As he started to leave, she called to him. "We can't just say goodbye—not like this." She made a fist and hit him squarely on the chin. He hit the floor with a thud. With her spiked heels she rolled him over and shoved him into the hallway. She stood over him. "Now that's a proper goodbye." Returning to her apartment, she slammed the door behind her and slumped to the floor, sobbing, not caring if she had hurt her delicate hand.

Chapter 67

The first thing Nick saw after he rubbed the sleep from his eyes was Clancy with the surgeon. Dr. Phelps checked his pulse. "Holding my hand again," Nick quipped. "Didn't know you cared."

Dr. Phelps shook his head. He turned to Clancy. "He's back to normal." He scowled at Nick. "And don't give the nurses a hard time." He headed for the door, waved a goodbye and called back, "I have an emergency. I'll check on you later. We have to talk. And for God sakes, stay off that foot."

"Foot? What foot?"

Nick sat up in the hospital bed, alarmed and confused. "Clancy, what's going on? What time is it? No, what day is it?" He swung his feet off the bed and winced with pain. "Wow! What the fuck! How did this cast get here?"

"You broke it, falling down the embankment to save Franny."

"What did they do to me? Shoot me full of tranquilizers? The last time I felt like this was the morning after I partied all night." He grabbed hold of Clancy's arm. "How's Franny?"

Clancy bit his lip, wondering where to begin. His voice indistinct, he said, "She's okay." Fright flashed in Nick's eyes. Clancy raised his hands reassuringly. "Don't get crazy, Boss. I swear she's okay. It's just that there are complications."

Nick pounded the bed with his fist. In a hushed tone he said, "I'm in control. Give it to me straight."

"First, the doctor's wife, Amelia Stern, the psycho who tried to kill her, drove off an embankment and drowned."

"That's good news. What about Franny?"

"Boss, please. Franny is resting comfortably, but there was an attempt on her life, last night."

"What?" Nick said sharply. "Don't tell me you didn't post security at her door. I can't believe you'd be so..."

"Of course I did. It was the first thing I thought of. Stubbs sat outside her door every second. But somehow this woman disguised herself in a nurse's uniform, got in and..."

"You said that Franny's all right, except for what?"

"Bear with me. I'll get to that in a sec. The intruder tried to smother Franny with a pillow, but Stubbs broke it up. He got kicked in the balls but managed to alert the nurse's station and security."

"Who was it?"

"She got away."

"Are you sure the crazy lady that drowned was Amelia Stern?"

"Yep, down to the DNA."

"So what's with Franny? And how come Dr. Phelps didn't tell me?"

"He's having specialists look in on her. And he knows...uh...how emotionally upset you can get." He eyed Nick. "She's blind, temporarily."

"Nobody's temporarily blind, Clancy. Thanks for trying to ease the blow. What I can't figure out is how the crazy lady missed killing Franny at such close range." He noticed the dark circles under Clancy's eyes. "You look like shit. You were up all night, right?" Clancy shrugged. "Now, Clancy, if you'll be so kind as to get my clothes out of the closet and find me a pair of crutches, I've got work to do. And take that look off your face. You don't think I'm going to sit in this bed while Franny's in danger, do you? You better get yourself home and sack out for a while. You've got bags under your eyes the size of Cleveland."

"No way, Boss. Someone just might kick the crutch out from under you. And there aren't many people who would help you up. No use getting pissed. I'm sticking to you like crazy glue."

Chapter 68

The sky turned gray and the wind made a whooshing sound around Lily's head as she opened the door of the limousine for Elaine. "Sit, Murphy," she said to her driver. "No sense you getting wet, too." Holding her umbrella with one hand, she extended the other to her friend. The wind snatched the umbrella, sending it soaring across the avenue, where it rested for a split second then took off again.

The driver sprang from the limo with his umbrella and held it over Lily. "Let me get you under the canopy, Miss Fitzgerald." He shut the door to make sure Elaine did not get wet. "I'll come back for you, Mrs. Benjamin."

Returning for Elaine, he said, "Take your time Mrs. Benjamin." He locked arms with her and supported her up the hospital steps.

Inside the lobby, Lily hesitated. "What?" Elaine said solemnly.

"I can't go up there yet, I'm too upset." "I'm on the verge of tears. I just can't face Franny."

Elaine nodded. "You took the words out of my mouth. You're right. How about we have a cup of tea or coffee in the cafeteria? This weather isn't exactly what the doctor ordered for my...condition."

"I was thinking of maybe..."

Elaine cut her off. She gave Lily a serious look. "No, Lily! No way are you going to start drinking this early in the day," she said, sharply. "You want to shorten my life even more?"

Lily returned with a tray. "Look, they had the Celestial tea you like. Chamomile, to calm you. And a no-sugar, no-fat, one hundred percent raisin-bran muffin."

Elaine took a deep breath and let it out with a long sigh. "Lily. Aside from Lew and Franny, and my girls, I love you more than anyone in the whole world. But I think you're losing it. Tea to calm me? You're making me feel like a basket case. I need the calming? Just take a look at you. You help me up the stairs like I'm on my last legs, handle me like I was made of glass, and get me special tea and diet bran muffins. I'm not dead yet, so stop treating me as if I were going any minute. And another thing. If you want to make me feel better, cut down on the wine, because that annoys the hell out of me." She ran her hands over her face, remembered how deformed they were and put them in her lap. Looking at her friend with compassion, she said softly, "I know you hurt, and you want to vent. Go ahead; it's your turn now."

Lily sat stunned. Her jaw dropped, and tears streamed down her face. "What has gone wrong, Elaine? It was only yesterday that God was smiling down at us. Suddenly, everything has fallen apart. Franny may never see again, Dash has left me, and you..." She dabbed at her eyes with a tissue. "It's like the world is closing in on us." A clap of thunder resounded throughout the cafeteria. "Geez," she said. "All we need is Nina Simone singing one of her sorrowful songs to put the finishing touches on this pathetic picture."

"It's not the end of the world, Lily. You still have your piano to keep you sane." She lifted the teacup with effort, her face revealing the pain she felt in her fingers, and set it down quickly. "It's strange. When you're young you think you will never die or grow old, that you will always be strong and healthy. One's life is very fragile." She shook her head. "Okay, sister," she said, tossing her scarf over her shoulder. "It's time to lose the blues and get the show on the road. Franny may not be able to see, but if we sound like we feel...well, she'll only get more depressed. We have to act up a storm. Think you're up to it?"

"Of course. If you can, so can I. I'm sorry I carried on. It was very selfish of me, and..."

Elaine interrupted, "We are all going to die, Lily, some a little sooner than others. That's the only difference. Let's not dwell on it." She held onto the table for support and stood. "Let's go."

"Elaine?"

"Yes, Lily."

"I need a drink."

Elaine's mouth curled to one side. She raised her hands and curled her deformed fingers at Lily as if she was going to claw her. "See these?" she said. "One more fucking word about the booze, and I swear I'll leave you scarred forever." She held Lily around the waist as they walked to the elevator. "You don't know how lucky you are, babe," she said. "Want to trade places with me?"

They stepped into the elevator as Elaine waved a Nancy Reagan *say no to drugs* finger at Lily. "No drugs, no alcohol. You beat the diet pills and you can beat the drinking, too."

"I know you're right, Elaine."

"That's for sure," Elaine said as the embarrassed passengers stared at the numbers that lit up as they passed each floor. "That's for sure."

As they left the elevator, the police officer raised his hand. "No one is allowed in this section of the hospital without special permission."

"Special permission?" Lily asked with a huff. "We were told that this is..." she checked her pass, "the floor that Franny Goldsmith is on, and let me see...yes..." she held the pass up to him. "This is the fifth floor, isn't it?"

"Yes, ma'am," he said politely. "But no one is allowed to visit with her.

You have to see the hospital administrator and have it validated."

"I don't think so," Lily insisted. "We are not schlepping all the way down to the lobby again. And why did they issue us the pass in the first place if the patient is not allowed visitors? Who's in charge?"

The officer started to speak as Clancy, overhearing their conversation, spoke up. "I'll handle this, Stubbs. Good morning, ladies," he said cordially. "Sorry about the mix up. Detective Pagliara did tell the office that the two of you, Miss Goldsmith's mother and Mr. Tripplehorn were the only visitors permitted to see Miss Goldsmith." He shrugged. "But the detective has everyone dancing on hot coals since the attempt on the patient's life last night."

"Attempt?" Elaine said, alarmed. "What attempt? Didn't Amelia Stern drown?"

Aware that they were attracting attention, Clancy leaned closer to them. "Let's go into the visitors' room. We can talk there."

•。

The door opened very slowly, making a soft whining sound as the rubber flap rubbed against the tile floor. Franny sensed someone's presence but said nothing, knowing the nurses constantly checked on her. But the silence in the room was not broken by the usual, "How are we doing" or 'Time for your pills" conversation. She sat up in bed and listened to the stillness of the room. "I know it's you two, you creeps," she said. "Come on, ladies, no tears for little Franny." She stretched her arms out. "Come over here and give me a big hug. I've been waiting all morning for you two to show."

No response.

"Oh, I know. It's you, Blanche. Only you would give me the silent treatment. Still punishing me, Ma?"

She still didn't get a response.

Alone in the darkness, Franny became frightened. She reached for the call button.

"It's me, Franny. Nick."

Surprised, hurt, but relieved, she answered with her usual Franny sense of humor. "Geez, are you trying to scare the shit out of me? Or do you think sneaking up on me like that will bring the light back into my eyes?" Trying to hold back tears, she said, "So, Detective Pagliara, what's happening back at the hoosegow?" She reached for a tissue but accidentally knocked the box to the floor.

The beat in his heart raced as he observed the bandages on her ear and eyes. He quickly picked up the box, removed a tissue and placed it in her hand; his finger's brushed against hers. "Here," he said, his voice breaking.

"You'll have to excuse my appearance," she said. "My eyes keep tearing. Doctor Phelps says it's natural for them to tear. I'm so lucky. I always complained that my eyes were dry, and now I don't have to worry about it anymore. Dr. Phelps has been really supportive. He says that there is a good chance I'll be able to see again. But between you and me, that's standard doctor-patient mumbo jumbo." She rambled on. "Your man Clancy is a really nice guy. Filled me in on what's happening. Who would have thought that sweet lady, Amelia Stern, was a killer? I asked him why they keep changing my room, but he's avoiding me. Are you here on official business? Go ahead. Fire away. Want to know something? Just ask Franny. She sees all, hears all and knows all. Well, we can forget about the seeing part."

"Franny, stop it!" he said flatly.

"Stop what? *You're* not talking. Since you entered my private room, unannounced, you've said all of three words. 'It's Nick, Franny.' And oh, yes, 'stop it.'" She didn't bother to blot the tears that now streamed down her face. "Well, Nick, you don't have to lose any more time than is necessary. You're excused. You paid your social call. Unless you're here on official business, you have my permission to leave. In fact, I wish you would leave."

"I don't want to leave. Please, listen to what I have to say."

"Don't patronize me just because I'm blind. I don't want your pity or your sympathy. Hey, we had fun, no regrets, right? You did what you thought was right. So, okay, I was hurt. Really hurt. But I lived through worse times, and I shall survive. Hey, good title for a song, don't you think?" She extended her hand. "Tell you what. No hard feelings. Let's shake, okay?"

Emotionally drained and guilt ridden, he bent down, his face almost touching hers.

A shiver ran through her as she felt his breath on her cheek.

"I don't want to shake hands, Franny. I want to take you in my arms, hold you and kiss you and for only one reason...because I love you. I always have. I made a stupid mistake, and I've more than regretted it."

He positioned himself on the edge of the bed and took her in his arms, holding her tightly against him.

She moaned softly, unable to speak, letting herself melt in his arms. "You're making a big commitment, Nick. You should be very sure. Pity is the last thing I want. You feel this way now, but in time you'll..."

"Let's only think of now. I hope in time you can find it in your heart to forgive this poor excuse of a man." He smothered her mouth with his.

She stroked the back of his neck. "I forgave you the minute we split. I just didn't want to believe it was over." She reached out to touch his face. "Can I ask you something, Nick?"

"Anything."

"I've been thinking."

He eyed her suspiciously. "This isn't going to be one of those kooky Frannyisms, is it? You know, like your mother is always saying, 'you're losing it again, Franny.'"

She ignored him. "I was thinking. If I'm going to be blind, and I know

I'll have to make adjustments…do you think I could have two, big Russian wolfhounds as 'seeing eye' dogs?"

"You can have Irish Wolfhounds, if you want, you screwball," he said, all the while his mind troubled by the thought that someone wanted Franny dead.

Lily and Elaine tapped on the door and burst in without waiting for an invitation. "Correct me if I'm wrong, but was that a scene from *An Affair to Remember?*" Lily announced. "Excuse our intrusion, but these hospital rooms are not soundproof."

Elaine joined in. "Too bad there isn't a back way out of this room. The entire floor is buzzing about the star-crossed lovers in room 501."

Chapter 69

Nick hopped briskly down the hospital corridors on crutches with Clancy at his heels, aware of the whistles and teasing remarks from the police officers and hospital staff. "Don't start anything, Boss," Clancy said, smirking. "They're only spoofing. You can't blame them. After all, you did leave yourself wide open. It was you who gave the order to make sure everyone kept an ear at her door."

"You mean they heard the whole scenario between Franny and me?"

"Uh huh. Except for a few smooches that didn't carry into the hallway." Clancy stifled a snicker. "One of the nurses almost got crushed by the crowd leaning against the door," he teased.

"Up yours, Clancy," Nick said with false cheerfulness and a hint of embarrassment. "And I suppose you didn't think it necessary to disperse the nosy fuckers?"

"I was outnumbered."

"You know something, big shot? You better watch your step."

Clancy spotted Mr. Tripplehorn coming toward them and turned to Officer Stubbs, giving him the okay to let the lawyer visit Franny.

The elevator doors opened as Nick turned and faced the onlookers, giving them the finger. They, in turn, reciprocated with a loud round of applause.

Franny said nothing but shuddered at the touch of Elaine's crippled fingers as they embraced. "So," she asked, "what have you two been up to?"

"We haven't been up to anything…because of you," Lily said.

Staring at Franny, Elaine added, "Yeah, who's had time to live a normal life? You, as usual, have taken center stage. First, you go on a wild automobile chase with that demented Amelia, then you and Nick do a *Romeo and Juliet* scene with a live audience listening right outside your door. What's next? Good thing Blanche isn't here. She would have said you're losing it again." They all laughed.

Franny frowned. "Speaking of Blanche, she hasn't visited me since I've been here. Isn't that just like her? Maybe the old man took a turn for the worse. You know something? I dreamed I had an argument with her."

Elaine declared. "Fighting is an everyday occurrence with you two."

"Why don't you call her?"

"I just can't get myself to do it."

Lily touched Franny's hand. "Well, I can do it for you, if you like."

"No," Franny said. "She should have the sense to come here even if the old man is dying. I *am* her daughter. Forget it. What do you think about Nick and me? Fabulous, huh?"

"I'm happy for you, Franny. By the way, Dash left me."

Franny sat up. "What? Just like that? What happened? What a creep. Never mind. Who is she?"

"Mariah, Mariah Tillingham. Her husband was investigated, and he is going to have a trial. It doesn't look too good for him."

"I think she's lucky. Don't you agree, Franny?" Elaine said. "The two men that screwed her are getting their just rewards. I give Dashel and Mariah no more than three months. They deserve each other."

"Right, Elaine," Franny said. "Never trusted Dash. His eyes are too close together. How are you taking it, Lily?"

"I thought I was going to end it all...but now with your condition and my addictions... Anyhow, I have no time for self-pity. More important, tell us, Franny, what do the doctors say about your ear and your eyesight?"

"Let's take one thing at a time. The ear, huh? Well, it's pretty much shot. No pun intended."

Lily shuddered. "Oh, no."

Elaine took in a quick breath and let out a mournful sigh. "My God! That was from the shot that grazed your ear?"

"Yeah, it did more than just graze my ear. They're going to run me through the mill, and then I'll know what gives."

Lily asked. "Do you know if it affected your hearing?"

"Not yet. They're probably going to toss a coin to see whether they'll do the eyes or the ear first. And plastic surgeons said they would even put a hole in the lobe so I could wear earrings."

Lily pulled two chairs close to the bed, and then motioned to Elaine. "Let's sit." Looking up at Fanny, Lily asked, "How can you joke about this?"

"Listen," Franny said, "are you girls here to depress me or cheer me up? Look at it this way. I'm lucky to be alive. It took a near-death experience to make me realize how fragile a person's life is. I've had lots of time to think, and I'm going to make a few changes—except for my big mouth. That would take a miracle."

"Good for you," Elaine said.

"Yeah, the doctor said I was lucky the bullet didn't hit a centimeter closer or I would be in big trouble."

"They say that I need corneal transplants, but it would still be a fifty-fifty chance that I would regain my eyesight. And like any organ, they would have to find the right ones and get them from an eye bank. Tell you the truth, ladies, I became confused with all the medical mish mash."

Elaine frowned. "It's important to know, Franny. What else did they tell you?"

Franny scrunched up her face, trying to remember. "Let's see…something about my cornea being damaged by the fall down the hill. And that I had a prolapsed cornea that's displaced from its socket…and my eyes are swollen and something about needing a bilateral corneal transplantation…I think…" She threw her hands into the air. "What is this, a quiz? That's what I remember. If you want to know more, go ask them yourself. To tell you the truth, I stopped hearing what they were saying after the third ophthalmologist's spiel."

Elaine edged closer to Franny. "Who is the neurosurgeon you spoke to? I mean his name."

"Who remembers?" Franny shrugged. "There were three plus Dr. Phelps and I think a Doctor Forester. Anyhow, I remember some months ago seeing a program about blind people on television and you know something? What they said was true. My senses are so much more acute and I'm aware of things and sounds I never even knew existed before."

"You're taking all this very well," Lily said.

"Actually, I'm numb. I must be spaced out from all the drugs they keep feeding me. And hey, what the hell, I got Nick back and that's what I wanted."

"Dr. Phelps is the doctor that Nick is so friendly with, isn't he?" Elaine said.

"Yeah," Franny said. "He's one of the top surgeons in the country. Nick knows him from all his dealings with the emergency procedures done here in the hospital. And he treated Nick's wife before she died. He and the Forester specialist are in and out of here all day."

"Then he should be here any minute, right?" Elaine asked.

Franny cocked her head to one side while Lily eyed Elaine suspiciously. "Why the sudden interest in doctors and procedures, Elaine?" Franny asked.

Elaine hesitated. "Oh, nothing. But you seem so unconcerned about getting a donor and restoring your eyesight. You're not going to just sit around and wait for your sight to return, are you? I only thought I would delve further...." She glanced at Lily. "We know how flighty you can be at times. After all, we are your best friends. Just thought I'd check on what the procedures are, and the like."

"What the hell does 'and the like' mean, Elaine?" Franny cried. "Lily, what is she up to?"

"Take it easy, Franny," Lily said.

Franny raised her voice. "No, I won't take it easy." She projected her voice toward Lily. "Lily, are you thinking what I'm thinking, and tell me I'm wrong, please."

Lily lowered the railing on the bed, sighed, and took Franny's hand in hers. "We are on the same wave length, Franny." She faced Elaine. "Are we on the same wavelength?" she asked gravely.

Elaine stepped up on a stool, sighed painfully and lay down next to Franny. "Come on, Lily," she said, locking arms with Franny. "Scoot over and put your body on the other side. I have something I want to read to the both of you."

GEORGE CORRENT M.D. PH.D.
MEDICAL SURGICAL SPECIALISTS
NAPLES FL. 34119

Dear Mrs. Benjamin:

As per our previous conversations and at your request, I am writing about the procedure we had discussed concerning the subject of a cornea transplant.

In regard to your question about the transplantation of an

eye, whole eyes cannot be transplanted. An eye cannot, at this time, be re-connected to an optic nerve, which would be necessary for it to send its images to the brain and also to obtain the vascular supply that it would need to function and survive.

The one part of the eye which can be transplanted is the cornea—the clear front tissue of the eye—essentially the *front window*' of the eye.

If a clear donor cornea is used to replace the patient's damaged one, this can restore vision—allowing the blind eye, or eyes, to see, as it were. So, if a person were to have their corneas badly damaged by trauma, for example in a fire, or by a mechanical or chemical injury, they might lose their vision. Then, a corneal transplant could restore the vision.

I hope this clarifies any questions you may have about transplantation.

If you decide to go ahead with the operation please call my secretary, Christine, to discuss preliminary procedures.

Sincerely,
George Corrent, MD Ph D

Chapter 70

Nick glared at Clancy. "Are you working solo now?" he asked accusingly. "When were you going to tell me? After she finished Franny off?"

"Take it easy, Boss. I wanted to be certain about the information before I made it official...you being all wrapped up with your...uh...personal affairs and your broken leg..."

"Thank you for your consideration, Father Clancy, but in the future try to remember who's in charge of this case." He eyed Clancy. "You're way out of line. Don't ever take it upon yourself to run the department for me. You check with me first, you understand?" He groaned with pain as he lifted his leg and rested it on the desk. "You realize, don't you, that she can still get to Franny?"

Clancy would have liked to tell Nick that his intimacy with Franny was blinding his perspective of the case. But he took the furthest chair from Nick and hung his head, sulking, hurt by his boss's sudden attack on him.

"Officer Stubbs," Nick yelled into the phone, "are you looking for early retirement?"

"No, Nick."

"You will address me as sir, you fucking moron. How could you let anyone into the room like that bitch who pretended to be a nurse?" Stubbs started to speak, but Nick spoke over him. "Open up the damn door and see who's in there with Franny. I'll wait." Nick tapped on his cast nervously with a letter opener, all the time glaring at Clancy.

Stubbs checked the room. "Just her two friends: the pianist and Mrs. Benjamin. That attorney, Mr. Tripplehorn, was here but he left. Oh, yeah, two specialists and Dr. Phelps stayed for quite a while with the three of them. And the nurse has been in and out constantly; she just left. Now the doctor is leaving."

"Listen, Stubbs. You're walking a very thin line. Check each nurse who goes in and out! What was Dr. Phelps doing in there all that time?"

What the hell is eating him, Stubbs wondered. "I don't know, Detective Pagliara," he said. "Dr. Phelps was just talking with them. I heard them laughing."

"Keep your damn eyes open." Nick said, his tone as cold as ice.

"I swear. I'm on top of it, Sir."

"I'm having Clancy and the boys put out an all-points alert for the woman," Nick said as he motioned a *thumbs up* to Clancy, who was already out the door, determined to snap the cuffs on this crazed dame and toss her sorry ass into the lock-up.

•。

Dr. Phelps looked from Franny to Elaine and back to Franny as they lay on adjacent gurneys, their hands tightly clasped. "Now, this is what I call a friend," he said, smiling warmly.

Tears flooded Franny's eyes. "Bet your sweet scalpel," she said. "They don't come any better. Drove me up the wall until I gave in. Are you going to stay during the operation?"

"Yes, of course I'll stay. Nick would have me arrested and put away on some trumped up charge if I didn't." He raised his head and greeted the surgeon who was to perform the operation. "Ah, Dr. Corrent," he said.

"Everything in order?"

Dr. Corrent, a tall man with an angular, pleasant face, sported a mustache and goatee. His brown eyes shined and his perfect white teeth gleamed as he smiled at Franny and then Elaine. "Couldn't be better," he said, his tone gentle and reassuring. "And how are my patients feeling?" He didn't wait for their reply. "Nervous and tense, I hope. Anything else would be abnormal." His smile vanished, and his voice took on a serious tone. "As I have said before, ladies, there are no guarantees. However, I've performed this operation many times. The chance that you will see again," he said to Franny, "remains to be seen. You may regain your sight immediately." He hung onto his words for a few seconds. "Or your sight may not return for weeks, or months or..." He shrugged. "I feel confident we have every chance for success."

Sighing, he turned to Elaine, a half smile lingering on his face. "What a wonderful place this world would be if there were more compassionate humans like you. You are the epitome of a true friend. Donating your sight to your best friend is...well, what more can I say." He took both their hands and held them for a moment. Turning to his assistant he said briskly, "Okay, it's time to scrub."

"Last chance to change your mind," Franny said to Elaine. "And thanks again."

"Change my mind? No way, Jose. And stop thanking me, or I *will* change my mind."

The hospital corridor seemed bleak and cold as the nurses parted the stretchers and wheeled them into the operating room. Her voice breaking, Franny called out. "I love you, Elaine."

"I love you, too," Elaine replied.

"I love you bigger," Franny countered.

"Okay," Elaine said. "You win."

Chapter 71

The silence was unbearable as Lew, Nick, Lily, and Trippy sat silently in the waiting room, each with their own thoughts, not saying a word.

Lily broke the silence. "I need a drink," she blurted in a low whisper. Everyone turned toward her. "Did I say that?" she asked. "I meant coffee."

"There's a bar down the block from the hospital," Nick said. "Maybe we should all go. The operation won't be over for a good two hours."

Lily stood up. "I'll be honest, I did mean a drink. But I promised myself that I would abstain. If Elaine can do what she is doing for Franny, the least I can do is go on the wagon. It just doesn't feel right. The three of us are supposed to share each other's happiness and grief, and I'm not doing my part. I could have volunteered *my* sight. Elaine is suffering enough."

Lew rose, his face showing the misery he felt, and embraced Lily. She collapsed in his arms, sobbing. "It wasn't meant for you to do any such thing," he said, trying to comfort her. "Elaine and Franny know that, and you should, too. Don't feel guilty. It's just the way the cards fell. We can't do anything about what life hands us. Let's pray that the operation is a success. We have to focus on the bright side."

Lily looked up at Lew. "You're a wonderful man, Lew," she said. "You're right." She sat down beside him and put her arm through his, sensing a warm, affectionate sensation run through her.

366

Nick eyed Lew. "And a brave man, too," he said. "I've got a confession to make. I've been blaming myself for Franny's narrow escape with Amelia, for almost being smothered in the hospital. I've been taking it out on every one I came in contact with. You're right, Lew. It's just the way the cards fell. We don't know how lucky we are until we lose what we have." He faced Lew. "I'm sorry, I didn't mean to bring up..."

"I know you didn't, Nick. You've had a hard time tracking down the killer, and then Franny being a suspect in the case...it must have torn you apart. I've known about Elaine's condition for a while now. And as much as it hurts to see her deteriorate a little more each day, I had to make a choice. Either I reconcile myself to it and just go on, or die a slow death until she... So I smile through the pain, living every agonizing day waiting...waiting..." He put his hands to his face and wept as Lily, her arms around him, tried to comfort him.

Trippy motioned to Nick to follow him. They walked along the hospital corridor. Trippy said, "You may think of me as an old fool but I, too, love Franny. Not in the same passionate way that you do, but as a man who was thankful to have tasted the fruits of youth that Franny shared with me. I knew from the beginning she was seeing me because she was devastated when you turned away from her. We used one another. I took her into my heart and she, in turn, made me feel gloriously young again. I tried to heal her wounds by making her feel wanted, secure and loved." He watched Nick's expression change from doubt to compassion.

"I knew that, but I was too jealous to admit it. And what riled me even more was the fact that you helped her while I hurt her. I heard of all the expensive gifts you gave her, and the lifestyle you afforded her, and it burned me like you wouldn't believe." He extended his hand to Trippy. "Now that I have come to my senses, you're one more person I have to thank...and ask for forgiveness."

Trippy clasped Nick's hand. "There's nothing to forgive, but I will be furious if I don't get an invitation to the wedding."

They returned to where Lily sat. She checked her watch. "It's been more than four hours. You would think they would have told us something by now."

"What we need is a break," Trippy suggested. "Food and drink. Is anyone hungry? I could send my chauffeur out and we could have a feast. Break up this torturous waiting."

"I couldn't eat a thing," Lily said. "Not the way I feel."

Lew looked up. "Trippy's right. We need a break." He turned to Nick. "Right?" he asked.

"Right," Nick agreed. "Come on, Lily, I bet you haven't had a thing today."

"Well, as Franny would put it, three's company but four's a hoot. Okay, I'll try."

"Who wants what?" Nick asked. "Pizza, Chinese, Italian or kosher?"

Trippy raised his hands. "Please let me take care of the ordering. Is anyone allergic or adverse to any particular type of food?" Everyone shook their heads. "Good, that makes it easier." He picked up his cell phone and dialed Le Grenouille. "Georgio, I need a favor.... Thank you. I knew you would. I need four complete dinners to be sent to the Eye and Ear Hospital, off Third Avenue. I leave the choice up to you. My chauffeur will meet your man at the side entrance. I'll need silver and linens. A fold-up table? Yes. Waiters will not be necessary. It's informal."

•₀

After they dined, Nick smiled at Lily. "I thought you weren't hungry. You polished off that lobster like..."

"Up yours, as Franny would say. And did you by any chance know what you had was lobster thermidor?"

"No kiddin," he joked. "Could've fooled me."

Lew managed a smile as he poured a demitasse for everyone while Lily held out a tray of assorted French pastries. "Fit for a king," he said, looking at Trippy. "Guess you eat like this all the time."

"Just about. I am fortunate to have my own chef at home."

Lily raised her eyebrows.

"Hey," Lew interceded. "It didn't come easy. You may not be aware that Trippy was a very poor kid back in England. He's worked damn hard for everything he's achieved." Trippy nodded, smiling appreciatively at Lew.

Nick chimed in. "That evens it out. Lew is a millionaire and Trippy is, too. That leaves you and me, Lily, the poor relations."

"Sorry to jump ship, Nick, but I have quite a bit put away from concerts and Tillinghams's gift of that ring. That leaves you the odd kid on the block."

"Figures," Nick said, shrugging. The door swung open and Dr. Phelps and Dr. Corrent approached. They looked at the uncovered trays of leftover food and then at each other. Dr. Phelps spoke first. "Nothing for the peons who worked their hearts out in the operating room?"

All eyes were focused on the physicians as silence encompassed the room. "It went well," Dr. Corrent said, raising his hand as everyone spoke over each other. "We will not know how successful the operation is until the bandages are removed." He hesitated. "And even then, all we can do is wait and pray." His eyes glanced at the left-over food and sighed. "Not even a crumb left for the working people. Well, Phelps, you and I are going to the corner Pizza Palace to dine, since we evidently have missed dinner."

Nick's mouth opened to speak but Dr. Corrent raised his hand.

"In answer to your next question, 'no,' you may not visit either of the patients at this time. Dr. Phelps will be in touch with you as to when you can. I suggest you all go home and relax for the next twelve or so hours." He started to leave, hesitated then viewed them seriously. "And remember...after the bandages are removed we must brace ourselves. The results may not be what we had hoped for."

Chapter 72

"I'm so excited I can hardly breathe," Lily said as Lew held the door of the taxi for her. "Thanks for being so thoughtful. I just didn't feel like using the limo today. I needed company." Actually, she had felt a twinge of excitement when he called and asked if she would like a ride to the hospital. She looked at him seriously as she slid into the seat beside him, aware of his cologne and thinking how good-looking he was. "Today's the day for the unveiling." Then remembering that it would not be a happy day for Elaine, she quickly said, "Forgive me, Lew. I'm such an idiot. It's not a good day for Elaine."

He put his hand on hers. "Don't apologize. Elaine knew perfectly well she would lose her eyesight by giving Franny hers. This was not a rash decision. We had gone over it a thousand times. I tried, you tried, but you know Elaine. Once she makes up her mind, forget it."

She wondered why he still held her hand, not that she wanted him to remove it. She thought, *this is Elaine's husband. Are you losing it?*

He sensed her discomfort and removed his hand. "Yes," he said. "This is a big day for Franny. And as far as Elaine is concerned, this is what she wanted. I know her. She won't complain. She has everything figured out."

"What do you mean?"

"Try not to get emotional, but since she decided to donate her eyes to

Franny, she tied up all the loose ends of her existence here on earth." He sighed deeply. "Down to the last detail of her life."

"Didn't she discuss anything with you?"

"No. She told me what she wanted to do. Oppose her? Why would I? We might have gone our separate ways for a while, but we never lost our love or trust for one another."

In the crowded hospital elevator, going up to Franny's room, he stood in back of Lily, inhaling her presence, telling himself he was a normal male and since he had not been with Elaine in months, it was only natural for his male hormones to rise to the occasion.

"I'll see you in Elaine's room, Lew. I want to use the ladies room," Lily announced.

But as he pushed the door open, his heart dropped upon seeing Elaine in a wheelchair, her hair in disarray, looking like someone's grandmother. "Sweetheart," he sang out as he fell to his knees and held her tight while smothering her with kisses. "How's my girl doing?"

He shrank back slightly as she answered, her voice cracking and hoarse. "Couldn't be better, darling. Is it time for Franny's bandages to come off? The doctor said I could be there...share the thrill of her being able to see again." She tried lifting her hands to caress him but she lacked the strength.

Still kneeling beside her, he took her hands in his and kissed her deformed fingers. Overcome with emotion, he blurted. "I should have stopped you. I never should have let you do this."

She leaned down as far as she could and kissed the top of his head. Speaking in a slow but determined tone she said, "Now, I want you to listen to me, Lew. When you're finished feeling sorry for yourself, I want you to pull yourself together. If Franny suspects that you're upset because of what I did, she'll feel miserable."

"You're right, sweetheart," he said, kissing her. "I'll wash my face and comb my hair in the bathroom."

Lily barged into the room, stopping short as she looked at Elaine. "Well, get you," she cried, trying to hide the shock of seeing Elaine's aged appearance. "How about a hug? How are you doing?"

"Stop the bullshit, Lily. I must look like something out of a horror movie. I feel okay. Tired and achy but otherwise... What can I say? And don't you start with the crying, too. I just got through with Lew slobbering all over me."

"I heard that," Lew yelled from the bathroom. "You never complained about my slobbering before."

"Then I wanted you to slobber. Now I just want you to treat me as normally as possible. Let's go. I want to be with Franny."

"Oh, there you are, Elaine," Dr. Corrent said, laughing robustly. "I was just about to alert the media." He looked around. "Are we all accounted for? God, I haven't seen so many spectators since Dr. Barnard performed the first heart transplant."

"That was before my time," Dr. Phelps quipped. "Where are Nick and Mr. Tripplehorn?"

Nick yelled from the doorway. "Present and accounted for, Doctor. Just some last-minute business. The arm of the law never sleeps."

"Thank God," Dr. Corrent said. "Now, let's move you up here, right beside Franny," he said to Elaine. "After all, you are the guest of honor. Mr. Benjamin, would you bring your wife over here? Thank you." The doctor clapped his hands three times and the nurse wheeled Franny into the room.

"I changed my mind," Franny said. "I've grown accustomed to the dark. You people with sight are missing a lot. Elaine, where's Elaine?"

Lew wheeled Elaine to Franny. "First, I need a hug from my best friend and a hug from my other best friend, Lily. And now a hug from Nick."

Dr. Phelps whispered to Dr. Corrent "I'm not sure we should be making this a three-ring circus. I think it's getting a bit overdone."

"Bernard," the doctor answered. "Don't worry. I have performed this surgery a hundred times."

Dr. Phelps shrugged reluctantly.

"And now for the unveiling," Dr. Corrent announced as though he were giving a seminar to his students. "Elaine, I will unwind the bandages, and you have the honor of holding them." He held his hand out and the nurse placed a pair of scissors in it. Slowly the gauze unwound and fell into Elaine's hands.

"I'm so excited," Franny cried. "I feel like a movie star who's had her eyes done over. Doc, maybe we should have thought about that."

"First things first, my dear. And besides, you are not ready for cosmetic surgery…except on your ear." He motioned to the nurses to close the blinds. "Now for the eye pads." Everyone edged forward. "Voila," he said as he took the last eye pad from Franny's face. "Now you may open your eyes."

"I'm afraid to," Franny said. "Maybe they won't open."

"They will open. Take your time."

"I'm afraid." Franny repeated.

"For God's sakes, Franny," Elaine said. "The suspense is killing me. Open them."

"Okay, here goes." She pried her eyes open and waited. "I don't see anything. Nothing." Her heart sank. "It's dark," she said. "As dark as before."

Chapter 73

Monday ran into Tuesday, and Tuesday into Thursday, without a trace of what had happened to Wednesday.

The telephone call from the hospital reminding Elaine she had a doctor's appointment left her in deep despair. A beeping sound disrupted her thoughts, telling her it was time to take her medication. She moaned as the pain traveled from her crippled fingers up her arm and into her neck. *This is not the way I want to spend the rest of my life,* she thought. *Dr. Kevorkian had the right idea. Why should anyone have to live with pain?* At night she tossed and turned and when she finally did fall asleep, it didn't last long. In the morning she asked herself what she had to look forward to today and tomorrow, knowing that the answer would be more pain.

The medicine kicked in, but the side effect that dulled her brain made her lightheaded and agitated. Lew had insisted on hiring a round-the-clock nurse, but she fought against it vehemently.

Lew stood over Elaine, trying to control his anger. "Franny has someone assisting her. Why are you so stubborn?"

"I don't want anyone hovering over me, cooking in my kitchen, and giving me baths," she contended. "I can manage very well, thank you." But she didn't. The bruises on her hands and legs were visual proof. "In fact, I get around the house pretty good for a lady that's learning to see in a new way." When he told her he was going to stay home with her, she threw a tantrum and finally gave in to a day nurse.

He suggested they get in touch with Celina in Guatemala and ask her to come back. A call revealed that Celina had gone to live with her sister who had developed cancer. The distressing news that her trusted friend and housekeeper could not come back and Franny's condition not improving plunged Elaine into more depression.

The only thing that brought her out of her despair were Lily's daily visits and Lew's undying devotion and attentiveness. She missed Franny's buffoonery and Lily's piano playing and cried, agonizing over her state of health. She shivered as she caressed the lace gloves she wore to cover her disfigured fingers. She knew her world was falling apart, and each passing day was a painful reminder her life was about to end.

Lew begged her to take the sleeping pills the doctor had prescribed.

"I can't stand those damn drugs. They make me sicker," she cried. "I'm up when I should be down, and down when I should be up. I'd need the whole bottle for them to work."

She turned to Lew with desperation. "Lew, darling, I want to ask you to do something ..."

He sprang up, his face draining of color. "Don't say it, Elaine. Don't think it. Don't even breathe it. I couldn't...please, sweetheart, don't ask me..." Tears streaked down his face as he ran to her and took her in his arms.

"You know there isn't anything in the world I wouldn't do for you, but please, not that."

"You don't understand," she insisted. "I dread getting up each morning knowing you have to look at me, crippled and blind, knowing the distress and agony you're going through. I just can't bear the pain. And for what? And for how long? Be honest."

She pulled the lace gloves off with her teeth and held up her hands.

"Look how misshapen they are. Pretty, huh? Look at my face. It's as round and swollen as a basketball. Look how fat I've become. And I have to use a ton of makeup to cover the blemishes on my face on the rare occasions when the girls force me to go out. I can't take the steroids any more because the side effects are shutting down my body's adrenal production.

She eyed him, trying to read his reaction. "The radiation has been stopped. I have trouble remembering things." She looked at him, her eyes pleading. "Is this the way a human being should live?" She put her arms on the chair and slowly raised herself, but the chair started to tilt.

"Elaine, my love," he pleaded as he ran to help her.

But she yelled at him. "Don't help me!" Feeling her way, she hobbled slowly to where she thought Lew stood. "See," she said removing a lock of her hair. "This is what you have to look forward to. We had a good marriage until I screwed it up. Thank God, we made things right. But Lew, I feel useless and—worse—I feel ugly. I can't stand for you to see me this way. I remember how pretty I was, and how you used to hold me and tell me I could be a movie star. And maybe I could have been but..." She hobbled toward him, holding her hand up, the lock of hair dangling between her crooked fingers, tears streaming down her face.

"If you love me, you will help me. Talk to the doctor. There must be a way to get around the law."

A gnawing hopelessness crept through Lew's very being. He held her in his arms and rocked her back and forth. "Oh, my darling, my love, how can I make you understand that I know and feel what you must be going through? But to take your life? I just can't." He sighed deeply. "Why don't you let me try another specialist? There must be others in Europe or even Asia that we could go to."

"Help me to the bed," she said. "Look, sweetheart. We've been to the biggest and the best. Let's face it. There is nowhere else to go. We've run the gamut."

"Aren't you supposed to take a pill?" he asked. "It's after eight."

"I ran out."

"What do you mean, you ran out? Didn't the nurse get you a refill?"

"I tried taking them myself, but I accidentally dropped the bottle in the bedpan," she lied. "Don't worry; she called the drugstore for a refill."

Frustrated, he shook his head. "How could you drop all the pills in the…?" He stopped short. "Never mind. It's eight o'clock. Where's her replacement?"

"Stop getting hysterical. She'll be here soon. Why don't you run down to the drugstore and pick up the pills?"

"Why didn't you tell me this before? You're supposed to take them as prescribed. Elaine, I have to tell you, you're a lousy patient." He walked toward the door. "I'll get on it right away. If you had a sleep-in nurse to make sure you behaved, you wouldn't…" He sighed, a helpless expression crossing his face. "Can I get you anything else?"

"No, sweetheart," she said. "Just a hug and kiss before you leave."

"How about two hugs and three kisses? Just to hold you until I get back."

She held on to him tightly. "I understand, Lew. Don't feel guilty. If I were in your place I probably wouldn't be able to do it either. I love you very much, and please forgive me for my infidelities."

His smile was sad. "Stop the foolish talk. We're even. Let's call it a draw, okay?" He turned away from her, tears filling his eyes, wary about leaving her alone. "Rest now, Elaine, I'll be right back."

"And, Lew, there's a letter on the foyer table. Mail it for me, please."

He picked the letter up and read to whom it was addressed. "You're writing to Lily?" he asked, puzzled. "What's the matter with the phone?"

"It's tickets for a charity bazaar."

"Who wrote this for you?"

"Loretta, next door."

"Rest, Elaine. I won't be long." Feeling apprehensive, he turned, hesitated. "You sure you'll be all right? I could ask Loretta to sit with you."

"Go already," she said, but she wanted so badly to ask him to stay, to take her in his arms and hold her forever. The door closed with finality, and she sighed a low moan, listening to the sound of his footsteps growing faint until they were heard no more.

Raising her hand in a farewell gesture, her voice catching in her throat, she breathed, "Goodbye, Lew. Goodbye, my darling."

Chapter 74

"Someone has to be home, Lily. The old man is on his last legs. Try again."

"I've been calling Blanche every hour on the hour, Franny. Maybe she took him to the doctor, or he could be in the hospital. Why did you wait so long to call her?"

"Why? I'll tell you why. Because I was too damn pissed at her for pulling a no-show all the time I was in the hospital. I know she's not rowing with both oars in the water, but not visiting her daughter who was going under the knife... I just can't get over it. It's inexcusable. The only understandable reason she can give me is if she was run over by an automobile or if her apartment went up in flames."

"Really, Franny. Cool it. You yourself said she's not always reliable."

"That's no excuse for what she did. Yeah, I guess the apple doesn't fall far from the tree, as the saying goes."

"Stop it. There's nothing wrong with you. A little high-strung, and at times, off-the-wall, and you talk before thinking sometimes...otherwise, you're almost perfect." She chortled. "Can I do anything for you before I go to rehearsal? I can wait until your help arrives. And by the way, the good looking, stud cop guarding your door...is he single?"

"I don't know which one you're referring to, and anyway, how would I know? No, I don't need anything. Thanks for the visit. Well, yes, there is something. Do me a favor. I get so messed up dialing. Call Nick for me. I don't know why I didn't think of asking him to check on Blanche. He's got the whole department just sitting around."

"You know they have telephones that make it easy for you to use. I think they're called, 'T T Y' phones. I don't know what the letters stand for but I guess they have raised numbers, like Braille. You could learn to do that."

"Yeah, I know, but I'm taking one thing at a time."

"I have to tell you, Franny, I'm very proud of the way you're handling your condition. Your attitude… it's unbelievable. I don't think I could do as well as you. If it were me I'd be a basket case."

"Go on. You'd be just fine. You have a head start. You could still play the piano. You hardly ever look at the keyboard when you play."

"I'll hand you the phone as soon as he answers, "Lily said, waiting for the operator to pick up.

The desk sergeant answered. "Sixty-ninth Precinct.

"Detective Pagliara, please. Miss Goldsmith calling." Lily turned to Franny. "The second he's hears it's you, he'll pick up."

"Yes, ma'am," the sergeant said. "He's in conference, but I'm sure he'll take your call.'"

"I always said, 'it's not what you know, it's who you know,'" Lily said, smiling. "You should see your face, Franny. It lights up at the mention of Nick."

When Nick came on the phone, Franny teased in her usual buffoonery. "Who are you in conference with? Some hot looking lady cop? I thought only businessmen had conferences…. I'm fine. Lily's visiting. What's wrong? You sound funny…. Why can't you tell me over the phone? Now you have me worried…. No, I don't want to wait until you get here. Anyhow, I think I know. It's Blanche, isn't it? Is she dead?… What! They can't find her or him?" She took a deep breath and let it out slowly. "Yes, Nick, I'm here. Can I put you on the speakerphone? I want Lily in on this. Okay, we're set."

Nick spoke. "We traced your mother and father to Las Vegas. They checked into the Mirage, paid cash for everything and checked out yesterday morning. As of ten minutes ago they've evaporated."

"Evaporated? The man can hardly walk. How about the hospitals?"

"Nothing, so far. We've alerted the train depot, the bus terminals, the airport, and we're investigating other avenues that would take them out of the country."

"Doesn't make sense. Whatever possessed them to take off like that? They didn't stick up a 7-Eleven, did they?"

Nick's frustrated sigh echoed over the loudspeaker. "Lily, will you convince her to let me come over and talk."

Lily eyed Franny, forgetting momentarily that she was blind and then said, "Maybe it would be better if he did, Franny."

"Uh uh," Franny said. "Why are you so insistent about coming over? There's something more, isn't there?"

Silence.

"Nick, you might as well get it all out while I have Lily here to lean on. What are you hiding?"

Lily agreed with Franny. "Might as well unload, Nick. You know who we're dealing with."

He hesitated. "You know, Franny, you can be a real ball-buster. Okay. You know the attempts that have been made on your life?"

"No, it slipped my mind," Franny chided.

"Stop with the quips. You're going to have to brace yourself for this one."

Franny held her hand out for Lily to grasp.

Nick spoke slowly, enunciating each word. "The intruder who tried to suffocate you in the hospital was…your mother.”

“You're fucking with me,” Franny said, stunned.

“I wish I were, baby, I wish I were.”

Lily dropped Franny's hand. “How? Why?” Lily managed to ask.

“That's not important at this time. Franny, are you sure you don't want me to come over? Lily, is she all right?”

Franny cut in. “I'm okay, Nick. Just digesting the news.”

“Nick,” Lily asked. “What did you mean when you said it's not important at this time. Is there something more?”

“I think I better come over.”

“Jesus, Nick!” Franny yelled. “Don't say that again!”

“Yeah, you're right,” he said. “By the time I got there you would probably have heard anyhow.”

“Heard what?” they asked in unison.

“Lily, go sit by Franny, will you please?”

Lily moved to where Franny sat and took Franny's hands in hers. “Lay it on us, Nick,” Franny said.

The stillness lay heavily in the room. After a few seconds, Nick spoke calmly.

“It's Elaine. She's committed suicide.”

Chapter 75

I lift mine eyes unto the mountains: Whence cometh my help?
My help cometh from the Lord who made heaven and earth.
He will not suffer thy foot to be moved;
He that keepeth thee doth not slumber.
Behold He that keepeth Israel doth neither slumber nor sleep.
The Lord is thy keeper; the Lord is thy shade upon thy right hand.
The sun shall not smite thee by day nor the moon by night.
The Lord shall keep thee from all evil;
He shall keep thy soul.
The Lord shall guard thy going out and thy coming in from this time forth
and forever.

~Psalm xxi

"I'm trying real hard to make sense out of this tragedy," Franny said to Lily, her throat sore from crying, her heart heavy with grief. She reached down and patted her German Shepherd, lying silently at her feet.

"I know what you mean, Franny," Lily answered, as if reading her mind. "It seems like it was just yesterday that we sat around the table at the therapy sessions—Thomas and Gerald fencing with each other, you mouthing off in your profane use of the English language, me spilling my guts out, and Elaine…" She shivered. "I can't believe she's gone."

Silent tears flowed down Lew's cheeks as he and Nick, their heads bowed, stood in back of the ladies, watching the casket slowly being lowered into the grave.

•.

No one spoke while the black stretch limousine wound its way up the tree-lined driveway for the funeral at the Benjamin's home in Armonk, New York. The chauffeur hurried to open the door, but Nick was already out of the car, taking hold of Franny's hand. "Careful, Franny," he said.

She pushed his hand away. "Get out of here, Nick. Why do you think I have a seeing-eye dog?" The dog immediately jumped from the car and waited obediently for her to exit. "Good boy, Max," she said, taking his harness. "Let me know if there are steps I should be aware of." Nick walked alongside Franny as Lew, Lily and Trippy, followed.

"You don't have to be so independent," Nick said. "I was only trying to be helpful. And use the cane for any obstacles in your way."

"You are the only obstacle, Nick. How am I ever going to get the hang of this if you keep helping me? I purposely left the cane in the car. I'm going to try and learn without it. If you're so worried about the cane, you use it."

"But…"

"But nothing," she said, raising her voice as Max voiced a low growl at Nick. She bent down and patted Max. "It's all right, Max, she said. "He means well." She hesitated for a second before asking, "Where are you, Lily?"

"Right behind you, Franny. We're all here. How are you doing?"

"I'm not sure I know how, or what I'm doing. I feel numb."

Lily sighed. "Me, too."

Franny stubbed her toe on the first step. "Okay, just this once, Nick, until Max and I work things out." She held her arm out for him to take. He smiled triumphantly as he led her into the house.

The wooden crate squealed as Franny sat down. The idea of the Jewish tradition of sitting Shiva and covering the mirrors throughout the house and sitting on crates gave Franny the chills. Petting Max's head, she asked Lily, "Did you ever think she would do it?"

Lily dabbed at her eyes. "Remember the day in the hospital when she asked you all kinds of questions about what the doctor told you concerning your eyesight, and the three of us cuddled on her bed?"

"Uh huh."

"I had an inkling then, but wasn't sure. I knew she was thinking about donating her eyes to you. But taking her life? Now that I think about it, it does make sense."

"Yeah, because she knew she had only a short time to live. Still, it was a brave thing to do. Not many people would donate their corneas."

Lily moved closer to Franny. "She had it all planned. Right down to the last detail."

Franny turned her head toward Lily. "What makes you say that? Did she hint about taking her life?"

"She didn't want to worry you because she felt you had enough on your mind. She sent me a letter."

"A letter? What kind of a letter? What are you talking about?"

"I received it a day after she... It was mostly about Lew."

"What about Lew?"

"She asked me to watch over him. She had this crazy notion."

"Like what?"

"That Lew and I should, well, get together."

"No shit. Why would she ask you and not me?"

"Because you had enough on your mind. She seemed to think he and I could be an item. And you *do* have Nick, you know."

"Leave it to Elaine to make sure Lew was taken care of after she died. What a grand lady."

"For sure."

"Are you?"

"Am I what?"

"Going to take care of him."

"Franny, Elaine's just been buried."

"Get real, Lily. That's what she wanted. Is there something I should know? You're hedging. If you and Lew have been playing spin the bottle, hey, I'm all for it; so don't hold back."

"Well, I have been sort of drawn to him. Maybe it's because of Dash. You know, the way he disappointed me. Anyway, one good thing came out of it."

"What's that?"

"I hated the reference everyone used to joke about. You know, Dash and Lily, like in Dashel Hammett and Lillian Hellman? I always felt I should be writing instead of playing the piano."

"Now that I think back, you always did favor Lew. In fact, I remember you telling me at your concert, and when we all went out to dinner, how much you admired him."

"I did?"

"Yeah. *Is* there some chemistry between you two? I mean when you're close to him, do you pulsate?"

"Pulsate? Yes, I guess so."

"Well, I'll be damned! That's awesome, Lily!"

"It is?"

"Of course it is. Now Elaine can rest in peace, and you can have a man of your own."

With a brief smile and a hesitant look, she asked, "What if he doesn't feel the same about me?"

Franny's mouth curled up in a half smile. "He will. I may not be able to see, but I can still be aware of things, sense them, you know."

Nick and Lew walked up to them. "Sorry about sitting on crates, but it's the custom," Lew said.

"Who cares?" Franny said. "I'm used to sitting on wooden boxes at Jewish funerals. Listen, Lew. Nick and I have some things to get straight. Why don't you take Lily and get some finger food or go for a walk in the garden? We need some privacy." Lew put his arm around Lily's shoulder and led her into the garden.

A puzzled look on his face, Nick asked, "What the hell was that all about?"

"I have my reasons. Have you heard anything concerning Blanche?"

"Yes. I was going to tell you."

"When? After she does me in?"

"She won't be doing anyone in. Your father died on a flight to the Cayman Islands, and your mother has been apprehended. As of this minute, she's being detained in a mental ward. Seems she tried to kill herself but wasn't successful."

"Jesus, they say it's hereditary."

"Not to worry, kiddo. I doubt you can get any crazier than you are. Oh, and one more thing."

She laughed. "You trying to give me a mental breakdown? Stop while we're ahead."

"This is good."

"Hallelujah!"

"We located the original videos of Dr. Kent's sexual encounters with his patients."

"I hope you destroyed them."

"No can do, precious. Police property. It would be against the law!"

"Don't yank my chain, Nick. You want everyone to see your future wife getting it on, in living color?"

"I'll make a deal with you. You teach me some of the tricks you did with the shrink and I'll think about having them confiscated."

Lew, holding tightly to Lily's hand, approached Franny and Nick. "Hey, is the heart-to-heart over?" he asked as he walked closer. He bolted as he accidentally stepped on Max's paw. Max yelped. His body weight forcibly pushed against Franny's crate and threw her off balance. As she fell to the floor her head hit the leg of a table and she blacked out. Nick turned pale. "Get a doctor," he shouted. "Dr. Phelps is in the other room."

Dr. Phelps rushed in and bent down over Franny just as she started to speak.

"What happened?" she said groggily. "Boy, did I see stars. I think I'm all right. Sit me up. And not on a crate this time." She felt the back of her head. "Geez, I'm growing horns."

"Wait a minute, don't get up," Dr. Phelps said. Examining Franny's bruised head, he sighed with relief. "Mmm, nasty bump. Doesn't appear to be serious. Could be a mild concussion. We should have it checked out."

The doctor stepped aside as Nick knelt down and cradled Franny in his arms. Everyone stood gaping while Nick angled his face close to Franny's. Searching her eyes, his voice breaking with compassion, he added, "You're a very lucky lady."

She grabbed hold of his suit lapels and pulled him closer to her, their noses almost touching. "You don't know how lucky I am, Nick." Tears streamed down her face. Her eyes alive with excitement, she breathed, "By the way, Nick, didn't I tell you I hate that black and white polka dot tie you're wearing?"